# ACCLAIM FOR PETER DELACORTE'S
## *TIME ON MY HANDS*

"A novel of pure wish fulfillment....The plot grows more and more provocative as we near the surprise ending."
— *The New York Times Book Review*

"Enormously fun. Delacorte's writing has a wonderful read-aloud quality, the plot is spiked with irony and action, and he manages period details perfectly."
–*Philadelphia Enquirer*

"Full of delicious ironies...especially for anyone interested in the politics and movies of the last sixty years."
–*Chicago Tribune*

"Enchantingly imaginative....A nimble tale of suspense and romance....Delacorte's prose is agile and brisk. Narrator Gabriel is a fluid and ironic observer, not only of Hollywood flimflam but also of his own boondoggled attempt to change history."
–*Publishers Weekly*

"A memorable, extraordinarily intelligent piece of fiction writing with a strong sense of time(s) and place(s).
–*Library Journal*

**Also by Peter Delacorte**

*Games of Chance*

*Levantine*

*Hero of the Revolution*

*Time on My Hands*

**And coming soon:**

*No Time to Lose*

(the sequel to *Time on My Hands*)

*For Bonnie*

## ACKNOWLEDGMENTS

Boundless thanks to Mika Kozma for conceiving and creating the cover. Copious thanks to Jody and Lisa Brown for showing me Memphis. Many thanks to Bonnie, to Dave Nelson, to John Koethe, to Erika and Kate Delacorte for reading every version of this book and never complaining. Thanks to Justine Underhill and her book club for their youthful perspective. Thanks to The Spun Yarn for providing more than a little inspiration. In memory of Mrs. Mary Jane Ray, who provided lodging, Memphis lore, and much valuable conversation. And in memory of Frank Woodward, who was a good friend.

*The events of this novel take place primarily between the First and the Fourth of April, 1968. On March 31, President Lyndon B. Johnson had announced he would not run for re-election in November. Johnson had been instrumental (and courageous) in pushing through Congress civil rights legislation initiated by President John F. Kennedy. Many believe that Kennedy—not as accomplished a politician as Johnson—might not have been as successful in bringing both the Civil Rights Act and the Voting Rights Act to fruition. Alas, Johnson became mired in another Kennedy legacy, the Vietnam War. Heeding the advice of Cold Warriors like Dean Rusk and Robert McNamara, Johnson saw Vietnam as a struggle between freedom and communism, good and evil— as opposed to a civil war in a far-off land. Johnson backed the corrupt South Vietnamese regime with an ever increasing number of troops, munitions, and bombing raids. The My Lai massacre had occurred in mid-March, although it would not be revealed for another eighteen months. As of April 1 1968 there were over 500,000 American soldiers in Vietnam. Johnson had come perilously close to losing the New Hampshire primary to the first anti-war candidate, Senator Eugene McCarthy of Minnesota. On March 16, Robert F. Kennedy, brother of the assassinated president, announced his own candidacy.*

PETER DELACORTE

# THE
# MOUNTAINTOP

# ONE

Not certain whether she's conscious or dreaming, Lydia hears Alex's voice. She opens her eyes; she happens to be on her right side, in a near-fetal position, facing Alex's side of the bed, which is devoid of Alex, as it has been all night.

It's dawn.

That *is* Alex's voice, outside the bedroom door. She did not close the bedroom door before going to bed, of that she's sure. So Alex has returned home after another of his crazy nights, and closed the door so she wouldn't hear him talking to himself. Or is it himself he's talking to?

She rolls onto her back, so neither ear is buried in the pillow. There is at least one other voice outside the door. She sits up, awakening very rapidly. Both of them, or all of them, are murmuring. It's not Alex's manner to be considerate; more likely there's something going on out there he doesn't want her to know about, or else she's going deaf.

This is the fifth or maybe the sixth time since she moved in with him that he's disappeared. Sometimes he drops acid and sometimes he crushes morning glory seeds into a paste and dissolves the paste in tea. She did it with him twice, but couldn't get past the nausea, couldn't let herself "fall into it," in Alex's words. Once, in February, she had to get him sprung from the mental ward at Bellevue after a woman found him sleeping in her car on Riverside Drive. In early March, three weeks ago, he was gone for 68 hours and returned filthy and barefoot.

"What about this over here?" The voice is not Alex's, but then she hears Alex clearly: "Hey, I said, keep it down." The first voice sounded Puerto Rican or Dominican to Lydia, who is something of an expert on Hispanic accents, having come to New York from Caracas when she was ten, and lived on the Lower East Side until she moved in with Alex on West 113<sup>th</sup> Street.

Now she hears more muffled dialogue beyond the bedroom door, and a small crash–something hitting the floor from a moderate height. The telephone? She gets out of bed and grabs her robe from the tattered armchair against the wall, puts it on, fits her feet into her slippers. Is she presentable? Does she care? She pads to the door, waits a few seconds, and calls, "Alex!"

All sound ceases. Then Alex's voice: "Yes, babe?"

"Would you come in here, please?"

She considers opening the door herself and getting a quick look at what she'll have to deal with, but before she's made up her mind Alex has opened it just wide enough to slip in. He's looking beatific, which is bad because it means he's high and good because nothing terrible has happened to him. He's barefoot again, unshaven, generally disheveled, but he doesn't look too awful. He's looked much worse. He says, "Hey, did we wake you up? I'm sorry." He moves to embrace her, but she steps back.

"Who's here, Alex?"

"Just some guys. Some guys I met. New friends."

"What are they doing here? At six in the fucking morning?"

"Don't worry about it, babe. It's cool. Everything is cool."

He's got that look, that saintly above-it-all look that she completely mistrusts, from experience. But as far as he's concerned, she knows, everything *is* cool. Just as everything was undoubtedly cool when the lady found him in her Alfa-Romeo and called the cops. He's still trying to hug her, doing this slow-motion stalking. She says, "Alex, are you giving away your stuff again?"

"It's all right, babe," he says, the expression unchanged–

2

a big, unwavering smile, red-rimmed eyes all glassy.

"You wanna introduce me to your friends, Alex?"

"Sure, babe," he says. "But just let me hold you, okay?"

She stops retreating and lets him put his arms around her. He envelops her. He's about six feet tall, she's a little over five feet. "I missed you," he says. "I wish you could come with me."

"Right," she says. "I'm gonna go out with you and hang around with some creeps all night, doing God knows what, and then I'm gonna come home and change my clothes and go to work."

"You know what I mean," Alex says, sniffing her neck.

"No, I don't." She pulls away. "Listen–is it safe for me to go out there?"

"Of course it is, babe."

Lydia glares at him, wondering for the hundredth or thousandth time in the last seven months what she's gotten herself into. Of course, last September Alex hadn't yet become all druggy, or if he had she wasn't aware of it, and her friend Maddy, who introduced them, wasn't aware of it. She's been on the brink of leaving several times, but the prospect of moving is always daunting, and this apartment is so nice, and Alex when he's not all fucked up is still ingenious and funny and...lovable. She says, "How many guys out there, Alex?"

"Umm...three."

"Where did you meet these guys?"

"At a place...a bar."

"At a bar where?"

"Shit, I don't know...on Columbus, in the Nineties...."

"Jesus," she says. "So you go slumming and you bring back some lowlifes."

Alex grins and says, "No, babe, these are not lowlifes.

3

These are gentlemen and fellow...searchers."

"Right. Searching for a sucker." Beyond the door she hears brief clattering, and someone says the word *pendejo*. "Okay," she says, "let's go out and meet your friends."

All three men appear to be in their early twenties. Two are sprawled on the couch; one stands by the front door, holding Alex's movie camera. It is perhaps a good sign that he didn't simply flee with the camera while Alex was occupied in the bedroom. He catches her eye and says, "Hey, sister." Lydia does not reply. She shifts her attention to the couch, where one young man, large and overweight, studies an *Incredible Hulk* comic book, while the other plays with Alex's Nagra tape recorder.

"Everybody," Alex says, "this is Lydia. Lydia..." He points to the man by the door. "...this is Rafael. Rafael is a poet." Rafael bows slightly and grins at Lydia. "And these two gentlemen are Flaco and...Jorge?"

"Julio," mutters the chubby man with the comic book.

Flaco nods in Lydia's direction and speaks to Alex, "You didn't tell us you had such a fine-lookin' old lady, man. Spanish chick, too, unless my eyes gone bad, right?" Flaco has very long legs, and thick, curly black hair. He turns to Lydia. "*Hablas español, mamacita?*"

Lydia ignores him. "It's very nice to meet you," she says to Rafael, making an effort to keep her voice cool and even. "I don't mean to be rude, but now I'm going to ask you to leave, because I have to get ready for work, and Alex should get some sleep. And I'm sure you guys have jobs to go to, right?"

Rafael speaks softly. "Yeah, we have jobs." He's short and slim, five-seven at the most, and wears thick-soled black boots and black jeans, and an expensive-looking brown leather

4

jacket with a fleece collar. "But Alex was gonna show us some more things."

"Electric guitar," says chunky Julio.

"Some other time," Lydia says to Rafael. "Right, Alex?"

"Right," Alex says to Rafael. "The lady is always right."

Rafael shrugs. "Okay, then. It is kinda late. I got no problem with that. We'll just take off, then."

Julio speaks to Alex. "You done with this, man?" He points to the comic.

"Sure," Alex says.

Julio gets to his feet and slaps Flaco on the knee. Flaco arises, still holding the Nagra. He is a foot taller than Rafael, a head taller than Alex. Rafael says to Alex, "Thanks for everything, brother," and turns the doorknob.

"Hold on," Lydia says, hearing her voice become shrill, "where you goin' with that camera?"

As large Julio and exceedingly tall Flaco shuffle toward the door, Rafael smiles and says, "I'm not lying to you. He gave us this stuff."

Lydia has a quick glance at Alex, who remains immobile by the bedroom door. Flaco holds the Nagra and Julio the comic book, the three of them now assembled by the front door. There is neither time nor purpose to bring Alex into this. "He can't give you what ain't his," she shouts. That is *my* shit. That camera and that tape recorder are *mine*. You want that fuckin' comic book you take it, but you put that other stuff *down*."

Rafael glances in Alex's direction. "According to him, he's a film student that just decided to quit, and he doesn't need his camera anymore."

5

"I don't give a shit what he told you." Lydia has advanced so she's directly in front of Rafael, with Flaco towering over her, on her right. "That camera and that tape recorder belong to me, and if you motherfuckers walk out of here with them, you're stealing, and I'm gonna have the cops on your ass in five seconds."

"*Chingale*," Flaco says to Rafael. "Fuck the bitch. Let's get out of here."

"Fuck *you*," Lydia says in English, glaring up at Flaco, "and give me back my tape recorder."

Flaco peers down at her, grinning. "You're a pretty brave little girl," he says, "with a *maricón gringo* for a husband."

"*No es mi marido*," she says in Spanish. "Give me my stuff and get the fuck out of here."

"Flaco, man, forget about it, okay?" Rafael says. He turns and flips the hefty sixteen-millimeter camera to Alex, who makes the catch, barely, and staggers against the wall.

"You kiddin' me man?" Flaco says to Rafael.

Rafael shakes his head at the bigger man. "No. Give the lady the tape recorder."

Flaco steps forward and places the bulky Nagra in Lydia's outstretched hands. As she accepts it, he runs his left hand down her right side, sliding through the opening in her bathrobe and brushing against her breast. She gasps and steps backward. Rafael says, "What the fuck you doing, man?"

"I had to get somethin' out of all this," Flaco says. "We coulda got fifty bucks for that thing. Maybe a hundred."

"I apologize for my friend," Rafael says.

"Get the fuck out of here," Lydia says, sobbing. Alex still stands against the wall, as if in a trance, holding his movie camera.

"*Me voy, putita*," Flaco spits, as he backs out the door, followed by Julio. Rafael performs a little bow. "Sorry about all this," he says, sounding neither ironic nor hostile. "I hope to see you around the neighborhood."

## TWO

Shapes!
Prosper is midway through the written test, sitting in a vast room in a standard-issue exam seat, surrounded by scores of young men armed with number-two pencils. The first two sections of the test have comprised twenty-five verbal questions--all preposterously easy--and twenty-five math questions an average fifth grader could have polished off in ten minutes. He's whizzed through both sections in half that time, but now he's looking at *shapes*.

Scanning the page, he believes for a moment that this portion of the test is devoted to non-representational art. How bizarre. Won't multiple-choice answers necessarily be very subjective?

He has ended up driving the forty miles from Riverside

to New Haven in his own car, having been given permission by a G.I. Joe-replica sergeant at the Stamford train station to forgo the communal bus ("You can swim there for all I care, long as you're on time.") He has consumed another couple of cans of Schlitz during the forty-five-mile drive, and downed another Dexedrine in the parking lot. He needs to pee.

He focuses on the page, on the first problem, the first shape, and after a good thirty seconds realizes that it's a two-dimensional figure which, if "folded," would become one of the three-dimensional renderings adjacent. He laughs to himself, partly because it's taken him so long to decode the very premise of the problem, but more because even in a less addled state he would not have a remote prayer of solving it, and perhaps even more at the recognition that there are probably forty or fifty guys in his immediate proximity struggling through the math and verbal problems who can look at these things and figure them out in a second.

There is no point, in any case, wasting his time on the art section. He flips two pages to part four, and encounters further wonderment. Tools! Here is an image of a tool and there, next to it, a choice of four possible objects for that tool. Just below, the process is reversed. An engine of sorts, for which one must choose among four possible tools. This is marvelous. Prosper scans the page. We're not talking about hammer/nail stuff here, but of wondrous, arcane devices juxtaposed with blurry, complex machines. Surely one would have had to apprentice for several years in deepest Anatolia or the steppes of the Kazakh S.S.R. even to get a glimpse at some of these devices.

He leans back in his chair and closes his eyes, opens them a moment later and scans the room. Everyone else, every last draftee-in-waiting, is hard at work, or at least giving that impression. Something else he notices in this moment: There are no men in khaki patrolling the aisles, making sure no one is cheating. Of course not--they want you to pass! They *need* you to pass. But what's he to do concerning this matter of the shapes and the tools? Leave the final fifty questions blank? That wouldn't be proper. Fill in a straight line of A's or B's? He opts, after a minute's contemplation, for an A-B-C-D-C-B-A pattern through the art section, and somehow it seems appropriate to give the tools a rhyme scheme: A-B-B-A, C-D-D-C, and repeat.

Done. It's taken him twenty-three minutes, according to the clock on the wall, to complete his Selective Service written test. If this were college he'd carry his booklet to the front of the room, hand it in, and spend the rest of the hour doing something constructive. But this is the military, so he has thirty-seven minutes to kill, and begins by writing a sort of prose poem in the margins of the test paper. He writes in the two foreign languages he knows, starting in French, proceeding until there's a word he can't find, whereupon he switches to Spanish, then back to French. The poem is about the night just passed, in which Prosper and his college roommate Ben stayed up all night drinking beer; and about Lyndon Johnson and Robert Kennedy and Eugene McCarthy, and about the boxer Muhammad Ali, who has recently expressed that he "ain't got nothing against them Viet Cong." *Moi non plus*, Prosper writes. *Yo tampoco*. At the top of the page he writes in block letters: A MAGDALENA, which of course--give or take a grave accent-- would have the same meaning in Spanish or French.

Nineteen minutes to go. From his inside pocket he takes three neatly folded pieces of lined notepaper on which several hours ago he had begun a letter.

9

Peter Delacorte

*April 1, 1968*

*Dear Mom and Dad:*

    *I'm sitting here at Aunt Catherine's kitchen table, just before dawn. Ben was helping me stay up all night before the draft physical, but he's fallen asleep on the living room couch. I've got to wake him in about an hour so he can make it to someplace in Harlem by eight o'clock. He's just taken a leave of absence from the Ford Foundation to work on the Kennedy campaign. I have mixed feelings about that, as you might guess. The "smart money" says McCarthy could never win, could never even be nominated, but now that Johnson's announced he's not going to run (I'm sure the news will have reached Senegal before this gets to you), it seems to me the doors are wide open for anyone, and there's such enthusiasm for McCarthy everywhere I go that I'm convinced he could've gained tremendous momentum if he'd had the anti-war platform to himself.*

    *Call me naïve.*

    *Anyway, Ben's asleep on the couch, and after I wake him I have to drive down to the Riverside train station and catch a bus to the Federal Building in New Haven. I'm going to see if they'll let me drive my car all the way there. That way maybe I can get back here at night if my strategy works...or maybe just head straight up to Canada if I pass the physical. But wait—Catherine isn't due back from her business trip till Friday, so I guess I'll have to stick around.*

    *Ben and I talked from about midnight to three. He says I've been procrastinating, I've been denying, I've been farting around, when I should've been making plans, committing myself*

10

*firmly in one direction or another. He should talk, right? Because his father was killed in WWII before Ben was even born, he's a sole surviving son, so this war could go on for 50 years and he'd never be drafted. Not that I'm bitter. Ben will help RFK get elected (opportunistic weasel that he is), and RFK will end the draft immediately...except it'll be about three or four months too late for me.*

*When we talked in Dakar at Christmas I hope I made my feelings about all this clear. I know you're behind me, and I know Dad's career prevents him from being as outspoken as he'd like to be—and of course one of the things I'm always concerned about is not stepping on Dad's career. Like if, God forbid, the Republican is elected in November and there's a picture of me refusing induction on page 8 of the Daily News— AMBASSADOR'S SON IS COMMIE PINKO TRAITOR—even if it happens that the ambassador in question is stationed in a little African country no one's heard of.*

*I know that my inaction doesn't show it, but I spend a lot of time thinking about this stuff—the war, and what the war means, and whether a person's first obligation is to his country or to his principles, or to some kind of higher order. One of the big hang-ups here is that evidently you have a real chance at Conscientious Objector status only if you can prove religious convictions. Do I have religious convictions? I guess you'd have to say that since I don't believe in God, the answer is no. But in the instance of this war, how am I different from someone whose religion prevents him from fighting?*

*I must know seven or eight guys from Princeton who (unlike Ben) believe that we have to kick the hell out of the Communists in Vietnam, but they've got better things to do. So a couple of these guys have deferments from business school, and a couple from law school, one from divinity school, two*

11

*who've used influence from their fathers or uncles or important friends of the family to get into National Guard units, which means that after their basic training they have to sacrifice a weekend every once in a while to march around the countryside or make believe they're shooting at each other.*

*I don't think the war is right. I don't think what's going on Vietnam has much to do with Freedom vs. Communism. I don't think that if we get the hell out of there the Commies will be all over Australia and New Zealand in a few months. I think they're having a civil war in Vietnam, and we have no place there. From what I hear, we're doing some pretty horrible stuff there, earning ourselves a reputation very different from anything we've stood for in the (recent) past—in the world's eye.*

*I'm trying to picture myself sitting here in 1941, or 1943, or 1945. Would I have been eager to go to war? Scared? Both? I know I wouldn't have felt like this—filled with this disgust for the people who run my country, and this sense of alienation from the huge numbers of my fellow Americans who either blindly obey their government or don't give a damn what it does.*

Prosper is pleasantly surprised that he could have written a coherent letter to his parents after a gallon of Schlitz. Is there anything to add?

*Later now, and I'm in the belly of the beast. By my own reckoning, just got 50 out of 50 on the verbal & math and 0 out of fifty on the other stuff, which had to do with tools and some offshoot of Cubism. Thanks for the genes!*

*To finish my thought of four or five hours ago: If Ho were like Hitler, if he were rounding up all the Christians, say, and hauling them off to death camps, I like to think I wouldn't*

*even wait to be drafted, I'd sign up right away in hopes that I
could help put the bastard in his miserable place.*

*Okay. My time is up. Maybe I'll write more later. I
hope they don't go through my pockets while I'm peeing in a
cup. Actually, maybe if they did read this they might conclude
that I'm not going to be the best gook killer, and let me go.*


He refolds the latter and slides it back into his pocket,
just in time for…the period of doing nothing. The military must
grade the tests to determine who's ready for the physical and
who's got to take the test again. According to Prosper's pals at
the War Resisters League, the passing grade on the written test
has decreased during recent months from sixty (of one hundred)
to fifty to forty, in order to meet the demand for new cannon
fodder. A random score, of course, would be twenty-five, so
with forty as the demarcation point, it's statistically quite
possible that a complete illiterate who's never even run across a
polyhedron or a Kurdish scythe could pass the test and go to
war.

On the sidewalk outside the Federal Building virtually
everyone smokes cigarettes. There is a group of young black
men, perhaps fifteen of them, and a smaller group of Hispanics.
The white boys keep to themselves or mingle in groups of two
or three. Prosper wonders whether it's time for another
Dexedrine, figures that it's best to wait another couple of hours,
wonders when he'll have his next opportunity.

A *de facto* segregation occurs. If the group consisted
of a hundred and fifty to begin with, a hundred and ten now
proceed to a locker room, where they're ordered to strip down to
their "undershorts." Virtually all the white guys have made the
cut, which is to say that the forty guys taking the written test

13

again are nearly all black or Puerto Rican. Prosper makes another observation, whose cultural significance is a bit tougher to identify: practically everyone in this group of primarily white test-passers is wearing white jockey shorts. Prosper himself wears blue boxer shorts.

There is more writing to be done: a long medical questionnaire. Have you had all the standard diseases? Have you had any of the less standard diseases? The venereal diseases? Broken any bones? Family history of dwarfism? Spent any time in a mental hospital? Ever been addicted to drugs? Are you queer? Prosper checks measles and mumps, and nothing else. There's no longer any percentage, his War Resisters League advisers say, in checking everything. It just makes the doctors angry, and less likely to be sympathetic to a legitimate reason for deferment.

The "physical" itself is far less comprehensive than what one might expect from one's own personal physician, but of course it takes a great deal longer because for every component there is the wait, the handing of one's sheet to the attending functionary, the recording of one's vital statistic. Prosper is seventy inches tall, as he has been for the past eight years, and weighs a hundred and forty-two pounds. In line just ahead of him, a very fat boy has engendered a low whistle from the corporal who's writing down everyone's weight and height. The corporal is about Prosper's age, with a pink, acne-scarred face and hair so short and fine that his scalp is entirely visible. "Two eight three," he has said aloud, before pointing to Prosper. "You could be two of him, buddy."

There is the inspection of one's scrotum by a middle-aged man wearing rubber gloves. Often in the past weeks Prosper has heard the supposedly true tale of the boy, always witnessed by a friend of a friend, or a relative of a relative, who

14

was expediently deferred after ejaculating on the doctor's hand.

Urine is produced. Blood is taken. Prosper wonders how the absence of this tablespoon or so will affect his blood pressure. Will it decrease because there's less of it to be measured, or will it soar as the remaining blood circulates that much harder? Getting to his feet after the blood-letting, he feels more than a little bit woozy. To be sure, this is the first time he's had a vein ravished after staying up all night and ingesting thirty milligrams of amphetamine, not to mention ninety-six ounces of the Beer That Made Milwaukee Famous. All at once his skin goes cold, and he returns to the stool much more quickly than he'd left it. The medic who'd just sucked his blood, a sallow young man with a thin, well-trimmed mustache, says, "Head between your knees. Okay. Deep breath. You're gonna be all right." He resists a strong but brief urge to vomit. He senses the blood returning to his head, and he says, "I'm okay."

"Not yet." The medic has a hand on his left shoulder. In a lower voice he says, "You get fucked up last night? It's all right, I'm not gonna tell nobody."

Mustn't his breath still stink of beer? "Little bit," Prosper says.

"I thought so. Okay. Get up slow."

Prosper obeys, rising from the stool in increments of inches, confirming as he reaches his full height that he will remain conscious. He nods a little thank you to the medic, who gives him a quick, conspiratorial wink. What is it exactly that they've shared here?

There's little time to consider it because the moment of truth awaits at the next station: and now, as he descends upon a new stool and a new medic slides the cuff up his right arm and begins inflating it, Prosper is convinced that his near swoon will

15

have neutralized the amphetamine, that his blood which until moments ago was on the verge of gushing from every orifice will now have been tranquilized into the low normal range, and it's only a matter of months before he'll be on his way to Saigon, or a matter of weeks before he's headed for Saskatchewan.

The cuff loosens and falls. Prosper remains inert until this medic hands him his chart and says, "You're done, pal."

This is the end of the line. There are three desks, standard issue gray steel, behind each of which sits an actual medical doctor, a reject from a *Marcus Welby, M.D.* casting call, wearing a white lab coat. Each is, by Prosper's reckoning, about fifty years old, the doctor on the left thin and balding, the doctor on the right chubby and bald. The doctor in the middle, it's slowly dawning on Prosper, is the first Negro, the first *black* man in this scenario who's wearing more than underpants. Prosper, who is seventh in the single-file line, who as yet has been unable to bring himself to read his blood pressure number on the document he holds, watches instead the routine: doctor peruses chart, looks over potential draftee, asks a few questions, looks over chart some more, sends kid on his way. The process tends to take about a minute and a half, which means that not a great deal of time has passed before Prosper's at the head of the line.

The fat boy, just in front of him, has drawn Doctor Thin & Balding, who has fixed his attention on a piece of paper stapled to fat boy's chart. He looks up at the great, hulking figure above him, rolls of fat spreading over white briefs. "Do you know what *morbidly obese* means?"

The boy's voice is barely audible. "Yes, sir."

"Tell me what it means."

"Means I'm overweight, sir."

"*Overweight?*" Doctor T&B's voice has risen to attract

16

the attention, momentarily, of the other two doctors and their victims. Doctor T&B resumes, his voice only slightly lower: "It means you're so fat you're could *die*, is what it means. Do you understand that?"

"Yes, sir," fat boy says.

"I'd like to see your records, young man," Doctor T&B snarls. "I'd like to see how much weight you've gained in the last, let's say, six months."

"I've always been heavy, sir," the boy says. For his part, Prosper wouldn't mind having a look at Doctor T&B's records. Is it ineptitude or some sort of misdirected patriotism that finds him, aged fifty, yelling at overweight draft dodgers in a squalid government building in New Haven, Connecticut?

"Next, please!" It's the black doctor speaking, and Prosper, who has been staring in the manner of the drugged and fatigued at the spectacle to his left, now must stumble toward his own fate. His chart handed over to the doctor, Prosper has been drawn anew into the ongoing exchange between the fat boy and the angry doctor when he realizes the black doctor is speaking his name.

"Yes," he responds, springing into something resembling attention.

"Do you have a history of hypertension, Mister Murphy?" The black doctor speaks in a voice that seems particularly soothing in contrast to his colleague's.

"Well, I wouldn't say hypertension, necessarily." Prosper is surprised to hear himself constructing such a complex thought. "But high blood pressure, yes, I think I tend to have."

"And what's the difference between the two?"

He doesn't know the answer to that. "Is it a matter of degree, maybe?"

"Do you know what's considered normal, for someone

17

your age?"

Prosper knows that a 145 over 75 or maybe 80 is where the Selective Service draws the line. "Not exactly, no."

"Well, let's just say it's way below yours. What's written on your chart here is one sixty-two over ninety-four. That's much too high for someone your age, your weight. That's dangerous. Are you on any kind of medication?"

A globule of sweat runs down his right side. "No, sir." Unless you count beer and Dexedrine.

The black doctor looks down at the chart, then back at Prosper. "Are your eyes always that bloodshot?"

It's impossible to tell whether the doctor is genuinely concerned for him, or simply on to his game. "I've been having trouble sleeping," he says.

The doctor now stares at Prosper's chart for quite a long time: fifteen seconds, twenty. The noisy exchange next door has ended, and the fat boy has moved on. Rivulets of sweat are now rolling down Prosper's sides, and he's suddenly aware of blood pounding in his head. "If I were you," the black doctor says, his gaze reverting to Prosper only now, "I would go visit my physician when I'm done with this. Do you have a personal physician?"

Prosper has not seen a doctor since the mandatory physical that preceded his freshman year at college. "Yes, I do."

"Why didn't he give you a note about your blood pressure?"

"I haven't seen him in a while."

"How long."

"Years."

The black doctor leans back in his chair and sighs. This is all marvelously ambiguous. Does he know? Does he care?

And the notion is beginning to creep into Prosper's head: maybe I *do* have high blood pressure. Maybe I didn't need the Dexedrine, and I'm in the process of killing myself. "You're not like a lot of the guys I see here," the doctor says, handing him back his chart. "You can afford to have a real exam somewhere. You don't want to end up in a wheelchair when you're forty, do you?"

"I don't," Prosper says, and he thinks: nor do I want to end up blown to bits when I'm twenty-four.

## THREE

Ben has the ability to function at close to full efficiency with just a few hours' sleep. It's something he takes for granted, something that consistently amazes his friends, and Maddy. When he was ten or eleven he used to sneak downstairs from his bedroom to the living room and watch Steve Allen on the *Tonight Show*. He'd fall asleep with the television still on, wake to a test pattern at sunrise, then tiptoe back upstairs and read until it was time for breakfast. It's not that he doesn't enjoy sleep, it's just that he doesn't need much of it.

19

Still, had he known Randall wasn't going to show up, he might not have been so cavalier about this morning. He fell asleep around four, sprawled awkwardly on Prosper's aunt's living room couch; Prosper shook him awake at perhaps six thirty, and not three hours later—as if in an anxiety dream—he found himself alone on the stage of the auditorium at the Frederick Douglass Youth Center on Lenox Avenue, looking down at a throng of black teenagers.

In the short time they've been working together, this has been Randall's job. He's the speaker. With his deep, resonant voice he ignores the podium and speaks from the edge of the stage, whether the audience is white boys at Yale, black kids here in Harlem, or a racial pot-pourri at CCNY. Ben has hung in the background, handing out buttons and stickers, occasionally helping answer questions afterward. Randall is habitually late, but this morning for the first time he didn't appear at all.

Profoundly conscious that he was the only white person in the room, Ben did his best to reproduce Randall's cadence and the call-and-response nature of his opening. Why are we here? *Kennedy!* What does Bobby Kennedy hope to be? *President!* Does he need your help here in Harlem? *Yeah!* The only rough moment came after he'd asked if anyone knew the important thing that had happened last night and a chubby girl in the front row said, "Your mama got laid." The kids burst into raucous laughter; Ben waited about five seconds before tapping the microphone and saying, "Yeah, but I had something else in mind." They laughed again, more softly. He said, "President Johnson said he wasn't going to run for re-election." Silence now. "So the field's wide open. That's good for us. It's good for Harlem, it's good for New York City, and it's good for the country." He had them.

20

He's in the process of handing out buttons and stickers when he spots Randall in the back of the auditorium, talking to the tiny black woman who'd introduced him. It crosses Ben's mind that this was some sort of setup, a test--that Randall was here all along.

Moments later they walk in the direction of Ben's Corvair, parked two blocks away on Lenox. "Where the hell were you, man?" He asks the question as affably as possible, not yet sure how much leverage he has with Randall, who until two weeks ago was a casual friend, a softball teammate, but now is his boss.

"You looked like you were pretty much in control of things," Randall says with a little laugh. "Like maybe you missed your calling. Maybe you could understudy for Adam Clayton Powell at the Abyssinian Baptist Church." Randall is twenty-eight, four years older than Ben. At six feet he's a couple of inches shorter, much slimmer in build than the former prep school quarterback. His skin is light brown, the fineness of his lips and the thinness of his nose suggestion of some Caucasian ancestry, his hair styled in a modest Afro.

"You there the whole time?" Ben asks.

"No, man, I wouldn't do that to you. I was downtown, working some things out. I hope you don't have too much planned for the next few days, maybe a week?"

"How come?"

"We're going to Memphis."

"Memphis?"

"Yeah, you've heard of it--sanitation workers strike, Martin Luther King, demonstration got rowdy, all over the papers..."

"Sure, I know...but why me?"

"'Cause you're good. 'Cause we're a team."

They continue briskly up Lenox Avenue in the cool late morning, Randall in a tweed overcoat and Ben in his coat and tie. "So...I've been promoted? Do I go on the payroll?"

Randall chuckles. "Not yet. But you get expenses."

Ben's heart beats a little faster. Does he in fact have anything to do for the next week? A party he's supposed to go to with Maddy and Prosper, but nothing else comes to mind. "When do we go?"

"Can you get us to JFK for a twelve-thirty flight?"

"Jesus. I've got to pack. A week, you said?"

"More or less."

"What do we do with my car?"

"Long-term parking's cheaper than a cab there and back. Unless you want to leave it with Maddy..."

Ben considers Maddy having to move the Corvair every night to avoid street-cleaning tickets. "Let's take it."

"All right, then, my man--let's get our asses to Memphis, Tennessee."

The Delta 707 is forty percent full, at most, so Ben and Randall have a three-seat row to themselves near the front of the coach section. Randall has been sorting through papers from his attaché case, open on the middle seat, while Ben, who's flown perhaps five times in his life, has been peering out the window at the receding northeast. "First stop, Randall says, "is Southwestern College. Heard of it?"

"Nope."

"Me neither, till this morning. Small liberal arts college affiliated with the Presbyterian Church. Practically all white. We talk to the student council. Then we go to Memphis State..."

22

"Heard of it," Ben says, "and that's about it."

"Second-largest enrollment in the state, after University of Tennessee," Randall says. "Hasn't been integrated all that long, as you might imagine, but now it's about eleven percent, twelve percent black. There's a Black Student Association that just started getting serious at the start of this academic year. And we've got Black Power coming to Memphis. There's this citywide thing called the Black Organizing Project, which is your uppity niggers, your *in*side agitators, which all of a sudden has a presence at Memphis State. Then there's this offshoot of the Bee Oh Pee called the Invaders, who started up last summer. Evidently named after the television show..."

*The Invaders* is one of the few programs Ben watches with any regularity. It's about a man--a white man--who's become aware, and is desperately trying to warn everyone else, that an immense band of (white) humanoids have arrived on Earth from a distant planet and are intent on taking over. "I don't get it," Ben says. "Do they identify with the aliens from outer space or do they identify with the white guy in the know?"

"Not everything makes sense," Randall says. "I think they just like the show." After a while, he says, "You spent much time in the south?"

"Are you kidding? I've been to Florida a couple of times. Does that count?"

"Yeah, some parts of Florida count. But probably not the places you've been to. Miami? Palm Beach?"

"Nope. Fort Lauderdale and Daytona Beach."

Randall chuckles. "Big difference. Except if you went to Daytona when they have that stock car race. Then *you* might feel like an alien, surrounded by all those crackers."

"What about you?" Ben says. "You spent much time in the south?"

23

Randall chuckles again. "Yeah, you might say. I grew up in Richmond. It's not exactly Dixie, but when I was a kid there wasn't much difference."

"I didn't know that," Ben says. "I always assumed you were from the north."

"Why?"

"I don't know. Because you went to Harvard. You don't have a southern accent."

"How about those kids this morning?" Randall says. "Did they have southern accents?"

"Sort of."

They had *black* accents," Randall says. "They may have been living in Harlem for two, three, four generations, but they still talk that way because everybody they come in contact with talks like that. So why don't I talk like that?"

"Jesus, Randall, what's the big deal? I was just surprised you were from the south."

"Where are you from, Ben?"

"You know where I'm from. Brookline, Massachusetts."

"Does everybody in Massachusetts talk like you? Do people in South Boston talk like you?"

"No, of course not."

"Why? Is it a regional thing? Do you cross a certain geographical line, and all of a sudden people have different accents? Why do you and the kid at the Esso station in Dorchester not sound the same?"

"It's a class thing, I guess. He's got a regional accent, a Boston accent. I've got kind of a homogenized American accent."

"Right," Randall says, irritation in his voice. "Me too. My father's a lawyer. His father was a lawyer. We don't sound like a lot of the other black folks because we've been middle

24

class for a few generations. But up until a couple of years ago we still couldn't use the toilet in the gas station down the street from my parents' house."

Ben examines Randall's face, which shows its usual absence of emotion. He says, "Look, I'm sorry I never took linguistics."

"It's not about linguistics, for Christ's sake. It's about knowing what's going on around you. It's about being prepared." He pauses, keeping his eyes locked on Ben's, and Ben wonders if he's expected to respond at this point. But Randall resumes. "You're a bright guy, Ben. You learn fast, you adapt quickly. That's why you're with me now. But I don't want you to think you know the way to black people's hearts and minds just because you made some time with those kids this morning."

"I don't," Ben says. "Of course I don't."

"What I mean is, I'd guess that things come pretty easy to you, am I right?" To agree outright would suggest vanity, so Ben performs a little shrug, which he immediately regrets because he suspects that it, too, suggests vanity. And Randall shakes his head. "You know what I mean--you're smart, you're confident, you can charm, you can be tough when you need to be. So I just want to warn you that you've been wading around in ankle-deep water so far, all this shit we've doing in New York. Now it's gonna get deeper in a hurry, and I don't want you to get in over your head. You understand what I'm saying?"

"I think so."

"Okay," Randall says. "Good. Now, tell me what's going on in Memphis."

Ben takes a deep breath and looks out the window, wondering if this is the last section of the exam, or if it's going to be like this with Randall from now on. "Okay." He tilts his head to face the teacher. "There's been a garbage strike going on for a while..."

"Sanitation workers," Randall interrupts.

"Sorry. Sanitation workers have been striking for...a few months. Just recently it's gotten a lot of national press because it's become kind of a civil rights issue, and Martin Luther King led a march a few days ago. It got kind of violent, breaking windows, looting, and the cops broke it up. They used tear gas...and Mace, I believe. The cops killed one boy, and there are...some questions as to the circumstances of his death. I read in the *Times* that the cops say he pulled a knife on them, but there are witnesses who say he was unarmed. Anyway, King says he wants to march again, and the city government is dead set against it."

"Good," Randall says. "Anything strike you as unusual about the whole scenario? Anything significant?"

Ben has to stop and think. "I don't remember any violence associated with King's marches in the past. Violence on the part of the demonstrators."

"Okay. And do you suppose the kids breaking windows and looting had much respect for Doctor King? For the movement?"

"I would think not," Ben says.

"All right, then. That's a start."

The young white woman at the Hertz counter does not appear even moderately reluctant to rent Randall a car, or surprised when he extends his American Express card. Ben knows the South only by reputation, but so far it doesn't seem all that different from the North. Indeed, even the weather here

26

on the first of April is pretty much interchangeable with what they left behind--cool and cloudy.

The car is a 1968 Mustang hardtop, dark blue, with just under three thousand miles on its odometer. Randall is content to let Ben drive, and Ben is delighted to do so. He's used to his '63 Corvair, which wasn't in great shape before he started parking it on Manhattan streets, and now suggests a project for a Third World body shop. The first few times he makes contact with this car's gas pedal he underestimates its power, and the Mustang surges forward.

It's a short trip into Memphis. Randall navigates with the aid of a little map provided by the Hertz people, and first takes them to Beale Street, where a number of shop windows are boarded up in the wake of disturbances four days earlier, and where perhaps forty men, all black, march in single file. Each of them has a large cardboard placard suspended from his neck; the placards read: I AM A MAN. The marchers' average age, by Ben's estimate, would be between forty and forty-five. The men wear overcoats and hats in the cool late afternoon. Randall says, "Hard to imagine these people putting on much of a riot." He turns to Ben, "You want to stay in the car for a minute? No place to park legally around here. I'm just gonna talk to one of these guys."

Ben watches as Randall walks alongside the marchers, out of earshot. Someone speaks to him, "Hey, nice car. Which engine you got in this?" He looks up to see two young men, late teens or early twenties, both in jeans and letter jackets. One, with dark hair in an updo befitting an extra from *Blackboard Jungle*, inspects the Mustang's grille. The other, with slightly shorter blond hair and residual acne, hunches down to the driver's side window. Ben says, "Not sure. It's a rental."

"So...you from outta town, drivin' round Memphis in a rented Mustang?"

"You got it," Ben says, growing a bit apprehensive, eyes on Randall, a hundred feet away.

After a pause, the young man says, "You enjoy watchin' niggers?"

How does one reply to that? "It's a hobby," Ben says.

The blond man guffaws and shouts to his friend, "Hey, Earl, this boy says watchin' niggers is his hobby!"

Earl joins the blond man at the window; Randall has begun making his way back to the car, but is still half a minute away. Earl speaks in a voice that might be interpreted as jocular, "You didn't come down here lookin' for trouble, did you?"

"Nope," Ben says, thankful that both rednecks are on his side of the car; Randall, his head now up, is perhaps twenty steps away. The car is running and ready to go.

"Check this out," Earl says, pointing at Randall. "He don't just like *watchin'* niggers, he's best friends with one in a suit!"

Earl, making a whistling sound, begins to move toward the front of the car, presumably to get to Randall, just as Randall reaches the door. Simultaneously, Randall says, "Excuse me, gentlemen?" and the blond man grabs Ben's left arm. With his right hand, Ben puts the car in drive and it lurches forward with enough force to free his left arm and to send Earl sprawling to the asphalt. Randall says, "Hey!" and Ben shouts, "Get in the car!"

Before Randall can close the door behind him, Ben has put the Mustang in reverse, then back into drive, and left the two rednecks behind. Randall says, "You want to explain that to me?"

28

"I didn't like the way things were developing."

They're a block down the road now, and Ben has slowed to normal speed. Randall says, "So you decided to knock a guy down with your car? There's a whole slew of cops back there, watching those gentlemen march. If they were looking in your direction, they wouldn't be hard pressed to see that as assault with a deadly weapon."

"Randall, Jesus, give me the benefit of the doubt..."

"I'm listening."

"Two tough kids looking for a fight, is what that was. Do I like watching niggers, and look here, his best friend's a nigger, and I don't believe the guy I knocked down had the best of intentions for you." He stops the Mustang short at a red light. "I saved us some trouble, all right?"

"In the future," Randall says, "you can let me take care of myself."

"Okay," Ben replies. "You're welcome."

**FOUR**

Save for Maddy and Lydia, the kindergarten and first grade teachers' room is empty. It's a small, windowless space with the sort of bland institutional furniture that is mass-produced in Grand Rapids, Michigan: one eight-foot long table with ten accompanying chairs, plus two smaller, square tables with four chairs apiece, on one of which is a coffee machine with cups in disorder all around it. Free-standing bookshelves against two walls contain long lines of textbooks and tall, thin children's books. It's a few minutes after noon, and the rest of the faculty, some twenty strong, is either still in class or supervising the children's lunchroom—a rotating task that is not anyone's favorite.

"God, I'm so lucky I get a chance to sit down with you," Lydia says. Before her on the scarred oak table is her fifth cup of coffee this Monday. Moments ago she's had a quick look at herself in the bathroom mirror and been surprised that she didn't look as dragged out and puffy as she felt.

"Not Alex again," Maddy says. Like Lydia, she is slender, brown-haired and brown-eyed. At five-foot four she is slightly taller than Lydia; her hair is straight—lank, in fact— where Lydia's is curly, and her skin is a pale Nordic white, while Lydia's is several shades darker, bordering on olive.

"Listen," Lydia says, "do you think you could get Ben to talk to him? Because I think Alex respects him. I can talk to him till I'm blue in the face and he's gonna nod and agree like *tomorrow* he's gonna stop all this shit, and maybe for a day or two he will, but then he's right back at it."

Maddy munches on a cheese sandwich she's brought with her from home. "Would you like some of this?" Lydia shakes her head. "You should eat something," Maddy says.

"I'm not hungry," Lydia says. "I have absolutely no fucking appetite."

A moment passes in silence before Maddy speaks. "I can try, but I think Ben is kind of fed up with Alex."

"*Now* you tell me. Jesus, Maddy, why did you introduce me to this guy?" Lydia was trying for a jocular tone, but she's afraid a bit of an edge crept in.

"I didn't know you were going to move in with him," Maddy says, with a sad smile. She pauses. "But it's not so much about Alex. Ben is just…so impatient, intolerant. His whole attitude is that he's got enough problems of his own…"

"What the hell problems does Ben have?" Lydia interrupts. "He's got piles of money, his family came over on the fucking Mayflower. He's got *you*."

"Yeah, but he's much more concerned with whatever happens to be concerning him at the time. His attitude is: Please don't bother me while I'm saving the world."

"So he couldn't spend just a little time helping to get his old friend off drugs?"

Maddy has another bite of her sandwich, and winces at her first sip of coffee. "Do you remember Prosper?"

"The other friend I met? Cute guy, right? Why didn't you introduce me to him first? Or isn't he into Latin chicks?"

Maddy smiles. "Alex listens to him. I can call him."

"Because this shit is getting scary," Lydia says. "It's one thing when he decides to stretch out in some lady's sportscar because God told him it belonged to him, or when he comes home all wet and dirty like some kind of Bowery bum. But when he starts bringing these lowlife Puerto Rican thugs into *my* fucking house…"

"I'll talk to Prosper," Maddy says.

Lydia feels tears welling in her eyes. "I have reached the point, Maddy, where I wonder what the hell am I spending my time worrying about this crazy bastard, where I am this close to just walking out the door, but then I think what am I gonna do with my stuff, and where am I gonna go? Back to

31

Avenue B? I don't think so. And if I leave, is Alex just gonna completely flip out?"

Maddy reaches across the table and touches Lydia's hand. "And the sad thing is," Lydia says, "when he's not all fucked up he can still be so smart...and so sweet."

Lydia's routine at the end of a school day is to walk from the old brick building at 104th Street and Lexington up to Madison Avenue, where she catches a bus that takes her across town to the West Side, just a few blocks from her and Alex's apartment on 118th Street, west of Morningside Drive. Today Maddy—who usually takes the 96th Street crosstown bus—rides with her, and they talk some more. She turns down Maddy's invitation to come home with her, to have dinner with her and Ben, and get away from Alex for a while. She looks forward to her bed and, in truth, she's more than a little worried about Alex, even if she's sick of his druggy bullshit.

The ride is a study in neighborhoods, as the bus travels from the edge of East Harlem past the northern tip of Central Park into the fringe of West Harlem, and finally to Morningside Heights, the predominantly white, middle-class enclave next to Columbia University. For now, between Madison and Fifth Avenues, she and Maddy are the only white faces in view. That is, if some hypothetical objective observer were to board the bus this instant and be asked to identify the only white people aboard, he would point immediately to the two young women. And indeed she thinks of herself as white. But if that objective observer could page through her ancestry, somewhere not too many generations back he'd find the offspring of slaves who was responsible for her too tightly curled hair and her full lips and her not fine enough nose. Her mother is fair-skinned and green-eyed, descended from Spaniards and Germans; it is her father who's a *mestizo*—a little bit white, a little bit Indian, a tiny bit Negro. She isn't ashamed of him, but she cringes when he jokes about his mulatto grandmother and her African superstitions. In Caracas, which she only vaguely remembers, the more European you look the better, but there is no great stigma to being a little mixed. In New York, to Lydia, it's terribly important to be white.

In the course of this mile-long trip the population of the bus transforms as Negroes, heading home from work on the East Side, or heading to late shift jobs on the West, dismount, and are replaced by white mothers and children returning from Central Park, or white teenagers in the midst of multi-transfer voyages, returning to Morningside Heights from their private schools in midtown.

Having given Maddy a little goodbye hug, Lydia herself debarks at Morningside Drive, where 110<sup>th</sup> Street is called Cathedral Parkway because it passes the gigantic Cathedral of St. John the Divine. It always strikes her as incongruous that this huge Gothic Episcopal cathedral should be here on the edge of Harlem, but then she supposes the neighborhood was a little different when it was built.

She hasn't taken ten steps when she sees an unwelcome face. Wearing the same boots, black jeans, and fleece-collared brown leather jacket, it's one of the Puerto Ricans from this morning: the short, skinny one named Rafael; the leader. He's changed his shirt. She tries to avoid eye contact, staring at the sidewalk, but when she glances up she realizes his eyes are locked on her. "Hey," he says, "Lydia, right? You mind if I walk with you?"

"How the fuck did you find me?" She walks briskly up Morningside Drive, picking up her pace to emphasize her lack of interest in him.

"Hard to miss a beauty like you," he says, keeping up with her. "You want me to carry this for you?" He touches the book bag slung over her shoulder.

She pulls away from him. "Not like you were waiting for me, right?" They're midway past the cathedral now.

"I live around here, too," he says. "You remember my name? Rafael?"

Lydia is silent for a moment, searching for the conversation's direction, or a way to end it. "Listen, I don't want you taking advantage of Alex. I told you, you're not gonna get any more of his shit."

Rafael chuckles. "I thought you said it was yours."

"What difference does it make? The point is, it ain't yours, and it's not gonna be."

"What if I wasn't interested in Alex's shit?" Rafael says, still hustling a bit to keep up with her. "What if I was interested in you?"

"Go fuck yourself." Lydia says.

"I didn't get the impression you and the trippin' boy were too tight, you know what I mean…"

"You got the wrong impression," Lydia says, continuing to stare straight ahead.

"Hard to figure you out," Rafael says. "You trying to pass? Or is Alex into Spanish chicks? Is he slumming?"

"Just fuck off, okay? If we pass a cop, you better watch out."

"Where you from anyway?" Rafael asks. "I like the way you talk. You ain't Puerto Rican, or Dominican. You don't sound Cuban to me. You don't have that sing-song thing like the Mexicans. So…somewhere in South America?"

"I'm from New York," Lydia says.

"Yeah, but I mean *originally.*"

"If I tell you where I'm from, will you leave me the fuck alone?"

"Maybe it's better if I just keep hangin' out with you and don't know where you're from."

"Whatever you like," Lydia says. She's spotted a green-and-black police car cruising down the street, a block away. "But I'm gonna tell those cops you're harassing me."

"Okay," Rafael says. "You win. So, where you from?"

"You missed your chance."

"Oh, hey, Lydia--come *on*. Just tell me where you're from, and I'm gone."

"Venezuela," Lydia says.

"No shit!" Rafael responds, and away he goes, southward at a good pace.

Alex is in the middle of the bed, eyes closed, legs crossed in the lotus position. He might be stoned again, or stoned still from the night before, or just doing yoga. Before she met Alex, Lydia had never heard of yoga. She tosses her book bag on the chair by the doorway, making as much noise as possible, and it works: Alex opens his eyes. "Hey, babe," he says. There is yet something about his voice that leaves her apprehensive.

Still standing by the door, she says, "So how was your day? You make it to school?" He shakes his head. "You had classes today, right? I know you have classes on Monday."

"It's cool," Alex says, his voice calm and level.

"What's cool?"

"Everything." He smiles. "Everything is everything." He gets to his knees and reaches toward her. "God, you are so beautiful," he says. "You are proof of the existence of God, so beautiful are you."

He expects her to come toward him, she knows, so he can move to the edge of the bed and put his arms around her waist and his head on her breast, but she doesn't budge. "It's not cool to be flushing your damn life down the toilet," she says.

His smile broadens. "The celestial toilet!" He laughs, catches himself, and gets serious.

"You did, didn't you? You took more of that shit. You're high again."

"High, I am," Alex says. "I am in touch with that which makes me high. I don't have to take any shit." He laughs, unable to help himself. "I don't have to take any of your shit, my beautiful, sexy *Venezolana*, but I would if you wanted me to." On his knees, he has ambulated to the edge of the bed, arms outstretched.

She takes a step backward. "How much do you pay Columbia, Alex?"

"I pay them nothing," he says. "Nada."

"Okay. How much does your dad pay them?"

Frozen in this pose of supplication, he moves his head slowly from side to side. "I don't know, babe. We've been through this, okay? Mom left me the money. Dad's in charge of the fucking money. It's like play money. Monopoly money. What do we care about that, anyway?"

Even in this sorry state, there is something attractive about him, with his two days' growth of beard and his black hair down below his collar, his eyes soft and glistening. But she's not going to give in.

"We care that *he* would care, is what. If he knew he's paying thousands of dollars for you to go to film school and you're just sitting around getting fucked up."

"Who's gonna tell him?" Alex says. "Not me. Not *you*."

He's got her there. There's no way in hell she's going to let the cat out of the bag and have this tight-assed Republican millionaire come up from Palm Beach, Florida to bust his son. On the other hand, if Alex doesn't get himself together, Dad's going to find out before too long. "What about when they send him your grades?" She says.

Alex cranes his neck and stares upward, as if something of great interest is happening on the ceiling. Very slowly he uncrosses his legs until he sits with them straight outward, and he looks at her. "What the fuck, babe? Are you just trying to bring me down? What *difference* does it make? It's my money. He can't do anything with it. What he pays Columbia's a fucking drop in the bucket."

"It makes a difference to me," she says.

He smiles. "Don't worry about it. Do…not…worry…about…it. Everything is cool."

"Everything is *not* fuckin' cool, Alex," she says, her voice rising. "I don't like what's happening to you. I don't like it that we used to talk about all your ideas, how you were gonna make this movie and that movie, and now you're trying to give your stuff away to some scumbags you meet on the street and you might as well be some goddamn wino I used to trip over on Avenue B…"

"I still have ideas!" His tone has changed abruptly. "What the hell do you know about my ideas? I can always get more stuff, for Christ's sake. My ideas are good. My ideas are beautiful."

"Tell me one," she says. "Tell me one fuckin' idea that you have!"

37

He narrows his eyes and smiles, his expression no longer suggesting its former benevolence. "My number one idea right now would be for you to get the hell out of my face."

"You got it," she says. She stalks out of the bedroom, slamming the door behind her. In the living room she checks her pockets for her keys and her wallet, and out the front door she goes, slamming that behind her as well.

## FIVE

The fat boy's physical is over. He's morbidly obese, and that's all there is to it. He'll be classified 1-Y, temporarily unfit for military service, which means he's in the clear for a while, probably a year, maybe for good. But it's no such luck for Prosper. Just as they keep giving the written test to all those guys back in the big room, knowing that by hook or crook—or simply the law of averages—a few will reach the magic forty percent, they plan to take Prosper's blood pressure a lot, hoping that once he's past all the stress of the physical he'll drop into the one-thirties. So they sequester him with two other hypertensive young men in a little room adjacent to the blood-taking area. There is nothing to read here, nothing to do but sit on plastic chairs designed to be as uncomfortable as possible and watch a succession of post-adolescents in underpants get stuck with needles. At eleven o'clock the corporal with the sallow, blotchy face, who this morning had pointed out that the fat boy was twice Prosper's weight, whose nameplate says DYBZINSKI, tells them to get up and follow him, and leads them approximately thirty feet to the blood pressure-taking area. This time Prosper checks in at 153 over 89. He has mixed feelings about the descent: he's getting better, and that's not all good. One of the trio, meanwhile, a chubby Latino named Mel, drops into the acceptable zone and soars into 1-A territory.

After another hour spent sitting in the little room, Corporal Dybzinski reappears and leads Prosper and Jimmy, an eighteen-year-old high school dropout from Bridgeport, back to the locker room. Get dressed, the corporal says, and go to lunch. He hands out little pieces of paper—chits that are evidently exchangeable for food in a dining hall on another level of this building—and he disappears without a word.

Are they actually on their own? For his part, Jimmy would just as soon go have some lunch. But Prosper turns left at the staircase and heads for the exit. There are a couple of uniformed men standing there, but they pay him no mind as he walks out the door and down the steps, into a cool and ominous midday, across the street to the parking lot and the Valiant.

At a luncheonette several blocks away he orders a BLT and a Coke, and swallows a Dexedrine. Not three minute later, before his sandwich has even arrived, the amphetamine enters his bloodstream like a marching band. Fifteen minutes later, filled anew with energy and confidence, he finds a *Times* in a storefront down the street, gets back in the Valiant, and returns to the Federal Building.

There is some confusion about whether it is necessary to undress again. Jimmy does so; Prosper does not. He sits in the little room, reading the *Times* and waiting. He offers Jimmy sections of the paper, but the Bridgeport boy prefers to sit and stare. Until 1:30, when a new trio of rejects from the latest busload joins them. So now they are four guys in underpants making sporadic, uneasy conversation in the company of one fully dressed guy with a newspaper.

Bobby Kennedy, says the *Times*, was told of Lyndon Johnson's decision to drop out of the presidential race while airborne, en route from one campaign stop to another. Kennedy, the story says, sat in silence, apart from everyone else on the plane, "amid the hubbub." Eugene McCarthy, meanwhile, has addressed the nation on NBC, has congratulated the president on his courageous decision, and expressed his hope that it will clear the way for a reconciliation among the American people. Prosper was an early fan of McCarthy, who had the guts to face down Johnson in the New Hampshire primary, and saw Kennedy's decision to run as an anti-war candidate as cold-blooded opportunism. Now he finds his attitude toward Kennedy softening just a bit.

He reads the editorial that praises the president's withdrawal, reads every word on the rest of the editorial page, turns to the sports section and scours it down to the agate print, checks the weather around the country and the world, reads the movie listings and the obituaries, looks to see if there is a used BMW 2000 in the classified ads, not that he needs a car or could afford to buy one.

Corporal Dybzinski breezes into the room at three o'clock; he gives Prosper a quick sideward glance, as if to say *why does this guy have his clothes on*, but says nothing. He leads the quintet on the short journey to the blood pressure area, where Prosper, even with the cuff tightened over his flannel shirt, scores 164 over 97, for a personal best. And now the weaselly Dybzinski takes Prosper and Jimmy aside. "You guys are done," he says.

"What?" Jimmy says, his face full alarm, "we don't get in the army?"

"Just for the day. You're done for the day." The corporal hands them each a piece of paper, another chit. "You take this over to the YMCA. Out the door, turn left, go four blocks. You can't miss it. You get a good night's sleep, you come back here at nine a.m. and we take your blood pressure again. You got that?"

There is not a chance Prosper will spend the night at the YMCA. He's in the Valiant at 3:20, on the Turnpike at 3:25, and back at Aunt Catherine's house at quarter after four, still feeling the giddy energy provided by his third Dexedrine.

Even on a miserable day it is a wonderment to enter the living room and encounter the dual picture windows. The view on April Fool's Day is hardly expansive, as the murky afternoon cuts visibility to a few hundred yards, but still there is a monochromatic beauty to the gray sky and the choppy gray-blue water, as if Winslow Homer had been transported to suburban Connecticut in his old age.

At the telephone stand, Prosper dials ABC and asks for Martin Snyder's extension; a female voice answers after seven rings. "Theresa? Did Martin leave early?"

"Prosper?" Theresa Impelliteri pronounces his name as if it ended with an *uh*. "He didn't even come in at all. He called at like ten and said he didn't see any point coming in if you weren't around to edit stuff."

"Well, *he's* got to edit stuff. I can't come in…"

"Oh, that's *right*, how did it go?"

"It went fine. But if it's gonna take me three days, then Martin's got to do the editing himself. I won't be in till Thursday."

"You wanna call him at home and remind him?"

"No. He knows what's going on. He just hates to do the shitwork. But I left instructions with Harvey for all the editing. Really all Martin has to do is approve everything after Harvey's finished the tapes. It shouldn't take more than an hour or two. I just don't want to come in there Thursday morning and have to edit those tapes."

"So why don't you call him?"

"I've had a long day. I'd like to take it easy now."

Martin Snyder is a big deal at WABC-FM, a man whose byline has appeared over a hip and eclectic *Village Voice* column for years, who has been hired by the American Broadcasting Company to provide some authenticity to its new FM venture. Nationwide there are only a few rock and roll stations on the FM band—all of them in big cities—in part because hardly anyone owns an FM radio. So while rock and roll rules the noisy, low-fidelity AM band, FM has been the province of classical music, jazz, and the spoken word. The pioneering FM rock stations, in New York and San Francisco, have tended to be free-form, to play lots of music, to play lots of different kinds of music in long blocks, to interrupt the music infrequently and briefly with commercials. This of course violates all the rules established over the last decade by AM rock and roll stations, and it is taken for granted by people in the business that if FM rock succeeds, it's only a matter of time before its anarchy is severely attenuated. ABC, which owns seven FM radio stations in major markets, is attempting in what is either a stroke of brilliance or an act of complete insanity, to get the jump on the rest of the industry by turning all its stations simultaneously into "progressive" rock outlets—not by hiring local hippies and visionaries and letting them pick their own tunes, but by putting one mellifluous guy in a studio in New York and having him tape intros to records and chatter about groups and such *for all seven stations*. And, if this seems too paradoxical, too counter-revolutionary, too capitalistically cynical, then...employ Martin Snyder, the newsprint arbiter of hip, to break into the programming twice an hour or so with a piece of Aquarian wisdom, or a snippet of his interview with Jim Morrison, or a prediction of the next big thing in rock and roll. And when Martin Snyder needs someone who can actually write these things, someone who knows a little bit about rock and roll and can think of some questions to ask Jim Morrison that don't concern how much money he makes, he turns to his man Friday, his ghostwriter, his indentured servant. And when Prosper can't make it into the office for some trivial reason, Martin does not exactly exhibit counter-culture solidarity.

Prosper dials a new number. To his pleasure, it is Maddy and not Ben who answers. The sultriness of her voice on the telephone always surprises him. "How did it go?" Maddy says. "Are you a free man, or are you heading for Vancouver?"

"Neither, yet. But it looks good. The pills work on the blood pressure, and nobody seems to give a shit whether I leave the building, so I can just keep taking stuff. Evidently I've got to do this two more days."

"So you're *home* now?"

"Right."

"And then after two days, what? You're out? You're deferred?"

"If my blood pressure stays up, then I'm 1-Y and technically they can call me back every year. But apparently in Connecticut they're not doing that. For now, at least."

"And it can only get better now, right? I mean, the war's not going to end just because Johnson's giving up, but if Bobby's elected it won't last long."

"If Bobby's elected."

"Hey, don't tell anybody, but Ben saw a poll the other day, downtown. They had Bobby against all the possible Republican nominees—Nixon and Rockefeller and Scranton, and that creep from G.E. Theater, Ronald Reagan, and it was just no contest. The closest one was Rockefeller and that was something like fifty-five to thirty-nine."

"I'm not counting any chickens," Prosper says. "What about Ben? Did he make it through the day?"

"He's in Memphis," Maddy says.

"He's in *Tennessee*?"

"Well, not Egypt would be my guess."

"No, I mean he didn't say anything about going away last night."

"It's news to me, too. I got home and there was about a three-line note. He and Randall are in Memphis for a few days, and maybe they'll meet with King."

"Martin Luther or Elvis?"

"I asked myself the very same question."

Prosper visualizes Ben in shirtsleeves, marching alongside Memphis garbagemen, while he's waiting in a windowless little room in New Haven for his blood pressure to be tested for the nineteenth time. Maddy says, "My God, I almost forgot...I had a long talk with Lydia at lunch today. She says Alex is getting high again. He was out all last night and came home with some Puerto Rican tough guys. He was trying to give away his movie camera and some expensive tape recorder, and she had to kick them out."

"Jesus Christ," Prosper mutters. "Good for her."

"I know, it's the last thing you need right now. She wanted me to get Ben to talk to him but I said he'd be more likely to listen to you." There is a brief silence. "She's really worried," Maddy says.

"Well, she's probably right to be worried."

"Will you call her, Prosper? Or call Alex?"

"I'll try," he says.

"One more thing," Maddy says. "Are you planning to go to Chip Boyle's party Wednesday night?"

"I'll probably be half dead Wednesday night."

"Ah, yes. How could I forget? Well, look, if you're still awake and you want to help a girl out, I don't particularly look forward to going over to the East Side alone."

"You're afraid you might get mugged by an investment banker?"

"That would be at Chip's place," Maddy says. It's the corporate lawyers roaming the streets I'm worried about."

## SIX

Where the fuck is she?

Alex vividly recalls his conversation, his argument, whatever the hell it was, with Lydia after she got back from school. At that point he'd been awake for a day and a half or two days, somewhere in between, and he was coming down with a thud. She walked out and he had a tall glass of Gallo from a jug that had been in the fridge for about three months, on the top shelf behind the milk and a quart bottle of Coke. That knocked him out and he fell asleep on the couch. Did he hear her come in after dark? He can't remember. He has long, amazing dreams after tripping and his head is full of them this morning, all jumbled up. A dream of his mother, before she got sick, sick in the sense of depressed. His father, the bastard, always uses the "sick" euphemism, as if it was some sort of unavoidable infection, as opposed to getting emotionally battered day after day by a fascist money-grubbing racist hypocrite. In the dream she was radiant, on the beach off Atlantic Avenue, looking as she did when he was maybe ten or eleven. Her hair blowing in the wind. He has inherited her black hair. Another dream about the place where they used to get drinks made of papaya juice and coconut milk and something else, and she would buy him a monkey's head sculpted from a coconut. His father threw them all out. In the midst of all this, Lydia speaking to him, or was that a dream as well?

He's wide awake now, with that familiar spinny hangover, not from the wine but from the morning glory seeds and not eating for two days. Not eating anything healthy, anyway. Some pork rinds with...who? He was hanging out with some guys, having beers with some Puerto Rican guys. Was that last night? No, last night he slept on the couch and had dreams about his mother and the coconut monkey heads. So it was night before last.

Why is the apartment so cold? This isn't an aspect of the hangover: It's freezing. The living room window is wide open; he staggers over and slams it down. He makes his way into the bedroom for a sweater and discovers *that* window open to its maximum as well. What the hell could he have been thinking?

## The Mountaintop

He wants to trip again, at least get a little stoned. What
time is it? He rambles out the bedroom door far enough to see
the clock on the kitchen wall. Six forty-five. What day is it?
Sunday night he was out all night, so yesterday was Monday.
Tuesday morning he has a nine o'clock class. Cinematography.
So the big decision is whether to crush some more seeds or
maybe smoke some dope, or to get himself together and go to
class. Breakfast would be a good prelude to either choice.

But where the fuck is Lydia? Is it possible she came
back and spoke to him, she tried to get him off the couch and
into bed, then she went to bed and now she's opened both the
windows and gone off to school? It's a comforting thought in a
way, that she hasn't spent the night elsewhere, but a queasy
thought as well that she may have come and gone and he
doesn't know for sure. He's going over all this, trying to run
the night through his head like a movie, as he looks through
kitchen cupboards for cereal. There are only some Grape-Nuts,
maybe half a bowl's worth, and God knows how old. He leaves
the open carton on the kitchen counter. The movie isn't
working because he can't separate what happened from what he
wants to have happened and—to some degree—what he hopes
*didn't* happen. Which is actually not a bad idea for a movie.
Next semester—if there is a next semester—he'll have a
screenwriting class and he'll have to remember the idea of that
three-way confusion. Probably he should write it down. But
first he's got to have something to eat. Is there bread? Yes! In
the little built-in bread enclosure there are a few slices of whole
wheat in a plastic bag and half a loaf of rye. Peanut butter in
the fridge. He chooses the rye and thinks about toasting it but
decides he doesn't have the patience. He smears peanut
butter—Jif, the cheap, lousy stuff Lydia buys—generously on

47

the bread and has a bite: the peanut butter is rancid and the bread is stale, but it will do.

He heads for the bedroom, munching on his breakfast, intending to write down his screenplay idea but already having trouble remembering exactly what it was. It had to do with Lydia and last night, the long mysterious, dream-filled night in which he saw his mother on the beach, and Lydia may have come home or that might have been part of a dream. Here is his pen and here is his thick, leather-bound notebook, a present from his stepmother. He rests the oozing peanut-buttered rye bread atop the dresser and he writes: *LYDIA where she was. Where is she? Did she come and talk to me, or did I wish she did?* He likes the sound of that. Perhaps he could eliminate a few words and make it a haiku. He is in the process of counting syllables when the telephone rings. This, for sure, is Lydia. Who else would be calling him at seven in the morning?

He stumbles back into the living room, leaving breakfast and the notebook behind, and gets his answer soon enough. "Alex? Hope I didn't wake you up..." Good God. It is his father, and there's no way out.

"Dad? No. I'm up."

"I wanted to catch you."

To *catch* me? Alex tries desperately to clear his head. "Here I am," is all he can think to say.

"Listen. I have it on good intelligence that you've been slacking off again." Christ! Did Lydia call him? Alex's father doesn't approve of her, has in fact called her a "spic," although not to her face. This despite the fact that his second wife, the stepmother, is Cuban, and even more despite the fact that his first wife, Alex's mother, was so dark that-- Alex has only recently come to believe--she was, she must have been, Negro.

Hair straight, but black as ebony, and dusky skin, as if she had a permanent tan. "Any truth to that?"

When could Lydia have talked to him? Why would she have? "I'm fine," Alex says. "Everything's fine. Nothing to worry about. How are you? How is Ofelia?"

"That's not what I hear," says the gravelly voice from a thousand miles away, in the sternly disapproving tone so familiar and so dreadful. "You'll recall, I didn't want you to go to this damn *film* school in the first place. You couldn't have gotten into a decent law school if you'd wanted to, but business school was an option. Still is. I could get you in at Gainesville for the summer session."

*What does he know?* is the thought that reverberates in Alex's mind, bouncing around and keeping him from transcending his general state of befuddlement. "Did Lydia call you?" is the best he can come up with.

"Did *she* call me?" He says, as if it's the craziest notion in the history of the world, but on the other hand, it's not exactly a denial. Alex is getting more agitated by the second, shivering in the cold, wondering what's become of Lydia, wondering whether she did come back and she called his father in the middle of the night. "Just *tell* me, Dad, for Christ's sake."

"Tell you what? If that girl is worried about you, then I certainly should be worried about you, wouldn't you think?"

"Dad...Did Lydia tell you she's worried about me?"

"I have this picture of you farting away your life, taking drugs, hanging around with hippies... How much did I spend on that camera and the tape recorder? Fifteen hundred dollars?"

His adrenaline goes berserk. "Why do you ask that?"

"What's the point of throwing away money like that, on top everything else, all that tuition, your goddamn club at Princeton, if you plan to live like some kind of hobo?"

"I bought all that stuff with my own money," Alex says.

"Jesus Christ!" His father says. "God help me! Your mother's turning over in her grave, if she's listening to this. You've never worked a day in your life. Your mother, in her blessed innocence, against *my* judgment, left you a bundle of money and you might as well be flushing it down the toilet."

"Dad...she committed *suicide.*" This Alex speaks not tactically, but as a sort of spontaneous, non sequitur rebuttal, and it seems to have an effect. There is silence at the other end of the line for several seconds.

Finally his father says, "What does that have to do with anything?"

Just everything, Alex thinks, starting to wake up, to focus, to transform this terrible antagonism he feels into something functional. "You make it sound like she's on her deathbed and you're giving her financial advice. That's complete bullshit."

"That's not what I said." There's a little less bite in his father's voice. "I advised her to put the money in trust for you. Years before she died. When you were fifteen or sixteen."

"And she did," Alex says. "It's not your money that pays my tuition, it's hers." Indeed it is. The financial situation is too complicated and too unseemly for Alex to try to understand, but he knows that his mother left him money outright, with which he pays the rent and buys his stuff, and she left him lots more money in trust, which his father can't touch except to dole out to Alex.

"All of it," his father says. "I told her, put all of it in trust, because the kid has no more sense about money than you do."

Alex's mind now works in two directions. One: He doesn't know when or even really if Lydia talked to his father, but it appears she didn't mention anything about the drugs, so this is just more of the same old crap, which is good, because— Two: He has been this angry, even angrier at his father in the past, but never felt as close to breaking through the barrier, of fighting back with as much full-bore malice as his father uses against him. He says, "At least she had a sense of decency. She was way ahead of you in that."

"Excuse me?" There is a familiar angry tremble in the old man's voice. "Is this my son, who lives like an animal with a girl from the slums, trying to lecture me about *decency*?"

"If she was turning over in her grave over anything I've done," Alex says, "then what do you figure she was doing when you shacked up with Ofelia a couple of months after she died?"

"That's a lie and you know it."

Alex is on to something, and he feels it. "When *did* Ofelia come into the picture, Dad? How long before Mom killed herself?"

"You know what I'm going to do?" His father says. "The minute we hang up, I'm calling Hank Lindstrom. Hell, I'm going over to his office. I'm going to break this trust. Have them take one look at you in court. Have a judge size you up, and see what he thinks of a deadbeat hippie living off his mother's family money."

"Did you *tell* her about Ofelia, Dad? Or did she catch you in the act? Is that why she took the pills?" The line goes dead. Alex drops the receiver and sprawls prone on the couch, gasping and sweating as if he'd just climbed seven slights of

51

stairs in a minute. He pounds his fists into the cushion and giggles like a ten-year-old until tears come to his eyes.

What's next? Again he feels the *frisson* that accompanies the thought of getting high: anticipation, excitement, guilt. In this case, the guilt's the main thing, overshadowing the image of himself tripping, heading outside on a spring day. But no, it's more important to go to class. Not because his fucking father wants him to, but to prove that he's capable. He's responsible. But he's got to come down a little bit. His heart's still beating like crazy fifteen minutes after his father hung up on him.

From the medicine cabinet he removes the big bottle of One-A-Day vitamins; below the top layer--the façade--of vitamins is an assortment of variously colored pills, and he grabs a couple of red ones, then rearranges so the vitamins are on top again and puts the bottle back on its shelf. He spots the peanut-buttered bread on the dresser and picks it up, leaving a sticky residue on the wood. He'll have to take care of that later. He washes the reds down with a big swallow of Coke from the half-empty quart bottle. The Coke is flat, but still pleasantly sweet. He finishes the bread and has another few gulps of Coke.

Back on the couch. It's nearly seven thirty now and class isn't till nine. Maybe a short nap? He should get the alarm clock from the bedroom and set it for eight thirty, but surely he'll only sleep for a few minutes. The reds are descending upon him like a slowly lowering shade. A velvet shade. Such a sweet image at such a sweet moment.

He awakens to the sound of a key in the lock. Lydia? Lydia! What time is it? Eight twenty-five. Far fucking out! He'll have time to greet her, hug her, apologize for whatever, tell her he loves her, and get to class. But her key doesn't seem to be working. It's a metallic scratching sound, like a key being inserted and re-inserted. He shouts, "Lydia!" and the noise ceases, but there is no response. Then the sound resumes.

He creeps to the front door, struggling against a bad case of Seconal grogginess. "Who's there?" he shouts. "Is somebody there? I'm gonna call the cops!"

There is no response. "Last chance," he yells, "before I call the police!"

Seconds go by. Then he hears, "Hey, Alex. Hey, man, it's Flaco from the other night."

Flaco? Alex shouts, "I don't know anybody named Flaco. Get the fuck out of here!"

"*Flaco*, man. We were havin' a few drinks together, you and me and Rafael and Julio. We came back here. You remember."

"No, I don't. Get lost. Go away."

Another brief silence. "Listen, Alex, I got a message for you from Lydia."

Can this be true? Why would this asshole have a message from Lydia? What if they've kidnapped her? "Okay," he shouts. "Tell me the message."

"Shit, man, I'm not gonna stand out here all day yelling through the door! Let me the fuck in, man!"

At this point Alex is about sixty percent dead set against opening the door to God knows what kind of mayhem, and forty percent concerned that this guy he can't remember might really know something about Lydia, who's been gone all night except if he didn't dream her appearance in the wee hours. "You give me the message, for Christ's sake, or tell me what it's about, and maybe I'll let you in."

53

No response for quite a while. His ear pressed against the door, Alex wonders if he hears murmuring, low conversation, Spanish. Or is he imagining it? He wishes he had a gun. He is in principle entirely opposed to even the idea of guns, but there are times when having a gun would be useful. He does have a brown belt in karate. There is a big carving knife a few feet away in the kitchen. Not very sharp, but this guy wouldn't know that. What if there are two of them out there? Then he wouldn't have much of a chance. "Hey!" he shouts. "Is it just you?" What the fuck was this guy's name? "Flaco? You alone?"

"Yeah, man, it's just me." The voice is softer, calmer. "Listen...Lydia had a accident. She needs you, Alex."

His heart races. "What kind of accident? Where is she?"

"Rafael took her to the hospital. To the emergency room."

"Who the hell is Rafael?"

"Aw, *fuck*, man! Don't you remember nothing? The dude in the leather jacket you liked so much. You said the dude was a fuckin' poet."

Alex suddenly has a clear image of the guy in the leather jacket—Rafael. He *did* like him. And the other guys, Flaco, very tall, and some fat guy who sat on the couch and took his *Incredible Hulk* comic. "Which hospital?"

"Saint *Luke's*, man. Where do you fuckin' think?"

The balance has tipped. Not that he's completely without suspicion, but now it's maybe sixty-forty the other way. He could tell them to leave, and he'd be along in a minute, but if they had evil intentions they could just wait for him by the building entrance. He can't go out the window because it's a fifteen-foot drop and even if he didn't break his ankles he'd be in a courtyard with no direct access to the street. He could wait them out, but if it's true that Lydia's hurt, wasting time is the worst thing he could do. What the hell. He undoes the deadbolt and swings the door open, recalling as he does so that he's neglected to ask what exactly has happened to Lydia.

There are two of them: Flaco the very tall one, and the big, fat guy who took the comic. Flaco saunters in and Alex retreats. He says, "What's the matter with her?"

"It ain't serious," Flaco says. "You remember Julio?" The fat guy nods at Alex and follows Flaco inside.

"Let's go, then," Alex says. "I want to see her."

Yeah, okay," Flaco says, "but first we wanna pick up that shit you gave us Monday."

"I didn't give you anything." He points to Julio. "He took my *Incredible Hulk*."

"The camera and the tape recorder, man. Where they at?"

Alex shakes his head. "No. I need that stuff. I'm at film school."

"Yeah, well, nevertheless, you gave the shit to us. You can buy new ones. Better ones..."   "What about Lydia?" Alex says with urgency. "Tell me what happened to her."

Julio has barged by Alex and gone into the bedroom. "I dunno, man," Flaco says. "She cut her finger. No big deal."

There is commotion in the bedroom. Drawers opening and closing. *"Los tengo,"* Julio calls, and in moments he appears with the Bolex sixteen-millimeter camera and the Nagra tape recorder, a good thousand dollars' worth of equipment. "Jesus," Alex says, "you can't steal those things. I have a class. I'm doing a goddamn *project*." He takes a position in front of the door.

55

"Don't be a fuckin' Indian giver, Alex," Flaco says.

"Look, if I said I was giving the stuff to you, I was high. I was wasted. I didn't mean it." Julio hovers over him by the door, clutching the expensive equipment, the symbols of Alex's renewed dedication to his craft.

"Tell you what," Flaco says. "I'll sell it back to you for...five hundred bucks."

Julio glares at Flaco and raises his chin toward the ceiling. "*Más,*" he says.

It crosses Alex's mind that he could write them a check, then stop payment on it. But then they'd surely come back. He could write them a check and be done with it, but they'd never accept a check, would they? Then he curses himself for even thinking about paying these bastards for his own camera and tape recorder. "I don't have that kind of money," he says, "and you can't take my stuff."

"Just get out of the way, man," Flaco says.

Standing in the doorway, Alex assumes a martial arts stance. When Flaco takes a step in his direction, Alex commences a kick whose target is Flaco's groin, but the tall, wiry Puerto Rican simply grabs Alex's ankle and heaves him at the doorjamb, where Alex crumples to the floor, semi-conscious.

## SEVEN

The word that comes to Ben's mind for this group is: *straight.* Seven of the eight boys in Southwestern's student council wear coats and ties, and the eighth sports a very unthreatening turtleneck. Hairstyles are two or three years back in time, and Bass Weejuns dominate. There are two girls, one of whom seems to have copied her look from a Lesley Gore album cover, except her skirt is daringly cut an inch above the knees. The other girl, Randall's characterization of the school notwithstanding, would appear not to be white. Her skin is lighter than café au lait but her hair is straight, and her features-- her lips and her nose--do not have a negroid fullness. Her eyes, too, are more green than brown, and all in all it is quite a picture. She is exotic enough, different enough, to be enticing, but not so much to fall outside Ben's definition of beauty. She wears a knee-length blue skirt over black tights, and a black v-neck sweater. While Randall makes opening remarks Ben cannot take his eyes off her. If this is a "white" school, what does that make her? Could she be Polynesian, or from somewhere in the Caribbean?

They're in a smallish classroom--Randall and Ben up on the stage, such as it is, Randall at the podium, and their audience seated below in fixed wooden chairs. "So the thing is," Randall says, wrapping up, "that in a lot of senses we're finding our way. It hasn't been two weeks since Senator Kennedy announced his candidacy. But it's been a pretty busy two weeks, you might say." There is laughter from the student council--good, friendly laughter. "The big news as far as the

57

campaign is concerned came yesterday, when President Johnson announced he was *not* running for re-election. And of course you folks have had some things happening right here in Memphis." There is laughter again, this time brief and tentative. Randall pauses, then says, "Can I ask how many of you folks consider yourselves Democrats? Can I get a show of hands?" Ten hands are elevated. "Can I ask how many of you will be eligible to vote in November?" Nine out of ten.

"Can I ask how many of you would be pleased if Senator Kennedy gets the Democratic nomination?" Five hands go up, including the café-au-lait girl's. Randall speaks to a burly, sandy-haired boy in the front row whose hand was not raised. "How about you. What's your name, and who should get the nomination?"

"Everett," the boy says. "And I would support Hubert Humphrey. I still kind of hope that President Johnson might reconsider, because I think he's done a real good job. I think Kennedy...I think Senator Kennedy's really running on one issue, which is the war..."

"And what do you think about the war?"

"Well, I can't say I'm a hundred percent behind it, but I do believe in the importance of stopping Communism..."

"Would you fight in the war, Everett? Do you plan to fight in the war?"

Everett, who has been quick to respond so far, now stops to consider. "*Would* I fight in the war? Yes, sir, I think I would. But after I graduate in June my plan is to go to law school, so I do have a deferment."

"So in all probability," Randall says, altogether affably, "you're probably not going to get that degree and *then* go to Vietnam." He pauses for a couple of seconds before saying, "Tell me what it is you like about President Johnson, Everett."

58

Visibly relieved to be off the hook, Everett jumps into this easy question. "I think he's in the best tradition of Democratic politics. He's dealt real well with labor and with big business, and he's done more for civil rights than all the previous administrations put together..."

"Right," Randall says. "And now that he's made sure we can vote and move into all the right neighborhoods, he's sending us all to Southeast Asia to get us killed."

There is a burst of laughter, spontaneous, but perhaps a bit nervous. Ben's eye is on the girl three rows back, who does not laugh, but smiles thinly. Everett, meanwhile, resumes the battle. "See, you're back to the war. It's the only issue you've got."

"I assure you it's not the only issue Senator Kennedy's got," Randall says. "But if you care about civil rights and racial equality, as I'm sure you do, you should look and see who's fighting this war for President Johnson. By and large it's *not* people like you and me, who have deferments, or families, or friends in high places who can get us into the National Guard. It's poor kids--and a disproportionate number of poor *black* kids--who get drafted, go through basic training, and *whoosh!* They're in Vietnam just like that. And they're in the infantry, which means like as not they're somewhere in the jungle fighting the Viet Cong on *his* terms."

A boy two seats to Everett's left raises his hand and Randall nods in his direction. "My name is Steven," he says, "and I want to say that I do care about civil rights, but I also care about the state of this country, and of this city, and I'm concerned about what's been happening for the last year or so."

Randall says, "Could you be a little more specific, Steven?"

59

Slender and clean-cut, Steven wears khakis and a blue blazer. "The riots in Detroit and Newark last summer. What happened last week here in Memphis. I'm afraid things could get out of hand..."

"And what would happen if things got out of hand?"

"Well, whole cities could burn up, for one thing. I don't know how close we came to that here, but I think if the police hadn't acted as fast as they did, it would've been a lot worse here."

Ben's eyes shift between the girl in the back, whom he very much enjoys watching, and Randall, who is being drawn into what seems perilous territory. Clearly, Randall could recapitulate some of their conversation on the plane, but in doing so would risk alienating Steven and probably several other members of the student council. "Tell me something," Randall says, focused on Steven. "In all those riots last summer--in Newark, in Detroit, in Los Angeles in sixty-five--did you hear anything about white people losing their homes? Did you hear anything about fires and looting in downtown areas. That was black people burning down their *own* neighborhoods."

"But the rioting in Memphis *was* downtown," Steven protests, "and the businesses that got vandalized and looted were white-owned."

"Do you actually call what happened in Memphis a *riot*?"

Now Everett, the big, sandy-haired boy, rejoins the fray. "The riots last summer--maybe they started in black neighborhoods, and maybe it was just good work by the police that kept them in black neighborhoods. Who's to say that the next one won't just explode? If Martin Luther King gets to hold that march here next week, who's to say this time the marchers won't be better prepared? Who's to say they won't bring in militants from all over the country? Who's to say they won't be carrying guns instead of just wooden sticks?"

A broad, incredulous smile has formed on Randall's face. "Do you really think that's what Doctor King stands for? Have you been living on some different planet from me for the last ten years or so?"

Ben thinks: probably so. Everett says, "Look, King may be preaching non-violence, but what happened here Thursday sure as hell wasn't non-violent..."

"Can I say something?" It's the girl sitting alone in the third row. Randall says, "By all means." She is silent for a long moment, perhaps conscious that suddenly all eyes are on her. Then she says, "Everett, you should listen to what you're saying. You should be ashamed of yourself. You've lived here all your life, just like me, and if you think Memphis has just turned into some kind of magnet for black revolutionaries, you've got to be crazy..."

"I *have* lived here all my life." Everett has twisted around in his seat so he faces the girl. "And I don't like what's happening here. I don't like it that they've picked Memphis to be some kind of battleground. Why do they all have to come here to do their damn marching and demonstrating? And rioting."

The girl doesn't hesitate this time. "What do you mean, 'they,' Everett? And what do you mean, 'rioting?' I was *there* Thursday, and what I saw was a peaceful march that got messed up because some kids and some criminals broke some windows, and that's where it should have ended. That should have been the extent of it. But if you ask me, it was the police force that rioted--running around spraying Mace in old ladies' faces, and ministers' faces, and trapping people so they had nowhere to go, and killing that boy, and then claiming he had a knife after they shot him in cold blood."

Now, as several people start to speak at once, Randall takes advantage of his superior position and says, "Hey, people, let's cool it!" Ben's gaze does not leave the girl in the third row. She still sits forward in her seat, knowing she's just said something unpopular, anticipating retaliation. Randall says, "Did anybody else actually *see* anything Thursday? Did any of you observe any looting, or any unrest?"

In the second row, a boy previously unheard from, the turtleneck-wearer, says, "Are you saying it didn't happen?"

"I just want to find out what you all saw, or experienced, as opposed to what you heard about."

The other girl, the white girl, who sits just behind Steven, says, "I was here at school when all this was going on, but the parents of one of my best friends own one of those stores on Beale Street--Lasky's Liquors--and she says the people who work in the store were scared for their lives. These boys broke the window, and then all of a sudden there were about ten of them inside the store, grabbing up bottles. They didn't get any money, but that was just because the manager emptied the cash register before they broke the window."

Her voice trails off, and after a few moments' silence Randall says, "Anybody else?"

The boy who'd spoken up a moment ago, the turtleneck boy, says, "Look, what's the point of this? We were all at school, how were we gonna see anything? We all heard stuff, we all know people that saw stuff, that weren't making things up."

"But it seems to me," Randall says, "that we've only got one eyewitness. What's your name, please?" He asks the girl in the third row.

"Delphine. Delphine Ennis."

"Delphine doesn't necessarily contradict what you all heard about. She just tells the story from a different perspective. I have no doubt that people were breaking windows on Beale Street, and taking stuff. I have no doubt that people were running amuck in other parts of town, later in the day. But Delphine tells us about what sounds like a very small percentage of a very large group getting out of control. And on the other side, probably also a very small percentage of the police reacting with far too much force. So can you picture that? All these orderly people on one side of the street. Then some bricks break some windows. That's a *loud* noise. Let's say there's just two or three cops poised for a confrontation, and they see the window breakers and they start running and Macing. So how do the orderly people react? They don't want to get Maced or gassed, so they take off running. Now how do the rest of the police react? They see their brethren Macing and gassing, and they see people running every which way, so *they* start Macing and gassing, and pretty soon they start clubbing, too. And pretty soon word spreads to the black neighborhoods that the cops are beating black people, and word spreads to the white neighborhoods that the Nigras are rioting, and suddenly you've got a city about to explode."

Randall pauses, making deliberate eye contact with everyone in his modest audience. He says, "Then what happened?" No one responds. He says, "Everett, tell me what happened next."

"The National Guard came. We had tanks rolling down Main Street, guys in uniform all over the place. Police everywhere."

"Steven," Randall says, "tell me what happened after that."

63

"Not much," Steven says. "They all left. Went back to Nashville, or wherever they came from."

Randall speaks to the turtleneck boy. "What's your name?"

"Wendell."

"Wendell--do you know that in Detroit, and Newark, and Watts, after the first outbreaks of violence, even after the National Guard came in, the fires and the looting got worse? Why do you figure that didn't happen here?"

"Because the police clamped down right at the start."

"Delphine," Randall says, "you agree with that?"

"No, sir, I sure don't."

"Explain it to me, please."

"It was because nothing happened here in the first place. Nothing happened except some stupid kids broke some windows and stole some stuff, and the police went crazy."

"What about the Invaders? What about the Black Power contingent? You think they had a hand in that window-breaking and looting?"

"No, I don't," Delphine says. "Contrary to popular opinion, I don't think it would be in their best interest to have people breaking windows and stealing liquor. I don't think that's what Black Power's supposed to be about."

"Stealing liquor wasn't the half of it," Everett breaks in. "Stealing guns is what worries me." There are murmurs of concurrence. Delphine shakes her head in disgust.

"So," Randall says to Everett, "I take it you disagree with Delphine? You think that was the Invaders breaking into the gun shop?"

"I can't say for certain," Everett says. "But I don't believe it's fair for her to say it wasn't them.

"Let me ask you this," Randall says to Everett. "If you had to apply one word, or two words, to what happened here Thursday, what would they be?"

"Riot," Everett says. He pauses for several seconds. "And anarchy."

"Steven--how about you?"

"Rebellion," says the boy in the blue blazer. "Chaos."

"Delphine?" Randall says. You have two words for me?"

"Prejudice," she says, "and distrust."

Ben watches Randall's face light up. This, he knows, is nothing theatrical. "Distrust!" Randall says. "Tell me about that word. How does it apply?"

"Both ways," the girl says. "What happened Thursday was pure distrust. The police didn't trust us. Not just Doctor King, but all those ministers out there, black *and* white, and all those people out making a point of being peaceful. And when a few of those redneck police got out of control we said, 'Oh, boy, here it comes again--white cops beating up innocent black people--and we ran."

Randall says, "Everett, tell me what you think of Delphine."

The thickset boy is caught off guard. "What I *think* of her? Well, in this case I think she's lookin' through rose-colored glasses."

"But what do you think of her in general. You get along with her?"

"Sure. She's nice. She's all right."

"Why do you suppose you have this difference of opinion?"

"Well...in this case, I guess because she's colored and I'm white."

65

"Can you see her side of it, though? Can you see it a little?"

"A little. I wouldn't be surprised if some cops got more violent than they should have. But I think it's asking too much of them to hold back and be careful in a riot situation."

"You see how they might have contributed to that situation?"

Everett responds after a few seconds, "It's possible."

"Good," Randall says. He takes an audible breath. "You see what we've just had here, we've had a dialogue, which is something I think we need a whole lot more of, because we've got an awful lot of distrust here. I'm not talking about Memphis, which you all know a lot better than I do, but about the United States in general. I think we've got to start talking to each other more than we have been, and I think we need a president who's going to encourage that kind of dialogue. Promote it. Take part in it."

Randall goes on in this manner for another five minutes. In their brief acquaintance Ben has never seen him so eloquent, so passionate. At the end, when Randall steps down from the stage and begins shaking hands with the student council, Everett first, Ben wonders how any of these young white southerners could support a candidate other than Robert Kennedy.

On a table in the back of the room there is a pail filled with ice and soft drinks, and a tray of pastries covered with powdered sugar. The girl, Delphine, holds a bottle of Coca-Cola and observes, along with several other council members, a conversation between Randall and Steven.

"Delphine?" Ben says, and she turns to face him. Perhaps it is because of the contrast with her mocha skin, but her eyes seem an other-worldly green. He says, "My name is

Ben Shelton. I wanted to tell you how much I appreciated what you said tonight."

"Thank you." This is the first time he's seen her broad smile. He waits for her to speak further. When she doesn't, he says, "It must have been pretty scary out there."

She gives him a quizzical look. "Tonight?"

"No. Thursday, at the march."

She laughs at her misunderstanding. "Yeah. It was the kind of thing, you know, you see it on television and you don't get any idea of what the tear gas smells like, or what it's like to be afraid of falling down and getting your head busted open by some cop's nightstick." She takes a sip of her Coke and she appears to look at him a bit more earnestly. "You're from New York too?"

She is perhaps half a foot shorter than he, a couple of inches taller than Maddy. "Massachusetts originally. Just outside of Boston."

"And have you known Randall long?"

"Couple of years. We were on the same softball team."

She smiles. "Does he ever give you a chance to talk?"

"Once in a while." He's about to start in on this morning's adventure with the black teenagers when he stops in his tracks, wondering whether it would be an appropriate anecdote in his current circumstances. So he stands there for a few seconds, uncharacteristically at a loss for words, and just then Randall catches his eye, nodding toward the door, telling him it's time to go. He says, "Listen, could I talk to you some more?"

"Of course," she says.

"I mean, we've got to leave now, for some kind of dinner. Maybe we could get together later."

"You're going to a dinner with Randall, right?"

67

"Yes."

"Well, you'll see me there. Dinner's at my parents' house."

## EIGHT

"Look," Maddy tells the man behind the desk, "it's very simple. I specified how I wanted my name on the checks. You got it wrong. Now you have to give me new checks."

"I'm sorry, Miss," the man says. He's about twenty-five. The nameplate on the desk says CORNELIUS MATTHIAS. Maddy wonders what qualities have elevated him here to this little cluster of sleek desks, as opposed to the tellers' cages across the lobby. Matthias has oily, receding black hair, and wears a brown suit with a narrow red tie against a white shirt. "I'm sorry, but what we did was we put your name on the checks just like it's on your account..."

"No, you didn't. My name on the account is Frances Magdalena O'Connor. What you have on the checks is Frances M. O'Connor."

"Yes, because the whole thing wouldn't fit."

"Look, I'm known as Magdalena O'Connor. Every two weeks I get a paycheck issued to Magdalena O'Connor. I don't need checks and deposit slips with Frances O'Connor on them.

If you'd written my entire name on the checks, it would have been all right. But you didn't. So you've got to give me new checks."

"Yes, I have agreed that we're printing you new checks, but we have to charge you the replacement charge for the new checks, which is three dollars for two hundred checks."

"Then I'm going to have to withdraw my money from the bank," Maddy says. "There's a Chase Manhattan two blocks down Broadway and I hear they're capable of printing checks right on the first try."

Cornelius Matthias wrinkles his upper lip. "You're gonna have to go through the whole process of opening a new account. Is that really worth three dollars?"

"You're damn right it is," Maddy says.

He looks across the lobby, as if seeking an escape route. "I'll have to talk to Mister Shapiro about this, okay?"

The apartment is a third-floor walkup on the south side of 91st Street, between Broadway and West End. The living room, by the standards of one-bedroom apartments in the price range, is huge--perhaps fourteen feet by eighteen--but this area includes the kitchenette, and of course the dinner table must double as living room furniture, the only other substantial pieces of which are a love seat and chair from Maddy's parents' house in New Jersey. (When her parents donated the furniture they assumed she was taking the apartment on her own; it was only after several months of Ben's happening to answer the telephone at all hours of the day and night that the official revelation was made, and it remains a fairly delicate subject.)

The bathroom door is adjacent to the refrigerator, not the most aesthetic arrangement, but the bathroom contains all the amenities--in miniature, to be sure. One may not stretch out in the tub, but one may take a bath as well as a shower, although one may not use the sink if the other one is sitting on the toilet. The bedroom is long and narrow: with the queen-size bed in its southeast corner there is a three-foot corridor between the bed and the west wall. If Maddy needs to get up in the middle of the night she must choose between crawling to the bottom of the bed or vaulting over Ben. (Prosper has suggested that the bed might be turned ninety degrees, putting its head to the east, which would leave space for maneuvering at either side and still two feet at the foot, but Ben prefers the bed exactly as it is.) At the foot of the bed is the tall chest of drawers that Maddy and her sister Jill shared as children, and beyond that the apartment's only closet, which is overstuffed with clothing that is, by Maddy's estimation, about seventy percent Ben's.

Both rooms look out on a little courtyard/garden outside the landlord's ground floor apartment. The garden features an apple tree, several rosebushes, and two little dogs who yap furiously at the slightest provocation. The Stillmans are in the habit of releasing the dogs sometime between one and four in the morning, and two nights in three they sniff out imaginary intruders and launch into fifteen-minute barkfests. Neighbors have called the police on more than one occasion, to no long-term effect.

Maddy deposits her school bag on the dinner table, puts the quart of milk in the refrigerator, puts the box of Post Raisin Bran in the little cupboard above the little stove. She has just turned twenty-three, and is less than a year removed from Sarah Lawrence College. She is five feet, four inches tall and quite good-looking, with straight brown hair that falls three inches or so below her shoulders. Like her sisters (Jill is a junior at Radcliffe, Bridget a senior in high school) she is slim and has soft, symmetrical features. But while her sisters have curly hair and blue eyes, like both parents, Maddy's hair is absolutely straight and her eyes brown, both traits inherited from her Spanish maternal grandmother, also named Magdalena.

The original Magdalena was killed in a train wreck in 1930, fifteen years before Maddy was born, but it is because of her that Maddy finds herself in the current arrangement. The original Magdalena was the daughter of a Spanish wine importer named Alvaro de Logroño, who moved his family to New York in 1897, when Magdalena was eight. His business ground to a halt during the Spanish-American War, but Logroño elected to stay on and ultimately became moderately successful. Magdalena eloped with an Irish accountant when she was twenty-one; they had two daughters, both of whom Magdalena raised bilingually. The older daughter lost interest in Spanish as a teenager, but Maddy's mother remained loyal, and was in fact a high school Spanish teacher when she met Maddy's father.

Maddy, naturally, majored in Spanish at Sarah Lawrence, and spent her junior year abroad in San Sebastián. In June of 1966 she stopped in Madrid for a week on her way home, and on the next-to-last day she met an American boy named Prosper Murphy at a café near the Prado. She rather liked Prosper, who was funny and good-looking, and quite a change from her intense and self-important Basque boyfriend of the year gone by. He visited her later in the summer, in Short Hills, and took her to the Apollo Theater in New York, where they were the only white people at a show headlined by Wilson Pickett. Afterwards they drove down to the Village to have a drink with Prosper's best friend, Ben Shelton. Ben was not as funny as Prosper but was strikingly handsome and projected a combination of self-assuredness and gentleness that Maddy found irresistible.

It made for a difficult situation. She was in no position to tell Prosper that she preferred his friend, not being anywhere near certain that Ben was interested in her. Perhaps he flirted with everyone. Nor did she feel comfortable with the prospect of calling Ben and asking him. So she waited, and for a couple of weeks found reasons to refuse Prosper's various invitations, until eventually Ben called her. He was full of apologies for the delay, explaining that he'd been unwilling to deceive his best friend, that he'd wanted to make clear to Prosper what was in the works. Maddy realized that Ben had not reciprocated her uncertainty, that he'd had absolutely no doubt of her interest in him.

Her parents, who had liked Prosper, loved Ben. He charmed her mother (even though he didn't speak Spanish) and his politics were almost identical to her father's. Maddy spent most of August with him, either at his apartment on West Eleventh Street or in Short Hills, with Ben sneaking down the hall into her room after her parents had gone to bed. After school resumed she spent virtually every weekend with him in the city, while he made frequent visits to Bronxville. From time to time she found disturbing evidence in his apartment: a poorly cleaned wine glass with lipstick smudges, a feminine umbrella in the closet. She did not confront him until the day she was changing the sheets and out tumbled a pair of women's underpants not her own. Ben confessed immediately, and with appropriate remorse: he had strayed with a Ford Foundation colleague; they'd had too much to drink, he'd invited her to spend the night, and one thing had led to another. In the morning they'd both felt thoroughly embarrassed by the whole thing. Maddy had been impressed by Ben's candor, found his explanation entirely credible, and forgiven him. Only later had it occurred to her: In the morning, when she was thoroughly

72

embarrassed, would the colleague have strolled out of Ben's apartment without her underpants? Or did this suggest some kind of planned rendezvous or regular arrangement, in which a change of underpants was brought along or available?

But those questions were never posed, and from that day in December there appeared no further alien garments or other objects of suspicion. On Maddy's twenty-second birthday-- March 25 1967--Ben suggested that they move in together when she was done with Sarah Lawrence, and she accepted without a moment's hesitation. He heard about the apartment on 91st Street in April, grabbed it, and moved into it on the first of May; she joined him in mid-June, after graduation and a week in Aruba.

Maddy spent the summer becoming certified to teach in various venues, but feared she would have to spend at least a year or two as an assistant at some private school, or as an on-call substitute in the public school system. She got the job at P.S. 72 because she was bilingual, and because she had a great interview with the Puerto Rican principal, who made fun of her Castilian accent but clearly saw her as a phenomenon.

When Maddy took stock of things, as she occasionally did either in moments of blissful satisfaction or in moments of anxious solitude, she concluded that she had a good life. She was twenty-three years old, she had a job she loved a fifteen-minute bus ride from an apartment she lived in a city she loved, where she lived with a man she loved. If there was a problem it was Ben's transition from the Ford Foundation to the Kennedy Campaign--from a job that paid well and epitomized stability to a job that paid nothing at all (at least for the moment) and, if he rose through the ranks as he expected, would involve a great deal of flux and travel, and ultimately perhaps a move away from this apartment and this city. Would she abandon her job here if the call came for Ben to move to Washington? For that matter, would Ben abandon her if the call came for him to move to Washington? Or would he be content with what she suspected to be his ongoing infidelities? She had no proof, no smoking guns, no panties in the bed, but she had plenty of evidence: late-night phone calls from female voices whose timbres didn't suggest business; late-night calls from people who hung up when Maddy answered; Ben coming home-- ostensibly from foundation meetings--smelling as if he'd spent a week doing research and development at Estée Lauder; Ben changing the subject abruptly and unexpectedly when certain names or places were mentioned, as if he didn't want her to get *near* something potentially incriminating. Nor did Maddy wish to get near it, most of the time. If the thought of Ben sleeping with someone else remained unproven and ethereal, she could live with it.

The phone rings at a few minutes before five. She's making Spanish rice because she's had a craving for it and Ben doesn't like it. She switches off the burner and runs to the phone. But it's not Ben; it's Prosper. She makes herself sound not disappointed and they talk for a while. He's just been through the first day of his draft physical and he sounds kind of…exhilarated. Maybe it's the drugs, she thinks. He hasn't heard from Ben either. She remembers to tell him about Lydia and Alex, which she's sure is the last thing he wants to hear. She asks him if he's planning to go to Chip Boyle's party night after tomorrow, which she'd intended to go to with Ben. Chip is an insufferable preppy who lives on the East Side, but there's something about his parties she finds irresistible—possibly the mixture of bohemian Princeton people and debutante-party-habitué Princeton people, or possibly just that Chip and his friends are so ingenuously mindless. In any case, Prosper says he'll go with her unless he's completely wiped out. She wishes him luck, and she thanks her lucky stars for the millionth time that Ben doesn't have to worry about getting drafted—ever.

She eats her Spanish rice straight up, with a glass of some sort of barely palatable white wine Ben has left in the refrigerator. She watches the news: lots of reaction to Lyndon Johnson's announcement that he's not going to run in November. It's great news for Bobby Kennedy and it puts her one giant step closer to her future, for better or worse.

Of course he's busy. Of course he's with Randall, and Randall has them doing some intense, important thing every minute. But how can he be so unmindful of her? Just the damn note, as if she were his sister, or his stepsister.

She goes to bed at nine, tosses and turns until eleven, gets up and watches the late news and has another glass of Ben's lousy wine, goes back to bed and eventually falls asleep well into the night.

The phone wakes her. What time is it? Five of six. 4:55 in Memphis. Would Ben be up this early, or this late? She catches it just after the third ring. It's not Ben; it's Lydia.

"Maddy? Did I wake you up? Oh, jeez, I am so goddamn sorry."

"It's okay," Maddy says, when for a couple of reasons it is not. "What's going on? What's the matter?"

"Mad...you're going to school today, right?"

"Of course I am."

"Listen, can you do me a favor? Tell them I can't come in till late, till noon?"

"Why don't you just call them yourself? What's the matter?"

"I don't wanna talk about it now, okay? Can you just do me that favor?"

"I guess so. Sure. But are you all right?"

"I gotta go," Lydia says. "Love you."

And that's that.

## NINE

The house is most impressive. It is a Georgian mansion on Parkway, a wide street lined with lush lawns and huge houses. Ben's first reaction has been to wonder silently at the rapid progression of integration--that a black family could own a house on a street like this. It will come out during the evening that while this block is testament to the existence of prosperous black Memphians, it is hardly--except in the loosest definition-- evidence of integration. All these stately homes, Ben will learn, were built during the twenties and thirties by prominent white Memphis families. The black middle class began moving onto Parkway in the late forties, but always remained south of Lamar Avenue, a major artery and a dividing line between Prosperity and luxury. It was not until the early sixties that the first house north of Lamar sold to a black family, whereupon in short order this entire block followed suit.

Delphine's father is a doctor--a general practitioner--and her mother a professor of English at LeMoyne-Owen, a black college in a less desirable area of Memphis. There are by Ben's count fifteen people including himself and Randall seated at a long table in a very large dining room. Ben, Randall, and Delphine are the only diners under forty, Ben and Randall the only non-Memphians. And Ben is the only white person in the room.

Not that this is exactly like going to the Apollo Theater in Harlem with Prosper in the summer of 1965, where Ben felt completely alien. Or that it is remotely like his experience of this very morning, when he was the person of the different color but he was in charge. Tonight he might as well be at a dinner party held by slightly younger friends of his mother and stepfather, given that he is surrounded by well-dressed, primarily well-educated people chatting about current events local and national. Except, it has dawned on him, that the air at this table is much more jovial, much looser than at any dinner party given by friends of his parents.

The Ennises have servants. It would be marvelous in Ben's eyes if they had *white* servants, but it's almost as strange that they have this couple--Willie and Ethel--perhaps married, he in a crisp white jacket and black bow tie, she in an elegant costume with frilly white cuffs, serving dinner. The first course was a Cobb salad, a dish previously unknown to Ben, identified for him by Delphine, who--mercifully--sits just to his right. She has changed clothes since the student council meeting; now she wears a strapless black dress cut quite low, so that when she leans forward Ben can see about sixty percent of her left breast and not much less of her right. The current course is a huge slab of delectable roast beef with Yorkshire pudding and spinach, probably the best, the richest spinach Ben has ever tasted. Mrs. Ennis--Betty Ann--summons the waiting team with a little gold bell. When she rings the bell, Delphine winces.

77

Delphine converses with Willie and Ethel as if they're her friends; everyone else at the table treats them as servants.

Dr. Ennis--Reginald, or Reggie--sits at the head of the table, with Randall, unquestionably the guest of honor, at his right. Mrs. Ennis is at the other end, with Ben to her right. She has begun the evening addressing him as Mister Shelton; when he insisted she call him Ben, she said, "Well, then, you call me Betty Ann."

"So, Ben, you've been with the senator for how long?" Mrs. Ennis is a striking woman, with Delphine's straight hair and green eyes. Her tan skin is liberally freckled, unlike Delphine's.

"About ten days."

"That short a time?"

"Well, the campaign itself has only been around for about two weeks."

"That's right. Of course. And what did you do before you joined the campaign?"

"I was with the Ford Foundation. I'd worked there for about fifteen months. Technically I'm on a leave of absence, and technically I'm a volunteer with the campaign..."

"So you're not getting *paid*?"

"Not yet. But I anticipate that I will be. And of course if the senator is successful..."

"As we know he will be..."

"Yes, of course. When he's elected president, then it would be wonderful to get some sort of job in the administration."

"What sort of job?"

What sort of job? Ben has always imagined himself, eventually, as a congressman, a senator--a dynamic, benevolent legislator. "Working with people. Something like this, I guess. Troubleshooting. Helping."

Betty Ann speaks to Delphine. "Sweetheart, maybe you should stick around Ben. He might be able to find you some work after you graduate."

"I'm very capable of finding work on my own, Mother," Delphine replies.

Betty Ann speaks to Ben. "She only calls me 'Mother' when she's reprimanding me. But I wouldn't say I'm completely unserious here. Doctor Ennis wants his only child to follow in his footsteps and be a doctor. But I believe Delphine would prefer to go into public service. Am I right, sweetheart?"

"Mother," Delphine's tone remains gentle, "you don't have to feel obligated to tell Ben my life story."

"Just some relevant pieces, sweetheart." Betty Ann smiles coyly at Ben, who realizes in this instant that she is the very picture of a southern belle, that unlike Randall she *does* have a southern accent, that she could pass for Blanche Dubois after a week in the sun.

Presently Dr. Ennis, at the other end of the table, gets to his feet; he is only slightly darker in complexion than his wife, and heavier set. In a deep and resonant voice he thanks all his guests for coming to dinner, and introduces Randall, whom he describes (in the evening's only concession to racial identity thus far) as "an earnest and responsible young brother."

Dr. Ennis sits down; Randall stands up. He too thanks everyone for being here, and then he proceeds to speak in a manner previously unknown to Ben, lacking the drama he'd shown earlier today at Southwestern, but altogether as effective. He reminds this gathering of presumably influential and well-to-do couples that Robert Kennedy is the brother of the late president, that he was Jack Kennedy's attorney general, adviser, and confidant, that while Lyndon Johnson pushed through all the groundbreaking civil rights legislation of the last several years, that legislation had been on Jack Kennedy's agenda, and that Robert Kennedy had been its proponent. People ask him, Randall says, if there are differences between the brothers, and Randall replies that yes, there are. While Bobby Kennedy can be charming, he certainly doesn't have his older brother's charisma; nor does he have Jack's ability to deal with people by using easy charm. *But*, Randall says--and he pauses for effect--there is one area, there is one aspect of character, where Bobby Kennedy has it all over his late brother. People describe Bobby Kennedy as ruthless, as opportunist, but what drives this man is *compassion*. Yes, he wants to be president, he wants to be the most powerful man in the free world, but Bobby Kennedy's ambition isn't self-glorification, it's the desire to employ all the principles that this country stands for, it's to make *liberty* and *the pursuit of happiness* available to *all* Americans for the first time.

Randall pauses, never having raised his voice much above a conversational tone, and there is spontaneous if genteel applause. Ben finds himself clapping. To his left, Betty Ann Ennis is beaming. He cannot see Delphine's expression.

Randall resumes, getting now to the nuts and bolts. Kennedy has joined the fray late. Governor Ellington and the Democratic machine will be squarely behind Lyndon Johnson's vice-president, Hubert Humphrey, in the contest for Tennessee's electoral votes. There's no primary in Tennessee, so it's likely that at the convention the state's delegation will lean toward Humphrey or some Johnson stand-in still in the race. But if black leadership is solid behind Kennedy, it can be at the heart of a coalition with young voters and antiwar liberals and turn the delegation around. Ben imagines that this is impossible, and imagines that Randall as well believes it's impossible, but it's a great way to raise money, and to build an organization.

What Ben wants most do is spend time with Delphine. What he must do, as this evening that began late now drags later, is chat with the guests. It's something he's made for, since once he hears a name he knows it cold, and he absorbs information like a sponge. The Madisons, Earl and Sheila, own a chain of dry cleaning establishments and have a son who attends the University of Pennsylvania. Did Ben know Bill Bradley at Princeton? Not really, but he saw him play for two years and thinks he's the prime example of how one extremely gifted and unselfish player can turn an ordinary team into a great one. The Floyds, Lee and Corrina, have a nightclub on McLemore Avenue, and they'd love it if Ben and Randall dropped in. Drinks on the house, and great live music (the band's name is vaguely familiar) on the stage. Ben figures that Prosper, were he here, would be in heaven.

It's just past eleven o'clock when Ben, now peripheral to a group that includes Randall, both senior Ennises, and the Madisons, notices Delphine heading for the kitchen. He takes a casual couple of steps backward, then turns and follows.

She's alone in this vast kitchen--Willie and Ethel and the cook having evidently gone home--and she's putting trays and glasses and ashtrays in the dishwasher. She smiles when she sees him, and he says, "Can I help?"

"That's okay. I'm just about done."

"It's a wonderful house," he says, leaning now against the counter, five feet from her.

"Did my mom give you a tour? She'll tell you where she found each piece of furniture."

"Not yet. I think she's still busy out there. Would you like to substitute for her?"

Delphine closes and latches the dishwasher door; she raises one eyebrow as she looks at him. "Sorry. I wouldn't do it justice."

"You don't like your house?"

"I like my house just fine," she says, still looking at him rather slyly, as if to imply that he's up to no good. "I just don't have Mom's enthusiasm for showing it off."

There's something about her tone that he finds inviting. He says, "I like your mother. I enjoy talking to her."

"She enjoys talking to you, too," Delphine says. "She's a charmer."

"Is it true," Ben says, "that you want to go into public service?"

"I don't know what I want to do. At this point all I know is that I don't want to go to medical school, and I do want to get out of Memphis."

"What's the matter with Memphis?"

Again she arches her eyebrow, turning her head slightly sideways at him, looking gorgeous in her strapless dress in this huge kitchen. "I couldn't begin to tell you," she says.

"I like what I've seen so far."

"You could do well here." Delphine has crossed her arms over her chest. "A charming young white man whose good looks would make up for his too-liberal attitudes. You can't even imagine the stuff I'd have to put up with if I tried to do anything in Memphis."

"Because of your color?" Ben says, plunging forward. "Your dad seems to have done pretty well."

Her hands drop to her sides and she shakes her head, but her smile is intact. "You've got a *lot* to learn," she says.

82

"I'd like to learn," Ben replies. "How would you feel about showing me around? I don't know exactly what our schedule is yet, but I'm sure I'll have some free time."

She resumes shaking her head, and laughs. "You're something," she says. "You have no idea what the rules are around here, do you?"

"I don't," Ben says. "I'll be the first to admit it."

Delphine nods, and looks away. She presses a button on the dishwasher and water begins to run. She looks at him again. "Where are you staying? The Holiday Inn downtown?"

"Right. Room two one six."

"I'm going to bed now," she says. "I have to get up at seven. I'll try to call you tomorrow, okay?"

"Fine," Ben says. "Wonderful."

## TEN

With only the vaguest sense of destination, Lydia walks south on Broadway. She's hungry, she's angry, and she's on the verge of despair because in the half-mile she's traversed she's come to recognize just how much her life is intertwined with—and dependent upon—Alex's. At the very least she's got to get away from him for a while. Maybe that will do him some good, make him think about his priorities. If not, then she mustn't mean much to him, and that's all the more reason to get the hell out. But to where? She can't afford her own apartment—not unless she moves up to Harlem or back to the Lower East Side or up to the Bronx. Each in its own way is a version of hell: Harlem close to work but dangerous—she could probably find a place, a one-bedroom, for under a hundred a month, but she'd need about eleven locks on the door and her whiteness would be a constant detriment; her old neighborhood would be cheap too, but back where she came from, enough said; the South Bronx close enough to work by subway but everything else like Harlem except more so; farther out in the Bronx it's nicer but the rents go up and she's spending forty, fifty minutes on the train each way. Does she want to move back in with her parents, even for a little while? First off, that's Avenue B again, second she's left all that behind, third it's like admitting defeat. So what she's thinking about is staying away for a week, maybe even just for a few days, hoping Alex will get some sense in his head, or maybe he'll go completely fucking nuts, he'll end up in a hospital somewhere, and she can have the place to herself. Jesus Christ—is she actually even thinking that? She's pissed off at the selfish, spoiled son of a bitch, but it's not right to wish him ill just so she has a nice place to stay.

Anyway, if she goes away for a few days, where does she stay?

The drugstore at 103$^{rd}$ and Broadway has a bank of phone booths in the back. Goddamn it…she has her wallet but not the little purse with all her change and tokens. Is there a dime hidden away somewhere in the wallet? No such luck. What she has is thirty-seven dollars and some checks. She eyes the man behind the counter at the front of the store: big, fat white guy with a stained t-shirt who looks like he hasn't shaved in three days. No way he's gonna give her change. So what can she buy that won't be a complete waste of money? She seizes on a little rectangular tin of Bayer aspirin: forty-five cents, and for sure she's going to need aspirin at some point.

She puts the tin on the counter and hands the guy a dollar. Without a word, without eye contact, he takes the bill, opens the register, and hands her two quarters. This segment of the transaction she had not anticipated. She hands him back a quarter and says, "I need two dimes and a nickel, for the phone."

Now he makes eye contact. He glares. "Why didn't you tell me you wanted dimes in the first place?"

Lydia does not need this. She waits until he's concluded the exchange, slamming the change down on the counter, before she says, "Why didn't you tell me you were gonna give me two quarters?"

"What the fuck else am I gonna do?" He yells. "Your change is fifty cents, I'm gonna give you two quarters every fuckin' time!"

She slides her remaining quarter onto the counter. "You can take this quarter," she says, "and shove it up your ass."

She dials Maddy's number and it's busy. She waits a minute; through the glass door of the phone booth she watches the fat man at the counter as—in pantomime—he describes to a new customer his exchange with the crazy girl now in the phone booth. She can tell because when he points to the booth the customer—an elderly white man wearing an overcoat and a homburg--turns to get a look at this audacious violator of drugstore protocol. She dials again and it's busy again. Should she just show up at Maddy's door? It's only a five-minute walk. But that *would* be an imposition. Maddy couldn't turn her down, and it's a tiny apartment, less than half the size of hers, or Alex's, and what's Ben going to think of her crashing on their floor? She dials once more, and it's still busy. Maybe she should head up to her parents' place, only for one night, but even at that what's she going tell them? That the guy they didn't want her to move in with turns out to be not just a rich kid with no intention of marrying her, but a crazy drug freak who tries to give away stuff it would take her dad a month's salary to buy?

She tries Maddy one more time: busy, no surprise. What if she just went back home? Alex would probably be asleep by now, judging from his condition forty minutes ago, and he'd sleep for a good ten hours. She could be out of the apartment at dawn, and walk to school, meet up with Maddy there, make plans. She reaches into her jacket pocket for a stick of Wrigley's Spearmint and comes out with the gum pack and a matchbook, on which is written *889-5255 ask for me*. She feels her heartbeat accelerate a bit, unaccountably. Rafael's handwriting is much nicer than his punctuation. Kind of artistic, with round, loopy eights. Does she really want to call a guy who twelve hours ago was on the verge of stealing her boyfriend's expensive shit? On the other hand, maybe he'll take her out to dinner and then she can call Maddy again before it's too late. She dials.

The voice on the other end says, "*Mercado González, buenas tardes.*"

She knows the place—something between a corner store and a supermarket—about five blocks from her place, in the wrong direction. She says, "*Rafael, por favor.*"

The voice says, "*Dígame, ¿quién habla?*"

"Rafael?" she says. "It's me, Lydia, from this afternoon."

"Lydia? Hey, how you doing? I didn't think you'd call so soon..."

"Yeah, well, I had some time on my hands. So—you work at that market?"

"Assistant manager," he says. "Listen, I get off at seven. You want to do something? Go out to eat?"

He's pretty sure of himself, not thinking she'd call so soon, when really it's out of left field that she's called at all. It's ten after six now and short of reaching Maddy what she'd like most in the world is to get something to eat. "I guess I could do that," she says.

"Where you wanna meet? You mind coming here?"

As she walks toward the front door, the fat man glares at her and says in a voice louder than necessary, "Don't you ever come back in here."

Lydia stops by the door and says, "Fuck you, you greasy son of a bitch."

The market is at Columbus and 109th Street and they decide to eat at a Cuban-Chinese place on Broadway and 106th, so she's just about made a round trip. But the night is not unpleasant and the neighborhood well populated and not particularly dangerous, although she's not sure she'd like to walk along Columbus Avenue after midnight. The food is cheap and pretty good: They have beef lo mein and *ropa vieja*, a shredded beef dish whose name means "old clothes" in Spanish.

"I'm not a thug," Rafael says.

"Who said you were?" She examines him for the first time not as an antagonist or a bother. He's kind of good looking, with skin just a tiny bit less European-white than hers,

87

with hazel eyes and curly black hair that falls slightly below his collar.

"You didn't want nothing to do with me this afternoon."

"I didn't meet you in the best circumstances, did I?"

Rafael smiles. "See, you thought I was a thug."

"I thought your friends were thugs—the big fat one and the one that felt me up. What do I make of somebody who has friends like that?"

"They're all right," Rafael says. They were pissed off because your boyfriend was gonna give us all that stuff. I ain't lyin' about that, you know."

"Yeah, but he was fucked up. You knew that. You knew you were taking advantage of him."

"Okay. Say some guy comes up to you on the street and says he wants to hand you five hundred bucks. You gonna turn him down?"

"It depends," she says. "I'm gonna be suspicious, at least."

Rafael shrugs and turns his palms up. "But you see my point?" She nods. He says, "So how come you're not with him now?"

"That's for me to know," she says.

"You serious about him, the white drug boy?"

"I sleep in the same bed with him, don't I?"

"Yeah, but..." Rafael shakes his head. "You and him, man. What a fuckin' waste, if you don't mind me sayin'."

"You don't even know him," she says.

He makes a little snort of a laugh. "You think it's like a stage he's goin' through? Around here people like him don't live too long, or they end up in Bellevue."

Lydia elects not to mention that Alex has already made one visit to Bellevue's mental ward. She says, "What kind of guy should I be with, then, so I'm not wasted?"

"How about a good-lookin' young Puerto Rican guy with a bright future in retail?"

"Listen," she says, "you call Alex the *white* drug boy, like I'm some kinda Negro. I'm just as white as he is."

Rafael smiles broadly. "White ain't just a color," he says.

They linger at the restaurant past nine o'clock. There is a pay phone in the grungy area by the bathroom, but Lydia chooses not to use it. Maddy's probably preparing for bed; Ben, she knows, stays up late, but she doesn't feel quite at ease calling him. Alex will almost certainly be asleep by now, so it'll be safe to follow the sneak-away-early plan, perhaps with her overnight bag and a few days' worth of clothing.

"You want to see my place?" Rafael says.

"Where's your place?"

"Just down the street, between Amsterdam and Columbus."

"I don't think so," she says. "I should get back home. I have to get up at six."

"So...stay with me. I don't get the feeling you want to hang out with the trippy boyfriend."

"I don't think so." She smiles. "I don't know you that well."

"I got a couch," he says. "Shit, I'll stay on the couch, you can have the bed."

"I tell you what," she says. "We'll compromise. You can walk me back to my place."

The apartment is exactly as she left it, except that Alex is curled up on the sofa, the near-empty half-gallon of wine that had been in the refrigerator forever is now open on the table, a glass next to it, so at least he wasn't drinking out of the bottle, and it's about a hundred degrees, meaning the radiator was on full blast with all the windows closed. She retreats to the front door and opens it. "He's out like a light," she says to Rafael. "You want to come in?"

"I don't know. I feel a little strange..."

"Don't worry about it," she says, and he steps inside.

"Jesus, it's hot in here," he says. She's in the process of opening the living room window wide. Alex groans in his sleep and flops over, so he's facing them.

It's just as hot in the bedroom; she opens that window too. How is she going to get to sleep? Rafael stands by the bedroom door, his leather jacket over his shoulder. "You don't want to stay here," he says. "It's like a fuckin' hothouse."

"Just what I was thinking," she says.

"So...my place?"

"Separate accommodations," she says. "You promise?"

"Cross my heart," he says, with a grin that's at best ambiguous.

"No, I mean it..."

"Me too," he says.

She takes the little cloth overnight bag from the closet and folds two days' changes of clothes, just in case. She takes her toothbrush and her hairbrush and assorted cosmetics, and her change purse. Rafael, gentleman that he is, takes the bag.

Of all things, as she's re-entering the living room Alex opens his eyes and stares right at her. "Hey, Babe," he says. "How you doing?"

## The Mountaintop

"Just great," she replies. Has he noticed Rafael? Is he even actually conscious? Whatever the case, the eyes slide shut, and Alex is gone again.

Rafael's building is an old brownstone with a stoop. The entryway smells faintly of urine and after that—as they ascend four flights of wooden stairs—the odors of must and Caribbean cooking alternate in intensity. Lydia is swept back to the apartments of her childhood; she was ten before her family moved into new public housing, a building with an elevator. She's left all that behind.

Rafael takes care of the three locks on his door with impressive dexterity and steps inside; she follows, and walks into a small room that's both cluttered and neat. There is a kitchenette with its miniature sink and appliances; the aforementioned couch—a loveseat, really—and a secretary desk with a wicker chair, a small table with two mismatched chairs of its own and--in a variety of freestanding cases--many, many books. "You want the tour?" He asks her.

The bathroom contains only a toilet and half-sized tub with a shower curtain; the bedroom is just about big enough for its double bed and a closet; crammed between the bed and the wall is a two-drawer chest with a large fan atop it. "Not as roomy as your place," he says, "but it's cooler."

There is a knock on the door and, quite suddenly, a hulking figure in the doorway. Lydia has a moment of cognitive dissonance—is this who she thinks it is?—and as she recognizes that it *is*, all her doubts about Rafael come back into focus.

"*Hola, Rafael,*" says Julio, the large man from early this morning. Rafael moves quickly toward the door, as if shielding Lydia, speaking in impatient Spanish as he goes, telling Julio

91

this isn't a good time, that he should get the hell out. Meanwhile, it's taken Julio a bit longer than Lydia to realize they've already met. *"Ay,"* he laughs, *"la chica de esta mañana."*

"Excuse me a minute," Rafael says to Lydia, and he ushers big Julio out the door, closing it behind him, whereupon the two have a brief conversation in muffled Spanish. She can make out words here and there, entire phrases sometimes when one or the other raises his voice—usually Julio. They're talking about her, what she's doing here; she hears Rafael say the word *amiga* several times, but she doesn't have much context. Julio frequently refers to the *gringo* or the *gringo loco* and that would be Alex. There are references as well to Flaco, the guy who groped her breast this morning, and it sounds as if Julio feels Flaco is unjustly being left out of something. The conversation ends with Rafael saying in a clear, loud voice: *"¡Ahora, no! ¡Definitivamente, no!"* Heavy footsteps followed by a slamming door.

She tries to interpret Rafael's weak smile. "He lives across the hall?" She says.

"Yeah."

"And Flaco?"

"Flaco's his cousin. He lives a few blocks away. We all went to school together."

"What was that about—you and him out there?"

"It was nothing. He's surprised to see you here…"

"Yeah, well, that makes two of us."

"Look—you don't have anything to worry about, okay?"

She considers going home; it's a ten-minute walk, fifteen at the most. But she doesn't want to be in the apartment with Alex, even if he's sound asleep, and having been up since dawn she's reaching a point of exhaustion here at quarter past ten. "I get the bed?" She says.

"Want me to change the sheets?"

"That's all right."

It's a siren that wrests her from sleep, and if it had been just the one she might have been able to drop right off again, but there must be a fire just a few blocks away because they keep coming, and eventually she's wide awake. Awake and disoriented, in the pitch darkness. It doesn't take her long to remember where she is, but it's still unsettling to waken in a strange bed with no visual frame of reference, and she flashes back to the first time she spent the night at a friend's house, except the comforting thing in that case was that after a few seconds she sat up and saw Ana Gutiérrez lying next to her. Just as well that Rafael is not.

She remembers the short route to the bathroom, but her eyes still haven't adjusted to the dark and she stumbles a bit at the door. There is a dim light from the living room, so she has no trouble finding the bathroom door's knob. The seat is down, meaning either that Rafael hasn't used the toilet since she did or that he's been thoughtful enough to put it back down after he peed, and that's certainly not in Alex's bag of tricks.

What time is it? She's still wearing her watch, and it's…two thirty-five, so she's slept for nearly three and a half hours. Is Rafael awake, she wonders, or has he fallen asleep with the light on? Should she just sneak back into the bedroom, or should she look in on him? She's wearing a flannel nightshirt that falls several inches short of her knees, her panties underneath that—not exactly modest, but hardly provocative.

He's sitting on the couch with a paperback book, and he looks up when she appears. "Sirens wake you up?" She nods, standing by the bathroom door. He says, "I bet it's pretty quiet on Morningside Heights."

"What you reading?" She says. He holds the book up. "Christopher Marlowe," she says. "Never heard of him."

"Guy who lived at the same time as Shakespeare," Rafael says. "I'm taking a course."

"No shit? Where?"

"CCNY."

"So...what, you're going for a degree?"

He chuckles. "Yeah, at this rate maybe I'd graduate in nineteen eighty. No, I just like learning shit. I took an English literature class in the fall and we read some Shakespeare, and I said hey, I could get into this stuff."

"Forsooth," Lydia says.

He laughs. "Right. See, you got it."

"So," she says, "don't you ever sleep?"

"I don't need much. Five, six hours. And I don't have to be at work till ten."

"Tell me," she says. "Your friends Julio and Flaco go to Shakespeare class with you?"

"Why you want to keep bugging me about those guys?"

"You have to admit it's kind of...incongruous, right? One minute you're with these scumbags trying to rip off my boyfriend's shit and the next minute you're reading some five hundred-year-old play?"

"You gonna stand there all night?" He says. "Why don't you come sit down?"

"I have to sleep," she says.

He shrugs. "Okay. That's cool. I was gonna lay down myself in a few minutes."

"*Lie* down," she says. "One of the most common mistakes in English grammar."

"Hey, I'm the one who's heard of Christopher Marlowe," he says. "And you probably got your degree, right?"

She nods. "B.A. from Fordham."

"In what?"

"Spanish," she says.

He laughs. "So you really had to work your ass off, huh? Spanish is like a real stretch for you."

He's teasing, she knows. "Fuck you," she says. "I had to read *Don Quixote* in Spanish, so Christopher what's-his-name's no big deal."

"Good," he says. "So come sit down."

She takes the few steps necessary to reach the couch, and sits on the opposite side from him, about a foot of upholstery separating them. She curls her legs underneath her, showing as little skin as possible. He says, "I like the way you move in that shirt. Very sexy."

"I've got to get up at six," she says.

"I'll get you up. Don't worry." He barely has to move to reach her exposed knee, and his fingers take a little exploratory walk up her thigh. "What if I carry you into the bedroom?" She smiles, but doesn't reply. "Then you could just curl up and go back to sleep, if you wanted. Or I could stay."

"Let's see what happens," she says.

He's massaging her neck and she's about half-conscious. It feels so good that she could just lie here forever. "Lydia," he whispers in her ear. "It's six o'clock."

"It can't be. I just went to sleep."

"Yeah. You went to sleep at five."

She opens her eyes. "Jesus Christ! It's six already?"

"It's about five...fifty-eight, for real."

95

She has no desire to move. "It was three o'clock five minutes ago."

"What time you have to be at the school?"

"Seven thirty, quarter to eight at the latest."

"So you could sleep for another hour. I'll treat you to a cab."

"No, I gotta be awake. I'm with all these goddamn little kids. I can't fake it." She sits up and is suddenly quite aware of her nakedness.

"Can you call in sick? You get union sick days, right?"

There won't be anyone at school for another hour at least. But Maddy, like her, is always up at six. "Where do I call from, Rafael? You don't have a fuckin' phone, unless you hide it somewhere."

"Julio has the phone. I pay half the bill." She gives him a look of incredulity, and he says, "Don't worry--he's not even gonna be up yet."

Julio in fact answers the door after Rafael's discreet tap, and Lydia has half a mind to turn and run back into Rafael's apartment. "Sorry," Rafael whispers. She's in her nightie and panties and a clean pair of mid-calf socks, and fat, unshaven Julio takes a good, long look. She heads straight for the phone, which is attached to the wall beside the grungy brown refrigerator. While Rafael and Julio converse in Spanish, she dials.

Maddy answers after the third ring, sounding more asleep than awake. "Maddy? Did I wake you up? Oh, jeez, I am so goddamn sorry."

"It's okay," Maddy says. "What's going on? What's the matter?"

In her peripheral vision, Lydia sees Julio checking her out; she should have asked Rafael for a raincoat. "Mad...you're going to school today, right?"

"Of course I am."

"Listen, can you do me a favor? Tell them I can't come in till late, till noon?"

"Why don't you just call them yourself? What's the matter?"

"I don't wanna talk about it now, okay? Can you just do me that favor?"

"I guess so. Sure. But are you all right?"

"I gotta go," Lydia says. "Love you."

## ELEVEN

The 24th Precinct is on 100th Street, between Amsterdam and Columbus. Alex's head is throbbing and his shoulder hurts. His intention had been to take a cab but when he couldn't find one on Morningside Drive he walked to Broadway and then figured what the hell, he might as well walk the rest of the way. It feels definitely weird to be entering this police station voluntarily, since he and the cops have had shall we say an adversarial relationship of late. Of late, hell. The cops were never exactly on his side in Palm Beach, either, pulling him over about every ten minutes because "the car didn't match the driver," especially when he was driving his stepmother's nine-hundred horsepower Cadillac, trying to blow some of the carbon out of the exhaust system because Ofelia never took it over twenty miles per hour. But of course the good side of that was that once they realized he was his father's son they'd always let him go with a warning.

He doesn't have a terribly vivid memory of the Alfa Romeo business, just that it landed him in Bellevue and that he's always loved that car, the red Spider roadster, and he wonders how people are stupid enough to park a car like that on the street in Manhattan, where it's going to get banged up and broken into and generally trashed. What supposedly happened was that he was in the car in the early morning when the owner came—a woman—and he wouldn't get out. What supposedly happened was that he told her and then he told the cops that God had told him the Alfa was his car, and all she had going for her was the registration. So the cops threw him into the back of their squad car—*that* he remembers—and they hauled him down here and talked to him for a while and then took him to Bellevue, where he was locked up for a day before Lydia managed to get him out. It helped that he was completely lucid, which obviously he hadn't been before, but you'd think that the cops would have a little understanding of different states of consciousness and not just throw somebody in the loony bin when he claims to have been communicating with God, if indeed that was what he had claimed. There was no damage to the Alfa, anyway, and the woman didn't press charges, so everything was cool and as if it hadn't happened except that he got a bill for something like $750 from Bellevue, which he tore up.

## The Mountaintop

This morning he is perfectly respectable and he's going to lay out exactly what happened. He stops just short of the station house and peers at himself in the long outside mirror of a van parked at the curb. Maybe he should have shaved; he hasn't since Saturday. And maybe it would've been a good idea to wear something other than the clothes he slept in, but neither of these is cause to go all the way back to the apartment, so up the stairs he goes. He tells the cop at the desk he wants to report a crime and the cop tells him to have a seat in an area where several other citizens are waiting. "Am I going to be behind them in line?" Alex asks in his best Ivy League voice, "Because this is a matter of urgency, and I should talk to someone as soon as possible."

It's a little after ten when he takes his seat, and indeed by eleven no one has seen to him and he's getting pretty impatient. He considers asking the elderly woman a few chairs away if she'll hold his place while he goes out and buys a magazine or has something to eat. There's a pizza place up around the corner on Broadway and at 96th there's a guy with a hot dog cart. He's on the verge of asking her when a cop appears and he thinks: Ahh, at last. But it turns out to be the elderly woman the cop's interested in, so now he's completely out in the cold.

It is exactly 11:37 by the clock on the wall when another cop—a stocky man about forty—walks up and speaks his name. Alex nods and stands up to shake the cop's hand, and as he does so the cop gives the once over and says, "You remember me?"

"No sir, I'm afraid I don't," Alex says.

"Six, seven weeks ago. They dragged you out of a car on Riverside Drive. I was the one decided to send you to Bellevue."

"I'm sorry," Alex says, "but I don't remember you."

99

"I'm not surprised you don't remember me, the state you were in. How did that go, with Bellevue?"

"I went home the next day."

"You did, huh? You got friends in high places?"

This notion, especially the use of the word "high," amuses Alex, and he giggles. "No, I was okay. There was nothing wrong with me."

The cop's expression becomes sterner. "So you convinced some headshrinker you weren't crazy as a bedbug, huh?"

"I'm fine," Alex says, finding himself in a difficult position because he can't really tell the cop his condition was the result of taking illegal drugs.

"You don't look fine to me," the cop says. "You look like somebody who's been on a three-day bender, or living on the streets."

"Look," Alex says, "I'm okay, and I need to report a robbery."

"I'll bet you do. What'd they take? Your sportscar? Your other suit?"

"A movie camera. A Bolex sixteen-millimeter. And a tape recorder, a Nagra Four."

The cop looks him over again. "You telling me these things belonged to *you?*"

"They're mine. They were mine. I'm in the film school at Columbia."

"Right," the cop says. "And I'm in the Swiss Guards. You got receipts? You got proof of who you are?"

Alex checks his pants: nothing but a pocket full of change and a filthy handkerchief. Jesus fucking Christ—his wallet is in the jacket he didn't wear because he put this sweater

on because it was so fucking cold in the apartment. He strains
to make eye contact "Not with me."

"Tell you what," the cop says. "You get your sorry ass
outta here right now, I won't send you back to Bellevue."

He slides into one of the phone booths in the back of the
drugstore on Broadway and 103$^{rd}$, and first he calls his own
number, hoping Lydia will answer. She doesn't, but of course
that was pretty much a waste of time because she'd be at school
now anyway. So he calls P.S. 72; it's just past noon and if
things are normal she'll be on her lunch break. She's called him
from school in the past, so he knows it can be done. When he
gets the receptionist he asks for the kindergarten teachers'
room. An unfamiliar voice—belonging neither to Lydia nor to
Maddy—answers, and for a moment Alex is paralyzed. *Hello?*
the woman says for a second time, and Alex says, "I'd like to
speak to Lydia, please."

"Lydia? I'm afraid she didn't come in today."

That's not good. His heart pounds. Were the Puerto
Rican hoods telling the truth about the hospital? Before he can
compose his next question, the line goes dead. Should he call
back and ask for Maddy?

Outside the phone booth is a hinged device that contains
the two immense volumes of the Manhattan telephone directory.
Alex opens the White Pages and looks up St. Luke's. There is a
baffling catalogue of numbers, so he elects to call the main one.
He must concentrate very hard when he speaks to the initial
operator, asking to be connected to someone who might tell him
if his fiancée—the word seems more impressive than *girlfriend*
and more truthful than *wife*—has been admitted. She transfers
him to the emergency room, as it turns out, where a woman
with a Spanish accent tells him no one with Lydia's name has

101

been treated there in the past twenty-four hours. That's a relief. Or is it?

Next he calls Prosper's number in Connecticut, prepared to deposit more change for long distance if anyone answers. No one does, and Alex lets the phone ring for a couple of minutes while he tries to figure out his next move. It turns out to be another local call, and this time he gets through. "Elliot?"

"You got me," replies the drowsy voice.

"It's Alex. You around for a while?"

"Sure, man. I got class at two. Here till then."

"Everything cool?"

"Yeah, man. You?"

"I'll be there in fifteen minutes."

Elliot Shatzberg lives in a university-owned building on 111$^{th}$ Street between Broadway and Riverside. Columbia has been buying up a lot of property in its vicinity and spiffing up the buildings, which are mainly occupied by faculty and graduate students. This has come at the expense of tenements and residential hotels, sending previous tenants farther north, to Harlem and the South Bronx, but the neighborhood is a lot better looking than it had been. Elliot's doing his best to offset that, even if only by a bit. He shares a two-bedroom second-story apartment with two other first-year graduate students, and Elliot's quarters are the definition of squalor, with what appears to be several months' worth of dirty laundry carpeting the floor and take-out food containers covering most other available surfaces. Elliot is tall and scrawny, with scraggly facial hair that could pass for accidental. Alex has never asked him what he's studying, but guesses from the odd book here and there it has something to do with math. Elliot at this moment is listening to the long, album version of the Doors' "Light My Fire," which Alex finds tedious.

"Whatcha need, man?" Elliot shouts above the music.

"Could you turn it down?" Elliot does so. Alex sits at the foot of the unmade bed. "Thanks, man," he says. "Been a bad day. You got any of that stuff you had last month?"

"The Mexican shit? I'm out. But I just got some dynamite weed from Duchess County."

Alex laughs. "Duchess County, New *York*? You kidding me?"

"Don't knock it," Elliot says. He opens a drawer in the chest that supports the stereo and in an instant has provided a pipe, some vegetation, and a little butane lighter.

Alex lights up and takes a deep inhale, then passes the pipe back to Elliot. "Not bad," he says.

"Have another hit and then let it sink in for a few minutes."

After his second drag, Alex rests against the wall and closes his eyes, more aware now of the room's fetid smell and the banality of the Doors, yet feeling a kind of peace setting in. "This is good shit, you're right," he says.

"These guys are geniuses, man," Elliot says, and at first Alex thinks he's talking about the Doors. "They grow this stuff indoors. They take seeds from all these really far out strains, and they like *graft* this super pot, man. They do it indoors so they can grow all year long."

In his near-reverie, Alex visualizes Duchess County-- well up the Hudson River from the city--in February, with three feet of snow on the ground. "What do they do for sunlight?"

"They've got all these like zillion-watt bulbs, man. It's like walking around in Costa Rica up there."

103

"I hope the cops don't check their Con Ed bill," Alex says. "Gotta be about five hundred bucks a month in winter."

"Wow, man, enjoy the dope," Elliot says. "Don't get hung up on all this negative shit."

"Bad day," Alex says. "These Puerto Rican motherfuckers ripped off my movie gear. Got in my place, knocked me around, took my Bolex and my Nagra. And Lydia...you know her, right?"

"Yeah, man—good looking little chick from, like, Brazil?"

"Venezuela," Alex says. "She split. Got pissed off at me and I don't know where the fuck she is."

"Bummer, man. What're you gonna do about your stuff. Did you have insurance?"

Alex laughs. "You kidding me?" In retrospect, it seems like a pretty good idea to have had insurance, although that's the sort of thing his father would carp on. He wonders briefly what a premium would have cost, then feels a deep sense of rage overcome his nascent marijuana high. "I've gotta find those bastards," he says. "I know where they hang out."

Elliot says, "How many guys?"

"Three. Or two. Just two guys this morning, but when I met them there were three."

"When you *met* them?"

"Long story."

After a brief silence, Elliot says, "What're you gonna do when you find them? Call the cops?"

"Shit, no. Fucking cops don't want any part of me."

Another silence. "Sounds like you need a piece, man."

"A piece of what?"

"A *gun*," Elliot says.

*The Mountaintop*

Alex pictures himself confronting the two big Puerto Rican guys, enjoying the shock on their faces when this patsy, this pathetic hippie gringo, pulls out a pistol, maybe even shoots the fat one in the leg to encourage faster response. "Where do I get a gun? Do you handle that kind of thing?"

"Not normally," Elliot says. "But I could make some calls, maybe find you one in a few days…"

"No," Alex says. "By then they'll have pawned the stuff, for sure. Can't I just do it legitimately? Just walk into a store somewhere?"

Elliot emits a raspy chuckle. "You ever see a gun store in New York, man? You gotta have a permit here, and it takes like six years."

"What about New Jersey? Connecticut?"

"I believe," Elliot says, "that the nearest place where you can just walk into a store and buy a gun is Delaware."

Alex knows Delaware as the place at the end of the Jersey Turnpike, on the way to Florida—not that far away. "So…it's like buying groceries? You just walk in and hand them the money and they give you a gun?"

"You have to be a resident. You need i.d."

"Well, shit, then I'm back at square one. Where am I gonna get Delaware i.d.?"

"Tell you what," Elliot grins. "Give me a hundred for a lid of this shit, and I'll lend you my driver's license."

This is too much for Alex to take in. "A hundred bucks for an *ounce* of weed? And what good is your fucking driver's license?"

"Is this far and away the best shit you ever smoked?"

"Hard to say. It's pretty amazing, but…"

Elliot produces a wallet from his back pocket and pulls out a sheaf of card-sized papers; he selects one and hands it to

105

Alex. It's a Delaware driver's license issued to Elliot Shatzberg of 12 Arbuthnot Lane in Dover. Alex grins. "This is real?"

"Hundred per cent."

"Jesus. You're from Delaware?"

"Shit no. I've got a friend who lives there. Last year I got a couple of speeding tickets and I was afraid they were gonna take away my license in Jersey, so I went down to Delaware and took the test, handed over a few bucks, and there we go."

"Far out," Alex says. "But here's a problem--I don't have any cash on me."

"It's cool, man. Pay me later. Tomorrow. Service with a smile here."

## TWELVE

It's Prosper's strategy to drink another six-pack of beers and sleep for two or three hours at most before heading back to New Haven, but at one a.m.—after just three cans of Schlitz--he stretches out on the couch listening to the mournful and soothing "Cortege" by the Modern Jazz Quartet, and the next thing he knows it's dawn. He stumbles into the kitchen and sits at the table in a stupor. What to do next? He's eaten nothing since the BLT at noon; he's neglected to turn on the heat, and he begins to shiver, sitting here in his socks and his short sleeves. He could afford, in all probability, to descend to his bedroom and sleep another couple of hours. But then he'd arrive at the Federal Building in the bloom of good health.

So he retreats to the living room for his jacket and his Dexedrine, then back to the kitchen for a beer to wash down the pill. What else is in the refrigerator? Many cans of Tab. Some bacon, some skim milk, a pound of butter and four eggs. Catherine has not shopped before leaving on her business trip. Prosper removes two eggs, along with a little butter and a little milk, and by the time the eggs are scrambled he's feeling fine.

Just as he's finished the last morsel of egg he hears the newspaper truck crunching up the gravel driveway, followed by the thud of the paper against the door. It's a banner headline:

## JOHNSON AGREES TO CONFER WITH KENNEDY; STOCKS RISE STRONGLY IN RECORD TRADING

Thank God for the stocks. Senator Kennedy is "conciliatory" in a telegram to the president, but pledges to continue in his race for the nation's highest office. Not to be outdone on the graciousness front,

## MC CARTHY PRAISES PRESIDENT ON WAR

The latter headline is down the page a bit, as if the *Times* knows which way the wind is blowing. And let us not be premature about the war's ending. Here's another front-page headline:

### 60,000 Reservists Face Early Call

And another:

## U.S. Sets Bomb Targets
## 200 Miles North of DMZ

The last story addresses an apparent inconsistency in
U.S. military procedure. In his Sunday speech to the nation,
Lyndon Johnson had stated that American planes would cease
bombing above the "demilitarized zone" that separates North
and South Vietnam. But B-52s had continued pounding targets
well above the line, and the discrepancy had not gone unnoticed
by the press. In today's story, a "Pentagon spokesman"" is
quoted as saying that "any raids that have been conducted since
the president's speech are obviously within the framework of
the president's speech."

In his latest surge of chemical well-being and insight,
Prosper realizes that the "Pentagon spokesman" has created a
marvelous alternate logic. If the president says on Sunday that
bombing above the DMZ will cease, and then proceeds to
continue bombing above the DMZ, well then, the president has
evidently told a lie. If the Pentagon spokesman on Monday
states without flinching that said raids are within the framework
of the president's speech, he is clearly both acknowledging and
legitimizing the president's lie. Within the framework of a war
built on lies, he is attesting, it is quite acceptable and expectable
to tell another lie.

Prosper figures that Corporal Dybzinski—he of the bad
skin and the rodential overbite—is his age, or a little younger,
as well as his height, or a little shorter. Here in the little room at
about half past eleven, the corporal after a few minutes'
fidgeting has for some reason elected to converse with Prosper.
Perhaps it is because Prosper is sitting closest to the door, and

*The Mountaintop*

Corporal Dybzinski has a few more minutes to kill before
leading his flock to the blood pressure area once again.

"You graduate from college?" Dybzinski says.

"Last June," Prosper replies.

"I did a year at Hofstra," Dybzinski says. Prosper nods,
not knowing how to respond to the corporal's admission.
Dybzinski resumes after a few seconds, "I just got so fuckin'
tired of studying, you know? Like, all through high school, and
now I've gotta do four more years of this shit. Forget about it."

There is a long silence, perhaps thirty seconds' worth, as
Prosper searches for a role in this exchange. It's Dybzinski who
speaks again. "You against the war?"

Prosper looks around the room. He and Bobby, the
Bridgeport high school dropout, are the only holdovers from
yesterday, the only clothed members of a group of six, which
also includes two Negro boys and two white boys, none of
whom appears older than twenty, and none of whom seems
focused on this conversation. Prosper says, "Yeah, I'm against
it."

"How come?"

How come? Prosper says, "Are you for it?"

"I'm in the fuckin' army, right?" Dybzinski sneers.

"Okay…but does that mean you think the war's right, or
does it mean you just go along with whatever the army does?"

The corporal smiles. "I asked the question first."

"You want me to tell you why I'm against the war?"

"Right."

Where to start? Prosper says, "It's their country.
They're in a civil war and it's their business. We're supporting
a corrupt government in the south just because the north is run
by communists."

"Okay," Dybzinski says, "isn't that enough right there? I mean, I don't know how 'corrupt' the south is, but isn't the whole point of this shit to stop communism?"

"Stop it from what?"

"The Russians press a button," Dybzinski says, "and we're all dead in two minutes." He makes a sweeping motion with his left hand, indicating that the dead would include everyone in the little room: the good, the bad, and the innocent.

Prosper says, "What does that have to do with Vietnam?"

"Everything. Fuckin' everything!" Dybyzinski's voice has risen considerably. "Why can't you people get the fuckin' connection?"

"Because there *is* no connection," Prosper says. "The only thing North Vietnam and Russia have in common is a system of government. But okay--if you're right that there's a connection, wouldn't the Russians be less likely to drop a bomb on us if we *left* Vietnam?"

"That's a laugh," the corporal says, color rising in his sallow skin. "What they want to do is dominate. You know that as well as I do. And if you don't, you're dumber than you look. What do you know about it, anyway? I've got family in Poland on my dad's side. It's like a prison there. Your cousins from England, Ireland, wherever the fuck your family's from, they want to come visit you, no problem. My family's locked up in fucking Warsaw. *That's* your communists."

"I'm sorry about your family," Prosper says, "but I don't see what that has to do with Vietnam."

Dybzinski's eyes grow large. "The fuck you don't! You peace assholes act like it's all a game. Ho Chi Minh's your buddy. That son of a bitch would cut your throat in a minute, and your baby sister's too. And if you don't think he's in bed with Brezhnev, then I have pity for you, buddy."

Indeed, until a couple of years ago Prosper, like the vast majority of United States citizens, had considered Brezhnev, and before him Khrushchev, to be the devil incarnate. But the war, and especially the prospect of being forced to participate in the war, has provided a different perspective. Brezhnev may be a lying totalitarian bastard, but is he much worse than Lyndon Johnson or any of the other American politicians who routinely twist the truth or simply lie outright when it comes to Southeast Asia? Dybinski's analysis of the situation, disjointed and illogical though it may be, is no less lucid than what virtually any member of Congress tells his constituents regarding the war seven days a week.

"What I don't understand," Prosper says, "is how we help ourselves with Brezhnev by sending five hundred thousand Americans to fight against his best friend."

"Because that's the only thing they understand," Dybzinski says. "We didn't fight them in Eastern Europe in nineteen forty-five, when we should have. "Now we have a chance to stop them in Asia, and we damn well better do it."

The non sequitur is so grand, so magnificently off the wall, that Prosper has no response. Dybzinski continues to glare at him. "What do you *say* to that, huh, peace guy? Isn't the picture pretty goddamn clear?"

Prosper says, "I don't think killing half of Vietnam is gonna help get your family out of Poland."

Dybzinski takes two steps forward and leans into Prosper's face. "Don't you fucking talk about my family! What do you know about my family, college boy?"

Prosper does not reply. Dybzinski rises to his full height and backs away. He mutters, "Fuck you, anyway" to Prosper and then addresses the group. "All right, ladies. One more time."

Prosper and the young black man who has been sitting across from him trail Dybzinski and the other three by several feet on the short trip back to Blood Pressure Central. "I'll say one thing," his companion says. "Took some guts to put that cracker motherfucker in his place."

"You think I did?"

"I do. Probably not from his point of view, though."

Prosper chuckles. "You're right about that."

"My name's Leotis, by the way." He offers his hand to Prosper, who takes it and says his own name.

"But if I was you," Leotis says, "I wouldn't be rufflin' that corporal's feathers any more."

One-fifty over ninety-six: still well into the range of unacceptability. Leotis too stays in the running, unlike Bobby from Bridgeport who—much to his delight—drops into cannon fodder territory. Dybzinski leads the surviving quartet back to the little waiting room and orders them to lunch. He gives directions to the cafeteria, then actually follows his charges into the hallway, as if to make sure that no one breaks for the outside. There will be no trip to the luncheonette today, no supplementary Dexedrine. Why hadn't he simply secreted a Dexedrine in his wallet, or his sock, or his shirt pocket? What sort of excuse would now earn him a trip out to the car, and chemical salvation? Phone call to a sick relative? No--plenty of pay phones in the building. Incipient terminal claustrophobia? Dybzinski would never go for that.

He and Leotis share a table in the cafeteria. Perhaps ominously, Leotis's B.P. has dropped significantly since the early morning. Same as yesterday, Leotis assures Prosper; nothing to worry about. Leotis, it turns out, lives in Stamford, perhaps seven miles from Aunt Catherine's house in Riverside. He's a high school graduate with one year at Norwalk Community College who's been moving furniture for a living since he was sixteen. His ambition is to buy a truck, in addition to the van he already owns, and make his business a real concern. He has a knack, he says, for getting large, difficult objects in and out of small spaces. "This one lady had a desk, biggest damn thing you ever saw, she had it in a little room up on the third floor of this house, and there was no way nobody ever carried that desk through that doorway, you know what I'm sayin'? You could twist it this way and that, wasn't no way to get it out that room. Except. Except, if you took it out this big bay window. But then what you gonna do with it? You can't just drop the damn thing, cause you three stories up. So I say, Miss, you wanna give me fifty bucks extra, I get that desk out for you. I go and get like eight dollars worth of heavy-duty rope, wrap that son of a bitch up good, go up on the roof, tie the rope around this big-ass brick chimney, then lower that desk down to the ground like a feather."

Prosper finishes his second bottle Coke of the lunch break, and wishes he had another; Leotis nurses a cup of coffee. Feeling sanguine and feeling a fine sense of camaraderie with his anti-war brother, Prosper talks to Leotis about that most difficult of subjects: strategy. If his blood pressure doesn't fail the remaining day-and-a-half's tests and he's classified 1-A, he figures the best course is to declare for conscientious objector status, which will at least buy him some time, then wait to see if Kennedy gets the Democratic nomination.

"You think he will?" Leotis says.

"I think he's got a good chance. My best friend works for the campaign. He's convinced Kennedy can't lose."

"What about you? You like him?"

"Not that much. He's a big improvement over Johnson and Humphrey, but I think he's taking advantage of the work McCarthy's done."

"Yeah," Leotis says, "but ain't no way McCarthy could get elected, right?"

Prosper laughs. "You too?"

"The dude is like too straight," Leotis says. "You see the man on the TV, it's like that's your history teacher, you know what I mean? He don't have that *thing* politicians have, where they all smooth and cool and fulla shit—like Adam Clayton Powell--where you say, 'I know this man is jivin' me, but I'm gonna vote for him just the same."

"You think Kennedy has that?"

"Johnson got a good case of that. Kennedy, it ain't quite the same. It's like, maybe he really does care about shit."

"I hope so," Prosper says. "I hope you're right."

"But what if?" Leotis resumes. "You think Kennedy would end the war just like that?"

"I think he'd end the draft, and then he'd end the war as soon as he could."

"And what if Humphrey kicks Kennedy's ass? Then what would you do?"

"If I didn't get the C.O., then maybe I'd leave the country."

"And go where?"

Prosper closes his eyes and leans back in his chair. "Canada, maybe. I hear good things about Toronto," he says, "and my parents live in Senegal."

"Senegal," Leotis says. "You talkin' about *Africa*?"

"Right."

Leotis explodes in laughter. "You don't look like no African to me."

Back in the little room, Leotis tells Prosper that his girlfriend has recently broken up with him because he didn't want to get married. He wonders--if his blood pressure comes down and he's reclassified 1-A--whether she'd take him back and they could manage a quick pregnancy, but then he'd have to work fulltime, and so much for college. "What about you?" He says. "You work at the radio station, you live over in Riverside, your parents in Africa. What else? You got a lady in your life?"

"I wish. There's a girl I really like, but she lives with a friend of mine..."

"The guy that works for Kennedy? Down in Memphis now?"

"Right."

Still smiling, Leotis shakes his head. "So you snakin' on your best friend?"

"No," Prosper says. "It's not like that. I mean, she and I knew each other first, and we fooled around a little then, a couple of years ago. But since they've been together I haven't done anything..."

"But you'd like to?"

"Sure, and I'd like the war to be over. And I'd like to run the radio station."

"I tell you what," Leotis says, removing his wallet from his pants pocket. "What's her name?"

"Maddy."

Leotis hands Prosper a business card. It reads:

115

*Peter Delacorte*

## MIDNIGHT MOVERS
### We Move It For You!
### Leotis Telford President
### 203 324-6680

He says, "When you move in with Maddy, give me a call."


The next trip to the blood pressure area comes at two thirty, and Prosper drops to 145 over 85, which is ominous. His diastolic is now high normal, his systolic barely above the cutoff point of 140. Surely another couple of drug-free hours will do him in. Leotis, as he predicted, is back well into the safety zone.

At three o'clock, hardly half an hour since the latest return to the little room, a new, non-Dybzinski soldier pokes his head in. This, according to his nameplate, would be Corporal Martino. "You guys are blood pressure?" There is nodding all around. The current group is seven strong: Prosper, Leotis, the two holdovers from yesterday, plus three post-lunch additions. Martino enters and begins checking charts. "Okay," he says, "you four guys..." He points to Prosper and his three fellow veterans, one by one, "you guys are done for the day." He hands out chits, gives directions to the YMCA, and Prosper knows he's been saved by the bell.

## THIRTEEN

Tuesday morning, Randall and Ben have coffee in the Memphis State cafeteria with William Marchand, a graduate student and a friend of a friend of Randall's, who is also a leader of the Black Student Association at MSU. It is, as both Randall and Marchand make quite clear to each other, very much an unofficial meeting. Marchand appears to be about Randall's age; in fact, there is a great deal about him that is similar to Randall. They're built alike, and they're about the same height; Marchand doesn't wear a tie this morning, but other than that it strikes Ben that he and Randall are virtually interchangeable—in brown woolen trousers, black shoes, white shirts, brown jackets. They are themselves the same color, a medium brown, and Marchand possesses finally the same intensity as Randall. Neither man ever takes his eyes off the other, except on the rare occasions that Ben speaks, when both lock in on him.

"You hear about your man Powell?" Marchand asks Randall.

"*My* man Powell?" Randall replies.

"Your brother from the north. From Harlem."

"You mean Adam Clayton Powell," Randall says with a straight face. "I thought maybe you were talking about Bud. Or Dick."

Marchand laughs appreciatively. "You heard the latest?"

"I guess I didn't," Randall says. "What did that fool do now? Defect to Russia? Or South Africa?"

117

Marchand shakes his head. "In the paper this morning. Adam Clayton Powell, lunatic Negro congressman, stricken with unspecified illness in Durham, North Carolina."

"Stricken by whatever drugs he's been doing, would be my guess," Randall says. "You talk about a fall from grace. Just when we're starting to get a few things done, this washed-up old egomaniac can't leave well enough alone. Why the hell doesn't he just stay in the Bahamas?"

"Power," Marchand says. "He sees a link between Black Power and Adam Clayton Powell power, and those eyes light up like neon, brother."

For Ben, this like watching a friendly tennis match between a player he expects is very good and a player he knows is extremely good. It's a match that's a pleasure to watch--to be allowed to watch. Randall obviously feels at ease with Ben observing; what impresses Ben, what gives him a giddy feeling of achievement, is that Randall has somehow conveyed to Marchand that it's all right to be candid even though this white boy is sitting across the table from him.

"When I first started to pay attention to politics," Ben says, very conscious of his own voice as he speaks, "the only two Negro politicians I was aware of were Edward Brooke and Adam Clayton Powell."

There is a moment of silence before Randall says, "Black is the word now, Ben. Not Negro."

Marchand laughs. "Don't be givin' him a hard time, Randall. Boy makes a good point."

"He does indeed. I don't know how I feel about that. I sure did admire Powell when I was a kid. Wished I could grow up to be him, except I knew my skin could never be that light."

"I guess my question is," Ben boldly proceeds, "when he was a young man, when he was the only black man in

118

Congress, did he really represent the people, or was he always just corrupt?"

"I don't know," Randall says. "I wish I knew how to answer that. All I know is, the current version makes me sick. Still, you got to give the old bastard some credit for trying to bring the movement down in style. What did he say? Something like, 'The non-violent days are over and if we gotta die, let us not die like dogs in some inglorious spot.'"

Marchand bursts out in laughter and slaps his thigh; Ben, too finds himself laughing out loud, both at Powell's audacity and Randall's presentation. "Did you see him?" Marchand says. "Were you there?"

"Front row," Randall says. "Right there in front of the Theresa Hotel. I could've reached out and touched Charles Kenyatta, standin' there with his helmet on, he's got this machete with a bible impaled on it..."

"I got to say, I don't get the significance of that," Marchand says. "Is it like, the machete penetrates the bible, so it's the African weapon destroying the white man's holy book, or is it like, this is a representation of the joining of the two cultures, that's gonna scare the shit out of Mister Charlie?"

"That's a rhetorical question, right?" Randall says. "You don't expect me to answer that question. 'Cause as far as I'm concerned, that's all *nothin'* but theater. I'm not sayin' I'd like to encounter Charles Kenyatta in a dark alley, but if you ask me, the man is more after a crude dramatic effect than a political statement."

Sitting back in wonder and admiration, Ben can't help noting that the longer Randall socializes with Marchand, his mirror image, the more his northern trappings, his Harvard façade, slip away. "Tell me one thing, William," Randall says.

119

"This little Black Power group you got here--what do they think of our friend Adam Clayton?"

"The Black Organizing Project? Could be they never even heard of him, that's how isolated Memphis tends to be. But, yeah, the guys I know in the Bee Oh Pee, I wouldn't say they'd actually consider Powell a *role* model, but inasmuch as they're birds of a feather, I reckon they'd appreciate him."

"Birds of a feather?"

"Yeah...you know, the Bee Oh Pee guys are big on rhetoric, big on theatrics, on lookin' the part. Like when I was an undergraduate up in North Carolina, that was the shit we had goin' on six, seven years ago. Angry young black men callin' attention to ourselves. It's a good gig, man, but it's a little short on solutions. We grew up, we saw the light. All that stuff is new to Memphis, though. It's like, white Memphis has always been *just* good enough to its colored folks so they don't rise up and complain. A lot of brothers here would equate Henry Loeb, the mayor, with Lester Maddox, George Wallace, Bull Connor, but he ain't like them. This is a cat that's genuinely *hurt* by what's been goin' on, because he believes he's been real good to his Negroes. Henry Loeb is racist, yeah, but mainly he's a man that doesn't know what the hell is happenin' around him. And Memphis--compared to Jackson, say, or Birmingham--Memphis is like an oasis of enlightenment. But by the same token the movement couldn't get much of a foothold here, cause too many people were too complacent. Then along comes the garbage strike and *twice*, respectable people go out marchin' in the streets and get gassed by the damn police..."

"What was the first time?"

"February twenty-three. Peaceful march. Police car runs over some lady's foot, she starts screamin', people start rockin' the police car, and it's like *one*, these cops been readin' about uppity Negroes all over the south, and they're prepared to take care of business if any of 'em show up in Memphis, and *two*, they all just got issued these new cans of Mace, the miracle product that takes care of uppity Negroes like DDT does mosquitoes. Then you had people runnin' every which way, and a lot of the cops decided they'd emphasize things by clubbin' people..."

"So," Randall says, "you had a lot of respectable middle-class people who'd probably had no confrontations with the law, you had all these folks who only knew the movement from watching Bull Connor on TV, gettin' their heads split open and their eyes burned out."

"Exactly. And the Bee Oh Pee, these guys are sittin' up here, a few miles from the action, sayin', 'See, what's the point of all this non-violent shit? The man's after your ass one way or the other, so why not play the game by his rules?'"

"You figure there's anybody listening?"

"A few hundred kids, for sure. Beyond that, I can't say."

"You figure they'd talk to us?"

Marchand tilts his head a bit as his eyes remained fixed on Randall. "Why would you want to?"

Randall smiles. "'Cause it's my job, brother."

"Yeah, but tell me what you expect to *achieve*. You think you can sweet-talk the Invaders so they get their moms and dads to vote for Kennedy?"

"It's possible."

"Right," Marchand says. "And it's possible I'm the next mayor of Memphis." He leans back in his chair. "Look, you want me to talk to these dudes, I can do it. You want me to?"

"I'd appreciate it."

Marchand shrugs. "I'll see what I can do. But one thing..." He looks at Ben. "No offense, but for the welfare of all concerned, I'd leave your friend at home."

Randall nods, and smiles at Marchand. "Understood," he says.

It's another cool day in Memphis, overcast and windy, as Randall and Ben make their rounds. They have remained briefly at Memphis State for a meeting with the school's nascent Kennedy for President committee. Randall takes a breather here as Ben does most of the talking; this is, after all, a matter of preaching to the converted, who consist of five students, two white boys, one white girl, two black boys, all earnest.

They have lunch at a barbecue restaurant on Central Avenue with a group of ministers. It crosses Ben's mind that every gathering so far has been integrated (although to be sure last night's dinner was so only because of his presence), which in itself seems to have significance. Whether it applies to the south, or to Memphis alone, he's not sure, but he guesses that five black men and three white men could not have met so casually at a Memphis restaurant a few years earlier.

"Lawson's not here," Randall says to Ben as they make their entrance, ten minutes late. Jim Lawson, a Harvard-educated black Methodist pastor, has been largely responsible for making the sanitation workers' strike an issue in Memphis's black community at large, and for bringing nationally prominent black figures into the fray. Randall had been told there was a "seventy-eighty percent chance he'll make it."

He doesn't make it. While this may be disheartening to Randall, it doesn't detract from Ben's growing sense of involvement with what's happening here. Over huge platters of ribs and chicken the ministers discuss the lifting of the curfew, the exit of the national guard, the disparity between the Memphis represented in local newspapers and the Memphis experienced walking around one's neighborhood. "The headline is, 'STILL SCATTERED ACTS OF VIOLENCE,'" says the black Baptist minister. "Well, what do they expect? Look at the paper from any day of the week in the last twenty years, you're gonna have scattered acts of violence."

A municipal court judge has called for investigation into the transportation of young people (black boys) by ministers (black) to Thursday's march by taxi. If these charges are found to have merit, says the judge, the ministers will be charged with contributing to the delinquency of a minor. "Can you *believe* that?" says another black Baptist minister. "Contributing to the delinquency of a minor because you took some kids to see Martin Luther King?"

"This is what they do," says the black Church of Christ minister. "This is what the Henry Loebs of the world do. They intimidate and they inhibit. You're going to think next time before you take some children to a rally, because you might get charged with a felony."

"I don't think it's a *strategy* to intimidate," says the white Methodist. "I think Judge Turner believes in his heart that there's a conspiracy to commit disturbances, to upset the order in this city, and if we take kids out of school we're encouraging them to riot and steal."

Randall asks if anyone knows when Doctor King will be returning to Memphis, and what his schedule will be when he does so. The first black Baptist says it's his understanding that King will be arriving from Atlanta this evening, or tomorrow morning at the latest, because he's scheduled to be the principal speaker at a big rally in support of the strikers tomorrow night.

"And where's that rally?"

123

"At Mason Temple, in southwest Memphis."

"It's open to the public?"

"Open to one and all, and it's a big place. You won't have any trouble finding a seat."

Randall then says that he very much looks forward to seeing Dr. King in person, having previously done so only at a very great distance, at the March on Washington, and he proceeds thereupon to transform this ecumenical chat into a low-key Kennedy event. Randall says that he's been listening very closely to the conversation at this table, and that while much of it has been clearly specific to Memphis, if you were to change the details the conversation could really have been about any city in this country, north or south. Because there is a deep misunderstanding between the races in America, a distrust in both directions, a distrust that Senator Kennedy is acutely aware of, and that--along with ending the war in Vietnam and doing things for America's cities--addressing that distrust is Senator Kennedy's principal goal. In fact, Randall says, those three issues are so tightly interwoven that they all affect each other, so you can't think about racial disharmony without thinking about the racial imbalance of troops in Southeast Asia, and you can't think about poverty in the cities without thinking about all the money America is pouring into the war.

None of this is news to the assembled clergy, Ben would guess, but Randall has arranged it in such a supple, enticing package that it evokes a great deal of enthusiastic nodding and murmuring.

Some eighty minutes after their arrival--after a series of tough questions that Randall fields with typical grace and aplomb--he makes a final statement. He wishes, he says, that whatever twists and turns the struggle may take in weeks to come, that whatever recalcitrance the community faces from the

city of Memphis, and whatever disdain and violence from its
police force, that these pastors will themselves associate Robert
Kennedy with the movement, will imagine how much better this
country would be with him as president, and will impart that
message to their congregations.

"How'd that go?" Randall asks Ben in the Mustang.
They're on the way to LeMoyne-Owen College, the black
school where Betty Ann Ennis teaches, not quite a mile from
the barbecue restaurant, and another session with
undergraduates.

"You're asking me?" Ben says.

"I don't see anybody else in the car."

"Don't you know? It went great. It couldn't possibly
have gone better. Couldn't you feel the electricity at the end?
Those guys weren't just being polite. They weren't just *telling*
you how enthusiastic they were, for God's sake."

"Yeah," Randall says. "I thought it was good. I liked
those guys. It's good that in a city like this there's some kind
of affiliation--literally, I mean--between the white ministers
and the black ministers. You don't see that too much in the
north. Here it's so clear that they've got a common enemy."

Ben drives the car several blocks in silence, wondering
if he should ask the question, and finally does. "Are you serious
that you don't know how it went?"

"You think I'm fishing for compliments?"

"No, of course not. There's always the possibility this
could be one of my tests, to make sure I didn't sleep through the
lunch meeting."

Randall chuckles. "No test. I can't be entirely objective.
I'm sure you can understand that."

"Not really," Ben says. "You had those guys eating out of your hand. I can't believe you don't know that." Stopped at a light, he slaps the steering wheel for emphasis. "And it's not as if you were talking to librarians, or engineers. You were preaching to the preachers."

"To coin a phrase," Randall says.

The LeMoyne-Owen meeting is uneventful, except that Randall again gives Ben the larger role, allowing him to make the opening statement to a group of some twenty-five black college students. Strategically, it doesn't make a great deal of sense to Ben. It's not that he doesn't appreciate the opportunity, and it's not that he's intimidated at once again being the lone white face in a fairly big room. (In fact his only trepidation comes from the fear that Delphine's mother might wander in and manage to read his mind.) It just seems that Randall would be a more effective motivator here, and he wonders if Randall is throwing him a bone, or if this is a further test--just the perversity of it, of preppy pale New Englander Ben standing before all these southern black kids. It doesn't occur to Ben until afterward--after he's done a perfectly good job--when they're driving back to the Holiday Inn, that Randall may simply have been taking a break. With all this shifting of gears, and with the bravura performance at lunch, he's got a right to be tired.

At the front desk Randall checks for messages. Ben does not. Randall has had a call from William Marchand.

It's a few minutes after four o'clock. Randall says, "I could use a nap. You want to meet for dinner around seven? Seven thirty?"

"We've got nothing planned for tonight?"

"Not a thing, unless Marchand's got me fixed up someway."

126

"Actually," Ben says, "I'd made some plans."

Randall chuckles. "You'd made some *plans*? You were gonna drop in on a debutante ball, or what?"

Ben would just as soon not say anything about his hopes for the evening, but he figures he doesn't have much choice. "I had just kind of a tentative plan with that girl from last night, with Delphine."

Randall is silent for a moment, his expression suggesting surprise, at the least. "You telling me you have a *date*?"

"No, just a casual thing. She's going to show me around Memphis."

"*Damn*, Ben. You are one fast mover. You are one devil-may-care white boy, are you not?"

There has been no lightness to Randall's tone. "It's not a fucking date, Randall, okay? I don't even know if it's gonna happen. We were just talking after dinner last night..."

Randall interrupts. "You mind if I come along?"

"Of course not," Ben says.

In his room, adjacent to Randall's, Ben calls the front desk and asks for messages. The clerk tells him he's had a call from Miss Ennis, who left a number for him to call before six. It's just quarter after four now, and Ben finds his pulse accelerated despite lowered expectations for the evening. He dials the telephone not knowing quite what to expect. A female voice answers, lower-pitched than Delphine's. Who is this? Should he announce himself? He says, "Hello, could I speak to Delphine, please?"

The voice at the other end calls her name, and in ten seconds she's on the line. "It's Ben," he says. "I just got your message."

"It turns out I'm free tonight," Delphine says. "If you'd still like to do something."

"I'd love to do something," Ben says, and there is a quick rapping at the door to his room. He says, "Can I call you right back? There's someone at the door."

"Why don't I just hold on?" She says.

It's not an idea that pleases him. "I'll call you back in five minutes at the most."

"Look," she says, "my girlfriend's expecting a call. If it comes in the next five minutes, she could be on the phone for an hour."

The rapping is repeated. Surely it's Randall, and surely he's getting impatient. This is such miserable timing. Ben says, "Listen, is it all right if Randall joins us?"

There is a brief silence at Delphine's end, punctuated by Randall's insistent knocking. "It's fine," she says. "Should I pick you all up?"

"That would be great," Ben says. "What time?"

"Is seven all right?"

"Randall?"

"Yeah," says the muffled voice outside the door. "Who the hell else?"

He lets Randall in. "Sorry. I was on the phone. Delphine's picking us up at seven."

Randall plops down on the edge of the queen-size Holiday Inn bed. "Seven, huh? Okay. That'll work. I talked to Marchand. I'm gonna go meet with those Bee Oh Pee guys right now. If it's up to me, you'd come along. I don't believe in this black-only bullshit. You know that. But William set this thing up, that's the way he wants it, I have to honor that. Okay?"

"Of course," Ben says.

128

Randall gets up, paces, and stops. "I'm gonna take the car. I should be back in a couple of hours." He checks his watch. "I should be back...quarter to seven at the latest. You wait for me, right?"

"Of course," Ben says.

## FOURTEEN

How to get to Delaware fast? This is Alex's preoccupation as he walks briskly from Elliot's apartment to his own, the baggie with a lid of that incredibly good grass in his pants pocket. (Alex has never paid more than forty dollars for an ounce, but this stuff gets you twice as high twice as fast, so a hundred didn't seem unreasonable, especially with the Delaware license thrown in.) The little bit he smoked has already put him in a far better state of mind. He's not so worried about Lydia; she'll be back, he's pretty sure. Where else does she have to go? He's focused on those Puerto Rican bastards and getting his stuff back from them. And Elliot's idea—the gun—is so simple and perfect. Alex couldn't be more philosophically opposed to guns: three miserable years at military school had pretty much cemented that. But sometimes you have to go against your principles to achieve your goal, to

do the sensible thing, like Wilson deciding to join the war in
Europe in 1917.

Does he know anyone who has a car? Prosper, but he's
thirty miles away in Connecticut. Ben has that Corvair
rattletrap that might not make it to Delaware and Ben probably
wouldn't lend it to him anyway. Can he rent a car? He has a
vague idea that you have to be twenty-five to qualify, and he's
eight months from that. Bus would take too long. Train?
Maybe to Philadelphia, and then what? Hitchhiking would be
insane. He could *buy* a car—not a new one but a used one.
How much does he have in the checking account? No idea, but
it's got to be a thousand, or seven or eight hundred at least.
Does it make sense to buy a car for, say, five hundred bucks in
order to buy a gun in order to get back a thousand dollars of
equipment? Yes, it does! Plus, to buy a *new* Bolex and a *new*
Nagra would run him twelve hundred, thirteen hundred, maybe
more.

He's got the munchies something awful, and all he's had
to eat today was that gross peanut butter sandwich at six in the
morning, so a couple of blocks from home he stops for a slice of
pizza and it's the tastiest thing he's ever eaten, or close to it.

In the apartment he spends what seems like half an hour
searching for the Yellow Pages, finds the massive book on a
shelf in the bedroom closet where Lydia keeps her boots, and
turns to AUTOMOBILES—USED. There are some listings for
Manhattan but they're either new car dealers—who Alex
figures are going to be selling trade-ins at huge markups—or
they're in parts of the city Alex doesn't know, like way
downtown, which Lydia could help him with if he knew where
the hell she was. Lots of used car dealers in Brooklyn and
Queens, but that's the wrong direction, as is the Bronx. New

Jersey's where he needs to go. Cross the George Washington Bridge, buy a car, get straight onto the Jersey Turnpike, and Delaware here we come. What's just over the bridge? He's passed by there a thousand times…Fort Lee, then Leonia. Indeed, there is a big ad for Leonia Ford-Mercury, Right Across the Bridge, Right on the Price!

In high gear, he takes a quick shower and he shaves. Should he wear khakis and a sport coat? No, better his only suit, even though it's a cotton blend and the weather's hardly summery. White shirt, black wingtips he hasn't worn in God knows how long. A tie? Of course. For good measure, his slim black leather briefcase, in one of whose sleek folds he squeezes the plastic bag with the magical marijuana. He grabs a few assorted pills from his stash in the medicine cabinet, puts them in a little container with his prescription allergy pills; he collects his wallet, his checkbook, and his passport, and he's halfway out the door when he thinks about Lydia. It's difficult to determine whether it's anger or concern that dominates his current feelings toward her, but he figures that if she's trying to teach him a lesson by staying out all night—if in fact she *did* stay out all night—maybe he deserves it. And if something has befallen her, well…the least he could do is leave her a short note.

First stop: the Chase Manhattan branch on Broadway, where they know him, and cashing a seven-hundred dollar check is no problem at all; six hundred in fifties and a hundred in twenties. Back on the street, he lets pass a succession of legitimate taxis, and soon enough a gypsy cab cruises by, sizing him up. All Alex has to do is flick his hand for the guy to stop.

"How much to Leonia, New Jersey?"

131

The driver is a young Latino, dark-skinned. The car is a Chevy Belvedere, 1963 at the latest, with enough dents and gouges to keep a body shop busy for a week. "New Yersey?" He says, and examines his prospective fare for a good ten seconds. "How 'bout forty bucks?"

"You kidding me? Twenty."

"Twenty-five and you pay the toll. You pay my toll on the way back, too."

"Good," Alex says, and he climbs into the back seat.

For somebody who wants to buy a car fast and get on with his day, the used-car lot at Leonia Ford is unreasonably big, its contents not limited to Fords and Mercurys by any means. Alex must keep reminding himself that his goal is to find a serviceable car and get out of here as fast as possible. But look—there's an Austin-Healey that's almost a dead ringer for the one his father gave him for his sixteenth birthday, and over here what could be the very 1958 MG driven by his old girlfriend Laura in Palm Beach. If he had time, he'd look through the rows and rows of cars for an Alfa Spider. But where would he keep it once he got back to the city? For that matter, where will he keep any car he buys? That's not his concern right now.

He's examining a 1963 Studebaker Lark—sticker price within his range at $475—when he's approached by a man perhaps two or three years his senior. "Anything I can help you with?" asks the man, who wears a shiny suede jacket and has thick black hair arranged in the sort of ducktail that was out of style about five years before the Lark hit the assembly line.

"I need something dependable," Alex says. "Got to get to Delaware this afternoon."

The man checks his watch and looks back at Alex with a wry little smile. "Almost three now, pal. I don't think we got anything with wings."

"How far is it?"

"Jeez…maybe two and half, three hours to Wilmington. But we'd have to do the paperwork."

This isn't the sort of thing Alex wants to hear. "How about if I pay cash and we postpone the paperwork till tomorrow?"

"I'm Leo, by the way." The man offers his hand, and gives Alex a firmer shake than he was prepared for. "We could get you a temporary registration, maybe. I could talk to my boss about the rest."

"Tell you what," Alex says. "Let me take this Lark on a quick test drive, see what kind of shape it's in, okay?"

With Leo in the passenger seat, Alex tools the Studebaker on city streets forming a rectangle around the dealership. It handles okay, it accelerates surprisingly well. At a red light he stamps on the brake and Leo must brace himself with two hands against the glove compartment. "Sorry about that," Alex says. "It stops all right."

"Good, low mileage," Leo says, although salesmanship doesn't really seem relevant here.

Alex checks the odometer. "Seventy-three thousand. I wouldn't say that's so low."

"We've got all the service records on this baby," Leo says. "New clutch at fifty thousand, give or take. Brand new brakes all around. Guess you know Studebaker knew how to build a car."

"Right," Alex says. "But not how to sell one."

133

The car has a bit of a musty smell, but the upholstery is presentable. The radio works, as do all the controls. After a second trip around the block, Alex pulls it into the same curb cut he'd exited from. "Whattya think?" Leo says, expectantly.

"I'll give you four fifty," Alex says.

Leo nods. "I'll talk to my boss. Four fifty plus tax and registration fees, we're up around that four seventy-five on the sticker."

"I mean four fifty total," Alex says. He removes his wallet from the breast pocket of suit and counts out nine fifties. "Show this to your boss."

"Okay," Leo says, taking the money with a slight sideways movement of his head. "Let's have a look at your driver's license." Without giving it much thought, Alex hands him Elliot's Delaware license. With a little smile, Leo says, "So…going home for a visit, Elliot?"

"Right," Alex says.

"Okay," Leo says brightly, "let's go inside and talk to the man."

"I'm just fine here," Alex says. "Can I have the license back?"

"I'll need it for the paperwork."

"I'll give it back when the time comes."

Leo hands him the license and says, "Hey, come on. What the hell. Come in with me now. It'll speed things up."

"No, man." There's a bit of an edge to Alex's voice. "You just go and do whatever bullshit you have to do with your boss."

Leo shrugs, slides out of the car, and heads for the bunkerish little building that serves as the used-car office.

Alex sits nervously in the Lark, tuning the radio and setting its buttons. Having set all five, he listens to "Forever

Came Today" by the Supremes, in the middle of which he backs the car up, turns it around, and drives off the lot, heading for the Turnpike. Leo and his boss have his four hundred and fifty dollars, so this can hardly be construed as theft.

He pulls into the first service area, just past Exit 16, and fills the car with regular. It takes almost seventeen gallons, which means for one thing that this little car has a huge fuel capacity and for another that the bastards gave him a nearly empty tank. He buys a Coke inside the station and, back in the Lark, fishes a little brown tablet out of his pill bottle and swallows it. The Obitrol should keep him alert and happy to Wilmington and back.

Traffic is heavy on the northern, smelly section of the Turnpike, where the road is virtually surrounded by oil refineries, and then through the exits to bedroom communities as the rush hour approaches, but Alex keeps the car at a pretty steady sixty miles an hour. Then, after he passes Exit 9, to New Brunswick and his old stomping ground, Princeton, there's far less congestion and he gooses the Lark up to seventy, seventy-five, eighty. It occurs to him periodically that getting pulled over in his current circumstance wouldn't be a good idea—despite the suit, a state trooper might just be motivated to do a little searching upon discovering Alex has no registration. So he eases off to seventy, but soon he's unconsciously edging back to eighty, eighty-five.

He crosses the Delaware at five minutes past five--warmer, more comfortable, and better dressed than George Washington was. There's a Sunoco station just off the first exit past the bridge, and he wonders if posing the direct question will raise any eyebrows, set off any alarms. Why should it?

135

The grizzled attendant is in the midst of pumping another five gallons into the Lark when Alex says, "You happen to know if there's a gun shop anywhere nearby?"

"What kinda gun you need?" The old man doesn't even look up from the hose.

"Pistol," Alex says.

"Well, you drive down this road about two and a half miles. On the right, you'll see Sonny's Sport Shop. He's got good selection, pretty good prices. Stays open till seven."

Not halfway there, he spots a Kresge's five-and-dime; in the tobacco section he considers which might be deemed more suspicious—buying a cheap pipe, or a pack of rolling papers. What the hell, he decides, this is Delaware, and I'm in a suit. He goes for the papers, and in the car he rolls himself a mini-joint, ignites it with the Lark's cute little coil lighter, takes a couple of deep drags, and proceeds to Sonny's.

Maybe it's a sport shop, but you wouldn't come here if you wanted golf clubs or a tennis racquet, for example. Feeling very good indeed, the supernatural grass having enhanced the amphetamine's euphoric qualities, Alex is more amused than dismayed by this exposition of The Enemy—guns and more guns, boots for trekking through the swamps searching for runaway slaves or invading Vietnamese, camouflage outfits for befuddling the deer or hiding from the communists. It's not even his father's kind of place—too déclassé for that. But if he ever gets kicked out of his apartment he could drive down here, buy a tent, a cooking stove and a shotgun, and live off the land for a few months. Except that every square inch of land nearby is paved over.

The pistols are all under glass, and Alex bets the glass is plenty thick, else the aforementioned communists could bust through it and supply the revolution. He admires a couple of long-barreled Magnums, like modern manifestations of the Old West, but figures he wants something small and concealable. He wonders if the little snub-nosed ones can shoot straight, but then he's probably not going to be doing any actual shooting, although it certainly would be nice to put one in Flaco's leg, give the arrogant bastard something to think about.

"Can I help you?" asks the middle-aged, plaid-shirted man behind the counter.

"Looking for a pistol," Alex says.

"Can I ask what you need it for?"

How shall Alex interpret this? "Excuse me?"

"You gonna be shooting targets, or vermin, or what?"

"Ah, no. I live in…kind of a rough neighborhood…"

"Protection, then?" Alex nods affirmatively. "And how much were you planning to spend?"

"I guess fifty to a hundred, depending…"

"You'd probably want something on the small side, I'd say, if you'd be carrying it?"

"Yes," Alex says. "For sure."

"Well, we've got your old standby here." The man reaches into the glass cabinet and removes one of the snub-nosed guns. "This is your Smith & Wesson thirty-eight Special. A very popular handgun with an excellent reputation. Holds five rounds, and you can see it's real easy to reload. This is on the low side of your budget." He hands Alex the pistol.

Alex likes the feel of it, the heft of it. The pistol smells of oil and steel. "Does it shoot straight, with this little barrel?"

"If you want something a little bit more exotic, I've got an automatic here, a Walther PPK…"

"Wait a minute," Alex says. "James Bond's gun?"

The salesman smiles and hands over the sleek pistol. "One and the same. Well, not exactly. In the movies it's a thirty-two caliber. This one's a three eighty. Gives you a little more firepower, in case you'd ever need it."

Wow. This is no mere utilitarian weapon, this is double oh seven. Alex has half a mind to drop into a Bondian shooting stance, but elects to stay cool. "How much?"

"I've got this on special for a hundred even, and I could give you a little break on ammunition…"

Alex retrieves the final three fifties plus Elliot's license and plunks them on the counter. The salesman has a quick look at the license. "Dover, eh? Pretty area down there, Mister…Shatzberg?"

"Very pretty," Alex concurs.

He zips back up the Turnpike, taking the Hightstown exit and detouring to Route One because he has a sudden yearning for a hamburger at the Colonial Diner outside of Princeton. The two-lane highway is nearly deserted at quarter after nine and he has to restrain himself from grossly exceeding the fifty-mile-an-hour speed limit. Just outside of Princeton Junction, where as an undergraduate he caught many a train to ride into the city, he pulls onto a side road and rolls himself another little joint. Good God, this stuff is amazing.

He has WIBG from Philadelphia on the radio and they're playing Otis Redding's "Dock of the Bay." He leans over and pulls the heavy little cardboard box from under the passenger seat, grabs the gun and then one little box of .38-caliber ammunition. With great care he removes the Walther's clip, loads it, and clicks it back in.

Out of the car, holding the gun with both hands, he aims at a streetlight some twenty feet away, and squeezes off four

138

rounds, at the conclusion of which the streetlight is intact but the concussion of the final explosion lingers in the still night. Smoke rises from the barrel of the gun, or is it vapor? Dogs—several of them, none seemingly very close—begin to bark. Alex points the gun at a mailbox not six feet from him and fires the fifth bullet: It rips a sizeable hole in the metal mailbox, which reverberates on its wooden post for several seconds. That's enough for now.

## FIFTEEN

Victoria Sálazar, a stern woman whose family came to New York from Havana when Fulgencio Batista was still in power, is the vice-principal of P.S. 72, and it is she Lydia chooses to confront when she arrives at school just before noon. Mrs. Sálazar would have tracked her down eventually, Lydia figured, so better to get it over with right at the start. "It would have been courteous to give us some notice," Mrs. Sálazar says.

"Believe me, if I'd been able to, I would have." Lydia wears her most conservative school outfit: a knee-length navy blue skirt with a white blouse, stockings, and black penny loafers, as if she were interviewing for a secretarial job at Con Ed, say, in 1965.

"Why couldn't you call us yourself? Why did we have to hear from Miss O'Connor?"

"It was a family emergency, Mrs. Sálazar. I had access to a phone when I called Miss O'Connor, and I knew by the time school was open I wouldn't be able to get to one."

"A family emergency?" The scowling *Cubana* clearly wants Lydia to elaborate, but she knows she doesn't have to, so she doesn't.

"If you look at my record, I think you'll see I haven't been late once. I haven't taken any sick days."

The older woman glares at her, gives a little shake of the head. "I didn't have time to call in a sub. You compromise the children, you put extra pressure on your fellow teachers..."

"I'm very sorry, Mrs. Sálazar. It was unavoidable. I'll do my best to see that it never happens again." She senses that she's taken the words out of the vice-principal's mouth.

"Are you kidding me?" Maddy says. "One of the guys who wanted to steal Alex's stuff?"

"It wasn't the guy who felt me up, the creepy guy," Lydia protests. They sit in the break room, as they do nearly every early afternoon. Maddy has a cup of coffee and a Danish pastry, Lydia a chicken salad sandwich, which serves as her breakfast and her lunch.

"If I remember," Maddy says, "you described one guy who was in charge, the guy Alex said was a poet, and he made some kind of threat to you when they went out the door..."

"*No*," Lydia's voice rises, "it wasn't a threat. He said something about he would see me around the neighborhood, and he *did*. When I got off the bus yesterday he was there, on the street, and he was all sweet talk, and I was telling him to go to hell. So then I went home and I got all pissed off at Alex..."

"More pissed off at Alex," Maddy corrects.

"Yeah, well, he was stoned again, or still. So I just got the hell out of there. After a while. And I called you. And your line was busy forever…"

"What time?"

"I don't know—six, six thirty…"

"I was talking to my sister, Jill, in Massachusetts. I have to fill her in on everything."

"About what?"

"About Ben. There was a note from him yesterday when I got home. He went to Memphis with Randall, for the campaign."

"And?"

"And nothing," Maddy shrugs. "Not a word. When you called at six I thought it was him."

"Oh, Jesus, Mad, I'm sorry. I'm so caught up in my own shit."

"Don't worry about it. It's not as if it's out of character, for Ben."

"You're okay?"

"Yeah. He'll get around to calling me eventually. Tell me the rest of your night."

"I'm sitting there in this fucking drugstore on Broadway, okay, and the last thing I want to do is go back to Alex, I didn't bring any money with me, just a few bucks, I can't get through to you, so I called this guy, Rafael. You know, maybe he'd treat me to dinner…"

"And he did, sounds like."

"It turns out he's like an assistant manager at a bodega, a big place on Columbus and 109th…"

"I think I can picture it," Maddy says.

"And he's taking a fucking Shakespeare course at CCNY. You walk in his place and it's like a bookstore…"

Maddy smiles. "Who would have guessed? So…you went from dinner to his place?"

"No! Jesus, give me a break. I asked him to walk me home. We get there, and there's Alex passed out on the couch, all the windows closed, both the fucking radiators on full blast, it's like a hundred and ten degrees, and there's no way I'm staying there."

"So *then* you went to his place."

"Yeah, except the deal was that he stays on the couch and I get the bed. And he would've, too. I mean, he did, but then I got up to pee in the middle of the night and we started talking…"

"While you were peeing?"

"No, Mad…come *on*. We were just sitting on his couch, and the next thing you knew, he was carrying me to bed."

"He *carried* you?"

"He carried me. And then, listen—can I ask you a question? About you and Ben?"

"It depends."

"Does he ever…do the oral thing with you?"

Maddy laughs. "It has been known to happen."

"Is it good?"

"It's…um…interesting, is the most I'd say."

"Yeah…with Alex, I don't think he knows what's going on down there, if you get what I mean. But Rafael last night, it was like…the first thing. It was like…heaven."

"Wow," Maddy says. "So you found a guy who reads Shakespeare and makes you feel very good."

"Right. I keep thinking about the Beatles' song—now that you've found another key, what are you going to play? What the fuck am I gonna do now?"

"Sounds to me like you're fed up with Alex and you just met somebody you really like."

"Yeah, but I can't live in that shithole fourth-floor walkup. Did I tell you that one of the other guys from yesterday morning lives right across the hall from him?"

"Has he asked you to live with him?"

"No. I guess I'm just projecting. I'm thinking about how I'm sick and tired of Alex and all the drug bullshit, but that place is so nice and so convenient, and I was dreaming about how if I could get Alex to move out…"

"But the lease is in his name, right?"

"If I could get him to move out, and Rafael to move in, then together we could make the rent, and I really don't think the landlord would give a shit."

Maddy leans back in her chair, takes a bite of her Danish, and a gulp of coffee. "You don't want to get ahead of yourself, do you? This is a guy you've known for a little more than a day, and yesterday morning he was just about your worst enemy. I couldn't blame you for wanting to get away from Alex, but I don't think you should be too hasty with this guy Rafael, even if he does read Shakespeare."

The attenuated school day does not go well. She has a classroom full of kids speaking multiple varieties of Spanish and she can't concentrate, her mind wandering to erotic images of Rafael followed by Maddy's words of warning, followed by the inevitability of a confrontation with Alex.

On the bus, Lydia considers various tacks to take with Alex—from telling him flat out that they're through to ignoring him as much as possible—but in the end her fondest hope is for him not to be home. If that's the case, she asks herself, if she'd prefer not to see Alex at all, why *is* she going home? Rafael has given her a set of keys to his place, but the thought of spending several hours alone there doesn't appeal to her, nor does the prospect of running into Julio. Or worse, Flaco. Or worst, both of them.

As it turns out, Alex is not in the apartment. Again all the windows are closed. The heat comes on most forcefully at night, so it isn't oppressively hot in the late afternoon, but it's unpleasantly stuffy. She opens the living room windows and checks the bedroom. The bed looks exactly as it had late last night: slept in, but not recently, so Alex has evidently spent the entire night on the couch. Something else: the dresser drawers are all open, which is not the sort of thing Alex does. He may be a little disorganized and a little crazy, but he's neat. Feeling a growing sense of apprehension, she heads for the deep bottom drawer, where she'd stashed the Bolex and the Nagra the previous morning, and they're gone. Could Alex have taken them? He's got classes Tuesday morning and afternoon, but to the best of her knowledge neither of them requires equipment. And of course it's pretty unlikely that he went to class at all, which leads her to wonder where he is at this moment. She supposes that he could be out doing almost anything—getting dinner, buying milk, buying drugs. She knows he gets his marijuana from a fellow Columbia student a few blocks away, but she doesn't know the guy's name or address. There's no reason to worry, really, except that she was gone all night and now maybe she's beginning to feel a little guilty. She recalls her conversation with Maddy during yesterday's lunch break: Maddy was going to call Prosper, to suggest that he call Alex.

Perhaps this has come to pass, and Alex and Prosper are somewhere having a heart-to-heart. Or perhaps not.

Alex's leather-cased address book sits on the coffee table next to the phone. She looks up Prosper's number and dials. He answers almost immediately, so unless Alex took a train to Connecticut, they're not together. "Prosper?"

"Yes," he says, clearly unsure who she is. "Hello."

"It's Lydia. Listen, do you have any idea where Alex is? Has he called you?"

There's a brief silence before Prosper says, "No." Then, after a pause, "Well, he might have. But I've been in New Haven all day, at the draft physical."

"Oh, shit," she says. "I knew that. How'd that go?"

"Okay so far. It's not over. Is Alex missing?"

"I'm not sure. It's probably nothing to worry about." She wants to get out of this exchange as quickly as possible, but she feels she has to explain why she called. "I was just hoping to talk to someone he might have talked to."

"About what?"

She's not making any sense at all, she knows. "I'm just trying to figure something out."

"Can I help?"

"No…I'm sorry I bothered you." She sets the receiver down, feeling like an idiot.

Not only is the toilet seat down, so is the lid, because there's a piece of yellow notebook paper on it—Alex leaving a note where he was sure she'd see it? She reads the scrawled capital letters:
BABE—

WHERE THE HELL YOU BEEN? WELL, NO MATTER, WHATEVER YOU DID I DESERVED IT. MOTHERFUCKERS FROM YESTERDAY MORNING

145

CAME BACK AND RIPPED OFF THE STUFF. I WILL NOT
STAND FOR THIS! I AM OFF TO TAKE RETALIATORY
MEASURES. SEE YOU LATER TONIGHT. TU HOMBRE,
ALEJANDRO

If she was confused before reading the note, now she is
mystified. She reads it a second and a third time, and a great
deluge of emotions floods down upon her, not the least of which
is something at least resembling love for her man, Alex, who
has uncharacteristically given her a blank check of forgiveness.
Beyond that there is an odd sense of trepidation that something
terrible might be in the works, and a glowing ember of anger at
the "motherfuckers from yesterday." Could they possibly
include Rafael? Could he, instead of heading to the bodega this
morning, have met up with Flaco and Julio and come here? Not
likely, she thinks, but she fears that's just wishful thinking, and
almost as bad is a scenario in which Rafael—in the
conversation she only partially overheard at six a.m.—gave his
okay to the theft, perhaps even assured Julio he wouldn't have
to worry about her messing things up, because she'd be going
straight from his bed to school.

And what in God's name would Alex's "retaliatory
measures" be? Short of going to the police (extremely
unlikely), what action could he possibly take?

Rafael is at the cash register, and she has to wait for him
to ring up a series of customers before she can speak a word to
him. He's noticed her, given her a couple of little nods, but she
hasn't so much as smiled in return. She clutches Alex's note in
her right hand, and she waits.

"*¿Puedo ayudarte, señorita?*" He says when she
reaches the front of the line; it's half a joke, she figures, and

half because there are now several people behind her, waiting to be served. "I have to talk to you," she says in English.

"Now's a bad time," he replies in a pleasant, somewhat impersonal tone. "I've got customers."

"I have to talk to you," she repeats.

"I'm off at seven." He glances at his watch. "Just over an hour."

"I can't wait," she says. "You're the assistant fucking manager—get somebody to take over for you."

"Okay," he says. "Give me a minute. Outside, all right?"

When he appears, three minutes later at most, he tries to embrace her, but she steps back. She says, "What the fuck's going on, Rafael?"

"What do you mean?"

She has misgivings about showing him the note because somehow he might sense through it whatever residual feelings she has for Alex, but she figures it's about as succinct a summation of the state of affairs as there is, and she stuffs the folded yellow paper into his hand.

He reads. He studies. He says, "I don't know anything about this. What's going on?"

"You tell *me* what's going on, Rafael. The motherfuckers from yesterday—that's you and your worthless Puerto Rican friends. I don't know where the hell he is, and that movie camera and that expensive fucking tape recorder are gone."

He hasn't lost his cool, hasn't flinched. "You know where I've been all day."

"What about your buddies? What were you and Julio talking about last night? This morning?"

147

He reflects. "Okay. Last night, Julio said Flaco was still talking about how that stuff belonged to them, how they should go back and like, claim it. But I said definitely no. I said there was no way in hell they should do that. Swear to God, Lydia."

"Why didn't you tell me that in the first place, for Christ sake?"

"Because I never thought they'd do it. Do you *know* they did it? Do you know that crazy bastard didn't take it himself and stash it somewhere?"

"It crossed my mind. But that was before I saw the note."

"What about the note?"

"I can't explain it to you. You don't know him. I can tell when he's bullshitting."

Rafael's eyes are fixed on hers. She doesn't know for sure that *he's* not bullshitting, but it certainly doesn't seem that way. He says, "Okay, let's say you're right. I'll talk to those guys. They'll be straight with me. If they haven't already sold that stuff, I'll get it back."

"What if they have sold it?"

"Jesus, Lydia, how far do you want to push this?"

"I guess I want to know what I mean to you."

He breaks his gaze, stares out at Columbus Avenue for a moment, then focuses on her again. "Yeah, well I guess I want to know what he means to you."

"I've known you for a day and a half, Rafael. Maybe Alex is a little crazy, but I've been with him for, like, six months."

"Okay," he says. "So maybe I should back off from you?"

"I'm not saying that."

148

"What are you saying?"

She feels tears in her eyes. "I don't know. I'm worried about him. I don't want him to get hurt."

"All right," Rafael says. "You still want to spend tonight at my place?"

She has zero desire to return to her place. Rafael's bed is inviting, the rest not so much. "I'm not sure."

"Have dinner with me again," he says. "You can call him, tell him the situation…"

"If he's even home…"

"If he's home. If he's not, we can go over there together and wait for him."

## SIXTEEN

The temperature had been a few degrees above freezing when Prosper traveled east this morning. As he heads back to Riverside now it's a good twenty degrees warmer under a bright sun. Feeling very weary, Prosper opens the Valiant's window wide rather than take another pill, and makes it home in fifty minutes.

The first thing he does is call Maddy to report on the day's progress, but her (and Ben's) phone rings and rings. He considers calling the radio station, but decides he wants to speak to neither Martin nor Theresa. What next? It's a little past four o'clock and he suspects that were he to lie down he'd fall asleep inside ten seconds and remain unconscious until midnight--which might not be a bad strategy for tomorrow's final day. But if he's to accompany Maddy to the party tomorrow night he'd rather not be a complete zombie.

He switches on Aunt Catherine's stereo. The Marantz tuner is a recent addition, requested by Catherine that she might listen to Prosper's work, selected by Prosper at a midtown Manhattan specialty store called Harvey Radio, where it was a hundred dollars cheaper than Catherine would have paid at the swank music shop on Greenwich Avenue. The dial is set at 95.5, the frequency for WABC-FM, and as the amplifier and tuner warm up an electronic hum transforms into a second or two of static and then the strange backwards music at the end of "Strawberry Fields." God, Prosper thinks, if they segué from this into "Lady Madonna" I'll quit, or perhaps just go to bed. But they don't. They segué from "Strawberry Fields" to the flip side of "Lady Madonna," an equally bad song called "The Inner Light," but an infinitely hipper choice. Should this perhaps be the slogan of FM rock and roll at this stage of its infancy: *We Play the Other Side of Bad Music?*

Prosper is rescued from such speculation by the telephone's ringing; he turns down the Beatles and hastens across the cork-tiled floor, hoping this will be Maddy calling him as the first thing she does after getting home from school. But it's not.

"Prosper?" The voice belongs unmistakably to Theresa.
"It's me," he says.
"How're you doing? You sound okay. You haven't been drafted yet, it sounds like."

"That's right. Two days down, one to go."

"Wonderful!" She says with nasal enthusiasm. "We're all rooting for you. You know that."

"What does Martin want, Theresa? Hasn't he done the damn editing?"

"He says he's gonna do it tomorrow. But he says you have to come in tomorrow, too."

Martin, Prosper thinks, is sure as hell not going to intrude upon his evening with Maddy. "What the hell for? I have to be in New Haven tomorrow."

"He says he'll be here late, and he has to talk to you."

"Why can't I just call him?"

She doesn't answer immediately. They are allies in this, he knows, both subject to Martin's whims, to Martin's dictates, to Martin's rule. "He just says you have to come in. It's important."

"What about now? Is he there? Is he busy?"

"He was talking to Allen a few minutes ago, but I think he's alone in his office now. You want me to see?"

"Please."

After half a minute of silence, he hears Martin's unmistakable nasal voice. "Hey! I understand you're not in uniform yet!"

"Not yet," Prosper concurs.

"So, listen—what time do you finish tomorrow?"

"I can't come in tomorrow, Martin."

"What the fuck—you weren't here yesterday, you weren't here today. Why not tomorrow, just for half an hour?"

Prosper knows that Martin's half-hours can become two hours or three. "The arrangement was I'd get three days off if I needed them. What's the big deal?"

"I need your advice on something.

151

"Here I am."

"This would be much better face-to-face."

"I can't come in tomorrow, Martin. It's now or Thursday."

There is no immediate reply, and just when Prosper starts to think Martin has wandered off, he speaks. "I got the Cousin Brucie gig."

"Wonderful. Congratulations." Cousin Brucie is Bruce Morrow, a very popular deejay who does the evening shift on WABC-AM, whose clear channel signal can be heard in Cuba, Pittsburgh and, God knows, Prince Edward Island. Cousin Brucie has just scored a television show on the somewhat déclassé Channel 9, and he wants Martin to "guest" on this Saturday night's show. "So," Prosper says, "where does my advice come in?"

"If it goes well," Martin resumes, "it could be a regular feature. I'd come on every week and we'd rap about one thing or another. Like the interview with Jim Morrison. Like, 'Martin, I understand you just had a long conversation with Jim Morrison of the Doors. Why don't you tell us about it?'"

Martin has paused. Is it time for advice? "Do it," Prosper says. "Sounds like a piece of cake."

"Maybe you could write some stuff sometimes. Some of the clever stuff. I'd pay you for it. Not much, 'cause he's not paying me much. But it could be a break for you, too." When Martin is planning, foreseeing, he becomes intense. Even on the phone, Prosper can sense the aura about him, something magical, something that projects today's imagining into tomorrow's tangible cultural phenomenon. He says, "There's one thing that bothers me."

Exhausted, terribly eager to get off the phone, Prosper tries to anticipate: some kind of AM-versus-FM sensibility problem, some question of aesthetics that Martin must feel to be more in Prosper's field of expertise? Martin says, "He wants to call me Cousin Marty."

In an odd way, Prosper's analysis has been right on the money. He says, "I don't see what's wrong with that. He calls everybody Cousin Everything."

"Yeah. I don't think I'd mind Cousin Martin so much. But Cousin *Marty*.... I don't even let my mother call me Marty anymore."

"Then tell him he's got to call you Cousin Martin."

"He'll probably call me Cousin Marty anyway."

Prosper comprehends that this is a genuine quandary for Martin: an opportunity to broaden his fan base, to make some additional money, to be on *television* in the world's largest market; but on the other hand it's an independent station, a program hosted by a man whose persona borders on the buffoonish, a man who may refer to Martin as Cousin Marty, potentially endangering Martin's reputation with his friends in the art world. How can you be a legitimate *poseur* when you've been addressed as Cousin Marty by a second-rate Dick Clark on Channel 9?

"How about this," Prosper says. "Every time he calls you Cousin Marty, you call him Mister Morrow."

After ten seconds, verging on eternity, Martin says, "I like that. Mister Morrow." Martin's accent transforms *Mister Morrow* into *Miss Tomorrow*. Martin's laugh is high-pitched and staccato, and stops as abruptly as it had begun. He says, "So--when do we wanna spend a little time on this?"

"You're just planning to talk about the Jim Morrison interview, right?"

"Maybe. Maybe I'll need more. Maybe I'll do something else."

153

Prosper doesn't like the sound of this. Martin advertises himself as an idea man, but in these brainstorming sessions it's Prosper who's expected to come up with the ideas, or to take Martin's obtuse formulations and turn them into ideas. He says, "It's been a long few days for me, Martin."

"No shit. Who's been here doing what you normally do? What I pay you to do?"

"Look, do you understand that in a few weeks you may not be paying me at all?"

Evidently stunned by Prosper's non sequitur, or perhaps realizing for the first time that Prosper may be headed elsewhere, Martin is silent for a few seconds. "We'll cross that bridge when we come to it," he finally says. "For now, we have to find a time to work on this. How about noon Thursday, at my office? I could order us some food from the Armenian place." Martin's other office, his real office, is across Sheridan Square from the *Village Voice*.

"I can't get down there. Why don't we just meet at the station?"

"It's what—four extra stops on the subway?"

"I can be at the station at one on Thursday."

"I'm better at the *Voice*. I've got all my shit there. Jesus Christ, sometimes I wonder who's the boss here!"

"You're the boss, Martin," Prosper says. "If you want me to do this for you, I can do it Thursday at one o'clock, at the radio station."

After another silent interval, Martin says, "All right. But I won't buy you lunch." And he hangs up.

Not a minute later, the phone rings again, and again his hopes rise. "Prosper?"

For a moment he's not exactly sure who it is, but it's not Maddy. "Yes," he says, "hello."

154

"It's Lydia Urrutia. Listen, do you have any idea where Alex is? Has he called you?"

He recalls only now his promise to Maddy, that he'd call Alex and try to talk some sense into him. "No," he says. "Well, he might have. But I've been in New Haven all day, at the draft physical."

"Oh, shit," she says. "I knew that. How'd that go?"

"Okay so far. It's not over. Is Alex missing?"

"I'm not sure. It's probably nothing to worry about. I was just hoping to talk to someone he might have talked to."

This is fairly puzzling. "About what?"

After a few seconds she says, "I'm just trying to figure something out."

"Can I help?"

"No...I'm sorry I bothered you."

"It's no bother," he says, and hears her hang up.

He falls asleep on the couch moments later, regains consciousness briefly to "Purple Haze" by Jimi Hendrix. He wonders what time it is, whether Maddy has called during his deep sleep, whether it's still early enough to call her. All he knows for sure is that it's entirely dark in the house and he doesn't possess anything close to the energy to drag himself off the couch.

## SEVENTEEN

At five to seven Ben's in the lobby, staring at but failing to read the sports pages of the *Press-Scimitar*. There has been no sign of Randall. At ten after seven Ben begins to wonder if neither of them will show up, but a few seconds later Delphine comes through the front door. She wears blue jeans and a light denim jacket and penny loafers; her hair is tied in a ponytail. It's as if she's trying to look as unglamorous as possible; she can't fool Ben.

Five feet in the door she stops and scans the lobby; he sees her expression change when she finds him, walking toward her. "Am I late?" she says.

"Not very," Ben replies, standing close to her, taking her in. "Maybe ten minutes. It's good to see you."

"You too," she says, and they stand two feet from each other. "Where's Randall?" She says.

"He's always late."

She smiles. "I'm a little on the hungry side."

"Let's give him ten minutes," Ben says. "He's my boss." She shrugs. He says, "Is there somewhere around here you like? Maybe we can leave a note for Randall at the desk."

She tilts her head and fixes her eyes on his. "If we're gonna wait for him, I guess we could go anywhere around here. It would not be seen as a violation of the social order…"

"Yes," Ben says. "Of course."

"But I was originally thinking you and I could go to a place out near school," she says. "If you don't mind a drive. Ten minutes, maybe."

"I'll leave Randall a note," Ben says.

156

Her car is a Mercury Comet, a two-door compact about the size and vintage of Ben's Corvair, but much better kept and much more mainstream. It's not the sort of car any of Ben's friends would have. She drives smoothly but fast, in the manner of someone familiar with the territory and unwilling to spend extra time in transit. Ben does not feel as at ease with her as he generally does with women who attract him. He's aware of that--of something better described as tension than anxiety-- and it excites him. It's as if (were this a game) the stakes had been raised exponentially.

The radio plays an Otis Redding song Ben knows, "Try a Little Tenderness," and he sings along for a bit.

"You like this music?" she says.

"Very much," he responds, and the next thing that comes to his mind is to tell her about his friend Prosper in New York, who *really* likes this music, and thought Otis Redding was God --but what would be the point? She says, "You know Rufus Thomas, Carla's father?"

"Sure," Ben says, fielding an easy one. "'Walkin' the Dog'."

"He was a disk jockey on this station. Al Bell, the guy who runs Stax now, he was a deejay in Memphis too. So was B.B. King."

Ben has never heard of Al Bell and couldn't name a B.B. King song if his life depended on it, so he nods with enthusiasm and listens to Otis Redding.

She has chosen a place called Charlie's, on North Parkway, across the street from the Southwestern campus. It is nothing more than a college hangout, a malt shop, with formica-topped tables and booths equipped with mini-jukeboxes.

157

"They've got real good burgers here," she says, "and the best steak sandwich I've ever had, anywhere." There are twelve booths lining two walls, a like number of tables, some four-seaters, some two, spread around the floor. There are eight clients here at the moment, all of them young, all of them white.

Delphine orders the steak sandwich; so does Ben. He flips through the pages of the jukebox. Six songs for a quarter. He selects "Keep on Dancing" by the Gentrys and "Hold On, I'm Comin'" by Sam and Dave. "Pick a few," he says to Delphine. She plays "Candy" by the Astors and "I've Got No Time to Lose" by Carla Thomas, and both sides of "Tighten Up" by Archie Bell & the Drells.

"Keep on Dancing" comes up first, sounding tinny and nasal and excruciatingly white. "Are they from here?" he asks her.

"Yeah. They still play here all the time."

There is a period of silence, during which Ben regrets his choice. He breaks the silence. "You said last night that I don't know the rules here."

"Yes," she says.

"Tell me about the rules?"

She pauses. "You sounded like you were asking me out."

"I was," he says. "I did. Here we are."

Delphine smiles, raising her eyebrows. "Here we are is right. Why do you think I brought you to this place?"

Ben peers around Charlie's. "Evidently not because you like the steak sandwiches."

"Look," she says, "I could get all dressed up and we could go someplace downtown, where everybody'd look at us all night. With some people it'd be curiosity, and with some people it'd be staring daggers. I don't know about you, but that's

158

not my idea of a pleasant night on the town.  Or I could take you over to Beale Street, where everybody'd look at us too, and just maybe some half-drunk Stokely Carmichael disciple would try to pick a fight with you, or yell at me about how I may look white but I ain't white, and I should keep to my own people." Delphine says all this in an even, moderate tone.

"So you've had some experience along these lines," Ben says.

She shakes her head. "Except for the look white part, no. You're the first white boy I've ever been out with. But I know how things are here. And I don't particularly enjoy calling attention to myself."

After a moment he says, "I would think that looking the way you do, you couldn't help calling attention to yourself."

"What kind of a thing to say is that?" she says, her voice rising just a bit.

"I mean that you're so...striking. You must be accustomed to being stared at."

"Look," she says, "it's one thing to get looked at because you might be pretty and another thing altogether when the only reason they're letting you in the place is because there's a federal law."

"Of course," Ben says. "It was a stupid thing to say."

All of "Hold on, I'm Comin'" has played, and now the jukebox is midway through part one of "Tighten Up," its manic syncopation filling the booth during this silence, until Delphine says, "In a kind of simple-minded way it was a very nice thing to say."

A half-hour has passed; the steak sandwiches have been served and consumed. Ben has told Delphine about, or given her his impressions of, growing up in suburban Boston, going to

159

prep school in New Hampshire, and college in New Jersey. He's told her about his good-future job with the Ford Foundation, and how he took a leave of absence to work for the Kennedy campaign. Delphine has recounted to Ben the paradoxes of growing up well-to-do but not white in the mid-South; she has touched upon questions of identity and affiliation, talked about the confusion she felt in grade school when dark-skinned classmates taunted her, made fun of her, even once beat her up because she wasn't black, she wore expensive clothes, she talked funny; while she could sit in front of the television at home and recognize that she was watching manifestations of a culture other than hers, one to which her parents and their friends aspired but didn't quite belong. She suspects, she says, that she's going to encounter this feeling of in-betweenness anywhere she goes, but she expects that things have got to be better in the North.

"Yes," Ben says. "I mean, I have to admit this isn't something I've given a lot of attention to, but I know in New York it's just pretty loose. You and I could walk into the Four Seasons, say, and if anybody stared at you it would be because you're beautiful."

Delphine shakes her head. "What's the Four Seasons?"

"A restaurant. A really expensive restaurant. A place to be seen."

"Let's forget about restaurants, okay, and people staring at me for whatever reason." She smiles at him, as if to negate the edge in her voice. "What about jobs?"

This takes him by surprise, this un-Southern candor. It's disorienting as well that as he's settling into Memphis, getting beguiled by it and her, she seems so intent on leaving. He says, "What kind of job? You said last night you didn't know what you wanted to do, you just didn't want to go to medical school."

160

"What about something like the Ford Foundation?" she says. "If I walked in there with my resumé, would they just laugh in my face?"

"No, I don't think so. What are you majoring in?"

"Double major in political science and English."

"And you've gotten good grades and all that?"

"Straight A's."

"I'll bet they'd snap you right up."

"Would you help me? Would you put in a word for me?"

"Sure. Of course. I don't know how much good it would do."

"So if I came up there, I could count on you?"

He nods in the affirmative; he smiles; he leans back in the booth and looks at her, admires her. She is without question one of the best-looking women he's ever met; she's smart, she's exotic. Is he making some sort of commitment, by word or by implication? "You can count on me," he says.

What's next? It's not quite nine o'clock on a Tuesday night in Memphis. "We could go back to my house," Delphine says, "if you wouldn't mind sitting around with my parents. My dad goes to bed around ten, but my mom will stay up till all hours if there's something interesting around. That would be you."

"I've got a nice, comfortable room at the Holiday Inn," Ben offers.

"I don't know about that," she says. And of course Ben doesn't know about that, either. Randall will have returned, or will be returning soon, and for the moment at least Ben doesn't look forward to explaining why they left without him. So he

161

doesn't pressure her, which in itself must seem a good thing. He says, "Why don't you show me around town?"

She does. She drives him out to the Stax headquarters on East McLemore, not much to behold, but something to report to Prosper, who will be rampantly envious and think of all manner of questions Ben should have asked. She drives him past Graceland, where Elvis Presley lives when he's in town. It's an imposing house, but Ben admits that he has little interest in Elvis--has never seen an Elvis movie and hasn't owned an Elvis record since "Heartbreak Hotel."

She takes him through downtown Memphis, shows him several large buildings dedicated to the commerce of cotton. They drive by the Holiday Inn and do not so much as slow down. They cross the Mississippi on the Hernando DeSoto Bridge, and Ben finds himself in another new state, Arkansas. Oddly, the day has been growing warmer since late afternoon and now, approaching ten o'clock, the temperature must be in the mid-sixties. Delphine takes a cutoff that becomes dirt road after a few hundred yards, and stops the Comet in a field some hundred feet from the river. "Shall we have a look at it?" she says.

"Are there snakes out there?" Ben asks.

"Poisonous ones," Delphine says, "and freshwater sharks in the river."

She leaves the motor running and the headlights on, so their way is illuminated as they tread through the tall grass. There are perhaps no snakes here but there are all sorts of things scurrying around their feet. As they near the Mississippi it becomes more and more audible; when they reach the wall above it, it's majestic. It doesn't possess Niagara's roar, but it makes one very much aware that a few million gallons are passing rapidly by at any given moment.

162

## The Mountaintop

"God, this is something," Ben says, looking at the lights of Memphis across the river.

She's standing right next to him, her right forearm touching his left, so he makes half a turn and swings his arm around her waist, the heel of his hand now resting gently on the top of her right buttock, and he kisses her. Surely this is something she's been anticipating; as he feels the softness of her lips, he feels her tense and then relax. It's a long kiss, a movie kiss, without any intrusion of tongue from either direction, but to Ben it's intensely erotic, with the river rushing by fifty feet below and a huge sky full of stars overhead.

The question is where to go from here. He moves his hand laterally, across the top of her buttocks, then up her back, caressing her spine. Her hands, which had been at her sides, now clutch the neutral ground of his outer thighs, as if she's conscious that moving them either forward or backward at this moment might have significance. He's startled when she withdraws her lips, but relieved when she takes a deep breath. Her eyes are shut. He kisses her neck, and she inhales again, more quickly, just as deeply. Still holding her with one hand, he brings the other inside her denim jacket, until his fingers are against the side of her breast, all the while continuing to kiss her neck. He feels her hands move upward to his hips, then backward so they press against his upper buttocks, whereupon he moves his hand across her breast, pausing to feel the barely perceptible nipple underneath her shirt and her brassiere. He undoes the top two buttons of her shirt.

It is she who resumes the kiss, lifting his chin with her hand, and slithering her tongue between his lips, by which time he has penetrated the top of her brassiere with his thumb, and descended the slope of her breast to the nipple, which is exquisitely taut. She's now running her hands up and down his

163

buttocks, which arouses him past the point of any reserve. He wonders if she has a blanket in the car, or if he should just spread his jacket on the grass. He withdraws his hand from her breast and lets it slalom slowly to her waist, where all by itself it undoes her belt and pops the brass button of her blue jeans. Her tongue, which had been furiously exploring his, now slows a bit as his fingers begin creeping between her panties and her skin. When they reach the crest of her pubic hair she takes a quick breath, and she seizes his hand, then pulls it away. "That's enough," she whispers.

His lips are still against her cheek. He says, "I got a little carried away."

She takes a much deeper breath, and exhales. "You're not the only one."

They re-cross the Mississippi. In the course of the fifteen-minute drive Ben tries several times to restore the earlier mood, but her replies to his attempts are brief dead ends. She doesn't seem angry or aloof, just removed. As she steers the Comet into downtown Memphis, a few blocks from the hotel, he says, "Will I see you tomorrow?"

"I'm not sure," she says. "What did you have in mind?"

"Maybe we could go out and do something, hear some music, or go to a movie."

"Doctor King's speaking tomorrow night, or at least we hope he is" she says. "There's no way I'm gonna miss that."

"Of course," Ben says, having completely forgotten this morning's discussion of the Mason Temple rally and Randall's determination to attend. "Would it be all right if we went together, or is that against the rules?"

"I think that would be okay," she says.

164

## EIGHTEEN

Maddy chooses to walk all the way from school because she's in no hurry to get back to the empty apartment. She stops at Gennaro's, the Italian delicatessen on Broadway, and buys a loaf of rye bread, some sliced turkey and some mortadella, some potato salad and macaroni salad. She might as well celebrate.

At home, she reads the *Times* from front to back, partly to pass the time and partly looking for anything about Memphis. Indeed, there is a brief story about the garbage strike, but nothing about Martin Luther King and certainly nothing about the young Kennedy campaign workers who might have (or have had, for all she knows) an audience with him. For his part, Bobby Kennedy is in Indiana, where the Democratic primary will soon be held. She watches the news with Walter Cronkite on Channel Two, as Ben would do, as perhaps he's doing right now in Memphis. She makes herself a sandwich with her extravagant ingredients, accompanied by potato salad *and* macaroni salad, along with a glass of Ben's wine. She thinks only now about calling Kennedy headquarters and trying to track Ben down. Surely they'd know Randall's whereabouts, which would probably be the same as Ben's. Would anyone answer the phone now, at nearly six o'clock? Would she feel strange and embarrassed asking that person to tell her where in Memphis, Tennessee her boyfriend is? No doubt about it.

She reads a Donald Barthelme story in a weeks-old *New Yorker*. Normally she has too little time to read the magazine, so she saves them for a few months, then throws them out.

165

Tonight she has plenty of time, but she finds it nearly impossible to concentrate. She flips through all seven channels on the television and finds nothing worth watching. She stretches out on the living room couch and closes her eyes. The next thing she knows, it's nearly nine o'clock. Shall she drag herself off to bed now? She could certainly use the extra sleep, but more likely the nap will have thrown things out of kilter and she'll toss and turn until midnight.

She considers checking in with Lydia, but she doesn't want to call their number and get Alex. Then she remembers Prosper. He'll be up, if only because it's a vital part of his strategy.

But there's no answer after seven rings, eight, nine, and she's about to hang up when she hears his voice, sounding extremely groggy.

"Prosper? It's Maddy...did I wake you up?"

"It's okay. I dreamed you called."

"I figured you'd be up. I thought that was your plan..."

"Yeah, you've saved me, actually. I fell asleep by mistake."

"Me too," she says. "I was lying here after Walter Cronkite and I went into this deep sleep. I think maybe I was abducted by aliens because a couple of hours are completely missing. But tell me how it went today."

"I made it. Pretty safe margins. One more day and I'm good."

"Fantastic."

"Yeah. The only thing that worries me a little, I got into an argument with this corporal who's in charge of the blood pressure guys. He's this scrappy little bastard who has relatives behind the Iron Curtain and thinks we have to nail Ho Chi Minh

166

or his cousins will be trapped in Warsaw for the rest of their lives."

"Are you serious?"

"I'm serious. I mean, I'm sure if you asked him to explain the situation it would make more sense than that. But that's pretty much what he said."

"And you argued with him?"

"He goaded me."

"Did you make him look foolish?"

"I don't think so. We were so far apart, it was almost as if we were talking about different things."

"So what are you worried about?"

"I'm not sure. I guess I was just hoping to be invisible, anonymous, just get it over with, and instead I was William Sloane Coffin for about ten minutes."

"You have to deal with this guy again tomorrow?"

"Probably. Most of the time it's him, sometimes it's another guy."

"You want me to send the aliens after him?"

"I'd appreciate that," Prosper says. "How's Ben?"

"I wish I knew."

"He hasn't called?"

"Not while I've been home."

"Well," Prosper says after a few seconds' silence, "I guess he's pretty busy."

Maddy doesn't know exactly where to go from here. She wants Prosper's sympathy, wants him to assure her that Ben's just being Ben, but she suspects that Prosper would just as soon have Ben out of the way. On the other hand, if Prosper still had strong feelings for her, how could he and Ben have remained best friends? She says, "I guess so."

There is a slightly longer silence. "I don't know whether I should say this, but you know it's always going to be like this."

She's taken aback. It's the first time Prosper has said anything to her overtly critical of Ben. All she can produce in the way of a reply is, "How do you mean?"

"I shouldn't have said anything. I'm sorry, I'm half asleep."

"I don't know whether you should or not," she says, "but how do you mean?"

"He's just not the most...considerate guy in the world."

"Yeah, well I know that," Maddy says. "I know he's ambitious and he's self-involved, but I can see improvements."

After a few seconds Prosper says, "Okay."

"Wait a minute," she says, trying to sound more affable than inquisitive, "what was that about, that *okay*?"

"Look, I'm sorry. I should just shut up."

"No--you can't just leave it there."

After a few seconds, Prosper says, "First tell me about the improvements."

"He doesn't complain as much about areas where we conflict, like me not putting my clothes away, or me not dressing as elegantly as he'd like when we're out with his friends." Those seem fairly petty, insignificant, as she speaks them. "I have more of a sense that he's settling down." But does she? "I have more of a sense of fidelity on his part, which wasn't always there."

She waits for Prosper's response. She's about to ask if he's still there when he says, "Okay" again, this time with what seems like a slightly less skeptical lilt. "That's it?" She says. "That's all you're going to say?"

*The Mountaintop*

Another brief silence. "He's been my friend for ten years," Prosper says. "I value his friendship. I'm sure in some ways you know him better than I do…"

"Well, I'd hope so," Maddy interrupts.

A longer silence, as if Prosper might be gathering his thoughts, or wondering whether to hang up on her. "I just don't think there are certain things you can expect from him."

"Like what?" She says.

"Like thinking about you when he's a thousand miles away, understanding how much you'd appreciate it if he called you."

He's got her there. "But wasn't that the jumping off point of this conversation?"

"Right," Prosper says. "I guess it's kind of circular."

Now it's she who doesn't reply immediately. "Do you know something, Prosper? Something I should know?"

"No. Nothing specific."

"Okay," she says. "I'll leave it at that. Do you still want to take me to the party tomorrow night?"

"Assuming I'm intact, yes," he says.

After hanging up, she yearns to call her sister, Jill, who's a junior at Radcliffe and with whom she shares nearly everything. But of course Ben might have been trying to call for the last fifteen minutes, and might be about to call now. She pours herself another glass of wine and makes another run through the television channels, this one as fruitless as its predecessor. Finally, a few minutes before ten, she calls Jill. Her sister is studying for a Spanish mid-term and can't stay on the phone too long, but after Maddy has recounted her conversation with Prosper, Jill says, "Well, he's probably right."

169

"About what?"

"When he says Ben's not going to change."

"That's not exactly what he said."

"That's the impression I got from what you told me."

"Jill, is that what *you* think?"

"Well, yeah, from what I know of him. I mean, I really like him…you know that. But I get this sense from him that he's always going to do just what he wants to do. And hell, Prosper's known him since they were ten or something…"

"Fourteen."

"Same difference."

"But why is he telling me this now?"

"Partly, I'd say, because he's sweet on you."

"You think so?"

"It's always been pretty obvious to me."

"So…you think he's sabotaging his best friend?"

"No, I think he's telling you the truth about his best friend, kind of like this is what you're in for. But as for the other part, you've already pretty much told him you're not interested in him, right?"

"Not exactly."

"God, Maddy, who's the wise older sister here?"

She goes to bed at eleven, and sleeps fairly soundly until the dogs downstairs go into one of their berserk frenzies. What time is it? Just before two. The barking does not cease: two little dogs, one's voice slightly higher pitched than the other, taking turns barking at an imaginary burglar, an actual rat, who knows what. She gets up and pees, and is on her way to refrigerator when the phone rings. Her heart pounds from the sheer surprise of it.

. "Hi," Ben says, "it's me. I'm sorry to call at one in the morning..."

"Two," she says.

"Oh, Jesus," he says, "I forgot about the time difference."

"It's all right. I would have been asleep at one, and now I'm awake because of the goddamn dogs."

"I won't keep you," he says. "I just wanted to say that it's been really busy, and we've done a lot of exciting stuff. Randall's just incredibly good at this. I'm learning a lot. I wish you could be here."

"That's nice of you to say. I wish I could be there."

"What's going on up north?"

"I talked to Prosper. He said so far so good."

"Great. Fantastic. He's just got one day to go?"

"Yeah, I guess. We talked about going to Chip Boyle's party tomorrow night. Tonight, technically."

"I can't say I'll be sorry to miss it."

She's been waiting two days for him to call and now all she can manage is small talk. She says, "I miss you. It's funny to be in this bed alone."

A few seconds pass before he speaks. "You're not gonna believe this, but Randall's knocking on the door."

"It's okay," she says. "Let me say hello to him."

She hears the *clunk* as the phone on Ben's end meets a piece of furniture. The connection is remarkably clear. She can't hear Ben's voice, but she hears another, a woman's voice in the distance, and wonders if it's some sort of cross talk, someone in Juneau talking to someone in Texarkana, the lines somehow overlapping. Seconds pass, quite a few of them. She hears the phone again as it's scraped across a surface, and then there's Ben. "Sweetheart?" He says. "This is crazy, but I have

171

to go. I'll call you again," and he's gone before she can utter a word.

## NINETEEN

Randall is in his room, with Johnny Carson on the television. At the door, he says, "What've you been up to?"

"Sightseeing," Ben replies. "How about you?"

Randall retreats into the room, sits on the bed; Ben leans against the wall next to the television. "Got your note," Randall says. "How long you wait for me?"

"Half an hour, maybe, forty minutes. She was anxious to have some dinner."

"It's all right," Randall says. "I didn't get back till nine. Called your room to say forget about me, but you were already gone."

"So," Ben says, doing his best to hide a vast sense of relief, "how did it go?"

"It went well."

"Jesus, Randall, are you gonna tell me what the hell happened?"

"I met with these three guys, out in a house in a bad part of town. These guys were all militant when I came in. Like, we didn't shake hands, we saluted. Then we started talking, and once we got through the bullshit, it was all right."

"What bullshit?"

"You know, all power to the people bullshit. What they call *rhetoric* when they're talking about people they don't respect. When they refer to people who've been in the movement since before they were born as Uncle Toms and house niggers. You just have to wait for them to get through with that bullshit, and then you ask them what *they* have in mind."

"And what do they have in mind?"

"Not much. Fried chicken in every pot, two dashikis in every closet."

"Seriously."

"I'm telling you, they don't have much in mind.  You ask, you push, you demand specifics, and finally they start talking about having more black cops on the force, having black firemen, more civil service jobs, a civilian review board representative of the population, more black faculty at Memphis State. And then I say, hey, you guys ain't that far from the mainstream. I just happen to work for a presidential candidate who supports all of the above. Then I've got to provide some specific stuff that Kennedy has said. Two of these guys, named Edwin and Edward--and you better not call either of 'em Eddie-- I don't think they'd recognize a newspaper if you put in front of them.  The third guy, named Charles, was really getting into it. It was like he was sitting there thinking, hey, I'm talkin' to a dude that speaks for a man who could be *president* this time next year. It was dawning on him that if he played his cards right, maybe he wasn't all that far from the seat of white imperialist power."

173

"So what's the upshot? Are these guys gonna open the first Militants for Kennedy office?"

Randall chuckles. "Not quite. But we have a dialogue, my brother. We have erected a bridge, or at least the supports on which a bridge may be built." He leans back against the bed's headstand and cups his hands, stretching his arms high above his head. "A good day, wouldn't you say? I'm sorry you couldn't join me on this last part, but don't you feel we accomplished something today?"

"Without question," Ben says. "And do I get to meet these guys at any point?"

"Yeah, maybe you do. Charles and I talked about getting together with William and maybe some of the clergy, black and white. Possibly day after tomorrow, in the evening."

"I'd like that," Ben says. "Tell me about tomorrow."

"Easy day tomorrow. Back to Memphis State in the morning, ten o'clock. On our own for lunch. Then we do a thing at Christian Brothers University at one o'clock, and we hit a couple of white high schools later on."

"And the rally tomorrow night?"

"Right. Yeah, well, that's not part of the program. That's optional, but highly recommended."

Ben says, "I talked to Delphine Ennis about that. I thought we might go together."

Randall squints. "You asking my permission?"

"Not exactly. Just telling you."

"Why? Because we're in the south?"

"I suppose so."

Randall leans forward. "Did Delphine accompany you on your sightseeing tonight?"

"We had a sandwich together. She showed me Stax Records, and Elvis's house."

174

## The Mountaintop

"The sublime to the ridiculous," Randall says, and pauses for several seconds. "You and this girl are just friends. Would you say that's an accurate assessment?"

Ben does not hesitate. "I would."

"Because if you weren't, you could be causing a lot of trouble. I mean, among other things you're a married man, Ben, or the next thing to it."

"Of course," Ben says.

Back in his own room, he sits on the bed, considering switching on the television. But he has no desire to watch Johnny Carson, and imagines there isn't much else on. He's brought nothing to read, so he's pretty much alone with his thoughts, and he has little desire to deal with them. He lies back on the overstuffed pillow and tries to picture Maddy, but her image won't stay in his mind. He keeps drifting to a picture--in Sensurround--of himself and Delphine standing interlocked above the mighty river.

He falls asleep in his clothes, with the light on, and wakes up uncomfortable and disoriented. Having discerned after a few disturbing seconds that this is the Holiday Inn in Memphis, he finds the clock radio on the night table and sees that it's twenty minutes to one. He brushes his teeth, then takes a quick, very hot shower, and returns to bed. Now he's wide awake.

There is, as he'd feared, absolutely nothing on television. He thinks about going downstairs in search of a magazine, but imagines that everything from here to Washington D.C. is shut down tight. He picks up the telephone, dials nine for an outside line, and calls his number in New York.

175

Maddy answers on the second ring, but she sounds pretty groggy. "Hi," he says, "it's me. I'm sorry to call at one in the morning..."

"Two," she says.

"Oh, Jesus," he says, "I forgot about the time difference."

"It's all right. I would have been asleep at one, and now I'm awake because of the goddamn dogs."

They talk for a few minutes--chatting, really. Prosper's about to make it through the draft physical, things here in Memphis have been exciting and productive. Maddy says, "I miss you. It's funny to be in this bed alone."

Just as she says the word *alone* there is a knock at the door--a quick, subtle tap-tap-tap whose unexpectedness makes him jump. He says, "You're not gonna believe this, but Randall's knocking on the door."

"It's okay," she says. "Let me say hello to him."

Ben half sets and half drops the receiver on the night table and walks toward the door in his boxer shorts. Has there been some late-breaking change of plan? Is Randall seeking company after spending the past two hours pacing the floor of his room? Ben opens the door, completely unprepared for Delphine.

"I couldn't sleep," she says. "Did I wake you up?"

"No, not at all." Ben hears himself speaking in a whisper. "No, it's great to see you. Look...can you hold on just a second? I need to straighten up a little bit." He eases the door shut and hastens back to the phone. "Sweetheart?" He says. "This is crazy, but I have to go. I'll call you again," and he places the receiver gently in its cradle.

Having hung up the phone, Ben takes a step toward the door before catching himself. His explanation for closing the

176

door in Delphine's face was that he had to straighten up. Shall he now return to the door dressed only in his boxer shorts? Or is it time that's the element of importance here? But how long will it take him to pull on his pants and button a couple of his shirt buttons? About fifteen seconds, as it turns out. He pulls the door open anew, and there she is. "I'm sorry," he says. "The room was a mess."

She enters, just barely. She stands about two feet inside the door. "No, *I'm* sorry. I should've called first. I don't know what got into me." She is dressed exactly as she was before, is equally, breathtakingly beautiful in her jeans and her denim jacket, her southern girl's casual ensemble.

"I couldn't sleep either," Ben says. "I was just lying here, thinking about you." He closes the door, and she begins to move into the room; straight ahead of her is the unmade bed, beyond it the room's only chair. He says, "Would you like to sit?"

She nods, and sits down toward the foot of the bed, bringing her legs off the floor, sitting cross-legged. She says, "I shouldn't stay too long. I've got another busy day. I'd imagine you do too."

Ben sits at the top of the bed, perpendicular to her, his back to the headboard, his bare feet on the edge of the spread, his knees at chin level. "Easy day," he says. "Colleges, high schools, then we all go see Doctor King."

She swivels to face him. "Doesn't sound so easy to me."

He smiles. "Randall's going to be doing all the work."

Delphine leans in his direction, her elbows on her knees; he's too far away for her to touch him, so he assumes she's trying hard to say something. He's transfixed by her eyes, by their deep green, by the texture of her hair, recalled from hours ago at the river. She says, "Am I crazy coming here?"

177

"No. Of course not. Why would you...?"

"Why would it be crazy?" She's leaning closer, and smiling. "Why would it be crazy for me to get out of my bed at half-past midnight and drive over to the Holiday Inn—and kind of sneak past the desk clerk so he doesn't think I'm a whore-- and knock on some boy's door at one in the morning? Some white boy's door?"

Ben moves toward her almost unconsciously, sliding his legs flat on the bed. "*My* door," he says.

"Look," she says, "we've talked about this a little. I don't expect you to understand all the little details, but I hope you realize that I'm not interested in foolin' around. You know what I mean?"

"I think so."

"I'm thinking about changing my life. Do you want to help me do that?"

It crosses his mind that if he's to tell her about Maddy, if he's going to mention that he's been sharing an apartment with someone in New York, now could be the time. But it would require such a wrenching shift in gears; it might send this lovely train right off the tracks. "I'd love to," Ben says.

Beaming, she rises to her knees and moves toward him; sensing her intention he separates his own knees so she may progress to a point between his legs and then slowly lower her torso upon his. He cannot recall ever having felt quite this much desire. She touches his lips with hers, pulls them away, and says, "I like you, Ben."

He runs his hands down the small of her back and says, "I like you too, Delphine. I like you very much."

During the nine months or so he's been living with Maddy, Ben has slept with what...six other girls? Seven? With

178

the exception of a couple of ongoing casual relationships, the liaisons have tended to be spontaneous and brief, and haven't given his conscience much pause. He knows that if Maddy were to find out about any of these she'd be hurt, and angry; if she were to find out about all of them, she might move out. Would he blame her? Could he blame her? Could he, on the other hand, possibly explain to her that these things--these affairs, these trysts, whatever they are--are a form of recreation, a means, actually, of reinforcing their own union, because each time one occurs he returns to Maddy with a renewed passion.

It's not so much that he compares her to his transient lovers and finds her superior, it's that theirs is a relationship so much more profound than anything he could imagine with the other women.

He's asked himself questions over these nine months, the most frequent of which is: How would I feel if Maddy told me *she'd* had a lover, or several? And he doesn't fudge, he doesn't lie to himself. He knows he'd feel betrayed, he'd feel wanting, he'd be furious at her and the guy. But if Maddy did have a lover and *didn't* tell him, and were discreet about it so word didn't get to him by other means, then what of it? If it didn't affect their arrangement, or if in fact it improved their arrangement, so much the better. It's a strange sort of concept, he knows, and of course it's occurred to him that it could be nothing more than a way of rationalizing his own behavior, but ultimately he's felt that the adage does truly apply: *Ignorance is bliss*. And such bliss! To be living in a time when all the barriers are coming down, when you can meet a girl, or for that matter a thirty-five-year-old woman, at a party or at some lunchtime function....Your eyes lock, you exchange a few words, and then it's just a question of where you're going to do it. He's got that *and* he's got Maddy to come home to in the apartment on 91st Street, and Maddy's got just about everything. She's gorgeous, she's smart, she's probably the funniest, the cleverest person--male or female--he's ever met, she's great in bed, no inhibitions. If he were to construct in the abstract an ideal female body, Maddy might be slightly away from it, being a little flat-chested, but that's not so important in the big picture.

She's been in a category apart from all the other girls. There have been moments--as when he ended up in the Dutch girl's apartment on Jones Street and had just an amazing night, and she suggested that they do this on a regular basis--when he's felt constrained, when he's wondered whether the benefits of his living arrangement did truly outweigh the obligations. But even after the Dutch girl he was thrilled to come home to Maddy. He thought about the Dutch girl from time to time, but he never called her again.

So, how does he explain this thing? How is Delphine going to fit into his life? She's lying next to him now, at three o'clock in the morning, in the Holiday Inn on Third Street in Memphis. They've made love twice in the past ninety minutes; for Ben the first time was better than the second, but first times are always exhilarating, transcendent. The second time he concentrated more on her, really got into her, and she got pretty carried away, and of course that's almost as exciting as getting carried away oneself.

If she actually comes to New York, what will he do?

She rolls languidly onto her back, left arm at her side, right arm extended over the pillow. She is without question the most beautiful woman Ben has ever seen, as if God had recognized that the perfect European woman and the perfect African woman would both fall short of a fantastic combination of the two.

180

He slides down the headboard and turns on his right side, so he's against her, with his chest touching her left arm and his groin against her hip. He kisses her neck, then edges down to nuzzle her breast, and lick the nipple. She stirs, and stretches, and murmurs, "What time is it?"

"A little after three."

"Oh, God. Am I gonna stay here? I have to be on campus at quarter after nine."

"What about your parents," Ben says. "Would they give you a hard time if you stayed out all night?"

Still supine, she says, "I'm twenty-one years old, for God's sake."

"I know. But you live at home. Maybe you don't want to roil the waters."

She rolls over on her side, so they're face to face. "Are you trying to get rid of me, or are you just the most considerate guy on earth?"

"I'm guessing we'll spend more time together. I'm hoping. I'm imagining the difference in how your dad reacts to your coming home at three thirty and your coming home sometime in the afternoon, and maybe I don't want to get on his bad side."

"All right," she smiles. "Are you gonna carry me down to my car, Ben?"

"It would be my pleasure," he says. She sits up; he watches the movement of her breast as she does so, and feels himself stiffening again. If they made love a third time, what wonders might be in store? But then Delphine would fall asleep again; he too might fall asleep, and what would be the consequences? He kisses the small of her back as she tosses her legs over the side of the bed. He watches her as she dresses, appreciating every motion, every nuance.

## TWENTY

Alex cruises down Morningside Drive at a few minutes past midnight, looking for a place to park. This is the difficult thing, or one of the difficult things, about having a car in Manhattan: if you get back into the city anytime past, say, four in the afternoon, the only way you're going to find a legal space on the street is if you happen to drive by when someone is pulling out. At least he doesn't have to worry about the street cleaning rules, which require that one side of the street or the other be vacant of vehicles for a three-hour period in the morning or early afternoon. Sometimes the street sweepers— huge machines that squirt water and employ gigantic round brushes to disperse all the rubble and dogshit—actually come and do their job, but even when they don't the cops slap thirty-dollar tickets on every miscreant's windshield. So you have to be lucky to find a space and extremely lucky to find one that's good for the following morning, but the Lark has New Jersey dealer plates, so any ticket Alex gets will be a meaningless swatch of paper. Not that he should push his luck—parking too close to a fire hydrant or in a bus stop might get the car towed away, or attract the attention of a cop in a squad car, who could call in the plate number, and that would be the end of the Lark. Which reminds Alex that he's got to drive back to Leonia tomorrow, in his suit, and take care of the paperwork.

He cruises in ever-widening rectangles. Nothing. There's an empty metered space on Broadway and 121$^{st}$, which wouldn't be a bad fallback option; either he could get up before nine and move the car, or he could leave it there on the theory that a fifteen-dollar meter ticket he doesn't have to pay is preferable to a thirty-dollar street cleaning ticket he doesn't have to pay.

He parks beside the fire hydrant just west of his building. The last of his Obitrol high has withered away, and he's feeling the fatigue of a long, strange day. At this hour it would probably be safe to leave the car for a few minutes, run upstairs and see if Lydia has returned. He might take the gun with him and stash it in a safe place. He rolls another tiny joint and smokes it, listening to WWRL, the soul station at the top of the dial. They play Sam & Dave's "I Thank You" and the Temptations' "I Wish It Would Rain" back to back. What if life consisted of sitting in comfort, smoking excellent dope, and listening to the radio late at night, when the music is great and the commercials are few?

But why is he sitting here worrying about parking the fucking car, losing sight of why he bought the car and drove down to Delaware in the first place? He pulls the Lark back onto 118th and turns right on Morningside Drive, driving slowly, nearly coasting, on the slight downslope, past the huge St. John the Divine Cathedral, across Cathedral Parkway, onto Columbus Avenue. Somewhere along here (or was it on Amsterdam?) he ran into those Puerto Rican guys on Sunday night. He has little fragments of memory, like still frames from a movie, seeing himself sitting in a booth with the tall, thin guy, Flaco, and the big, fat one, Julio, the two guys who ripped him off this morning. The other guy, the shorter, skinny one with the cool leather jacket, he pictures on the street, on a side street. Did he meet that guy first, maybe? Did they get into a conversation about something, and then Alex was getting cold? They all ended up in the bar, they closed the place, which would have meant four a.m.

183

There are bars here and there, on both sides of the street. Columbus runs south, downtown, and there's hardly any traffic at this hour, so he can cruise at about fifteen m.p.h., keeping an eye out for cops because suit or no suit if they pulled him over they'd search the car and find the gun. Confiscate the gun, and then who knows what. Nothing looks familiar until he gets past 106th Street, and there on the west side of Columbus is a place called Flor de Cienfuegos. Flower of a hundred fires? He pulls into one of several empty metered spaces and stares at the place: it looks right.

He removes the Walther from its box, takes out the clip, and refills it. The gun fits nicely and discreetly in his right jacket pocket. He locks the car and heads inside.

The place is almost empty, but it's familiar. Past the bar is a bowling machine; turn left and there's a row of booths separated from the bar by a five-foot-high wooden panel. In one of those booths, he's ninety-five percent positive, he sat with Flaco and Julio, or maybe with all three of them. Now, he takes a stool at the bar. The bartender is a tallish man, white, but with thick black hair. "Can I help you?" He speaks with a slight Spanish accent.

"Draft," Alex says.

The bartender returns in a moment with a mug of beer. Alex takes a ten from his wallet and slides it onto the bar. He says, "Why the flower of a hundred fires?"

The bartender gives him a blank look, then says, "Oh…Flor de Cienfuegos? Because the owner's from Cuba. It's a town in Cuba, on the south coast."

"How about you?" Alex says, after a sip of cold beer.

"Me? I'm from Puerto Rico. San Juan. What about you?"

"Florida, originally. My stepmother's Cuban."

"Nestor," the bartender says, extending his hand.

Alex shakes Nestor's hand and says, "I was in here Sunday night, late..."

"I was working," Nestor says. "I don't remember you."

"I looked pretty different," Alex says. "I was kind of fucked up. I was with a couple of guys—a tall, thin guy named Flaco, and a big, chubby guy named Julio..."

Nestor laughs. "All tall, thin Puerto Rican guys are named Flaco."

Alex smiles. "Try to picture this, Nestor. Those two guys sitting with me, looking like I hadn't slept in two or three days. Maybe there was a third guy, in a leather jacket with a fleece collar..."

"Why you asking me this?"

Is Alex going to have to pay for information? Does Nestor take him for a cop because he's sitting at the bar in his blue suit? Would a cop be dressed in a blue cotton suit in a bar on upper Columbus on a cool night in April? "I'm at Columbia, at the film school. I met those guys on Sunday, and we talked about some ideas I had. And they had. The guy with the leather jacket...Rafael? Had some interesting ideas. I wrote down their information, but my girlfriend threw it out."

Nestor gives him a long, studying look. "There's a guy named Julio that comes in here most days, kind of on the heavy side, maybe twenty-five. He's got a tall buddy I see sometimes, but you know, every skinny guy is Flaco..."

"I think we're talking about the same people," Alex says. "Where can I find these guys?"

Nestor shrugs. "I don't think I'm tellin' any big secrets if I say Julio comes in here for a beer every day after work, five thirty, six o'clock."

"Where does he work?"

185

Nestor laughs. "I don't know where the fuck he works, man. Ask him yourself."

Wonder of wonders, there is a space on 118<sup>th</sup> just east of Amsterdam. It's on the wrong side of the street for the morning, and it's just big enough for the compact Lark to squeeze into, but that's fine. Alex pats various pockets to make sure that he's in possession of his wallet, his marijuana, and his Walther, and walks half a block to his building.

It's cool in the apartment, pleasantly so. Alex notes that the kitchen window is open about six inches, and he doesn't recall leaving it that way. Filled with hope, he treads softly into the bedroom, where Lydia will be sleeping. He can make out the bed in the darkness, but there's no one in it. He calls her name softly, as if she might be hiding in the closet, or under the bed.

Back in the living room, he sees a sheet of paper on the coffee table. Has she left a note for him? No—this is the note he left for her. She hasn't been here at all; he must have left the window open himself. Upon closer examination, he realizes that in fact she *has* been here: she's left him a note on the back of his note.

*Alex—Waited for you till eleven o'clock. I have to get up in the morning and go to work. I don't know what the hell you are up to. I'll try calling you from school.*
   *L.*

## TWENTY-ONE

Prosper awakens at four o'clock Wednesday morning, largely because he's failed to turn on the heat and it feels like fifty degrees in Aunt Catherine's huge downstairs den. He's curled up on the far end of a sectional sofa, where he'd fallen asleep watching the Late Show on Channel 2 sometime after midnight. So he's slept nearly four hours—that on top of the two on the upstairs couch before Maddy called.

He takes a hot shower and replays the conversation with Maddy as best he can, fearful that he grossly overstepped his bounds in being as candid as he was about Ben. What if Maddy makes up her mind that he's a scheming rat, eager to betray his best friend, and what if Maddy relays the conversation to Ben—that is, if he ever does call her—and Ben pulls the plug on their friendship then and there? It's comforting to recall that Maddy still expects him to take her to Chip Boyle's party tonight.

How's he going to feel when eight o'clock rolls around?

What about now? After the shower he's warm, at least, but he feels as if his feet are clad in cast iron and someone has taken a sledgehammer to his head. He scrambles the refrigerator's remaining two eggs and takes his first Dexedrine since the previous morning, and by four thirty he's slithered into that familiar amphetamine state of well-being. Too bad these things are so bad for you, because they do make life easier to tolerate.

There is a spring in his step as he travels back to the living room in search of *The Crying of Lot 49*, arriving just in time for one of Martin's pre-recorded spots on WABC-FM. This is one of a series about hip places to visit in North

America, and Martin is telling pimply-faced kids in Detroit, Pittsburgh, etc. about the artists' colony in San Miguel de Allende, Mexico. For Martin's benefit Prosper had written the town's name out phonetically: SAHN MEE-*GHEL* DAY AYE-*YEN*-DAY. To no avail. If any of Martin's listeners are inspired to make it to Mexico, they'll be looking for San Meegwell day Alendy.

The newspaper truck arrives just before six, and it's a good day for the Times. The front page banner:

**M'CARTHY WINS WISCONSIN;**
**POLLS 57% TO JOHNSON'S 35;**
**G.O.P. GIVES 80% TO NIXON**

To be sure, Eugene McCarthy has just trounced a man who'd announced two days earlier he was out of the race, and Robert Kennedy's name wasn't on the ballot in Wisconsin, but Prosper wonders whether the great size of the margin doesn't mean that McCarthy still has a chance, especially because hardly anyone seems to have written in Kennedy's name. As to the Republican primary, Nixon was running virtually unopposed, as he will at the convention unless Rockefeller chooses to rejoin the race, or Ronald Reagan (God forbid) opts to rally the right wing.

Adjacent on the front page:

**U.S DEFINES BOMBING LIMIT**
**AS 225 MILES ABOVE DMZ**
**IN REPLY TO WIDE OUTCRY**

And below that:

**Fulbright, in Debate, Calls
Curb on Raids Misleading**

and:

**HANOI PRESS CALLS
PEACE BID A FRAUD**

and:

**White House Claims Johnson
Had 20th Parallel in Mind**

These are all, of course, pieces of the same puzzle. In
his withdrawal speech, Lyndon Johnson had magnanimously
avowed that bombing above the DMZ would cease. When it
did not, the Pentagon maintained that in saying bombing above
the DMZ would cease, the president *meant* that bombing two
hundred miles above the DMZ would cease. Now, when all
sorts of important people, friends and foes alike, have taken
note of the two-hundred-mile discrepancy, the Pentagon
clarifies things once and for all: no more bombing will occur
two hundred twenty-five miles above the DMZ. Senator
William Fulbright, the Democrat from Arkansas whose civil
rights record is spotty at best, but who is becoming one of the
loudest voices protesting the war, has not appreciated this round
of Pentagon triple-talk, and the North Vietnamese press have
gone a step further, calling Johnson's pledge to seek peace an
unadulterated lie. So the White House has attempted to clear
everything up: when the president said "DMZ," he had intended
to say "Twentieth Parallel." A simple and understandable
mistake, as if when the president said "Baltimore," he had
intended to say "New York;" when he said "apples" he had
intended to say "watermelons;" when he said "Thunderbird" he
had intended to say "Edsel."

Corporal Dybzinski's morning greeting to Prosper is:
"You look like something the cat dragged in." In a perfect
world, Prosper would be able to respond, "You look like a
pizza-faced Neanderthal," but as things stand he limits himself
to, "Thanks."

The early returns: Systolic 143, diastolic 91. It's the
closest he's come to falling within the acceptable, which he
attributes to the five hours that have elapsed since he took the
first Dexedrine of the day. He won't make yesterday's mistake
again, meanwhile, having secreted another capsule in the little
watch pocket of his Levi corduroys. Not that he imagines even
Dybzinski would order him searched, but the vestigial pouchette
seems an excellent hiding place for a tiny gelatin tube.

Leotis comes in at 155/101, so he's looking like a sure
thing at this point, although he's got another full day to go after
this one. Back in the blood pressure room he says, "I see your
man McCarthy won in Wisconsin. Won big, too, looks like."

"Right. Probably would have been a little closer if
Johnson hadn't dropped out two days earlier."

Leotis chuckles. "So how come Kennedy didn't run in
Wisconsin?"

"I guess because he didn't want to spread himself too
thin. He's just gotten into the race so he didn't even have a
chance to campaign in Wisconsin and he figures he can win the
next one, in Indiana."

"How'd you feel about him winnin' in Indiana?"

Prosper mulls that over. "Good, I guess. I think it's a
pity McCarthy did all the work, came out against the war,
showed how weak Johnson was because of the war, and now
Kennedy's gonna reap the benefits..."

190

## The Mountaintop

"So you figure it's gonna be all over for your boy, even after Wisconsin?"

"I hope not," Prosper says, "but I don't see how McCarthy can stand up to Kennedy. He's got the name and he'll have the money. But yes, if he wins in Indiana it's a good thing because it means two anti-war guys have won two big primaries, so it gets harder and harder for the party big shots to stay behind Humphrey..."

"You don't like Humphrey?"

"I liked Humphrey fine until the war. He's Johnson's vice-president, so maybe he's for continuing the war, or maybe he's against it and he's scared to say anything. Either way, I don't want any part of him."

If the other occupants of the room have any interest in this discussion which, while low-key, is audible to all, they don't show it. Of the four holdovers from yesterday, two have made the grade this morning; five have joined the group from this morning's new crop, so the hypertense in underpants outnumber their fully dressed brethren by one. The racial breakdown (Prosper and Leotis included) is six black, three white. Beyond that, nothing is known. Everyone looks young— eighteen, nineteen, twenty at the most. Everyone appears scared or bored, and no one seems motivated to do anything but stare at the floor, or straight ahead.

Dybzinski arrives early for the late-morning session. "Ain't got nothing better to do is my guess," Leotis murmurs to Prosper, who nods in response.

The corporal turns in their direction. "You boys enjoyin' yourselves?" He says, and when neither Prosper nor Leotis answers, he adds, "You deaf, or you just don't want to talk to me?"

Prosper can't restrain himself. "It didn't work out too well yesterday." Leotis gives him a subtle elbow in the ribs.

"You know," Dybzinski says, "some guys here are hard-asses. They make everybody strip down to their drawers no matter how long they've been here. You two should be happy I'm a nice guy."

"Thanks," Prosper says, trying to sound sincere.

"You know what else? Some guys wouldn't let you have that book. You're not supposed to have anything in here—no books, no magazines, no newspapers..."

"Why is that?" Leotis says.

"Because that's the rules." Dybzinski takes a step toward Prosper. "Can I see that book?"

"You confiscatin' his book?" Leotis says.

"Shit, no. I just want to see it." He extends his hand, and Prosper forks over the paperback. Dybzinski studies the front cover, then the back. "What is this, some kind of hippie bullshit?"

"It's about an auction," Prosper says. "Rare stamps."

"Sounds, um...gripping," Dybzinski says, and he flips *The Crying of Lot 49* back to Prosper. "See? Told you I was a nice guy."

The second blood-pressure check of the day occurs just before lunch, but lunch is the variable. It seems to happen whenever Dybzinski wishes it to happen, or perhaps that's the wrong way around. Maybe it's a matter of Dybzinski—in a quite unmilitary fashion—varying the timing of the BP taking just to trip up people like Prosper, to upset their regimen, to cause them to ingest whatever artificial pressure raisers they're taking too early or too late. Or maybe Prosper's just being paranoid, and the irregularity of the checks reflects nothing more than a general aura of chaos at the New Haven Federal Building.

In any case, the important thing is to get another Dexedrine into his system at least ten or fifteen minutes before the next time they tighten the cuff on his biceps, because if his systolic drops just a couple of points he'll be draft bait. And the problem is that Dybzinski keeps hanging around—chatting with anybody who'll exchange words with him, paging through the national edition of the *Daily News*—and Prosper can't risk even a quick dip into his watch pocket and a swift, liquidless swallowing of the capsule.

Eleven o'clock comes and goes. Eleven thirty. Possibly, Prosper thinks, the mere stress of sitting here worrying will do the trick. But he'd rather not take the chance.

At twenty to twelve, Dybzinski stretches theatrically and announces, "Gotta piss." Glancing at Prosper he says, "Don't you boys go anywhere."

"Right," Leotis says quietly to Dybzinski's back. "Same to you, motherfucker."

Prosper doesn't dawdle. A quick scan of the room reveals that no one is looking in his direction; he seizes the pill between thumb and forefinger and tosses it into his mouth, keeping his hand there as if stifling a yawn. He feels the drug working before Dybzinski has returned.

He soars to 161/99, while Leotis drops a bit, to 148/86, and then it's lunchtime.

"You notice somethin'?" Leotis has just completed a scan of the cafeteria. "All those other tables, you got white boys with white boys, black boys with black boys, white men and ladies with white men and ladies, black men and ladies with

193

black men and ladies. "And the army people too…" He gestures to a cluster of tables far across the vast room, where indeed several black men in uniform sit at a single table amidst five or six occupied solely by whites. From this distance it's hard to tell who might be Puerto Rican, Dominican, or Mexican, but Prosper imagines they have their own tables, too.

"Where I went to school," Leotis says, "it was maybe fifty-fifty, white kids and black, but I didn't have no white friends. It wasn't like I didn't want to, it was just a thing that didn't happen. We didn't hang out with them, they didn't hang out with us. It was black tables in the lunchroom, white tables in the lunchroom. Wasn't no fights or nothin', and, you know, there was some white kids I would talk to, even some white girls, but no way we was friends. But you," he smiles, "you *grew up* in Africa."

"No." Prosper shakes his head. They've finished lunch and he's on his second cup of coffee. It's a beverage that doesn't normally appeal to him, but the caffeine will reputedly boost his blood pressure a few points.

"That's what you told me yesterday."

"No, I said my parents live in Africa."

"So, what, you grew up separate from your parents?"

"My father's in the foreign service, so I grew up all over the place."

"Like where?"

"We lived in Washington till I was eight. Then Honduras till I was eleven. Then Buenos Aires till I was fourteen. Then I went away to school, so wherever my parents were I was here half the year, anyway…"

"How do you mean you went away to school?"

"I went to school in New Hampshire."

"Why the hell you go to school in New Hampshire?"

194

"Because that's where my father went."

"So, you like...fourteen years old and they just put you on a plane from South America?"

"Pretty much."

"*Man*...I'd think bein' in South America a pretty cool place to be." Leotis consumes the last of a glazed doughnut. "So what came after that?"

"When I was fifteen we went to Dahomey."

"Now, that's a place I never heard of."

"It's a little country in Africa. In central Africa, on the Atlantic coast."

"Seems like a comedown from Buenos Aires."

"Actually it was a promotion. It was my father's first ambassadorship."

Leotis whistles. "Damn! So your daddy was a hot shit, number one American in...where?"

"Dahomey."

"How many people in Dahomey?"

"Two million, maybe two and a half million."

"So--probably four times as many people in New York City than in that whole country."

"Right. I don't think the whole country was as big as New York State."

"What did you do in Dahomey?"

"What did *I* do? I wasn't there much. A few weeks in the summer for three years. It was hotter than hell. A hundred degrees every day. Humidity. When the electricity worked we had air conditioning."

"Nice house, I bet."

"Yeah...it was a big house. Lots of bugs, though. Big roaches. Huge roaches."

"Servants?"

195

Peter Delacorte

"My parents weren't big on servants, but yes, there was a cook and an assistant cook, and a married couple who took care of the house. Antoine and Marie-Claire."

"What language they speak? African language, or English?"

"French. It was a French colony, so the official language was French, so everybody who went to school spoke French."

"But not everybody went to school?"

"No--not by a long shot."

"Why was that?"

"Because there weren't a lot of schools, because there wasn't a lot of money. But the real reason was that France didn't want educated people growing up in the colonies and making trouble..."

Leotis nods, and glances at Prosper. "A lot of African countries belonged to France, right?"

"Right. France, England, Portugal, Belgium, Germany..."

"And they didn't treat the Africans too good, right?"

"Some better than others. I guess they all had pretty much the same objective, which was to spend as little money as possible to keep the country running, to maintain order, and to bring as much money as possible back to Europe. We were actually there...well, I wasn't there but my parents were, when the French government was giving gradual independence to Dahomey, which went really smoothly. No violence. But then when the French left there were only a couple of hundred people who had any idea how to run things. There were only a few thousand people who knew how to read and write."

"So...everything got all fucked up."

"Right. The other big problem was that once the French were gone, all the different tribes started jockeying for power, so it was a mess..."

"But you got out? Your daddy went someplace else?"

"Another promotion--just up the road, to Senegal."

"Things in better shape there?"

"Nope. Bigger country, pretty much the same problems."

Leotis leans forward in his chair. "You were on the west side of Africa, right?"

"Right. Both countries."

"West side, right where it kind of slopes in. That's where all the slaves came from."

"Yes," Prosper says. "We lived maybe a mile or two from the docks in Porto Novo, in Dahomey. Two or three hundred years ago it was one of the biggest slave ports. Maybe the biggest. It was an independent kingdom, actually. A black African kingdom that got rich and powerful selling slaves to the New World."

"That's what I call black *power*!" Leotis says, and laughs his throaty laugh.

## TWENTY-TWO

Ben awakens to a rapid knocking at his door; halfway out of bed, he glances at the clock radio on the night table. It's seven thirty-four, which means it's eight thirty-four in New York, and Maddy's already gone off to school, so he won't be calling her back until tonight at the earliest. He snatches his boxer shorts off the floor and slips them on, incorporating this rather complicated procedure into his progress toward the door.

This morning it is Randall, who's already in his work clothes, holding a newspaper. "Damn," he says, "thought I was gonna have to knock till noon. You take a sleeping pill, or did you go deaf in the middle of the night?"

"Sound sleeper," Ben says, as Randall cruises by him into the room. Ben turns, watching him. "Did you sleep well?"

"Like a baby," Randall says, sitting near the foot of the bed. "Turned off the TV at what, eleven o'clock, went out like a light, didn't open my eyes till six." This is good news, of course. Ben grabs his shirt off the floor, where it had been sitting next to his underpants. His pants, he realizes, are on the floor to Randall's left, at the foot of the bed. Randall says, "You usually so cavalier with your clothing?"

Ben knows that Randall knows he's not; he buttons the shirt. "Guess I wasn't expecting to fall asleep as soon as I did," he says, aware of his non sequitur. "Have you been out?"

"Yeah. It's spring here. Gonna be seventy, seventy-five degrees today. May be some big storm coming through tonight, though. This is a weird part of the world in April. One minute everything's all bright and placid, birds singing and God's in his heaven, next minute all hell breaks loose and they got funnel

198

clouds suckin' up mobile homes and anything that doesn't have a foundation."

Ben picks up his pants. "We don't have to be anywhere till ten, right?"

"Right. I thought we might go out and get some breakfast and talk a little strategy."

Should he put the pants on? What he'd like to do is take a leisurely shower and get dressed in clean clothes. "You want to give me about half an hour, then?"

Randall sits on the bed, peering sideways at Ben, who stands three feet away, holding his wrinkled khakis. "I imagine I could do that," he says.

"So," Randall says, "I figure we should stay for the march, assuming the march is gonna be in the foreseeable future." Randall has a fairly Spartan breakfast before him; he's finished his Special K and now he's working on two poached eggs with rye toast.

Ben has a huge ham omelette accompanied by a small family of sausages, a little bit greasy by his standards, but tasty just the same, and a pair of rich, sweet muffins. He says, "What do we know about that?"

"Well, you know Doctor King and the SCLC people would like to get it scheduled as soon as possible. He's got the whole Poor People's thing in D.C. on hold because all of a sudden this is so important, all of a sudden he's got to prove his movement hasn't been taken over by militants, and he can still have a peaceful march..."

"But Memphis has a restraining order, right?"

"Right. The SCLC's lawyers go to court here tomorrow to argue against that."

"Some local judge?"

"Right."

"Shouldn't that just be kind of automatic? Why should a Memphis judge rule in the SCLC's favor? Isn't that just giving them permission to march?"

Randall smiles. "Just because it's black and white doesn't mean it's all black and white. I can't say I'm familiar with this guy, but I imagine there are some judges who are capable of rising above local attitudes and deciding an issue on its merits. Like, do these people have a right to mount a peaceful demonstration? Isn't that kind of thing guaranteed them as American citizens?"

"Sure," Ben says, "but isn't the assumption here that any demonstration is *not* gonna be peaceful, and the militants are gonna burn the city down?"

"Shouldn't be," Randall says, smiling again. "Doctor King, I'm sure you know, is a very persuasive man, and I'm sure he's got very persuasive lawyers."

Ben, as often, doesn't know whether Randall is being inscrutably wise or foolishly optimistic. And of course he has more than a passing interest in this matter. "So if the lawyers persuade the judge, and he removes the restraining order, then when's the march likely to be?"

Randall shrugs. "I don't guess it would take them too much time to organize things. Possibly they could do it Friday--more likely early next week."

Early next week. Another four days, five days with Delphine. To be sure this is all virgin territory for Ben, but his guess is that there would be little or no official business over the weekend. Randall says, "How would you feel about meeting the man?"

## The Mountaintop

"Meeting Doctor King? How do you think I'd feel, meeting somebody who's been one of my heroes since I started paying attention?"

"Could just happen," Randall says. "Maybe tomorrow evening, maybe Friday sometime."

"I thought tomorrow evening we were meeting with William Marchand and the Bee Oh Pee guys."

"Yeah, I have to make some calls about that. But if we get a shot to sit down with King, far as I'm concerned everything else gets cancelled. Anyway, it's more likely we'd see King Friday, if the march doesn't happen and if he doesn't go back to Washington." He takes a modest sip of his black coffee. "If the Senator wins in Indiana, and if King can pull this march off, we could have us a good thing going."

At Memphis State, Randall addresses a huge Political Science class and Ben's participation is limited to sitting on the podium and looking attentive, which isn't that easy to do because what's going through his mind over and over is his time in bed with Delphine. Just the way a song will occasionally pop into his head with full orchestration, he can virtually feel her body, feel himself inside her, recreate the sensation in a kind of abstract totality, feel himself at that delicious moment just before he comes, and picture her face as she came, her eyes shut tight, mouth open wide, head tilted back, the veins in her neck standing out. As Randall speaks passionately to perhaps a hundred and twenty students--a surprising number of them black, perhaps twenty-five or thirty--using words like *commitment* and *reconciliation* and *dedication*, Ben sits fifteen feet away hoping his erection will subside before the time comes to stand up.

201

*Peter Delacorte*

During lunch with much of the Poli-Sci department, Ben manages to slip away and call the Holiday Inn. Although there is a pay phone just outside the dining room, he wanders out into the campus because the day is so beautiful. It's windy, to be sure, but the temperature must be in the mid-seventies; he imagines himself and Delphine back in the tall grass in Arkansas, disporting themselves under the sunshine with the river rushing by.

Are there any messages for room 216? There are not. Nor are there when he calls after their stop at Christian Brothers University, where Randall once again does the honors, speaking to a smaller, whiter class.

They are en route to Washington High, Ben at the wheel, when Randall says, "Everything all right with you?"

"With me? Sure. Everything's fine." He pulls the Mustang up at a red light. "Why do you ask?"

"You just seem a little detached," Randall says. "A little out of it. Not your usual self. Anything you want to tell me about?"

The radio is tuned to WDIA, Delphine's station, and the DJ is talking about the imminent storm. The volume is low and Ben is torn between turning it up and paying attention to Randall. "Nothing," he says. "Nothing I can think of." The light changes and he accelerates away from the intersection. The DJ is in the process of reading a list of counties, counties in apparent danger of being struck by tornadoes. Ben does not know what county Memphis is in. He'd like to get this conversation over with as quickly as possible. "When you're doing your stuff, there isn't much need for me to participate. That's fine with me, of course."

"That's not what I'm talking about," Randall says.

## The Mountaintop

Late afternoon, the DJ says, continuing into the evening. Ben's probably never been within a thousand miles of a tornado. "What *are* you talking about?" There's more irritation in his voice than he'd intended, but fifteen or twenty seconds go by without a response from Randall and he begins to assume his inadvertent tone has ended this line of discussion, so he concentrates on the radio, to which Randall seems completely oblivious. The DJ now comes right out and says there's a tornado warning--a strong chance of a tornado touching down-- in Memphis. Ben tries to imagine the Holiday Inn, or Mason Temple, or wherever he happens to be at the time, being sucked up into the sky.

As to the line of discussion, no such luck. Randall says, "I'm just gonna take a shot in the dark here, Ben. Is there something goin' on between you and that girl?" He pauses for a couple of seconds. "Between you and Delphine?"

What now? There is music, all of a sudden, on the radio. "I like her," Ben says.

"I like her too, but my eyes aren't all glazed over, and I'm not sneakin' off to use pay phones in a town where I'm acquainted with almost nobody."

Ben's first thought, first strategy, is to tell Randall he was trying to call Maddy. It would be perfect, except Randall knows that Maddy would be at school in the middle of the day. Ben could insist, could say he'd been intending to call her but had fallen asleep, which was true, and now in his guilt he tried to call her on her lunch hour....But no, this is stupid. It's inevitable that Randall will figure things out, will recognize that *something*'s going on, so why not get it over with?

The Mustang sits at another light, on Central Avenue. Ben turns his head and makes eye contact. "I called her. I'm trying to make plans for tonight. She's coming with us to Mason Temple."

There is another brief period of silence. Again the car proceeds down Central and again Ben wishes that this is the end of it, and again his hope is in vain. Randall says, "Tell me one thing, would you? Are you *sleeping* with this girl, Ben?"

Now it seems that lying, or evading the question, would be pointless. He takes a deep breath, exhales, and says, "Once."

"*Once!*" Randall shouts. "Like *once* makes it not so bad, like it could've been an accident? *Jesus*, Ben..."

When they have traveled another couple of blocks and Randall has said nothing more, Ben decides to take a chance. "I have to say, Randall, I don't see why it's such a big deal."

"Oh, you don't." Randall's reply is immediate. "You don't see that there's one aspect of it that's a little troublesome, which is that you're a white boy down here in Memphis screwin' around with a black girl, who happens also to be the daughter of a very influential family we scarcely want to alienate. And there's another aspect of it that's even *more* troublesome, which is that you *live* with somebody, you share an apartment and a *life* with someone who, unless I miss my guess, would not be pleased to learn that you'd been having sexual relations with some other girl. And you see how these two aspects might kind of *dovetail*, Ben?" Randall stops, meshes his fingers, separates them, and says, "I'm getting ahead of myself. Did you tell her about Maddy?"

"No." Ben considers leaving it at that, then adds, "Not yet."

"You think she might be serious about you, or is this just a fling for her?"

"I'm not sure."

"I didn't get the impression," Randall says, "that she was the kind of girl who'd fool around with transient political types just for the sake of it."

"No," Ben says, and then after a moment's deliberation he ventures, "but I don't think she's a babe in the woods, either."

"I don't think I like the sound of what I just heard," Randall says. "I don't think I like the sound of that at all."

*What* doesn't he like the sound of, for Christ's sake? Ben has an urge to tromp on the accelerator and send them tearing through traffic, but instead he pulls the Mustang into the Texaco station on the next corner and slams on the brake, causing Randall to shoot his hands out against the dashboard. Ben turns to face him. "What's the *matter* with you, goddamn it? Who the hell do you think you are? What gives you the right to pass judgment on me?"

Evidently taken aback by Ben's outburst, Randall says nothing at all; nor, however, does he take his eyes off Ben's. "I am *not*..." Ben says, coming down very hard on the *not*, and then stopping completely.

After a respectful while, Randall says, "You're not what? You're not gonna take any more of my shit? You're not gonna drive me around Memphis anymore? You're not a sleazy, cheating son of a bitch?"

What Ben wanted to say, what he couldn't find the words to say, was that he wasn't playing with Delphine's affections and he felt that she knew she was taking a calculated risk in sleeping with him, that she perhaps saw him as her way out of Memphis, and maybe he might be just that, but he didn't know yet. That was much too complex a thought to express, and even if he were to find a way to articulate it, Randall, he suspects, would not be sympathetic. He says, "I'm not a bad guy, Randall. I'm not doing a bad thing here, I promise you."

"That's a pretty subjective evaluation, don't you think?"

Ben stares out at the gas pumps beyond the windshield. Here in the Texaco station, little vinyl pennants strung from pole to pole jerk and contort maniacally in the wind, and it's *hot*. When he speaks again, it is in uncharacteristic bursts. "It's not just a matter of cheating on someone. On Maddy. I'm sorry about that part of it. I'm sorry about the circumstances. I don't want to hurt anybody. I'm not trying to screw things up. I wish you'd get off my case...give me the benefit of the doubt. Things *happen*, for Christ's sake."

## TWENTY-THREE

This early morning when Lydia awakens she is stark naked and lying next to Rafael in his bed. He doesn't stir when she slides out of bed and takes the very short walk to the bathroom. It's a strange mixture of ease and unease that she feels here: The place itself is squalid in its condition, its tininess, its mustiness, a history of first-generation immigrants in the odors of the staircase and the hallways. But if you sit in the living room (such as it is) and you squint, you can picture yourself in a used bookstore somewhere way downtown, and that's not such a bad thing. Most of all what makes it bearable for her is Rafael himself, whom she's known for something like forty-four hours. This is nuts, she knows, but she imagines that for the first time in her life she's found someone she can depend on, someone she doesn't have to take care of, someone she doesn't have to worry about. A lot of it is intuitive, of course, because she hardly knows him at all, and in her most objective moments she asks herself how much of it is wishful thinking. But what kind of man is it who would sit with her for two hours in her relatively opulent apartment, waiting for her rich, crazy lover to appear? What kind of man would stand on the sidewalk and take her worst shit, accusations that would have sent any thin-skinned Latin *macho* into rage or flight? What kind of man would fuck her silly twice last night and twice tonight, and after the first one tonight, when she was ready to fall into blissful sleep, go down on her with a suave adroitness that Alex, for all his self-styled personal liberation, could never manage in a million years?

When she climbs back into bed, Rafael turns over and softly runs his left hand from her neck to her navel. Moments later, she falls back to sleep with his hand on her breast.

In early daylight, in and out of shallow sleep, she is aware first of Rafael's absence, which is not altogether a bad thing because it allows her to stretch out on the bed that's not really big enough for two. Then she smells coffee, hears the toilet flush. She's awake enough at one point to peer at her watch and see that it's not yet seven. Next she hears voices, in Spanish, and it's almost like waking up in the small apartment of her childhood, listening to her parents trying to be quiet in the early morning. Except in this case both voices are clearly male: one of them is Rafael's and the other belongs to…Julio? No, it's not Julio, because Rafael is referring to Julio in the third person. "I told him, definitely no. I didn't want him doing that."

The other voice is deeper. "Why should I give a shit what you want? Why should you be giving him orders? Who the fuck do you think you are?"

"I think I'm your friend," Rafael says. "I think maybe I know what's right and what's wrong better than you do."

"The hell with that!" The other voice has grown louder, and Lydia almost simultaneously deduces and hears that it belongs to Flaco. "This ain't about what's right and wrong, this is about you making time with his chick."

"Bullshit," Rafael says, still keeping his voice down. "The guy wanted to give us his stuff. The girl said no, so we backed off…"

"*You* backed off."

"We backed off because it was the right thing to do…"

"You had your eyes on her right then, didn't you?"

"Tell me this," Rafael says, "when you went back, was he *happy* about giving you that stuff?" If Flaco responds, Lydia doesn't hear it. "Then you stole it, asshole," Rafael says.

"So what?" Now Flaco makes no pretense of being quiet. "When did we start giving a shit about something like that? If some rich fucking gringo give us something and then takes it back, when did we start saying oh, sorry, mister."

"Did you pawn it or sell it?"

"What difference does it make?"

"If you pawned it, give me the ticket and I'll redeem it."

"You fucking pussy. We sold it. Of course we sold it."

"Buy it back, then."

"Are you kidding me? Are you crazy? You blinded by her cunt? What do you care, anyway? What does she care? If she's left that sick bastard for you, what difference does it make to her?"

"It makes a difference to me. If you care about our friendship, you're gonna buy that stuff back."

"If *you* care about our friendship," Flaco says, "you don't talk to me like that."

Lydia hears the door slam, which comes as a relief. She hasn't been looking forward to leaving the bedroom and encountering Flaco.

Rafael appears in the doorway. "Sorry," he says in English. "Did that wake you up?"

"I was awake," she says.

"Did you hear all of that?" She nods. "I can talk to Julio," he says.

"Rafael," she says. "Don't worry about it. Don't get in trouble because of this. You know what? Alex had it coming."

She has promised herself to stop by the apartment before going to school, but when Rafael gets back in bed they make love again, and then he prepares a chorizo and egg breakfast, so by eight o'clock she hasn't even gotten dressed.

"Why is it so important to go there?" Rafael asks.

"I don't know," she says. "I feel guilty about him."

"He got himself into this bullshit, you didn't."

She smiles. "That's what I told you an hour ago."

It's too late now to walk the half-mile up Morningside Drive, and Alex—if he's even home—would be sleeping. So, she promises herself anew, she'll go there after school.

She has a good morning with the kids. It's a complex and tricky job, and it's fortunate she got to spend last year as a teacher's assistant, learning to gauge which children were capable of some communication in English, which were limited to Spanish. Virtually all of them speak only or primarily Spanish at home, which simplifies things to the extent that there are no kids who speak only English. One of the purposes of the kindergarten program is to achieve a level of bilingualism at school year's end so that the kids—who will be learning to read in Spanish as first graders—can converse comfortably in English. Although she grew up surrounded by Puerto Rican children, she has never lost her Venezuelan accent, so often she has to make an effort to be understood, and more often to understand. Plus, there are several kids from the Dominican, who occasionally use words that mystify her. So almost nothing is second nature. Virtually every sentence has to be well considered before it's spoken. Yesterday, even after her morning off, was a disaster, the combination of fatigue and not being able to get Rafael out of her mind, then the conversation with Maddy, leaving her frequently tongue-tied in a room of five-year-olds.

Today it's much better. There is a reversal of roles at lunchtime, as with some sanguinity Lydia tells Maddy that any doubts she may have had regarding Rafael are no more. Maddy voices mild skepticism, but mainly wants to talk about her own problems. Ben has finally called her—at two in the morning— and talked for a couple of minutes before excusing himself to answer a knock at the door, and then after a brief apology, hanging up on her.

"And I could swear I heard a female voice," Maddy says. "Maybe it was just a phone thing. You know—when you hear part of another conversation in the background?"

As far as Lydia is concerned, that pretty much wraps up the package, but she's not going to come right out and say it. "Who'd be knocking on his door at two in the morning?"

## The Mountaintop

"He said it was Randall, his boss. He's...kind of intense. I wouldn't put it past him to think of something in the middle of the night and decide he had to tell Ben right away."

"But he hung up, and he didn't explain?"

"No. He said he had to go. That was it."

"Jesus, Mad, why didn't you call him back?"

"I wouldn't have known where to call."

"He still hasn't fucking told you where he's staying?"

"No. I don't think that's intentional. It's a kind of...oversight."

"You serious?" Lydia says.

She takes the bus up 110th Street to Cathedral Parkway as she has every school day since she moved in with Alex. She gets off at Columbus, and here she is sorely tempted to cross the street and walk a few hundred feet to the bodega, but instead she dutifully turns right and heads uphill on Morningside Drive.

She stands outside the apartment door for the better part of a minute, listening; if Alex were home there would probably be music—Ravi Shankar or the Ronettes—but there is no sound. Maybe he's asleep. Maybe he was tripping again last night, got in at dawn as usual, and is sleeping the day away. She almost hopes that's the case, because it would toughen her resolve.

She lets herself in and immediately checks the bedroom. She can't be absolutely sure, but it seems to be in slightly different disarray from yesterday—the bed unmade in another way. And of course: the bedroom window, which she'd opened, is closed. The note she'd left on the coffee table is no longer there, nor is there any apparent reply. Is it possible he's gone to his Wednesday afternoon class?

211

## TWENTY-FOUR

Having smoked another joint and swallowed another Seconal while listening to *Chet Baker Sings* until well past two, Alex sleeps the sleep of the dead until mid-morning. He awakens briefly at ten, remembering (1) that he has a car, and (2) that it's parked on the wrong side of the street. But is it an eight a.m. till eleven a.m. zone, or an eleven a.m. to two p.m. zone? Had he even checked last night? Whatever, they're not going to tow the car away and he won't have to pay the ticket, so it's not worth worrying about. The interior of his mouth feels as if bacteria with muskets have re-enacted the War of 1812. He is soon unconscious once more, and it's past noon when he wakes up again.

A quick survey of the apartment shows no sign of Lydia. Should he call the school? What's he going to do about the car? He runs his tongue along his inner cheeks, which are like a topographical map, the result of having spent much of Tuesday clenching his jaw and grinding his teeth thanks to the Obitrol. He's aware of an incipient headache. He constructs a joint and smokes it, sitting on the couch and staring at the wall. What's he going to do about the car? He's tempted to drive it back to the Leonia and leave it on the lot, but then he'd be out $450 or whatever the hell he handed that salesman. Maybe he can negotiate a deal on the phone. What salesman wouldn't appreciate getting back a car with a just a couple of hundred new miles on its odometer along with a nice bit of cash? A hundred and fifty? He's ferociously hungry after the joint, so he gets dressed in Monday's clothes—jeans, a work shirt, derelict boots—and walks toward Broadway and the West End,

212

where they have fat, succulent burgers. On the way, he stops at the Lark and plucks the parking ticket off the windshield. He reads it as if inspecting some sort of minor document—a receipt for a toaster, perhaps—and discovers it was issued at three minutes after eight. So this cop was on his toes. Alex pictures all the owners of cars unfortunate enough to have license plates sprinting down the stairs and up the street to reach their vehicles before this punctual cop started handing out citations. He tosses his ticket in the big metal trash basket at Amsterdam and 118<sup>th</sup>.

Back home, burger consumed, headache only mildly annoying, Alex is barely inside the door when the phone rings. This must be Lydia. Except…it's nearly two o'clock, well past her lunch break and not nearly late enough for her to be done.

"Hey, Alex?" It's Elliot's voice.

"Elliot? Yeah—how you doing?" Alex is eager to report yesterday's events.

"Listen, man, I just got a call from a fucking car dealer in New Jersey. I don't suppose you'd know anything about that?"

Alex is a little confused. He's spent much of lunchtime working on a strategy for the salesman in Leonia, and now Elliot's telling him *he* got a call from a car dealer. Is this a coincidence? He's about to reply that no, he doesn't know anything about that when he remembers that he handed the guy Elliot's license.

"Hold on," he says, "was this guy's name…Leo?"

"I don't know what his fucking name was, man. All I know is out of the blue this bastard calls me up, asks me if I'm Elliot Shatzberg, and starts telling me I stole a car. I tell him I don't know shit about any car in New Jersey and he can go fuck

213

himself. Then I remembered I loaned you my Delaware license."

Jesus Christ, Alex thinks, Leo must have memorized the license, which was in his hand for all about twenty seconds. "So you hung up on the guy?"

"Yes, I fucking hung up on the guy."

"Cool," Alex says. "There's nothing to worry about, okay? I didn't steal the car. I just didn't sign some papers…"

"You showed this motherfucker *my* license, man? What the fuck got into you? The last thing I need is any heat, for Christ's sake."

"I'm gonna take care of it right now, Elliot. Don't sweat it. There's no way this is gonna come back to you."

"It better fucking not, man."


Alex spends a few minutes pacing the floor, walking from bedroom to living room and back, and back again, trying to concentrate. He rolls his second joint of the day and sits on the couch, smoking and scribbling in his leather notebook, which is usually reserved for creative entries. But then, this is a matter that requires imagination. He writes: *Leo*, and then he pauses for a long time, sucking in the marijuana smoke and keeping it in his lungs until they're ready to burst. Then he writes: *2 ways to go/either offer give him back car, get most of money back/or maybe he just wants me come back and sign papers.* Anything else? Any strategy? Anything to anticipate? He can't think of a thing.

What did he do with the fucking phone book? Ah…it's right where it was yesterday, on the shelf in the bedroom closet, surrounded by Lydia's boots. He returns to the couch, finds the number and is about to dial when he remembers the matters of license and identity. He picks up the notebook and writes: *I am*

214

*elliot unless I am coming in to sign papers/then I have to be alex.*

    He dials. He asks the woman who answers the phone if he might speak to Leo, and there is a long wait. Finally, "Hello, this is Leo Passaglia speaking."

    "Leo, hey, this is Elliot from yesterday, with the Lark?"

    A brief moment of silence. "Yeah? What the hell did you think you were doing, drivin' off the lot? That's grand theft auto, pal."

    "I paid you for the car, Leo. I gave you a fair price."

    "Do you know the shit we had to go through? *I* had to go through. Boss put me through the fuckin' wringer. I had to call information in every fuckin' area code within two hundred miles. We found one guy in New York with your name, that evidently wasn't you…"

    "Here I am, Leo. Sorry for the inconvenience. I had to get to Delaware."

    "We're *this* close to callin' the cops," Leo says. "Local *and* state…"

    What's going through Alex's mind is that he holds the cards here. Leo doesn't have any idea where he is; the only thing he knows is that the Elliot Shatzberg he called isn't the guy who took the car. Alex is tempted to hang up on the spot, but he doesn't want to do anything that would endanger his status as Elliot's preferred customer. He says, "I paid you for the car, Leo."

    Another brief silence. "You got a bill of sale, Mister Shatzberg?"

    "You know I don't."

    "Tell you what I'll do," Leo says. "The sticker on that car was four seventy-five. You give me a hundred for tax and license and two hundred for my trouble, we'll call it even."

Alex laughs. "Why the hell should I do that?"

"Cause if you don't, there's gonna be a warrant for your arrest in about five minutes."

A warrant for Elliot's arrest, or more likely no warrant at all. But is that a risk Alex can afford to take? "How about this?" He says. "I'll bring the car back. You can have the car. Give me three-fifty, and keep a hundred for your trouble."

"That car's depreciated," Leo says. "How about this: You give me a hundred for tax and license, and *three* hundred for my trouble."

"A minute ago you said two hundred."

"Yeah, and the price is gonna keep goin' up until you stop dickin' around."

"I don't need the car," Alex says. "Give me back three hundred, you've got the car and a hundred and fifty bucks."

"Listen, asshole. Understand one thing: You're screwed here. You stole a car. You can do time for that. You can't *sell* the car without a pink slip. You want to get out of this, you come in with another four-fifty, everything's legal, we'll forget about the grand theft auto."

Alex tries to imagine the worst-case scenario: Some authorities somewhere find Elliot's name in the Delaware DMV files. They talk to the people who actually live at that address, who *might* know where to find Elliot. They talk to Elliot, who *might* tell them he gave his license to Alex. Probably not on the first *might*, and only under great duress on the second *might*. Worst case, Alex has to find someplace new to buy marijuana. He says, "Leo...how about this? Go fuck yourself." And he hangs up.

Delighted with himself, he breaks into spontaneous laughter and pounds his fist on the sofa cushion until he's created a small cloud of dust. He's got to tell somebody about this. Lydia wouldn't appreciate it, but Prosper would. And, by God, Prosper in all probability will be at Chip Boyle's party tonight. Alex hadn't planned to go but now, especially with Lydia among the missing, he figures why the hell not? For the moment, he's got time to make it to his Modern American Film class at three—the first class he will have attended in two weeks. He resists the temptation to have another quick smoke, grabs his notebook, and heads out the door.

## TWENTY-FIVE

On the brief traverse from the blood pressure test area to the little waiting room, Corporal Dybzinski normally leads the pack. This afternoon he chooses to walk alongside Prosper, which does not put Prosper at ease. "High again, huh?" Dybzinski says.

"I'm sorry?"

"You're way up there on the blood pressure again? What was it this time?"

"I don't really need to tell you, do I?"

"Nope. I checked your chart. One sixty-something over ninety-two, give or take. Way up there. Kinda scary for a young guy like yourself, right? Healthy, in pretty good shape, but…Jeez, you got blood pressure like a seventy-year-old geezer. Is that an inherited thing, or what?"

Prosper chooses not to reply. "They tell me," Dybzinski says after a few seconds, "that some of your anti-war types, or cowardly pricks as I prefer to call 'em, will take drugs to keep their pressure up. You hear anything about that?"

Prosper is already visualizing himself taking a urine test or, God only knows, a *blood* test, seeing himself conferring with the ACLU. He senses his heart pounding, his blood pressure doubtless soaring now, when it doesn't count. He says, "I wouldn't know anything about that."

"Don't let the motherfucker get to you," Leotis says, back in the now overcrowded and increasingly claustrophobic little room. "They done all the pee tests and blood tests they gonna do. All you got to do right now is have high blood pressure one more time, and that's it."

"What was yours this time?"

"One forty-five over eighty-eight," Leotis says.

Prosper shakes his head. "That's close."

"Too damn close."

Dybzinski comes and goes, lingers and hovers. Prosper converses intermittently with Leotis, periodically checks the blank expressions of their numerous fellow testees, tries to read *The Crying of Lot 49*, but can't concentrate. It's two thirty now; the next trek to the blood pressure area might be at three, three thirty, four o'clock. There doesn't really seem to be a system to it.

At quarter to three Dybzinski reappears, and speaks. "College boy?" Prosper glances around the room, hoping someone else might respond, but no one does. "Yeah, you, with the book." Prosper makes eye contact. "How do you think we're doing in Vietnam?"

"I don't want to get into this."

"Hey, I know you're against the war, but I'm interested in how you think we're doing. You read about it every day, right? I'll bet you know more than all these other guys put together."

"I doubt it," Prosper says.

"Shit, don't be modest. You're a bright boy, I can tell. Too bad you don't know about the world."

Leotis says, "He know a hell of a lot more than you do."

"He do, huh?" Dybzinski says. "Why won't he talk to me?"

No one speaks for a minute or so, long enough for Prosper to hope the conversation is over, but then Dybzinski resumes. "It makes me sick, you assholes here when right now a few hundred of our guys are over in Khe Sanh in this fuckin' battle that's been goin' on for three fuckin' months…"

"What about you?" Leotis says.

"What about me?"

"I don't see you over in no Khe Sanh. You sittin' here with us."

Dybzinski takes a step forward. "You think I wouldn't like to be over there, instead of pullin' this bullshit? Huh, wiseass? Black boy?"

"Take it easy," Prosper says.

Still glaring at Leotis, Dybzinski points to Prosper. "He talks! I got the son of a bitch to talk!" Now he shifts his attention to Prosper. "You know what the casualties are? You know how many guys we've lost at Khe Sanh? And you know how many *they've* lost? Ten times as many. I don't know,

219

twenty times as many. They just keep pourin' the troops in, like they don't give a shit how many get killed…"

Prosper says, "Doesn't that tell you something?"

"Damn right! It tells me about the value of human life we have versus the value of human life *they* have. It tells me about democracy, where we care about keepin' people alive and healthy, and communism, where it's all about fuckin' robots who don't give a shit whether they live or die, as long as their system wins out."

"That's the craziest thing I've ever heard," Prosper says. "Those people are fighting for their country, not their goddamn system, and they want to get the Americans the hell out of there."

"Give me a fucking break!" Dybzinski is on the verge of shouting. "Tell that to the people in Saigon. Tell that to people we're protecting all over the south…"

"Yeah," Leotis interrupts. "How come those people can't fight their own damn war? How come they need us to do it for them?"

"You, my friend," Dybzinski says to Leotis, "are fuckin' ignorant." He points to Prosper. "He's crazy. He's politically fucked up. But you have the brains of a monkey."

Leotis gets to his feet and takes a step toward Dybzinski, who's about three feet away. Prosper quickly stands between them. "I don't think you're supposed to do this," he says to the red-faced corporal.

"Fuck both you guys," Dybzinski growls; he turns and stalks once again out of the room.

"*Damn,*" Leotis mutters. "You tell me who's got the brains of a monkey."

## The Mountaintop

All this turmoil can only cause the blood pressure to rise, Prosper muses, but that notion fades as time passes. If it were purely anxiety being measured, he'd be off the charts as four o'clock comes and goes. It's now been how long since the last Dexedrine? And no chance of getting out to the car to purloin another one. Why hadn't he secreted two? Or three— one for Leotis, who might need it more than he. What if they keep him here into the evening? Do they do that? Is there a special blood pressure night shift? He should have called the radio station during the lunch break to find out if Martin has seen to the tape editing. And Maddy. If he's out of here by five, he tells himself, he'll still have time to get back to Riverside, change clothes, do the reverse commute into Manhattan, pick her up, and get to the party.

It's ten after four when Corporal Martino, Dybzinski's benign counterpart, appears in the little room. Recalling that Martino's sole duty yesterday was to announce that they were done, Prosper feels his spirits rise. But Martino is here only to lead them once more unto the breach. Once more the motley brigade—twelve this time in underpants, two in mufti—makes its way out of the room, into the hallway. Once more the sleeve tightens around the biceps, the heart pounds, the sleeve loosens. Sometimes the PFC on sleeve duty writes the life-or-death numbers on the chart in silence, sometimes he announces the news, good or bad. This late afternoon Private Adams, a tall white man who looks about twenty, says, "One forty-eight over eighty-six, chief."

That's it. The 86 doesn't matter; by eight systolic points Prosper has failed the final test. He's won. He's out. He's a free man.

He waits for Leotis, who has somehow fallen two behind him. He watches the sleeve go on and off, and listens, but the soldier silently hands Leotis his chart.

"So?" Prosper says.

"I can't look at it, man. Read it for me."

Prosper scans the chart, focuses on the bottom number. "One thirty-five over sixty-eight," he reads aloud. He feels a surge of cortisol as the significance of the numbers sinks in.

"Shit," Leotis says, shaking his head, "I didn't even make it close."

It is Martino who leads them back to the room, Martino who divides them into two groups: four, including Leotis, who've just fallen into passing range, and seven who will be returning tomorrow, to whom the corporal hands out YMCA vouchers and instructions to report at eight. Prosper assumes he's in neither group because he's the only one of the twelve who's completed his third day, so he waits.

Martino doesn't have much to say to the draftees-to-be. They'll be getting notices of their reclassification shortly; they have the option to enlist in any of the armed services; if they choose not to, they'll most likely be drafted into the army; for now, they're free to go.

"You need a ride?" Prosper asks Leotis. "You're on my way."

"No, man. Got my van. Thanks anyway."

"What are you gonna do?"

Leotis looks at his feet. "Not sure. Don't think I'm gonna enlist. Don't think I want to get drafted..."

"You want to get together and talk about it?"

"Sure. Why not?"

222

"How about tomorrow? Tomorrow night? Maybe you could come into the city and we could do something with Maddy."

"Sounds good. I may have a job in the afternoon, but I should be done by five or six. You got my card, right?"

"Yep. Midnight Movers."

"All right, then. You call me."

Prosper stands above Corporal Martino, who's busy with paperwork. He says, "Is there anything more I have to do? I've got stuff to do tonight."

Martino doesn't look up. "Your buddy wanted to have a word with you."

"My buddy? The guy who just left?"

"Nope." Martino points to the doorway, where Corporal Dybzinski has materialized. Dybzinski makes a slow, cinematic come-hither gesture with his right index finger, as if he were Oliver Hardy's malevolent doppelgänger.

"What's this about?" Prosper says.

"Come with me," Dybzinski replies.

"I'm not going anywhere with you. I'm done. Four times today, three days. I'm finished."

"You're not finished till I say you're finished. You're not signed out."

"Sign me out, then. I've got work to do. I've got a job."

"I want to make sure we do right by you," Dybzinski says.

Prosper turns to Martino. "Can he do this?" Martino shrugs and looks away.

"Come on," Dybzinski says. "Nothing to worry about. I'm not gonna take you out in the alley and beat the shit out of you. Five minutes, and you're on your way. Cross my heart."

It is with as much a sense of mystery as of dread that Prosper follows the wiry little corporal. Are they going to have another chat about the war? About the plight of Dybzinski's relatives in Warsaw? Down the familiar hallway they go, Dybzinski with clipboard in hand, until they reach the blood pressure area, where PFC Adams is packing up for the day.

"Not just yet, huh, Mikey?" Dybzinski says.

"Did him already," Adams replies.

"Give him a bonus round for me. A going away present."

Dybzinski has led Prosper to the chair and now pushes him down into it, like a dog trainer with a recalcitrant subject. Prosper has two thoughts in rapid succession: (1) they can't do this to me; and (2) even if they *can* do this to me it'll make no difference, because my heart's pounding like a bongo drum and my blood pressure must be higher than ever. He says to Adams, "This isn't right."

"He's the boss," Adams says, slipping the cuff on Prosper's right arm.

Prosper feels himself slipping into an odd sort of calm, as if he's endured everything he had to and now he's made his way into a different dimension, where no harm can befall him. He says, "This doesn't count, right? I've already done it four times today."

Adams inflates the cuff, and Dybzinski says, "We'll see if it counts."

"One three eight," Adams says, "and eight four."

Prosper is processing very slowly, not quite capable of converting Adams's individual digits into complete, relevant numbers. He notes that just to his left, Dybzinski is using his pencil's eraser on the clipboard, and he realizes almost simultaneously that Adams has just articulated a reading of 138 over 84, and that Dybzinski is substituting that spurious, illicit figure for the legitimate 148/86 of half an hour ago.

"You made it, pal," Dybzinski says. "You're in."

How quickly can one make the journey from nearly placid to absolute panic? "For Christ's sake," Prosper says, "they'll *see* you erased that."

"Not a chance," Dybzinski replies with a victor's grin. "Nobody gives a shit."

## TWENTY-SIX

It's just past four and the sky is seriously clouding over when they finally return to the Holiday Inn, and Ben is exhausted despite having pretty much just tagged along all day. He didn't get a lot of sleep last night, but that's par for the course. The tension between him and Randall is something new. They've known each other nearly two years, but it's been in the last couple of weeks, since they've been working together, that they've become fairly close. It's a kind of intimacy Ben values, and it's disturbing that Randall is so upset with him. Upset? Displeased? Disappointed? He understands that in certain ways he overstepped his bounds, that there are aspects to this romance that are tactically not ideal, and that Randall is fond of Maddy. But he's only even *met* her, what...twice? Three times? Ben is accustomed to a sort of fellowship in which men are uncritical of each others' conquests or infidelities--in which most men of his acquaintance in fact boast of them. That's not his style. The pleasure is in the act, not the telling.

Sitting cross-legged on the bed in his room, he has a sudden image of himself in Prosper's car Sunday night, driving back from a beer run to Port Chester, and Prosper getting on his case for making out with a girl at the bar. Well, obviously Prosper's still got a thing for Maddy, so that's understandable. With Randall is it mostly Delphine's color, or is it Maddy, or is it worrying that if the Ennises get pissed off that could be a lot of money and votes down the drain? He could do his best to convince Randall that he's not just fooling around with Delphine--but if Randall's main concern is Maddy, that would backfire.

He picks up the telephone and dials the front desk, asks if there have been any messages. There have been none. Should he call Delphine at home? Should he call Maddy? It's now seventeen minutes past five in New York, so she should be home. He stretches out on the bedspread, supine, and falls asleep inside twenty seconds.

It's the telephone that wakes him. He rolls over and glances at the clock radio, which reads 5:11. As he picks up the receiver he's just more than semi-conscious. "Hello?" He hears himself sounding groggy.

"Ben?" It's a female voice, mid-range. Maddy.

"Yeah," he says, sleepily. "How are you doing?" He's thinking about what he's going to say to her, what excuse he'll make for hanging up last night.

"I'm doing fine. A little tired. How about you?" Wait. The inflection, the accent aren't Maddy's. He's waking up. He's ninety percent sure it's Delphine. Seeking something neutral, some insurance just in case this *is* Maddy, he says, "Did you get any sleep?"

"I slept till almost nine. Missed half my nine thirty class." It's Delphine, for sure. "But it wasn't a big deal. Since then I've been runnin' around all day. Thinking about you."

"Me too," he says. "God, have I ever been thinking about you. Did you get any trouble from your parents?"

"Both gone when I got up. I'm still at school now. But I think they're used to me being out late by now."

He wonders whether to tell her about Randall. What good would it do? He says, "So...what about tonight? Can we get together for dinner?"

"I don't think so," she says. "I've got a few more things to do here, then I should get home and change. Why don't I just meet you at Mason Temple a few minutes before eight?"

"Sounds good," Ben says. "It starts at eight, right? Are we gonna have trouble getting seats?"

"I doubt it. It's a huge place. And the weather will keep a lot of people away."

The weather. "What about that?" Ben says. "Is it like *The Wizard of Oz*? Is the whole place gonna get sucked up into the air?"

She laughs. "It happens every spring. There might be a few trailer homes and barn roofs and doghouses floatin' around, but I think Mason Temple should stay put."

A few minutes after Ben hangs up he goes into the hallway, puts his ear against Randall's door, and hears the murmur of the television. He knocks, and Randall answers, in his stocking feet. Ben says, "You get some sleep?"

"A little," Randall replies. "Enough. You want to come in?"

Ben sits in the chair in the corner of the room, by the window, and Randall bounces down near the head of his bed. Ben says, "Do we have dinner plans?"

"Not so far. What's going on with Miss Ennis?"

"She's meeting us at Mason Temple."

"Well, then, why don't we just get us some room service? No point in going out before we have to." Randall nods toward the window. It's not raining yet, but the wind's howling is audible through the thick glass. "People on the TV say this is gonna be one son of a bitch of a storm. I wonder if they call stuff off when this happens."

"Delphine says it happens every spring. She says the Temple's a big, solid place."

"Yeah, I know," Randall says. "But what if some big damn funnel cloud doesn't wait till we get *in* the Temple, and just picks that Mustang up and drops it down somewhere in Arkansas?" Randall scoops up the newspaper to his left, folds it into something capable of flying, and tosses it across the room to Ben. "Look at the bottom of the front page."

Expecting something about the weather, Ben unfolds the *Commercial Appeal* and discovers instead an Associated Press story in which Roy Wilkins, the distinguished head of the NAACP, voices great concern about Martin Luther King's Poor People's March. Wilkins notes that a certain "unruly" element has infiltrated the civil rights movement of late, and wonders whether the time is right for a huge gathering of Negroes in the nation's capital. He fears there is a "real danger" that, as in Memphis a few days past, things will get out of control and the movement will be dealt another blow.

"What do you think?" Randall asks Ben. "With people like Roy Wilkins lining up on the other side, what do we need with George Wallace and Lester Maddox?"

What Ben thinks is that perhaps he and Randall are friends again.

## TWENTY-SEVEN

She is awakened by the first loud ring of the telephone, and her first strong impulse is to ignore it; but this might be Ben calling from Memphis; she peers at the little alarm clock on the bedside table and sees that it's twenty minutes after seven; she's been out for an hour and a half, a much-needed nap after a night of little sleep. Where is Prosper? She rolls over to the edge of the bed and gets to her feet, stumbles into the living room, makes it to the phone just as it's beginning its sixth ring. She tries to make her voice sound as perky and awake as possible.

"Maddy?" It's not Ben, it's Jill. "Kristin said you called earlier. Did Ben ever call you?"

Indeed, Maddy had called her sister soon after getting home, when she was wide awake and eager to tell her closest confidante about the two a.m. misadventure. Rehashing it once more doesn't appeal to her, but she can't simply tell Jill it didn't happen. So she recounts the tale of the two a.m phone call.

"My God," Jill says. "And has he at least called you back?"

"Nope. Not yet." The sudden loud, discordant buzz of the intercom shocks her.

"Is that your door?" Jill says. "Jesus, how can you stand that sound?"

"I can't stand it. Can you hold on? I think that's Prosper."

"Who needs Ben?" She hears Jill say as she puts the phone down and heads to the front door. Maddy presses a button and shouts, "Who is it?" She releases the button and listens as a voice that might be Prosper's or might be the Shah of Iran's says something altogether unintelligible. Maddy presses the other button, the one that sends the electric signal to unlock the building's front door, and just to be safe she steps out on the landing and calls out Prosper's name. "Yeah, it's me!" he yells from three stories down.

She leaves the door open and returns to the phone. "We're going to a party," she says. "Did I tell you?"

"You did. Some gay boy who lives on the East Side, right? Why don't you just stay home and neck with Prosper? Ben deserves it."

"It's tempting," Maddy says. "But you're the one who's hot for Prosper. I wouldn't want to break your heart."

Prosper's clumping up the stairs has ceased; she waves as he appears in the doorway, dressed in his suede outfit and looking very sharp. She is suddenly self-conscious, in the remnants of her school garb, barefoot, unkempt. Prosper smiles broadly as he sees her. She cups the phone's mouthpiece with her hand and says, "What's the verdict?"

Still smiling, he shakes his head. It's a mixed signal, and in her confusion, wondering whether to ask a follow-up question or tell him it's Jill on the phone, she takes a step toward him and yanks the telephone off its table, sending it crashing, jangling to the floor. Prosper hastens past her to pick it up, and she speaks into the receiver, "Jesus. Are you still there, Jill?"

"I'm here. Can I talk to him?"

Handing him the receiver, Maddy says in a loud whisper, "What *happened*?"

Prosper smiles wanly as he takes the phone. The smile, by her interpretation, is not an indication of good fortune. "You don't know, or it's bad news?" He simply shakes his head again, now with the phone against his ear. "*Tell* me. Tell her you'll call her back."

But Jill, it would appear, has already begun speaking to Prosper, who makes a gesture of placation to Maddy. So she shrugs and walks past him into the bedroom, where she sits for a moment on the bed, then gets up and opens the closet door. Her wardrobe is not extensive: three dresses, one fit only for summer weather; three skirts; two fairly dressy pairs of pants; three pairs of jeans; assorted tops. At Chip Boyle's parties the minority population is the arty crowd: some people from work, and Prosper, and a couple of other college friends, while the majority population is the preppy crowd. As a member of the arty crowd, Maddy shouldn't have to be terribly concerned about what she wears, but perhaps because she's been conditioned by Ben, she suspects that all her clothes are shit. Once a month, on average, Ben takes her along to some political function or some New York social gathering, and invariably just

231

before they walk out the door he says something like, "You sure you want to wear that?" Or, "You think that's right for tonight?" As if she could turn around and pull her Dior out of the closet.

She half-listens to Prosper's side of the telephone conversation, and realizes when she's tuned in that he and Jill are speaking French, which is Jill's means of flirting with him. She unbuttons her school shirt and her school skirt and tosses them on the bed. She selects her purple cotton top, a narrow-cut buttoned shirt, and puts it on. She selects her navy blue denim mini-skirt, and puts that on. She kneels to open the bottom drawer of the tall chest, and fishes among her rather limited hosiery selection for the black tights, which should be cool enough for the party and warm enough for a trek through the park. Does she want to wear them over her underpants? No. She is in the process of unhooking her skirt when Prosper taps on the door. She stops. From without, he says, "Are you decent?"

"If you mean *adequate*, I guess I'd hope for a little better than that." She pushes the door fully open, the black tights in her left hand. Prosper still holds the phone against his left ear. His eyes roam from her eyes to her toes and back to her eyes.

"You look terrific," he says. He points to the phone. "She's getting her Larousse because she needs to ask me about a word."

Anticipating a bit of a delay, Maddy ducks back into the bedroom and closes the door behind her. She wonders, as she often has before, whether Prosper really is as much of a sweetheart as he seems to be, or if it's just that they don't live together. She unhooks the denim skirt and pulls it off along with her underpants, then maneuvers her way into the black tights and puts the skirt back on. She returns to the chest and brushes her hair; there is no mirror in the bedroom, but then her hairstyle isn't particularly intricate. She reopens the bedroom door and watches Prosper listen to Jill for a time, during which Prosper frequently looks at her and smiles. Eventually he speaks several sentences in rapid French, after which he asks Jill if she needs to speak to her sister again. That much Maddy can decipher. Evidently the answer is no, because Prosper says, "Okay, bye," and hangs up the phone.

"Tell me," Maddy says.

"We were talking about a movie she just saw."

"*No*, Prosper—tell me what happened today, for God's sake."

"You want the long version or the short version?"

"Whichever you want."

"Okay. Monday they tested me four times, Tuesday they tested me four times, I had high blood pressure every time. Today they tested me four times, I had high blood pressure every time. I was all set to go. It was five o'clock. They were closing the place down. This corporal I told you about, the guy who kind of goaded me into an argument..."

"Oh, Jesus," Maddy says.

"Yeah. He took me back one more time. The Dexedrine must've worn off, I don't know. It was as if the whole thing was a dream..."

Maddy takes three steps and hugs him. She feels his arms around her. "Can they do that? Don't they have some kind of protocol? Is this guy some kind of renegade sadist?"

"That's what I've been thinking about for the last three hours. I'll call the War Resisters League tomorrow, but I don't think there's anything I can do. I mean, there's no court of appeals, there's nobody I can report this guy to."

"So what happens now? They don't just pick you up and put you in a uniform?"

"No, it takes a while. I've got a few weeks to try to figure things out, maybe a couple of months..."

She releases him and stands back. "How are you doing?"

"Okay. I'm a little wasted, a little shellshocked, maybe."

"You want to forget about the party?"

"No, let's go. I'd like to drink some beer and see some people."

"You're the boss," she says. "Do we take the Eighty-Sixth Street crosstown?"

"I've got the car. It's just around the corner, on West End."

"So we could spend the night looking for a place to park on the East Side," Maddy says.

"No, I think God owes me one."

Prosper says, "Has Ben called you back?"

"No," she replies. "Let's not talk about Ben."

They're on the 86th Street transverse through Central Park, which separates the West Side from the East Side. To Maddy, who has lived in New York for three-quarters of a year, the West Side is a wondrous mixture of bohemia and ethnic weirdness, a constant source of surprises and challenges. The East Side--this part of it, as opposed to East Harlem, where she works--is sleek and cool and clean, uninviting and intimidating. She says, "Do you ever wonder how Chip can afford to live in that apartment?"

"He makes a lot of money," Prosper says.

## The Mountaintop

Chip is the up-and-coming star of the production department at Time-Life Books. Maddy has no knowledge of, nor interest in, what he does. "But that place has got to rent for seven or eight hundred a month. How much could they possibly pay him?"

"Fifteen hundred a month, at least," Prosper says.

Maddy quickly calculates that that's nearly four times what she makes. She and Ben pay $248 a month for their rent-controlled apartment. Her take-home pay is $430 a month, Ben's used to be about $600, so before he changed jobs they paid about a quarter of their income for housing. Chip must pay half of his, give or take. She says, "What's the story with him and Nicola Murray?"

"How do you mean?"

"They strike me as a very unlikely couple."

"He's always had the hots for Nicola. She's been going out with various people, friends or acquaintances of his, and now they're together. What's unlikely about that?"

Prosper brakes the Valiant as the light at Fifth Avenue turns red. Maddy says, "Well, I guess if you don't look too closely, they're kind of made for each other. She's actually more superficial than he is. But the whole thing is a charade."

"How do you mean?"

"Prosper, if there ever was a man who wouldn't have the slightest sexual interest in a woman, it's Chip."

Prosper is silent until the light changes. He turns right onto the avenue and says, "You're not being a little presumptuous?"

"Jesus," Maddy says, "just take a look at him."

Chip Boyle is tall and slender, with curly blond hair, a strong chin, an aquiline nose. He is dressed impeccably, a

235

vision in blue, tonight's ensemble comprising a European-cut dark navy suit made of brushed cotton, a lighter blue shirt, a fashionably wide tie with yellow sunflowers against an azure background, and cordovan loafers with slightly elevated heels. After Chip's outfit, the first thing Maddy notices is the music. It's the first Mamas and Papas' album—the one with them all crammed into the bathtub—which happens to be her least favorite record of all time. Standing by the open front door, Chip says, "Prosper and Madeleine! Come in out of the cold! And where's Benjamin?"

"In Tennessee," Maddy says. Chip knows full well that her name isn't Madeleine; it's his back-formation nickname for her.

"Doing good deeds?"

"I hope so."

"And Prosper? I'm assuming you're here because you haven't been drafted?"

"I can only stay a few minutes," Prosper says. "The MPs are waiting outside for me."

"Seriously," Chip says, "are you drafted or not?"

"Nothing conclusive yet," Prosper says, not altogether untruthfully.

"So—we'll say that no news is good news?"

"We'll say that."

"My gosh," Chip says, beaming, "don't let me forget! There's someone here asking for you. I invited him, but I never expected to see him here."

"Alex?" Prosper says.

"On the first guess," Chip replies.

This should pep things up, Maddy thinks. She says, "He's not here with Lydia, by any chance?"

"Solo," Chip says. "And looking rather respectable."

"I don't see him," Prosper says.

"He's probably in the bedroom," Chip replies. "I think people are smoking something in there."

It seems in fact that only the respectable contingent, the preppy contingent, has arrived so far. There are twelve or fifteen well-dressed young people seated or on foot in the living room or the kitchen, most of whom Maddy recognizes from previous parties or other Princeton gatherings. The apartment is the lowest level, technically the basement, of a townhouse owned by a wealthy widow who herself occasionally attends Chip's parties. It consists of this spacious living room, an actual kitchen with full-sized appliances, and a bedroom of reasonable dimensions on the other side of the kitchen.

"I don't see Nicola," Maddy says.

"She'll be here in good time," Chip says. "Go get yourself something to drink."

There is a wondrous selection of booze on the kitchen counter: bottles brought by guests and left there on the honor system. Maddy, who is no expert on such matters but knows the good stuff when she sees it, spots a Haig & Haig Pinch, a Chivas Regal, a couple of Wild Turkeys, a variety of liqueurs unfamiliar to her, in elegant bottles. She and Ben and Prosper tend to stick to the beer, which Chip generously supplies. Tonight there are four six-packs of Heineken on the bottom shelf of the refrigerator, untouched. Prosper removes two green bottles, uncaps them with the oversized church key on the counter, and hands one to Maddy.

They are approached by a man in a gray three-piece suit--tall, blond. She's met him before, but he's interchangeable with several other of these Princeton boys. He raises his drink in their direction and Prosper says, "Hi, Roger. You know Maddy, don't you?"

"Of course," says Roger. "Prosper, I heard you'd been called for your physical."

Prosper shakes his head. "Not me. Where'd you hear that?"

"I ran into Ben last week. He told me he'd just quit the Ford Foundation and joined up with the Kennedy campaign, and I could swear he said you had your physical coming up."

"Nope," Prosper says, "I'm sure I would've heard something about it, and I haven't heard a thing."

Maddy says, "Where do you stand with your draft board, Roger?"

"I'm getting a doctorate in divinity at Columbia, so they can't touch me."

"You're going to be a minister?"

Roger chuckles. "Oh, I don't think so. But say, where's Ben?"

"Ben's in Memphis."

"Memphis? What in God's name is he doing in Memphis? You don't mean Egypt, do you?"

"I'm pretty sure it's Tennessee, but now that you mention it, it might be Egypt. I'll check his pockets when he comes home and see if there are any scarabs."

Roger smiles appreciatively and lifts a pack of Gauloises from his shirt pocket, He extends the blue cigarette pack to Maddy and Prosper, who both decline. Still holding the drink in his left hand, Roger manipulates the pack so a cigarette pops up; he seizes it between his lips, takes a Zippo from his pants pocket, and lights the Gauloise. "Does it have anything to do with Martin Luther King and the garbage strike, and all that business?"

"I wouldn't be surprised," Maddy says.

"Don't you think that's dangerous ground?"

*The Mountaintop*

"How do you mean?"

"Well, for Bobby to associate himself with King. Let's say he gets the nomination, which I don't think is a sure thing. He's won himself some Negro votes in the north, but he probably had them anyway. He's won himself some votes from people on the left who might have sat the election out. Then you've got that solid south that always votes democratic. How are they going to feel about a candidate who's identified himself with someone like Martin Luther King?"

"Roger," Maddy says, "we're just conjecturing, for God's sake. But can't you imagine that even somebody running for president is capable of an act of conscience?"

"Wouldn't we all like to think so?" Roger says.

"I'd like to think so," Prosper says, "but I don't."

Maddy gives Prosper a theatrical elbow in the ribs. "Thanks for helping me out."

"What *do* you think?" Roger says.

"I think it would be both an act of conscience and a political act. I think at this point Kennedy's just trying to get the upper hand on McCarthy. McCarthy showed that Johnson could be beaten, Johnson saw the handwriting on the wall, and now Kennedy wants to put McCarthy away as fast as possible so he can concentrate on Hubert Humphrey. I don't think Kennedy's particularly concerned about the South. I think he figures he can win without the South."

"Prosper," Maddy says, "are you giving up on McCarthy?"

"Not completely," Prosper says. "I still think he's the best man. I think he has the most integrity. I think if Ben weren't working for Kennedy, or if you weren't involved with Ben, you'd like McCarthy as much as I do."

239

There is a moment during which no one speaks. Prosper and Maddy drink from their Heineken bottles in unison. Roger exhales a plume of French cigarette smoke and says, "How about Nixon?"

"God help us," Maddy says.

"I like him," Roger says. "Like him a lot."

Someone, probably Chip himself, turns the stereo up just as "I Saw Her Again" begins, and Maddy says, "Boy, do I hate this song. Let's find Alex."

Their search is not a lengthy one. Alex sits cross-legged on Chip's double bed, wearing what appears to be a blue summer suit, accompanied by two hippyish couples in bell-bottoms and buckskins. The aroma of cannabis is strong and unmistakable, and Maddy has a moment of admiration for Chip's tolerance. Prosper says, "Hey!"

Alex turns and says, "Prosper! How the fuck are you, man?"

"Good," Prosper replies. "How about you?"

"Great, man. Hey, Maddy…where's Ben?"

"In Memphis."

"Wow…Tennessee, or Egypt?"

"I've heard that one before," Maddy says. "But you know what? If he ever comes home, I'll see if he's got any hieroglyphics in his wallet."

"Seriously—what's he doing in Memphis?"

"Working for Kennedy."

"Right--I forgot," Alex says. He turns to the other people, whom Maddy doesn't know, and says, "Guy had this great job, and he quit to work for Kennedy."

"Somebody's gotta do it," says a tall, bearded man who wears huge black boots. "Hey, Prosper," he adds. Prosper introduces Maddy to Jake, the man in the boots, and Terry, who play in a band they organized at Princeton, and Jake introduces the two girls as Monica and Eileen, both of whom wear extremely short skirts and lots of eye makeup. Jake, who has been holding a joint, passes it to Prosper, and Alex says, "Check this stuff out, man, it's unbelievable." Prosper takes a drag and hands the joint to Maddy, who sucks in a tiny bit of smoke and passes the joint to Alex. She's not much of a marijuana aficionada, and after about fifteen seconds she's as stoned as she's ever been. She'll stick to Heineken for the rest of the night.

## TWENTY-EIGHT

Alex keeps remembering that he wants to ask Maddy about Lydia, but then someone will say something that distracts him or he himself will go off on some sort of ramble. Then he'll remember again. Obviously she knows what's up with Lydia because she sees her every day and they hang out together. There's a little break in the conversation; everybody's just been laughing about something, and he's on the verge of talking to Maddy, but what exactly is he going to say? Like: Hey, Maddy, do you know where the hell Lydia's been spending the night the last couple of days? He's already told Jake and Terry, and whoever these two chicks are, that Lydia

241

just didn't feel like coming tonight. So the thing to do will be at some point to take Maddy aside and just casually ask her.

Other than the Lydia problem, Alex is feeling pretty great. He went to class today. He's going to go to class tomorrow. He stopped by that bar on Columbus, the Flor de Cienfuegos, on his way over here, sat on a stool for half an hour with the pistol in his pocket, chatting in his more than passable Spanish with a different bartender, but the guy Julio never showed up. So he'll check out the bar again tomorrow. But right now he's feeling really mellow. Sure, he'd like to know what's going with Lydia and sure, he'd like to get his camera and his Nagra back, but he's still got a baggy with half of Elliot's incredible dope and he keeps replaying the conversation with Leo, the used car salesman, and in his head Leo sounds more and more like a New Jersey Italian version of Sylvester the Cat, all flustered and sputtering and ineffectual.

Here in Chip's bedroom, Maddy has been trying to explain to Jake what exactly Ben does for the Kennedy campaign, and Jake's talking about how cool it is that Ben's on the front lines. Ben has always been a little too straight and upstanding for Alex's taste, but in the last few months he's been a real pain in the ass. Alex will acknowledge that they've been going in different directions, and that Ben has the right not to approve of what Alex chooses to do in the spiritual and recreational arenas, but it feels to Alex that if they were approaching each other on the street, Ben would cross to the other side to avoid him. Prosper, on the other hand, is a true and dependable friend. Which reminds him that he keeps remembering and forgetting to ask Prosper what's going on the with the draft thing.

Jake says, "I mean, shit, I keep going to school just to get my deferment. That's fucked up frontwards and backwards.

242

If it wasn't for the war, I could concentrate on music and forget about school. And if Johnson decides they need another fifty thousand, a hundred thousand troops over there, my draft board's gonna reach a point where they say hell, let's go after all those assholes with the student deferments."

"They're doing it already," Prosper says. "Everybody's got a quota. They're taking married guys in more and more parts of the country."

"So the thing is," Jake says, "I fucking admire what Ben's doing, but if I dropped out of NYU and went to work for Kennedy, they'd draft me in five minutes."

Alex says, "Ben doesn't have to worry about that, does he. They can't touch him, because his father was killed in World War Two."

Prosper says, "How do you mean that, Alex?"

"Just what I said. Ben's free to do anything he wants to. The rest of us aren't."

Maddy says, "Alex, if you didn't have to worry about being drafted, would you be out working for someone who's trying to stop the war?"

This Alex finds consummately amusing, and he bursts into a sharp chortle, but quickly recognizes that no one else is laughing. He can't put into words what's so funny—whether it's the image of himself wearing black shoes and a Kennedy button or the very notion of a hypothetical situation in which he'd be doing anything other than exactly what he's doing. He says, "It's all bullshit."

"What's all bullshit?" Maddy says.

"Look, maybe Kennedy's a little different from Johnson. Maybe this politician is a little different from that politician. It's like saying…maybe this fart doesn't smell quite as bad as that one." He laughs at his own analogy; so do Jake, Terry, and the two chicks, but not Prosper and Maddy, who says, "You don't think Kennedy wants to end the war?"

"I think he's using the war to get elected, which is fine. If I voted, I'd vote for him. But look, his brother *started* the fucking war..."

"He's not his brother," Maddy says.

"No, but I think if it weren't..." He searches for a word, and after several seconds resumes, "...*expedient* to be against the war, it wouldn't be very high in his priorities."

"I think that's completely wrong," Maddy says.

"Well, sure. You think he's an idealist. People always make that mistake. They think politicians are idealists because some politicians pretend to be idealists, they seem to be idealists. But all they're interested in is power. It's human nature. To be a politician, to *want* to be a politician, you have to be an egotistical asshole. They seek power, and power corrupts, so when they get powerful they become *corrupt* egotistical assholes."

Prosper says, "That's some pretty profound stuff, Alex."

It hasn't come out as lucid as Alex intended it, which is one of the disadvantages of being utterly stoned, but he feels he's gotten his point across. "At least it's right," he says.

Moments later, Chip appears in the doorway and invites everyone outside for a game of Henry James, which is an incredibly boring word association game Prosper and Ben used to play at Princeton. Alex stays put, assuming Jake, Terry, and the girls will too, but they all exit to the living room. Whereupon Alex remembers yet again that he hasn't asked Maddy about Lydia, and whether she'll still feel like talking to him after he's insulted Bobby Kennedy.

If she won't, there's not much point to sticking around here. He'd like to talk to Prosper, but this Henry James game might go on for hours, so maybe what he should do is stick a couple of Heinekens in his pockets and go home. Or not. He's leaning back on Chip's bed when he hears a discreet tapping on the open door. He looks over to see…what's her name, Chip's girlfriend, who was a fixture at Colonial Club in Princeton when she used to go out with some other preppy asshole. "Hey," he says. "Bathroom's available."

"Actually," she says, "I heard there might be some pot available."

"That too," Alex says, getting a good look at her as she moves toward the bed. She's not bad looking, if you don't mind the style. She wears a fairly conservative skirt, just above knee-length, and those whitish stockings that kind of turn him on, and semi-high-heeled black shoes, and pink lipstick, and her blond hair and her eyebrows look as if they're starched, as if they were manufactured for a mannequin. He says, "I wouldn't have figured you for a dope smoker."

"Why not?" She says, sitting across from him on the bed.

"Because you're more of the Chivas type."

"Are they mutually exclusive?"

Good question. "I suppose they aren't," Alex says, "except I guess I mean not so much that you'd *drink* only expensive Scotch, but it's like you walked out of a magazine ad for expensive Scotch."

"Is that bad?" She asks.

He's begun rolling a new joint. "Not bad at all. I just never figured you for a dope smoker."

She says, "You're Alex, right? I'm Nicola."

Of course. "Sure," he says, "You and Chip."

245

"You're Ben and Prosper's friend. And you go out with that...Spanish girl?"

"Venezuelan," Alex says.

"I haven't seen her tonight."

"Nope. Me neither." He licks the edge of the rolling paper and seals the joint.

"So...all's not well?"

"Not really sure," Alex says. He hands her the joint and clicks open his Zippo. She takes a huge drag and sucks it in. He half expects her to explode in coughs, but she knows what she's doing. She hands him the joint and he tokes modestly, inasmuch as he's as high as he wants to be. She's closed her eyes and leaned against the headboard, so the two of them are parallel, and after holding the smoke in for a good thirty or forty seconds she exhales, then breathes quickly for another twenty seconds or so before she says, "Wow."

"Pretty good stuff, eh?"

"Amazing," she says. She takes the joint from him and has another drag, this one not nearly as enormous. After a moment she says, "God, I feel tingly all over." She wears a white blouse made of silk or satin or some such fabric that Alex would at first have classified as conservative, but as he gazes at her now he realizes it's fairly translucent, and he can perceive the outline of her breasts. She wiggles first her left foot and then her right until both her shoes are off. "What do you do these days?" She says.

"Film school. Columbia," he replies. "How about you?"

"I work at an art gallery a few blocks from here, on Madison." She offers the joint to Alex, but he shakes his head. She takes another quick drag, holds the smoke in for a few seconds, and talks as she exhales. "Summerfield Gallery. You know it?"

"Nope," he says.

"Pop art. It's a lot of fun because some of it's real bullshit and some of it's just kind of bullshit, and nobody knows which is which."

"What about Warhol?"

"I'd say…just kind of bullshit."

"Why?"

"Why just kind of bullshit as opposed to real bullshit, or as opposed to not bullshit at all?"

"I think he's great."

"He's a great promoter," Nicola says. "He's kind of the Aquarian P.T. Barnum, except instead of Siamese twins and elephants, he's got silkscreens and soup cans."

"What about his films?"

"Would you rather watch twenty-four hours' worth of the Empire State Building, or a long closeup of a man's face as he's getting a blowjob? Allegedly."

Alex laughs. "You're pretty hip." The word "blowjob" is still sinking into his brain, and he likes what it's doing there.

She says, "Do you want any more of this?"

He takes the joint, licks the tips of his thumb and forefinger, and extinguishes it between them, then drops it in the bedside ashtray. Propped on his elbow he leans above her. He's on Chip Boyle's bed, this is Chip's girlfriend (allegedly), and Chip is right outside, but what the hell. He gives her a tentative kiss on the lips, figuring the worst she can do is pull away. If she tells Chip, what is there to lose? She doesn't pull away, not by any means; she opens her mouth a bit, and Alex is happy to provide his tongue.

Things proceed rather rapidly. He unbuttons the silken blouse and spends a fair amount of time first touching her breasts, which in his current state is an exquisite experience in itself, and then licking them, which is altogether different but just as enjoyable. She runs her fingers through his hair and softly coos; he feels her heartbeat, which seems extraordinarily fast, and that excites him further. With his head still on her chest, he moves his hand down the fabric of her skirt until it ends, then begins crawling along those lovely, erotic white stockings, until he reaches leg's apex, where he pauses. "Yes," Nicola says. "Don't stop."

"Should I take them off?" It's not clear to Alex whether he's referring to her stockings, her panties, or all of her clothes. He'd accept a *yes* to anything.

"Close the door," she says.

He slides off the bed and has to walk around it, dealing with a huge erection, to get to the door, which he closes gently, muting the voices and the music from the living room. When he turns around, Nicola, still on her back, has bent her knees and hiked her skirt up enough so she can pull down her stockings and panties. He would have enjoyed doing that, but this is hardly a bad development. He undoes his belt and begins to unbutton his blue suit pants when she whispers, "No!" He stops. "Not on the first date," she says.

Is this a joke? She slides to the far side of the bed, away from the door to the living room, near the door to the bathroom and says, "Come here," she says, more as an invitation than a command, and Alex does so, conscious of the bulge in his pants. She sits now on the side of the bed, skirt at mid-thigh, legs naked, and says, "Do you remember what the little cake says in *Alice in Wonderland*?"

What the fuck is she talking about? What does *Alice in Wonderland* have to do with Nicola lying here pantyless on Chip's bed? The little cake? Ah! He says, "Eat me?"

She gives an appreciative nod. He is certainly aware of the expression in this connotation, but never imagined he'd hear it from the likes of Chip's pink-lipstick-wearing girlfriend. "I'd like that," he says, and in a flash he's knelt between her legs. It's dark in here, but he knows his way around, to an extent. It's not difficult to get his tongue inside her, but once he's there he's not entirely sure what to do, dealing with this warm, soft, salty area. After half a minute Nicola says, "Not there," and Alex reflexively starts to back out, until he feels her hands at the back of his head. "Up," she says, and his tongue ascends the hollow an inch or so. "Up, up," she says, and he goes by gradations until he's nearly at the top of the cleft and there's this little protrusion. "Yes," she says. "Stay there. Yes."

## TWENTY-NINE

The origins of Henry James are not exactly clear, but it is an evolution of a game Prosper and Ben used to play in prep school, and it was they who introduced it to Chip, who refined their version and turned it into a party game. Henry James has no connection to the eponymous literary figure beyond his being one of the more prominent possessors of two first names, and thus two names that can be built upon in either direction. So Player One begins the primitive version of the game by saying, "Henry James." Now Player Two, who may add a name at either front or back, says, "O. Henry James." And Player One says, "O. Henry James Madison." And Player Two says, "Sadaharu Oh Henry James Madison." Now Player One, in a move that would be abjured by purists, says, "Sadaharu Oh Henry James Madison Avenue." The purist argument is that the additions must be limited to names of people. The revisionist argument is that the game is a lot more fun, and lasts longer, when it's wide open.

Chip's party variation of the game may be played with unlimited participants; everyone is given a piece of paper and two initials, the latter chosen at random from a book or magazine or newspaper, whatever happens to be handy. Players then have three minutes to construct as long and interesting a chain as they can, the one stipulation being that front and back additions can be no more than one name/word longer than each other.

For her part, Maddy found the original version boring and frustrating, because Ben has a bottomless knowledge of minor figures of American history and baseball players, while Prosper knows the name of every person ever to have recorded a rock and roll song and is Ben's equal on baseball players. But give her this free-association game and she's not bad at all.

Prosper has acquired his third Heineken; Chip has turned down the music (Sam & Dave's *Double Dynamite*) and handed out pencils and paper. Maddy and Prosper sit cross-legged near the front door. She looks around the room: There will be perhaps twenty players, the bulk of whom are Chip's preppy friends; little competition there, nor will there be from the two bedroom longhairs and their girlfriends, she imagines.

Prosper says, "This is going to be interesting."

"How do you mean?" Maddy asks.

"I mean a couple of things, I guess. One is that this is a pretty weird group to be playing Henry James, and two is that I think my brain may have stopped working."

"But you could drive your car."

"Yes. I could drive my car. You want to drive somewhere with me?"

"I didn't mean that. I meant that your brain was working well enough so that you could drive your car."

"I know," he says.

It sinks in that Prosper's made a sort of proposition, which is unlike him even under the canopy of banter. If indeed it was a proposition. She turns to face him, and gains no edification; Prosper wears the grin of someone who's consumed two and a half beers and smoked some strong marijuana. He is rather better looking in this state, Maddy observes, when his facial muscles are relaxed.

Chip holds a copy of *The Fountainhead*. How preposterous, Maddy thinks. He flips it open with his left hand, points with his right, and announces, "The first letter is a...*C*. And the second letter is a...*W*." There are scattered groans from cognoscenti. Roger--the Richard Nixon admirer from the kitchen--shouts, "Do it over, Chip. Those are shitty letters."

"More challenging this way," Chip says, and Maddy realizes that Chip is quite a bit more tipsy than when she and Prosper arrived. She had seen Nicola in the kitchen when they first emerged from the bedroom, but now a quick scan of the living room shows no sign of her. Perhaps she's in the bathroom. Maddy, for that matter, wouldn't mind a quick trip to the bathroom herself, two Heinekens having gone through her rather rapidly. But the game is about to start. A girl unknown to Maddy, sitting on the couch, agrees to be timekeeper, which involves giving warnings at the one- and two-minute marks. She stares at her watch for what seems like a day and a half before saying, "Go!"

The only C.W. Maddy can think of is Christopher Wren. Where can she go with Christopher Wren? Was there a baseball player named Joe Christopher? What about the man who married Richard Burton's ex-wife after Burton and Elizabeth Taylor ran off together? He was Something Christopher. Next to her on the floor, Prosper writes frantically for a few seconds, then grumbles. Around the room, no one's pencil appears to be doing much. Jake from the bedroom catches her eye; he whispers, "Fucking impossible." She thinks of Richard Burton's wife's name: Sybil. And then immediately she thinks of Christopher's name: Jordan. That would give her Jordan Christopher Wren. Big deal. She needs a first name to go with Jordan. Jordan Almond, Jordan River. Would they accept the actor Louis Jourdan? But wait! She has an inspiration just as the timekeeping girl says, "Two minutes." *Saint* Christopher. *Eva Marie Saint* Christopher. *Christmas Eva Marie Saint* Christopher. Would they allow that? *Hail Merry Christmas Eva Marie Saint* Christopher Wren. She's stretching the rules with abandon. *Nathan Hale Merry Christmas Eva Marie Saint* Christopher Wren. But she's done everything in one direction; it won't count unless she can make additions on the *Wren* side. She thinks of birds. But of course if she knew any names of wrens, they wouldn't have surnames. It would be *Humphrey's Wren*, not *Wren Humphrey*, although *Wren Humphrey* wouldn't be a bad title for the lost manuscript of Tobias Smollett.

## The Mountaintop

"One minute!" announces the timekeeping girl. Prosper writes something more. Terry from the bedroom has stretched out on the carpet, supine, eyes closed. Maddy silently sounds out the words: Kris-toe-fer-ren, renna, renno, *rennay.* Christopher *René Descartes*! But that's not going to get her very far. Descartes before the horse? Is there another René in the house? *René Clair. René Clair Booth Luce. René Clair Booth Luce Woman. Of the Night. Errant.*

"Time!" There are murmurs of disgruntlement around the room. Jake, as if the cannabis has attenuated his vocabulary, mutters, "That was fucking impossible." Prosper says in Maddy's ear, "How'd you do?"

"I think it might be a good one," she says. "How about you?"

"Slow start. But I got a little rush at the end."

Maddy is suddenly aware that her need to pee has become urgent. Chip says, "Okay, who's going to start?" He looks in her and Prosper's direction and Maddy violently shakes her head, pointing toward the other side of the room. "Andrea?" Chip calls to a girl on the couch. "How about it?"

Maddy whispers to Prosper, "I have to excuse myself for a minute."

"What if it's your turn to read?"

"I'll be back in two minutes, unless Alex wants to explain politics some more."

She gets to her feet and moves along the perimeter of the room, into the kitchen, noting that the bedroom door is closed, as it was not before. Alex seeking peace and quiet? Alex napping? She makes the softest little tap on the door and opens it cautiously. No Alex at all, it would seem, just the rear view of someone female—Nicola, from the hairdo—leaning somewhat backward, hands behind her on the bed. It's possible

253

that Nicola is murmuring, making some sort of sound, but the greater audio from the living room makes that doubtful. Maddy feels enough trepidation so that, all things being equal, she would back out the door and wait a few minutes. But short of squatting in the kitchen sink, there is no other place to pee.

She pads quickly around the bed. Indeed that is Nicola murmuring—purring is more like it. "Excuse me," Maddy says. "So sorry." And as she turns the corner she can't help seeing someone kneeling on the floor, his head under Nicola's skirt. Someone in Alex's blue pants. Of all the things in the world she never imagined she'd see, Alex with his head between Nicola Murray's legs is very high on the list. There is no retreating. "Very sorry," she says, averting her eyes, as she slips into the bathroom. Inside, she immediately turns the cold water tap on full blast.

She takes way longer than she needs, giving them a good three or four minutes to get themselves separated and reassembled, and when she leaves the bathroom the bedroom has been deserted.

\*\*\*

Alex is really getting into it, feeling a fine sort of rhythm building as he works his way in this new territory, aided by occasional whispered directions from above. "Faster, yes, little faster, just there, good, yes." It's all the more exciting as he pictures how Nicola will reciprocate, with those luscious, pink-tinted lips. He senses the muscles in her upper thighs beginning to stiffen; this is new, and he has to restrain himself from upping the tempo. Just then he hears a voice, not Nicola's. "Excuse me…So sorry." My God, is that Maddy? Should he stop? Seconds later, from nearer by, "Very sorry." He feels her footfalls as she passes by, hears the bathroom door open and close just behind him, hears the water start to run. Was it

Maddy? Did she recognize him? Of course she did. Will this get back to Lydia?

"Don't stop," Nicola whispers. "*Do not stop.*" Alex obeys. Maybe he speeds things up just a little. Certainly his hands, which have encompassed the top of her buttocks all the while, increase their grip, and yes, those thigh muscles tense in earnest, squeezing his ears so they burn. "Oh, God," Nicola says, in a voice exceeding a whisper. She repeats that four, five, six times as her fingers rake through his hair. This goes on so long that Alex is convinced Maddy or maybe not-Maddy will emerge from the bathroom with Nicola still in mid-orgasm.

But the water keeps running, the toilet doesn't flush, Nicola's thighs ease up, her hands come to a stop, and she says— again in a whisper—"Okay."

Alex slides out from under. He suspects that his knees have gone to sleep. Nicola says, "Get up!"

He gets up, somewhat shakily, his mind focusing again on the next act. They'll have to leave, then perhaps subtly come back. Lock themselves in the bathroom. Nicola's pulling on her panties. She says, "That was lovely."

"I certainly enjoyed it," he replies.

"Look," she says, "we have to get out of here. Can you do something about that?" She points to the protrusion in his crotch.

"I was hoping you would."

She's finished pulling up her second stocking. How do they stay up? "Some other time, okay?" She says. "I owe you one."

***

"Everything okay?" Prosper says.

"Yeah. I got delayed," Maddy replies. Jake is reading his Henry James entry, which is brief and incoherent.

255

"Alex still ranting?"

"Right," she says. "Well, not exactly. How's it going in here?"

"I read mine."

"Oh, God…sorry I missed it. How was it?"

"Not bad. I had William Carlos Williams in the middle and Roger said it was illegal because the C. W. had to be a person's entire name, not just the last two thirds of it…"

"An interesting point," Maddy says.

"But Chip said I invented the game, so I could do anything I want. It gave me a sense of power."

"How are you otherwise?"

"Not bad. A little drunk. And Alex's dope was pretty strong."

"I'll say." Maddy spots Nicola across the room, standing next to Chip, looking her customary pink-lipped, white-stockinged proper self. A girl Maddy doesn't know reads, "Clint Walker Percy Dovetonsils." Not bad, but ineligible because nothing precedes the mandatory C. W. in the middle. Where is Alex? Lurking in the corner of the kitchen; somehow she missed him when she left the bedroom.

"Madeleine," Chip calls. "There's no one left but you."

She reads: *Nathan Hale Merry Christmas Eva Marie Saint Christopher Wren é Clair Booth Luce woman of the night errant.*

Silence. Are people stunned, or didn't it make any sense? Eventually, Prosper says, "Wow!" and Chip claps his hands. A few other people pick up the applause, and Maddy catches Nicola's eye; she's nodding, perhaps approvingly, perhaps as some sort of warning.

"That was amazing," Prosper says. "Possibly the best party Henry James ever."

256

## The Mountaintop

In an unnecessarily loud voice, Roger says, "Will someone please explain for me—is there a dessert named after Christopher Wren? Is this something I don't know about?"

By ten thirty or so the party has thinned out considerably. It's Wednesday night, and people have to get up in the morning and go to work or school. In Maddy's case, of course, it's both, but she's not eager to go back to the apartment. It's difficult to imagine at this point which would be worse: getting another middle-of-the-night call from Ben, or not getting a call from Ben at all. Prosper is involved in an animated conversation with Alex, Jake, and one of the short-skirted girls. From afar, Maddy had witnessed a brief kitchen encounter between Alex and Nicola that didn't appear to end amicably.

She's opening her fourth Heineken when Alex intercepts her by the refrigerator. "Hey, Maddy," he says, "I meant to talk to you earlier…"

She waits for the sentence to be completed, but it doesn't happen. She has a sip of beer. Alex seems to be staring at her feet. He says, "Was that you in the bedroom?"

"It was."

"Look, I don't know what happened. It was…spontaneous."

It's her turn to talk, but she has no idea what to say. "I didn't figure it was something you'd been planning," she says, with no malice intended.

"I was going to ask you about Lydia," he says.

"Okay…"

"Do you know where she's been? I haven't seen her since Monday morning."

"I have a pretty good idea," Maddy says.

257

"Well…" Alex shrugs his shoulders and briefly makes eye contact. "Is she all right? Is everything okay?"

"She's fine, Alex. She's pretty upset with you. I guess you know that."

"You're not gonna tell her about this?"

"I'll tell you what—I won't say anything about this to her as long as you don't expect me to tell you anything more *about* her."

Alex appears to be mulling that over. It's an awfully good deal, by Maddy's estimation. "Will you tell her that I've been going to class?"

"She'll be happy to hear that."

It's past eleven, and Prosper sits in an armchair across from Chip and Nicola, who are on the couch. The apartment is in remarkably good order, in part because Chip has made the rounds every twenty minutes or so, collecting empty bottles and used plastic cups, emptying ashtrays. Maddy stands behind Prosper's chair and says, "We should go."

"We were just talking about the four of us getting something to eat."

Chip says, "Do you know about the papaya place at Eighty-sixth and Third? Best hot dogs in the world."

"It's too late, Chip," Maddy says.

"We could drive over there," Prosper says. "Be there in five minutes."

"I have to be up at seven," Maddy says.

Nicola says, "I'm pretty wiped out, too."

"Okay," Chip says. "Some other time, then."

"It was a lovely party, Chip," Maddy says. "Nice to see you, Nicola." She immediately regrets her choice of words, but Nicola simply smiles and says, "Nice seeing you too."

## The Mountaintop

It's a brisk, clear spring night as they walk along
Madison Avenue on the short trip back to the Valiant.
Prosper's looking just the slightest bit unsteady, and Maddy
asks him if he's okay to drive. "I'm fine," he says. "But if
you'd rather drive that's good with me."

"That's not the part I'm concerned about, driving across
town."

"Then drive me back to Connecticut."

She laughs. "Seriously. You've stayed on the couch
before. It's comfortable enough, right?"

"I'm serious too," he says. "You're in a union, aren't
you? You've got sick days. Come spend the night in my aunt's
seaside villa, take the day off. I'll drive you back tomorrow
afternoon."

"I've got a union, but I've also got to deal with Mrs.
Sálazar. She puts you through endless shit if you don't give her
three days' notice that you're going to be sick. I had to tell her
Lydia would be late yesterday morning and she treated me like
a conspirator. Which I was, in a way."

"Kind of defeats the purpose of sick days, doesn't it?"
Prosper says.

Maddy finds herself weighing Victoria Sálazar's grim,
suspicious visage and the apartment, the call from Ben she'd
rather not answer even if it comes, and it probably won't, the
little dogs waking her in the middle of the night anyway—
versus Prosper's aunt's house on the Long Island Sound. There
are other reasons not to go: She hasn't brought her wallet, so
she has no money or identification. She has parent-teacher
conferences tomorrow night and her school bag is sitting by the
front door in the apartment. She says, "You think you could get
me back to school in time for the first period after lunch?"

259

## THIRTY

When Ben asks for directions at the front desk, the young man in his Holiday Inn blazer says, "Mason Temple? You sure you wanna go *there*?"

It's not really a bad part of town, though, just a couple of miles south of the hotel. There isn't a white face to be seen as they approach the huge, rectangular brick building—not many faces at all, actually, with the rain already falling fairly hard and the wind strong enough in gusts to make the Mustang shudder. But in front of the Temple itself there is a throng of folks with umbrellas, waiting to get in. And there's no place to park within a two-block radius.

"Jesus," Randall says. "This is gonna be trouble later on, if this storm gets all biblical and we're parked half a mile away."

They're stopped behind a bus, a private bus unloading scores of black men. "How shall we do this?" Ben says. "You want to get out now, and I'll park?"

"Or I could park it," Randall says. "You've been doing all the grunt work."

"I don't mind," Ben says. "Delphine said she'd be waiting at the front entrance for us. If you could just look for her. It shouldn't take me more than fifteen minutes to park and walk back here."

He chooses to drive east, away from downtown and the river, and indeed he finds an ample space on a dark street not five blocks away, then walks briskly back toward the Temple, a white boy in a black neighborhood in inclement weather. Ben, who always packs so carefully, has not thought to bring a raincoat, so he and Randall have both picked up cheap umbrellas at the hotel gift shop. The night remains surprisingly warm, but the wind is in his face and its gusts are intermittently spectacular; he wonders if his umbrella will survive the short walk. A block from the Temple he stops at the curb to let traffic pass, and looks upward: this is as foreboding as any sky he has ever seen.

Nearing the building, he's not sure whether to be on the lookout for Randall or Delphine or both, and he's suddenly conscious that normally when he's trying to pick Randall out of a group, the first priority is to look for the black guy. That won't work tonight.

It's Delphine who waits for him, in any case. Look for the very light-skinned girl. Under an umbrella of her own she waits by the front entrance to the Temple, as promised; she wears a dark, modest skirt and a white blouse buttoned nearly to her neck, and lipstick. She sees him several seconds after he's spotted her, and she smiles and waves. Ben's first instinct is to embrace her, but he thinks better of it. There are forty or fifty or sixty people in their immediate proximity and none of them are white. He extends his hand instead, feeling foolish, and she takes it. He says, "Did you see Randall?"

"He went in," she says, as they turn and head up the stone steps. "He saw some ministers that you all had lunch with. They're saving us seats, right up front, they said." He lets his arm touch hers, and he says in a voice slightly lower than normal, "You look beautiful."

"Thank you," she replies. They've entered the Temple and it's huge--a vast auditorium containing what Ben guesses must be a couple of thousand people. Above the ground level there is a balcony, that too filling up. Delphine says, "I should tell you that evidently there's a good chance Doctor King isn't going to make it."

They're at the beginning of an aisle, at a bottleneck, waiting for people to file into their seats. "But everybody's here to see him, right?"

"It's a rally," Delphine says. "There's gonna be all kinds of speakers, from the union, and labor people from New York, and local preachers. But yeah, I don't think half this many folks, a tenth this many folks would've showed up except for Doctor King."

They're inching down the aisle now. "What's the problem?" Ben says. "Is it the weather? Is the airport closed?"

"No. This is just what I heard from the ministers talking to Randall ten minutes ago. One of them talked to Jim Lawson, who kind of got all this whole strike organized, and he said Doctor King was back at the motel, just exhausted, and he was hoping to skip this thing and get a good night's sleep."

Ben is of course not interested in listening to the labor leaders and the local ministers. He wants to see the great man, Martin Luther King, and short of that he'd just as soon not be here, especially when the alternative could be several hours spent alone with Delphine.

He is now conscious of what must be a great flash of lightning, inasmuch as its light penetrates the huge, opaque windows high above them sufficiently to illuminate the vast Temple. He touches Delphine's arm and manages to say, "Lovely weather we're having," before being interrupted by an extraordinarily loud clap of thunder, at a frequency not attained by the northeastern thunder he's known--at a higher, more savage pitch that hurts his ears. He has jumped, or twitched, or shuddered, because Delphine, grasping his wrist, says, "We're okay in here."

262

## The Mountaintop

It is the worst kind of frustration, this double denial.
There is no sign of King, so surely it's true: he's not going to
speak. And as speaker after speaker drones on, Ben cannot
suppress these intermittent surges of arousal, sitting virtually
pressed against Delphine, their legs touching, her breast
brushing his shoulder when she shifts in the pew. Randall is at
her other flank; the integrated, ecumenical queue is to Randall's
right. Ben has no idea who these people are to his own left,
here in perhaps the twelfth or thirteenth row--excellent seats for
a show you don't want to see. Delphine has identified for him
most of the people sitting on the stage, including Ralph
Abernathy, King's second-in-command in the SCLC, and the
man who will take King's place tonight. There are a couple of
white men seated on stage, northern union officials, two white
pastors in this very row, and that's about it. There would be, in
the abstract of Ben's imagination, something thrilling or at least
exotic about being the only white guy at a *real* Negro church
service, with a pastor preaching fire and brimstone and the
congregation shouting back encouragement. But there's no
intimacy here. The place is too huge, and while the weather
outside has gotten more and more violent, as if trying to provide
drama, it seems instead to detract from the proceedings inside,
in that whenever someone onstage gets going, elicits a few calls
of *Amen!* or *You tell it, brother!* from the crowd, he is upstaged
by a crash of thunder or a ninety-mile-an-hour wind gust.

It is a few minutes before nine o'clock when Ben is
suddenly conscious of a collective murmur around him, and
before he's had the opportunity for much conjecture, Delphine
squeezes his arm and whispers, "There he is." Ben spots a
figure making his way to a chair on the stage, just behind the
pulpit, and realizes that this, without question, is Martin Luther

263

King. The murmur becomes a buzz, as all around Mason Temple people are surely nudging their friends and loved ones and pointing out their leader's arrival.

For his part, Ben feels a chill of anticipation, and brushes his hand across Delphine's knee, as if to apologize for his unspoken complaints, to reacknowledge his desire, to attest that he too cherishes this moment, and what's to come--and an instant after this precarious touch there is another lightning/thunder combination that rattles the building.

All that stands between Martin Luther King and his constituency now is the Reverend Ralph Abernathy, who has taken the pulpit to introduce his boss moments after King's arrival, and has rambled on for (by Ben's calculation) twenty-three minutes. Abernathy has provided a sort of synopsis of King's career, which has of course not been entirely uninteresting, but Ben wonders whether Abernathy isn't doing this for Abernathy's benefit, seizing his moment in the tornado and making the most of it. Ben looks again at his watch; it's twenty-five minutes past nine now, and surely it was just nine o'clock when Abernathy started talking. Ben glances to his right; Randall and the ministers, and Delphine, remain rapt. Is it courtesy, or do they actually enjoy listening to this gasbag? The rest of the audience isn't exactly in his sway, if the increasing incidence of coughing and throat-clearing is any indication.

But here comes a crescendo. Abernathy's voice rises; the crowd senses it. Yes! He's actually speaking the words, "... the Reverend Martin Luther King, Junior!" and here is King, smiling broadly, beaming, Ben would say, walking to the pulpit.

There is a phenomenal moment, just as King stands ready to begin to speak, when there is absolute silence among the audience, and the storm is still, and the only sound in the building is provided by two huge window fans that have been turned on sometime quite recently. It is as if Heaven and Earth have silenced themselves in respect, while the rumbling fans contribute a twentieth-century flourish, a poor substitute for sounding trumpets. All of this combines, in any case, to send a major chill down Ben's spine. He's sitting thirty or forty feet from one of the men he most admires in the world, sitting leg-to-leg with this fabulous girl Delphine, and life is as close to perfect as it ever might be.

"Something is happening in Memphis," King says in his rich, mellow preacher's voice. "Something is happening in our world." He pauses, and there are shouts of encouragement from the crowd. "If I were standing at the beginning of time and the Almighty said to me, 'Martin Luther King, which age would you like to live in?' Strangely enough, I would turn to the Almighty and say, 'If you allow me to live just a few years in the second half of the twentieth century, I *will* be happy.' Now, that's a strange statement to make, because the world is all messed up. The nation is sick, trouble is in the land, confusion all around. That's a strange statement, but I know somehow, that *only when it's dark enough* can you see the stars. And I see God working in this period of the twentieth century in a way that men in some *strange* way are responding to..."

King is speaking extemporaneously, it strikes Ben; unless he's memorized these words, this is all off the cuff. He's been doing that for years, was of course a preacher in Atlanta before he became a leader in the civil rights movement, and that can account for the pace, the rhythm of his speech. But the structure of what he's just said is so intricate, so artful, bouncing from Memphis to the world to himself to God, and beyond that

King casts a mood of such *serenity*. How is it possible for a
man to be simultaneously so intense and so peaceful?

"Something is happening in our world. The masses of
people are rising up, and wherever they are assembled today--
whether they are in Johannesburg, South Africa; Nairobi,
Kenya; Accra, Ghana; New York City; Atlanta, Georgia;
Jackson, Mississippi; or Memphis, Tennessee--the cry is always
the same: *We want to be free!*"

As Ben is considering King's choice of locations, their
apparent randomness, but the sense of balance, the exotic mixed
with the nearby, there is a brilliant flash of lightning, followed
in a fraction of a second by a booming thunderclap; then
silence, as King pauses and the crowd is left mute.

"We've got to give ourselves to this struggle until the
end. Nothing could be more tragic than to stop at this point in
Memphis. We've got to see it through. When we have our
march you need to be there, if it means leaving work, if it means
leaving school. Be there. Be concerned about your brother.
You may not be on strike, but either we go up together or we go
down together. Let us develop a kind of dangerous
unselfishness."

King pauses again. Delphine is leaning forward, her
elbows on her knees. Beyond her, Randall appears mesmerized.
Ben wonders where the phrase "a kind of dangerous
unselfishness" comes from, whether it something King has
come up with on the spur of the moment, or whether it is
something he uses regularly. It's a wonderful phrase.

"One day a man came to Jesus, and he said to Jesus,
'Who is my neighbor?' The question could easily have ended up
in a philosophical and theological debate, but Jesus pulled that
question from midair, placed it on a dangerous curve between
Jerusalem and Jericho. The Jericho road is a dangerous road.

266

## The Mountaintop

The first question that the priest asked, the first question that the
Levite asked: If I stop to help this man, what will happen to me?
But then the good Samaritan came by, and he reversed the
question. If I do *not* stop to help this man, what will happen to
*him*? That's the question before you tonight: If I do not stop to
help the sanitation workers, what will happen to *them*?"

King pauses again; Ben realizes now where King was
headed with dangerous unselfishness, and realizes that he's
always thought of the good Samaritan as someone who wasn't
in too much of a hurry to stop.

"And they were telling me: Now...it doesn't matter now,
it really doesn't matter what happens now." What's this a
reference to? To the situation in Memphis, or to King's place in
the civil rights movement? "I left Atlanta this morning and as
we got started on the plane--there were six of us--the pilot said
over the public address system, 'We're sorry for the delay, but
we have Doctor Martin Luther King on the plane, and to be sure
that all of the bags were checked, and to be sure that nothing
would be wrong on the plane, we had to check out everything
carefully, and we've had the plane protected and guarded all
night. And then I got into Memphis, and some began to say the
threats, or talk about the threats that were out, about what would
happen from some of our sick white brothers."

While King hasn't lost the glorious rhythm of his
delivery, this anecdote is a definite departure from everything
that preceded it, the syntax rougher, the direction unclear. It
strikes Ben that King must be awfully tired.

"Well, I don't know what will happen now. We've got
some difficult days ahead. But it really doesn't matter to me
now, because I've been to the mountaintop. I don't mind. Like
anybody, I would like to live a long life. Longevity has its
place. But I'm not concerned about that now. I just want to do

267

God's will. And he's allowed me to go up to the mountain, and I've looked over, and I've seen the promised land. I may not get there with you, but I want you to know tonight *that we as a people will GET to the promised land.* So I'm happy tonight. I'm not worried about any thing, I'm not fearing any man. *Mine eyes have seen the glory of the coming of the Lord.*"

This last has taken Ben completely by surprise--taken everyone here by surprise, it would seem, because there a communal outburst, an explosion of emotion, of fervor. Ben is first conscious of Delphine getting to her feet, then of everyone in the temple rising until finally, a second late, he stands up, clapping, as are all around him. King turns and leaves the pulpit. The ovation continues apace for several seconds, and then quite spontaneously stops, just like that.

Delphine has sat down and Ben realizes she's weeping. He makes brief eye contact with Randall, and sees that tears are streaming down his face. Heedless of repercussion, Ben sits and puts his arm around Delphine's shoulder. "All right?" he whispers in her ear.

She nods, half a smile on her face.

## THIRTY-ONE

Alex has a bad case of lover's nuts, blue balls, call it what you will, standing here in Chip's kitchen, wondering what to do, where to go. Periodically he glances at Nicola, who ever since they left the bedroom has hovered around Chip. He tries not to stare. Alex fears he has alienated both Prosper and Maddy with his political observations, on-the-money though they may have been, and Maddy of course must have known it was him with Nicola in the bedroom, and his fine mood of an hour and a half ago has turned into a state of frustration, sexual and spiritual. He misses Lydia, no way around it, misses the certainty of her being at home, misses her compact, sexy body. It keeps crossing his mind that this would be the perfect time to go home and get high. Just a little acid, so he'd be okay for his ten o'clock class. But he knows how one thing leads to another; he can imagine himself staying up all night, tripping, and then what if Lydia chose to come home in the morning and found him stoned again?

Chip and Nicola are moving this way, he notices. Chip stops to talk to Prosper and what's his name—Jake—and Nicola keeps coming. Not having even looked in his direction, she stands five feet away at the kitchen counter, pouring herself a glass of white wine. "Hi," says Alex.

"How are you doing?" She replies.

"Could be better."

"I'm sure you will be."

"Listen," Alex says, "we kinda started something in there that we didn't finish. I'd really like to do that."

"In due time," Nicola says, smiling at him.

269

"We could take a cab to my place," he says. "Or you know what? I've got a car now. We could drive someplace." Even as he's speaking those words, it strikes him as the most inane thing he's ever said.

"I have to be work in the morning," she says, still smiling.

He says, "Do you and Chip…make it?"

"Do we *what*?"

"I've always figured he wasn't into chicks…"

"That is none of your fucking business," Nicola says. "Don't push your luck, okay?"

A while later he talks to Maddy and asks her not to say anything to Lydia about the business with Nicola, which seems cool with her. He thinks about thanking Chip for the great party before he leaves, but Chip's with Nicola again, so Alex just takes off.

He's a block away before he realizes he's forgotten to ask Prosper about the draft thing. Maybe he'll reach him tomorrow at the radio station.

He waits ten minutes for the crosstown bus at 86th and Madison, starting to shiver as the early spring night air penetrates his summer suit. A couple of cabs go by, occupied. He starts walking west without thinking much about a plan of action; when he gets to Fifth Avenue he has a choice of going north—which means continuing to walk, because traffic runs south—or keeping westward, which means walking over to the transverse at 85th or resuming waiting for the fucking bus. On the other hand, he has a loaded pistol in his jacket pocket, so what the hell—he lifts himself over the wall and begins walking across Central Park in the dead of night.

## The Mountaintop

The sky's clear, so it's not as if he's in pitch black. It's kind of thrilling, sighting on a well-lit building he figures must be on about 87th and Central Park West, walking rapidly through the wide open spaces, encountering nothing but small wildlife—and that heard only, not seen. Maybe it's squirrels, maybe it's rats, but for sure it's not young toughs out to steal his money and what remains of his bag of marijuana.

Emerging from the park unscathed but chilled, he heads a block south to the subway entrance at 86th; miracle of miracles, a train comes almost simultaneous to his arrival on the platform, and he rides the warm car three stops to Cathedral Parkway.

He's had no other intention than to go home, but when he finds himself standing on the Columbus Avenue sidewalk he turns south instead of north, toward the Flor de Cienfuegos.

Nestor is back behind the bar, and Alex orders a draft. "I came in this afternoon," he says, "but that guy Julio wasn't here."

Nestor shrugs. "What can I tell you? Most days..."

There is a brief silence. Alex is the only patron at the bar, but there are voices from the booths behind the partition. Nestor fidgets. After a while he says, "The other guy, there's a guy named Flaco in the back. Like I said, there's lots of guys named Flaco."

Alex descends from the stool and with his glass of beer walks around the partition to a point where he can see the occupants of two booths. Indeed, the copper-skinned, curly-haired man—with two others unfamiliar to Alex—looks in the dim light very much like the guy who stole his Bolex and his Nagra and slammed him against the doorjamb. The three speak rapid Caribbean Spanish he can't follow.

271

By the booth now, Alex says, "Hey, Flaco?" The curly-haired man, who is solo on his side of the booth looks up, puzzled. "My name is Alex, remember? From yesterday morning?"

Flaco smiles in recognition. "Right! How you doing, man?"

"Doing okay," Alex says. "I was hoping I could get my stuff back from you."

"Your stuff?"

"Yeah. My camera and my tape recorder."

"You gave me that shit, man, remember?"

"Well, I want it back."

Flaco says something unintelligible to his two companions and then slides out of the booth. He's a full head taller than Alex. "Let's talk about this," he says.

Alex follows him to the back of the bar, where Flaco sits on the edge of the bowling machine. "We gotta get one thing straight. You gave me those things, I did not steal them."

"Okay," Alex says, "what if I said I gave them to you?"

"Then maybe I could sell them back to you."

Alex laughs. "*Sell* them back to me."

"Yeah, for a lot less than you'd have to pay to get new shit, and a lot less than I could sell them for to somebody else."

"Like how much?"

Flaco shrugs. "Five bills."

"They're still in good condition?"

"Just like when you last seen them."

"I'll give you two hundred," Alex says.

Flaco laughs and shakes his head. "No, man. You know what that stuff is worth."

"Three hundred."

"Five bills is my deal," Flaco says, "or tomorrow I sell it to somebody else for a grand."

Alex has no intention of paying anything at all for what is rightfully his, but he's enjoying the conversation, relishing the notion that Flaco, who thinks he's stringing him along, is himself being strung. He says, "How would we go about this?"

"Go *about* it?" Flaco chortles. "Man, you got a fuckin' way with words. How about, you give me three bills up front, I bring you the shit, and then you give me the other two bills?"

"Let me see the stuff first."

"Why? You don't think I wanna collect my other two hundred?"

"I want to see it first," Alex says.

Flaco nods repeatedly, as if cogitating. "Okay," he says. "Follow me."

Alex drains the remainder of his beer and nods to Nestor as Flaco walks out the front door. He pats his right jacket pocket, as if to assure that the little Walther is still there. On Columbus, Alex says, "Where are we going?"

"To see your stuff."

"Yeah, but where is it?"

"Not too far." And that's the last Flaco speaks until he turns right at the end of the block, on 106th. It's an ill-lit, dingy street, completely deserted at one a.m. or thereabouts. Flaco stops abruptly and says, "Let me see some cash."

"Don't have it with me."

"Let's see your wallet," Flaco says. This seems as good a time as any, so Alex reaches into his pocket and removes the pistol. Flaco takes a step back and says, "Jesus Christ, man, what is that? A damn toy? Don't be fuckin' with me!"

"Where's my stuff?" Alex says.

273

"It's just down the block, man! You remember the guy with the leather jacket, Rafael? It's at his place."

"Why'd you want my wallet?" Alex says. "You were gonna rob me again."

Flaco shakes his head. "How do I know that gun is real?"

"You'll have to take my word for it." Alex savors the moment. His heart may be beating a little faster than usual, but his hand is steady. He hasn't had any smoke since the last joint on Chip's bed, with Nicola, nearly four hours ago, and he's thinking about as clearly as he ever has. "Why would you steal my stuff and then give it to Rafael?"

"Rafael's my buddy. He lives nearby."

"Bullshit," Alex says. "Where do you live?"

"What the fuck difference does it make where I live?"

"Cause that's where the stuff is, if you still have it." Flaco takes a step in his direction, and Alex says, "Stay back."

"I just wanna get a better look at that gun, man, see if it's real. It's like a fake James Bond gun."

"Stay back," Alex repeats.

"Half a block up," Flaco says, "is Rafael's place. Come with me and I'll show you something."

"Tell me what."

"Come with me."

What the hell, Alex thinks. If Flaco takes off, or does anything treacherous, he can shoot him. "Walk slowly," Alex says.

They head north up 106th Street, the tall Puerto Rican moving as if measuring his steps, Alex perhaps ten feet behind, starting again to shiver a bit in the cool night. At mid-block Flaco says, "Gotta cross the street here, okay?" Alex nods, and they cross.

The building is an old brownstone with a stoop. Flaco climbs the four steps as Alex remains on the sidewalk. "I'm gonna buzz him."

"Go ahead," Alex says, "but if you go in, you're dead."

Flaco presses a button. "He'll be sleepin' now, but if I buzz a few times, he'll wake up."

"Why are we here?" Alex says.

Flaco buzzes a second and a third time. "I told you, I'm gonna show you something."

"Just tell me."

At this point the tinny speaker below the buttons produces an indistinct sound that could be, "Yeah?"

"*Es Flaco. Hay problemas, hombre...*"

The speaker crackles again, and this time it sounds like, "Go away."

Flaco says, "*Estoy aquí con el maricón gringo, amigo, de Lunes..de tu chica. Tienes que ayudarme...*

Flaco's speaking slowly and clearly enough that Alex can understand him, and he's trying to sort things out. *I'm here with the gringo faggot*, Flaco has just said, *from Monday, from your girl*. Just then the speaker crackles again. It sounds like, "Get the fuck away and let me sleep." Then there's an electronic pop, and silence. Flaco slumps, appearing near despair.

Alex says, "What did you mean...the part about his girl, his girlfriend?"

"What the fuck you talkin' about?" Flaco says. He hits the buzzer again.

"You told him you were here with the *maricón gringo*— that's me, right?—and then you said *tu chica*. You talking about Lydia?"

Flaco has the look of a man who's just turned over his hole card by mistake. He glares at Alex and says, "He's ballin' your old lady, man! That's what I wanted to show you!"

Alex's synapses are running amuck. Is *this* where Lydia's spent the past two nights, with one of the assholes who tried to rob them Monday morning? He gets what Flaco was up to, trying to distract him, trying to redirect his attention, his anger, by leading him to the scene of the tryst, but now he's even angrier because he's been cuckolded for sure, he doesn't understand it, and he still doesn't know what's become of his Bolex and his Nagra. "Where's my stuff, for Christ's sake?" He says.

"Forget about your stuff, man. Get new stuff, okay? Let's just call it a night."

Alex stands slack and preoccupied on the sidewalk, the gun's barrel facing concrete, and suddenly Flaco's long body is hurtling through the air. Alex has time to raise the Walther and fire once. There's no way he'll miss, because Flaco's not three feet from him when he pulls the trigger.

The bullet, however, cannot interrupt Flaco's momentum, and in an instant Alex is violently propelled to the sidewalk, blanketed by six and a half feet of dead or wounded Puerto Rican. The impact causes his head to ring and spin, and for a moment he's afraid he's going to pass out. He takes deep breaths and slowly releases the air, as if he's performing yoga at the bottom of a football pileup.

It's soon clear that Flaco is not dead, but neither is he in very good shape. He moans, but he doesn't make any appreciable movement, certainly nothing retaliatory. Alex is aware of noise—of windows opening, voices calling. He squirms and heaves and manages to wriggle out from under Flaco. He gets to his feet and looks quickly around. Flaco continues to moan. Alex says, "Where are you shot?" Flaco mutters something, probably in Spanish, but Alex can't make it out.

He locates the Walther on the sidewalk and grabs it, puts it back in his pocket, then begins walking at a good clip back toward Columbus Avenue.

## THIRTY-TWO

Rafael has sat bolt upright in bed and Lydia, half awake, says, "What's that? Your buzzer? Somebody downstairs?"

"Yeah. Probably somebody trying every buzzer. Some wino wants to sleep in the hallway down there." The buzzer sounds again. "Shit," Rafael says. "I gotta check it out." He gets out of bed, naked, and Lydia listens as he pads to the front door.

"Yeah?" She hears him say, and then there's a garbled sound from the intercom. It's like standing on the subway platform and trying to understand some unintelligible announcement about why the trains are late. "Go away," she hears Rafael say.

"Who is it?" She shouts, as if she'd know anybody who'd ring Rafael's buzzer at one o'clock in the morning.

"You don't wanna know," he shouts back, so of course she does want to know. The intercom squawks again, and this time she thinks she hears *maricón gringo*. She doesn't like the sound of that: It's what the tall, scary guy called Alex Monday morning. She hears Rafael say, "Get the fuck away and let me sleep!" Fifteen seconds later he's back in bed.

"Was that your friend Flaco?" She says.

"Yeah. I'm sorry. He's drunk."

"What did he say about Alex?"

"He didn't. He said he was with the *maricón gringo...*"

"That's Alex."

"Yeah, I guess it could be. Except he said he needed me to help him."

"Jesus," Lydia says, feeling a wave of trepidation, and about two seconds later she hears a gunshot that sounds as if it comes from directly below. If it was in fact Alex down there with Flaco and one of them got shot, certainly it wasn't Flaco.

Rafael is out of bed again, already pulling up his pants. She gets out on her side and begins dressing. "You stay here," Rafael says, stepping into his shoes.

"What if it's Alex who got shot? What're you gonna do?"

"You stay here by the window. Open the window. If somebody got shot, I'll call up to you, okay?"

"Then what do I do? You don't have a fucking phone, Rafael!"

He's fully dressed now—at least he's got his pants and his shirt and his shoes on—and he's moving toward the door. "Knock on Julio's door. Wake him up. Start screaming. I don't know—do whatever you have to do."

She watches him take the stairs two at a time, until he disappears. She trots back into the apartment and tugs the window upward; it will only open a few inches, not wide enough for her to squeeze her head through and look down. Maybe, she thinks, Flaco refers to all white guys as *maricón gringo*. What would Alex have been doing with him, or vice-versa? It's conceivable that Alex was trying to get his fucking camera and his fucking tape recorder back, but he hates guns. He equates guns with everything he hates about his father. He says guns represent everything that's wrong with America, that no civilized country would allow its president to be shot down in the street.

She hears a siren, then another, and in a few seconds she can see a police car's flashing red light reflected in the windows across the street. Quickly, she puts on her socks and shoes and finds Rafael's leather jacket hanging on a hook inside the bedroom door.

A small crowd has gathered. From the stoop she can see Rafael by the curb, talking to a pair of cops. The second siren belonged to an ambulance, which has pulled up behind the police car. "Rafael!" She shouts. He looks up at her and shakes his head. What the fuck is that supposed to mean? Go away? Alex is dead? I didn't see anything?

She descends the steps and stares briefly at what looks like blood on the sidewalk—not too much of it. The ambulance restarts its siren and pulls away. People—maybe fifteen or twenty of them—continue to mill around, speaking Spanish in low voices. Doubtless one or more of them called the police. She catches the eye of a middle-aged woman about her size and asks her in Spanish if she knows what happened. The woman tells her a man was shot. What did the man look like? The woman shakes her head and says all she knows is a man was shot.

She climbs back to the top of the stoop and waits. Finally Rafael finishes with the cops, one of whom has been writing in a notebook. Looking grim, he joins her on the stoop. He says, "It was Flaco. He's dead."

"Oh, my God," she says, and then after a respectful moment, "Did you tell them anything? Did you mention Alex?"

"No," he replies. "I didn't see any point."

"What were you talking about, all that time?"

"I told them he was just ringing my buzzer, trying to get in. I told them I thought he was drunk, and I had to get some sleep. I told them he was a pretty nasty guy sometimes, but he was my friend."

Lydia thinks: He was a friend you're better off without.

## THIRTY-THREE

Prosper has made the drive from Manhattan to Riverside countless times, but rarely as a passenger, never as a passenger in his own car. He's considered giving Maddy directions for his special route, but at this hour it wouldn't save any time, just fifty cents in tolls, and if he got her on the Cross County, for instance, and fell asleep, they might end up in Vermont. As it is, he directs her to the Third Avenue Bridge and Bruckner

Boulevard, and from there he figures she can pretty much find her way.

He's drifting off when she says, "Is it named after the composer?"

He has no idea what she's talking about. "What composer?"

"Is Bruckner Boulevard named after Anton Bruckner?"

Prosper doesn't know the answer. It's never occurred to him that the Boulevard might be named for the composer, so he chooses to let himself fall asleep.

He wakes up, partially wakes up, when the car stops at the first tollbooth, on the New England Thruway. He wonders for an instant where he is, why he's in *this* seat, then remembers everything: he's just been classified 1-A; that's Maddy in the driver's seat, taking him home. The amalgam of very bad news and very good news sends a little tingle through his body, but it's not enough to keep him from falling back to sleep.

He wakes up again at the next tollbooth--this one between Exits Two and Three of the Connecticut Turnpike-- because Maddy is slapping his left knee. "*Prosper*...do you have a quarter, for God's sake?" They're in an exact change lane; he finds coins in the pocket of his suede jacket, hands her a quarter. She flips it into the wire mesh receptacle, and they're off.

"How are you doing?" Maddy says, looking straight ahead.

"Fine. Still a little drunk, I guess. Maybe more stoned than drunk. How are *you* doing?"

"I'm okay. We're almost there, right? Exit Five?"

"Right. About three minutes up the road."

"I couldn't possibly find it from the exit, so you're gonna have to stay awake, okay?"

281

"Okay. I'm awake. I could even drive us home from the exit, if you like."

Maddy shakes her head. After a moment she says, "How are you in the broader sense?"

The broader sense? He watches her in profile; she squints a bit, perhaps in deference to the headlights of westbound trucks. Her shoulders are forward, some two inches from the seatback. In the twilight of the Valiant's interior her straight brown hair glistens, and when the car encounters a bit of rough road, as right now, he sees her breasts move under the purple blouse. He wishes that he could lean left and just fall into her lap. But meanwhile, there is a question on the floor. "I guess I'm pretty much okay in the broader sense, too."

"But what are you going to do? What's your plan?"

What *is* his plan? His plan was to fail the physical. "Let's not talk about it now, okay?"

"God, I love this room," Maddy says, standing in front of the east-facing picture window. On this clear night in early spring the window does indeed present a tableau: the lawn, the seawall, the reeds in the foreground, and beyond them the calm bay, with the peninsula leading to Greenwich Point visible in the moonlight, a couple of miles away. The duck colony, perhaps forty feet beyond the seawall, mutters and quacks intermittently, and somewhere not too far away a mockingbird runs contrapuntally through his repertoire. Prosper sits on the floor by the record cabinet, looking for something just right.

Maddy says, "There didn't use to be mockingbirds around here, did there? I don't remember them when I was growing up in New Jersey."

"Last year," Prosper says, considering the Four Tops' *Greatest Hits*. He knows Maddy likes them, especially

282

"Bernadette," but wouldn't they be a little raucous for this moment?

"Last year?"

"Last summer, in June. I called the Audubon Society in Greenwich. I said either some maniac is playing birdcalls in the middle of the night or there's a mockingbird right outside this house, and the lady said yeah, they've been moving north at some incredible rate, like a hundred miles a year. They just move into areas, into neighborhoods, and take over. In about five minutes they're the dominant bird."

"Jesus," Maddy says. "So they're bird Nazis."

All of this puts Prosper in mind of Charlie Parker; but his Charlie Parker records, he knows, are in Dakar. In Africa. Ah, but what about the next best thing? He's got *Kind of Blue* and *Sketches of Spain* and *Jazz Track* and the ancient *Workin' with the Miles Davis Quintet*, with its marvelous blue monochrome cover. He places the record on Catherine's turntable, puts the tonearm gently on "It Never Entered My Mind." The mockingbird, no doubt in deference to the combination of Miles Davis *and* John Coltrane, shuts up.

In his stocking feet Prosper pads across the cork floor until he is directly behind Maddy. "I like this music," she says. "You've played this for me before, right? Is it Miles Davis?"

"Right," he says. He played it for her twenty-one months ago, in this house, a few days before he introduced her to Ben. He thinks now, oddly, of Ben's dislike for this record, and for Miles Davis in general. "That fucking anemic trumpet." Prosper now in an act of no premeditation puts his hands on Maddy's shoulders. She doesn't flinch, or move at all, so he begins to massage. This, it strikes him, is the sort of thing that Ben does so easily, casually touching a girl in a manner that could be interpreted as either intimate or simply friendly. He

283

kneads the soft skin between Maddy's shoulder blades and her neck, and after a few seconds she hikes her shoulders slightly and says, "That feels good." He continues to knead, his face about half an inch from her hair, so he smells the vague perfume of her shampoo

Prosper massages a bit more deeply now, and Maddy murmurs something not particularly verbal. He allows his nose to touch her hair, and then to intrude between the tresses to her neck. Has he passed the point of friendliness and entered intimacy? His hands, as if possessed of a will of their own, all at once cease massaging; his thumbs meet for an instant behind her neck, and then his hands slide slowly, gently down across her collarbone, their tips sensing the slight incline where her chest begins to protrude. His left hand is over her heart, and feels it thumping. Down his hands continue, across the fabric of her purple cotton top, until each palm is centered upon a breast, a nipple, and Maddy takes a long, deep breath, and exhales. This Prosper interprets as license of a sort. He is by now intoxicated in every sense: tired and residually drunk and stoned, touching forbidden parts of the girl he loves, has loved. He kisses her neck, and again she lifts her shoulders, and again he permits his hands to descend. Where are they going? For now, to the point where shirt meets skirt. He fits his fingers underneath the skirt's waistband. Is it possible that she's inhaling, helping him? His fingers untuck the shirt and feel the smooth skin of her midriff, and for the first time he's conscious of how tremendously aroused he is. He continues to nuzzle her neck as his hands move upward again, now cupping and then caressing her breasts without cotton's impedance. It occurs to him that she has made no sound since he was rubbing her shoulders, but of course neither has he. And the texture of her

284

nipples would indicate that she too is excited, or at least not altogether uninterested.

Where does he go from here? Miles Davis and the Quintet finish "Four," the up-tempo song, and begin "In Your Own Sweet Way," which shortly will feature a great Coltrane solo. Prosper wonders if now he should reposition himself, somehow get in front of Maddy. But how? Would he just let go of her and walk around her as if she were a statue? Or twirl her a hundred and eighty degrees as if she were a ballerina? Here's the Coltrane solo, and Prosper's hands begin again to descend, not exactly in time to the music, but going down faster than they'd come up, and again they reach that *terra misteriosa* of the waistband. How is the skirt fastened? Fingers under the shirt: is it a clasp? A button? His fingers pull fabric in opposing directions, to no avail; his fingers are suddenly shunted aside by hers, which make quick work of whatever device it was. Maddy does a little shimmy, which increases Prosper's arousal exponentially, and the skirt falls to the floor.

What's this, now? The elastic waistband of her tights, and underneath that...nothing but Maddy. Clearly he's been given a green light, so he lets his fingers make quick work of the remaining territory: the briefest of visits to the navel; a half-minute's grazing among the wonders of the pubic hair; an exploratory traipse by the left index finger to the tip of the cleft. This is about the full extension of his arms, unless...he bends his knees slightly, giving himself a bit more reach, and with the middle finger of his right hand attains the edge of the promised land, and slides barely in. Whereupon there is a sound from Maddy--something between a sigh and a gasp--which he interprets as encouragement to delve further.

He has never been here before. When he and Maddy dated, or whatever it was they did, first for the last several days of his trip to Spain and then during the summer before he went back to college, they kissed, they fondled, but nothing more. Was it because he held her in such awe? There hadn't been, to his recollection, any signal for him to go just so far. And of course he wondered ever after whether she would've hopped into bed with Ben so quickly if *they*'d been lovers. But here he is, in any case, feeling celestial, standing behind the girl of his reveries, with his maximum erection pressing against the small of her back and the middle finger of his right hand exploring this wondrous, smooth, moist part of Maddy. In he goes, and down, and out a bit, and in again, and finally up, and here she stiffens. Has he done something wrong?

"There." Maddy whispers.

There? He maneuvers his finger again near the peak of the orifice and she breathes in sharply. "Yes," she says in the exact same tone of voice, and he realizes where he is, what he's found.

He stays there, massaging once again. She shifts her weight so that all of a sudden he is peering over her right shoulder, and he can see them in the window. What a fine picture this is! Maddy in her tights and her purple shirt; his own hands, both of them, deep within the tights; his own head staring back at him; and best of all Maddy's face--her neck craned slightly backwards, her eyes closed.

Her breathing is audible, and accelerating. His finger has found its spot and will not stray. "Yes," she says again, and again, and then, "Oh, *God*!" She inhales a monster breath, and tautens. Prosper withdraws his finger and slides his hands up past Maddy's hipbones. He doesn't want to let go of her, and so clasps his hands around her waist. She lets her body slacken, and he wonders for a moment what his role is now. Shall he pick her up and carry her to the couch, or to his bedroom? The last cut on the first side of *Workin'*, a short tune called "The Theme, take one," finishes, and the tonearm can be heard lifting off the record and setting itself down on its cradle. There are the ducks again, staying up late.

"*La fiesta de los patos*," she says, in her sibilant Castilian.

"Thank God they invited us," Prosper says, looking at her reflection in the window.

Maddy performs a little dance and descends to her knees. What's she doing? She's stepped out of her skirt, which had been lying in a clump around her feet, and now she's picking it up and tossing it on the chair. As she stands up she turns, so when she's upright she faces him. She kisses his lips and simultaneously fishes for the fly of his suede pants. It's a subtle zipper, but she finds it, and undoes it, and just as quickly locates the aperture in his boxer shorts. Not so fast, Prosper wants to say, as she grasps him with her right hand. This is his dream, his fantasy, coming true, and he doesn't want it to be over so soon. With both hands he slides her tights several inches down her legs, and attempts to lower himself toward her, but there is clearly no way she's going to relinquish her grip. He withdraws his lips from hers for an instant and says, "Maddy, let's..." But she presses hers against his anew, all the while tugging at him with her right hand. All this arousal, all these minutes; he doesn't stand a chance, and after no more than forty or fifty seconds he simply explodes.

When Prosper returns from the kitchen with a paper towel and two cans of Schlitz, Maddy has moved to the couch, where she sits cross-legged, looking over her shoulder out the southern picture window. She has pulled her tights back to waist level, but made no further effort at reclothing herself.

287

This Prosper takes as a good sign. And it excites him. He stops where they had been standing moments earlier and drops the paper towel on the floor; he proceeds to the couch and says, "Hi," to Maddy.

She turns her head and accepts a can of Schlitz. "How are you doing?" He says.

"I'm okay." She has a sip of beer. "You wouldn't be planning to do some laundry, would you?"

"It wasn't at the top of my list. Why?"

"Because I'm gonna have to wear this stuff to school tomorrow, unless you want to take me home first, in the morning."

"Let's do some laundry," he says

Prosper's got two weeks' worth of darks in the huge Maytag washer with Maddy's purple top and blue denim skirt and black tights. She has dissuaded him from including his white and yellow Oxford shirts and his white socks, although God knows he's washed them with indiscriminate colors before. She sits on the couch in the living room, wearing his madras Bermuda shorts and a plain white t-shirt. Is it the outfit, is it the fact that so much of her is visible, or is it just that she's sitting here with him at two thirty in the morning, and they've just done what they've just done, that fills him with such a mixture of lust and longing?

She says, "You're sure you'll be all right in the morning?"

"I'm fine," he says. "I got four or five hours' sleep last night, by mistake. It probably did me in, too."

"Does it work that way? Your blood pressure goes up or down depending on how much sleep you've had?"

288

## The Mountaintop

Prosper sits on the floor by the couch. When he returned from the laundry room, Maddy was in the bathroom. He put Charlie Byrd's *Blues Sonata* on the turntable, found his beer on the floor by the couch, and sat down beside it. Maddy reappeared seconds later and reclaimed her former position on the couch. "I don't know," he says. "I just reached a point where I figured the more fucked up I got, the higher my blood pressure would be, and it kept working. Then last night I fell asleep on the couch. Everything else was the same. I took the Dexedrine, two pills, and all of a sudden I was normal. I was a soldier-to-be."

"But not right away," she says. "It stayed high all morning and all afternoon, and then the nasty guy made you do it one more time. Maybe you were in shock."

"Does your blood pressure go down when you're in shock?"

"I don't know," she says, "but there was obviously something about that whole series of events that messed you up. If it was just getting too much sleep, why wouldn't you have been normal first thing in the morning?"

He shakes his head, which is perhaps five inches from her toes. He is fond of her toes, and of the smoothness of her feet, of the bluish veins that stand out in them. He is fond of the curve of her legs. Whenever she moves, whenever she shifts her weight a bit, her breasts move perceptibly under his t-shirt, filling him with a sense of giddy elation.

He searches for words. "Maddy...what we just did...what was that?" The moment he's uttered the words he regrets having done so, and that feeling is augmented when she makes no immediate response. He looks up at her, trying to see her eyes, but she's turned her head toward the window. A minute goes by, and he begins stroking her foot. "I don't want

289

to spoil the mood," he says. "I don't want to be pushy." He pauses; he strokes. "I don't know about you, but that was..."

"It was lovely," she says.

It's a relief that she spoke, that she said what she said. He tries to clear his head as much as possible, suspecting that his choice of words in the next few minutes might be extremely important to his future. He says, "Do you know how I feel about you?"

She's still not looking at him; not quite. "I think so."

"You know Ben's been my friend since we were fourteen, my best friend most of the time. So I wouldn't do something like this...capriciously. Or spitefully."

"Drunkenly?" Maddy says.

"No. I'm not that drunk. How about you?"

She shakes her head. "Not drunk. Maybe a little spiteful."

He wishes she hadn't said that, although it's just about a given that if Ben weren't a thousand miles away and messing around as usual, Maddy wouldn't even be here with him. After quite a while he says, "So that was to get even with Ben?"

"No," she answers right away. "It wasn't to get even. It was...I guess, to acknowledge that there's a whole new set of rules."

Nor is this what Prosper wants to hear. "A whole new set of rules? Anybody can screw around with anybody, and it's not a big deal?"

"No." She makes eye contact with him. "*Not* anybody can screw around with anybody. Well, they can if they want to. I don't care. But the new rules as they apply to me--if I'm attracted to you and I'm clearly not involved in a monogamous relationship, then why shouldn't I act on my attraction to you?"

It's getting better, but it's not quite good enough. "Would you want to be in a monogamous relationship?" Their eyes still meet, but she says nothing. "Because I would," he says. "With you, I mean. There's nothing I'd want more than that."

"Not even to be 4-F?" Maddy says.

"Not even that."

She leans forward and kisses the top of his head, puts her arms around his neck. "What time is it?"

"I don't know," he says. "Three o'clock, quarter after?"

"I've been up since seven yesterday morning, Prosper. Can we get some sleep, for God's sake?"

"What about the laundry?"

"I'll put it in the dryer when I get up to call Mrs. Sálazar. Is there an ironing board?"

"In the laundry room. The iron's on the shelf next to the washer."

Prosper's room is downstairs, off the large room with the television. Because the house is built into a slope, the downstairs is at most half the size of the upstairs. There are two bedrooms upstairs in addition to Catherine's. When Prosper's entire family used to visit here, his parents stayed in one of the upstairs bedrooms, his sisters in the other. He has always stayed downstairs; and since his father was posted to Senegal, when Prosper was a junior at prep school, he has spent most of his vacations in this house, in this room. It's almost home.

"I don't think I've ever been in your room," Maddy says. "My God, you've got a view of the water." She stands by the window, which faces south. It's not the majestic view available in the living room, but at just above ground level it's a strange perspective. If the seawall a hundred yards away were perhaps ten feet higher, the Long Island Sound would be invisible.

It's cool down here, and humid, because the room is virtually subterranean. There are twin beds, some five feet apart; there is a built-in cabinet under the window and a built-in bookcase against the west wall, which contains all of Prosper's books as well as the comic books he has accumulated and hoarded since 1956. There is no other furniture, and no other accoutrement save a self-contained radio/phonograph atop the built-in cabinet, and a clock radio on a shelf between the two beds. Maddy says, "Can I borrow your toothbrush?"

"In the drawer to the right of the sink," Prosper replies, "there are about twelve toothbrushes. Brand new."

He's wondering whether to pull the beds together or whether just to invite Maddy to sleep in his when she speaks from the bathroom. "Prosper, it's a little drugstore in here!"

She's opened all three drawers on the right side of the bathroom cabinet, and discovered Catherine's cache of every cosmetic or over-the-counter medicinal item a guest could possibly desire--from deodorants (roll-on, spray, pad) to toothpaste to tooth *powder* to hydrogen peroxide to Band-Aids (and Curads) to antacids and laxatives. "Bunion pads!" Maddy says.

Prosper stands in the doorway. "She's very thoughtful."
"Your aunt?" She continues sifting through the bottom drawer.
"Mercurochrome. Vitamin C. Lomotil. Are you sure this isn't just your idea of a party?"

"I'm more an enema and truss kind of guy," he says.
"Not at the same time, I hope."

She is such a vision, even in this odd costume, even standing here bantering in the cold bathroom at three thirty in the morning, or perhaps especially standing here at three thirty in the morning. He says, "Do you want to sleep in my bed?"

"The two of us?"

"Right."

"I don't think so. No offense, but I think I'd like to stretch out and get some sleep."

"I'll pull the beds together, then?"

She smiles. "Sure."

## THIRTY-FOUR

Ben says, "Why don't I just give him the keys and we can take your car?"

"And go where?"

The rally is over. It's been at least half an hour since King left the pulpit and God knows how long since the audience started filing out of Mason Temple. Ben and Delphine took the left exit from their pew, assuming Randall was leaving on the right, but Randall and the assorted clergy have remained in a cluster in the aisle, in animated conversation, while Ben stands here with Delphine near the main entrance. There isn't much to say, as it turns out, about what they've just witnessed. But why? Ben knows he missed something--whatever it was that left Delphine and Randall in tears--and he fears that if he voices his white boy's admiration for what he did get he'll seem foolish, or ignorant, or simply *different*. The storm outside, meanwhile, seems to have blown itself out, or just moved east. People leaving by the main entrance tend to pause at the door and open their umbrellas, but the furious tempest that reached its crescendo while King was speaking is no more.

"We could go back to the Holiday Inn," he says.

Delphine shakes her head. "I don't think so."

"Just for a drink. Just to talk."

"Well, Delphine!" The voice belongs to a burly black man in an expensive-looking black suit. "And this is Ben, right?" The man offers his hand, and Ben shakes it, wondering for an instant whether Delphine has been spreading the word of their liaison. Then he realizes he knows this man, from dinner at the Ennises' night before last. Delphine says, "Ben, you remember Mr. and Mrs. Floyd."

"Of course I do," Ben says, as the handshake continues. "Good to see you again, sir."

"Call me Lee, would you? Delphine can stand on ceremony, but you don't have to." Lee Floyd releases Ben's hand. "And this is Corinna." Mrs. Floyd is probably a foot shorter and a hundred pounds lighter than her husband. She nods pleasantly at Ben, who's searching for a response when Corinna says, "What did y'all think of Doctor King's address?"

"Amazing," Ben says, and the word seems oddly inappropriate the moment it's out of his mouth.

"He does know how to move a audience, doesn't he?" Corinna says. "Delphine, honey, did your parents come tonight?"

"No, they couldn't make it. Always busy, you know."

## The Mountaintop

Lee Floyd says, "Where's that colleague of yours, Ben? Where's that Randall? That's a young man can deal with a audience himself."

"Right over there, sir." Ben gestures down the aisle.

"Surrounded by preachers in the house of God." Floyd laughs a deep ho-ho-ho, like a black Santa Claus, at a joke Ben isn't sure he gets. "Listen," Floyd resumes, "y'all want to come hear some music?"

Ah, yes. This is the guy who owns the nightclub. Delphine says, "I should probably be heading home. Don't want to be out in that weather any longer than I have to, and tomorrow's a school day."

"Honey," Corinna says, "seems to me like that storm's about done with."

"How often you have a chance like this?" Floyd says. "Show a couple of boys from New York the real Memphis? What you think about it, Ben?"

"Fine with me," Ben says.

Floyd focuses on Delphine. "Drinks on the house, little girl. How can you say no to that?"

Smiling, she shakes her head. "I really shouldn't."

Corinna Floyd wraps her arm around Delphine's waist, "Come on, child! Let yourself have a good time!"

The Floyds have moved on; Randall's group is finally, gradually dissolving. Randall has in fact looked in their direction and waved. Ben says, "What do you think? You feel like going to that club?"

"If you'd like to go, sure. Why not?"

There's not a great deal of enthusiasm in her voice. "I'd like to do whatever you'd like to do," he says. "I'd just like to spend some time with you."

295

"Let's go, then," she says in that same, listless voice.

His urge is to embrace her, but that's out of the question. He says, "Delphine, what's the matter."

"Nothing's the matter. I'm fine."

"Look, if you don't want to go out tonight, just tell me. We can do something tomorrow. I'm probably here through the weekend, at least."

"No, let's go. I've been to the club and it's a real nice place. You shouldn't miss it."

Tentatively, he puts a hand on her shoulder. The temple has almost cleared out. He runs his hand down her arm. "You sure you're all right?"

She looks him in the eye for the first time during this conversation. "Look, it was an emotional thing for me, okay? Seeing him make that speech. I don't think there's any way you could understand."

She's right on the money there, but still it hurts him that she *knows*. "Tell me about it," he says.

"Tell you what?"

"What you felt. What it meant to you."

She shakes her head. "I can't. It's just that he's..." She shakes her head again, as tears suddenly pour down her cheeks. By concern, by passion, by reflex, Ben spontaneously puts his arms around her; for an instant she accepts his embrace, but then she tenses and pulls away.

"Hey!" Ben hears Randall's voice behind him; the exclamation is a greeting, nothing more, but it causes Ben to jump, and to understand Delphine's withdrawal, or to think he does. "What goes on here?" Randall says. "Did I see you all talking with the Floyds?"

"You did," Ben says. Delphine has just now turned to face Randall. On the composure scale Ben would give her perhaps sixty-five out of a hundred. He says, "They'd like us to come over to their club and hear some music. Drinks on the house."

"Sounds mighty fine to me," Randall says. "Did you accept?"

"I said we'd talk it over with you."

"Well, hell, let's do it." He speaks to Delphine. "Where is it? How far from here?"

"It's on McLemore, maybe half a mile. Five minutes."

Randall nods. "You up for this, Delphine? Forgive me for saying, you look a little wiped out."

"I'm fine. I guess I'm having a little trouble...switching gears."

"King get to you?"

"He did."

"Got to me, too. Got to all of us in that little group. We were just talking about it, trying to figure out what he meant when he said he might not get to the promised land with us. It's not like him to come right out and compare himself to Moses."

"I know," Delphine says, "and that's only the half of it."

"Well, let's not dwell on this now. There's soul music to be heard. I assume the Floyds don't run a country and western place."

Delphine laughs, which puts Ben more at ease. Randall says, "How are we gonna do this? Did you drive here, Delphine? Did you park nearby?"

"Right around the corner."

"You mind taking us all?"

"Not a bit."

Ben sits in the Comet's back seat with three wet umbrellas. Up front, Randall and Delphine chat about music,

297

bandying names of Memphis musicians, a few of whom Ben recognizes, most of whom he doesn't. Randall goes off on a tangent about somebody who plays drums for both Booker T. and the MG's and Al Green, whereupon Delphine oohs and ahs a bit and compliments him on his knowledge. Randall says something Ben doesn't understand which causes Delphine to burst into laughter and slap Randall's knee. Ben keeps hoping they'll talk about King's speech, but they don't.

Delphine parks not a hundred feet down McLemore from Corinna's. The rain has by now diminished to a light drizzle, so much so that the umbrellas are left in the car. There is a modest cardboard sign in the corner of the club's big plate-glass window that reads:

## LEROY TELFORD & HIS MUSTANGS
## WEDS-SAT AT CORINNA'S
## $2 DOOR--NO MINIMUM

A badly reproduced photograph of the band, just below the lettering, shows seven black men in identical checked jackets and identical Afros. Randall says, "Wait a minute--Delphine, you know this group?"

She studies the sign. "Leroy Telford? I don't think they're from here."

"I saw Leroy Telford up in D.C. maybe three years ago. I only remember that because I saw them last year in New Haven, and it was one of the best damn shows I've ever seen. It's got to be the same guys, because they were wearing these outfits."

"So they were real good?" Delphine asks.

"You bet your ass they were good," Randall says. "They didn't do anything original, but they were a hell of a cover band.

298

Did the Curtis Mayfield songbook--the up-tempo Major Lance stuff, and the Five Stairsteps. You get all that down here in Memphis?"

"Sure we do," Delphine laughs. "But there's something wrong here. You all come down in the rain to hear some Memphis music and Lee Floyd's got a cover band from up in Connecticut."

Randall looks at Ben, certainly aware that Ben couldn't tell a Connecticut cover band from the Philadelphia Symphony Orchestra, and says, "How about it, preacher, do we go in?"

"Fine with me. I could use a beer."

"Delphine?"

"Yeah, why not?"

The man at the door, squeezed into a suit several sizes too small for him, could easily pass for an NFL lineman. Delphine says the Floyds' name and her own; the big man nods, opens the door to the club, and motions for a hostess. This woman in a long black dress and lavishly styled hair leads them to a table perhaps thirty feet from the slightly elevated stage, directly in front of what Ben assumes to be the dance floor. The band is evidently taking a break; loud, recorded music plays through speakers on the stage. The club is no more than a third full--presumably because of the weather--but still noisy and extremely smoky. It's bigger than Ben expected, probably close to a thousand square feet, and better kept.

"Not bad," Randall shouts over the music. "Not a bad looking joint."

Ben hears a voice behind him say, "So y'all made it down here." He's in the process of getting to his feet when Lee Floyd puts an arm on his shoulder and says, "That's all right, son. Relax yourself." Floyd eases into the vacant fourth chair at their table and shouts, "Damn! Music's so loud in here you can't hear yourself think!" He signals to the bartender, flattening his hand and moving it up and down, as if petting a very tall dog, and the bartender makes the same signal to someone unseen; within ten seconds Otis Redding has been muted to a near whisper.

"Sorry 'bout that," Floyd says. "I tell them, let people talk between sets, but they got to turn it up."

Randall says, "Fine place you got here, Lee."

"Thank you, sir. I'm proud of it. Like to have a place where people can come and have a few drinks and listen to music. Speakin' of which, what y'all want to drink?"

Randall looks at Delphine, who shrugs. "Beer all right with you?"

"I'm not gonna have much of anything," she says.

"I got some real nasty sour mash bourbon," Floyd says. "Save it for the specialest occasions."

Randall looks at Ben, who smiles and shakes his head. "Afraid not, Lee. Afraid you got a table of beer drinkers here."

Floyd signals the bartender again, and inside a minute a waitress arrives with a pitcher that holds at least a gallon. Randall says, "Lee, is this the same Leroy Telford that I would've seen up north a couple of times?"

"You heard him? What you think?"

"Best cover band I ever heard."

Floyd nods pensively. "Yeah, that's about right. Leroy showed up here maybe three years ago, tryin' to set up gigs. I called around, heard good things about him, booked his band for one night in the summer of sixty-six. I said, man, you cats are *good*, but you got to write some original material, get you a record contract. I passed the word around to the Stax people-- come on down and listen to these guys."

"Did they?"

Floyd shrugs. "Well, you know Stax is right down the
street here, so it's always some boys from the studio, a horn
player, a engineer, stuff like that. But did Hayes, Porter, any of
the producers come down here? No. And *now*, of course, they
goin' through some changes over there."

There is a break in the conversation, and without much
premeditation Ben seizes the opportunity to say, "I've got a
friend who works at a radio station in New York." All eyes are
suddenly upon him.

"Who's that?" Randall asks.

"Prosper."

Randall chuckles. "That's the wrong kind of radio
station, Ben."

"Yeah, but he loves this music."

"So what?"

Lee Floyd sits to Ben's right, Delphine to his left, both
their gazes earnestly fixed upon him, waiting to hear his
inspiration. The best he can come up with is: "So, maybe he
could do something for Leroy Telford."

"Jesus Christ, Ben," Randall says, "get on a handle on
the situation. I'm sure Lee here knows all kinda people at
WDIA, at every R and B station from here to Nashville.
Prosper works at a station that plays hippie music."

Ben has no response. He's somewhat shocked by the
anger in Randall's voice; he'd thought they'd gotten past that.
But Randall's right, without a doubt. Why couldn't he have
been content just to observe? Floyd now says, "Well, you never
know, now, whether Ben's friend might be connected, in some
way..."

"He's not connected," Randall says. "He just likes soul
music. Knows a hell of a lot about it, but so do I, and I sure as
hell couldn't get Leroy Telford a record contract."

Ben feels Delphine's hand under the table, on his knee. That's some considerable solace. He drinks half his glass of beer in one extended gulp.

"But say, Randall," Floyd says, doubtless sensing the tension around him, "what did you think about Doctor King's words tonight?"

"What did I think? Well, I think the man is about this close to a saint and about this much beyond a genius, and I think along with Senator Kennedy he's about the best hope we've got in this country right now."

"Amen," Floyd says. "You know, I've heard him talk before--many times on the TV, and here in Memphis just in the past couple of months, and there's always somethin' about that voice of his, they way he talks..."

"Serene," Randall says.

"Yeah...you got it--*serene*. It's like, that man could walk into the most vicious argument between two fools in*tent* on killin' one another, and in three minutes he'd have 'em shakin' hands. Hell, he'd have 'em huggin'. But tonight...you know what I'm talkin' about? Tonight, it was different. It was like he started out preachin', and then midway though it was like all of a sudden he was just sittin' in the parlor, talkin' about the plane ride. Then at the end he went back to preachin', except it was somethin' more..."

"Intimate," Randall says.

"Yeah, intimate, but also like he had some kind of vision. Not like when he said he had a *dream*. That was a speech. Don't get me wrong, that was one hell of a speech. But it was like that was somethin' he wrote down and practiced. This was more like he was standin' at the podium and it came to him. I been to the mountaintop and I seen the promised land. I may not get there with you, but it's all right. Like he's done, he's tired, he's thinkin' about quittin'."

"He's tired," Randall says. "That's for sure. The schedule that man must keep. Washington this morning, Atlanta tonight, Memphis tomorrow, New York the day after that..."

"But I mean tired in a different way. Tired of all the bullshit. Tired of havin' to deal with motherfuckers--pardon my language, Delphine--like our mayor Henry Loeb. Tired of tryin' to keep everythin' together when all this Black Power shit is comin' down."

"Afraid the movement's slipping away from him," Randall says.

"Yeah, but I mean just *weary* of it all. Like, I've *done* my part, y'all are on the verge of gettin' somewhere, now pardon me, I'm just gonna step aside."

"But he's got the whole Poor People's thing comin' up this summer," Randall says. "Maybe the biggest thing he's ever done. Branchin' out, gettin' more political..."

"I know, I know," Floyd says. "I'm just tellin' you what I heard the man sayin' tonight. What *I* heard."

## THIRTY-FIVE

Maddy sits on a wicker chair in the screened porch of the summer house in Cape May. Some fifteen feet from her, in the dining room just beyond the porch, her sisters engage in an animated game of jacks, which is annoying because she's trying to concentrate on what's happening here. Her mother says, "Doctor King, could I get you something to drink?"

It's awfully hot. In a soft, mellow voice Martin Luther King says, "If you have a glass of lemonade, Mrs. O'Connor, I'd appreciate it."

With her mother gone, Maddy is excited to have their visitor to herself and anxious because she doesn't know quite what to say to him. The way King looks at her, as if he's staring benignly into her soul, puts her immediately at ease, and she says, "My boyfriend is in Memphis. He's with the Kennedy campaign, and he's a great admirer of yours."

In the dining room, or perhaps in the living room beyond it, someone has turned on a radio that's playing "I Think We're Alone Now," by Tommy James & the Shondells. King leans toward her and speaks in a low tone, "You don't have to..." She can't make out the rest of what he's said. It's as if someone has lowered the volume on his voice and raised the volume of the radio. She says, "Excuse me, I didn't hear you." King resumes speaking, but now he's completely inaudible. "Pardon me," Maddy says, standing up. She heads for the dining room, intending to tell her sisters to take the damn radio and go to their room, or even better to go outside. But where are they? Where is the radio?

The radio, of course, is on a shelf just to the left of her head. She turns over and in the morning light searches for the button that will shut it off. Farther to her left, Prosper doesn't stir. He is soundless and inert. She fumbles and gropes, and finally interrupts Tommy James in mid-verse: "...the beating of our har..."

It's quarter to eight. Already her dream has become more of an impression than a narrative. She was on the porch in the house on Cape May. The *old* house, so at the latest it would have been 1957, except she was her current age, but her sisters were the ages they would have been, and she was talking to someone. It was unbelievably hot, which it certainly is not here in Prosper's bedroom, where it feels like about fifty degrees. She's exhausted, and it would be extremely easy to curl back under the covers. But she's got to call school; she's got to put her clothes in the dryer, else she will return to Manhattan dressed as Prosper in midsummer.

In his t-shirt and socks she scampers up the stairs. At this level it's fifteen degrees warmer. She can't resist a side trip into the living room and a look out the picture window. The ducks are quiet, perhaps sleeping in after their late night, and there is no sign of the mockingbird, but there's a great deal of activity around the birdfeeder on the lawn, highlighted by the presence of a pair of pheasants nervously pecking at seeds strewn down by smaller birds.

Her and Prosper's clothes are in a great damp lump at the bottom of the washer. If, after putting them in the dryer, she goes back to sleep for, say, two hours, will her skirt and top be so wrinkled as to be unwearable? Will she have time to iron them? Should she wait and dry them when she's up for good? What the hell--she gathers the soggy laundry with both hands and tosses it in the dryer. It takes her a couple of minutes to figure out the controls, but she gets the thing running.

It's time for the dreaded phone call. It's just before eight and Mrs. Sálazar will be in her office. She stops at the picture window for a quick look at the view and the birdfeeder; alas, the pheasants have departed and there's nothing to keep her from the telephone.

"Mrs. Sálazar...Hi, it's Maddy O'Connor. I'm sorry to give you such late notice, but I had to drive a sick friend to Connecticut late last night..."

"Are you telling me you won't be in?"

"No—just that I'll be late. I have to get back into the city..."

"How late, please?"

"I'll be there by lunchtime. I'm terribly sorry..."

"Miss O'Connor, you called me around this time Tuesday to tell me Miss Urrutia wasn't coming in. Is there a pattern here?"

"No, really. If I'd had any idea....It was midnight, and I had to..."

"Obviously there's nothing we can do about it now. Miss Urrutia will just have to double up. I assume she *will* be coming to school this morning?"

"Of course. As far as I know..."

"See me when you come in, please." And the line goes dead. That didn't go as smoothly as Maddy had hoped, but it's done.

It's no warmer downstairs than it was twenty minutes ago, and by the time she's brushed her teeth again she's freezing. She's left the covers down on her bed, so it's going to be preposterously cold. Prosper is lying on his side, all the way to the left of his bed. She pulls the covers back slightly and slides in next to him. He's naked. He stirs, and rolls over, opens his eyes. "Maddy?"

"Just me."

"I was dreaming about you." His smile is broad and sleepy. "Did you call the school?"

"I did. Everything's fine."

He's pressing against her, and she likes the warmth, but she's not at all sure about the rest of it. "Did you put the laundry in the dryer? I forgot to show you how to work it."

"Everything's fine. Let's get some sleep now, okay? We have to get up in an hour."

"Okay."

Now she turns over, so her back is to him. His body is against hers, immobile, but still it causes her to think of their liaison hours earlier, when he stood behind her and their bodies meshed. If they had somehow been seized and plunked down in this bed, they would be in precisely the position they're in now. He says, "Maddy?"

"Uh-huh?"

"That was an amazing round of Henry James. The best ever."

"Thanks. You said that last night."

"I wanted to make sure you knew." She feels his hand on her midsection. "Do you ever think about how much we have in common?"

"Like what?"

His fingers make little circles around her navel, and her skin begins to tingle. "We're both half-Irish."

"What else?"

"We both speak Spanish. We both like making fun of people at Chip's parties."

"So far I'm not very impressed."

307

Prosper is silent for a moment; his fingers extend the radius of their circle. He says, "We're both pissed off that Ben isn't faithful to you."

This turn in the conversation doesn't please her. "That's not fair," she says.

"And he never will be," Prosper says.

"Let's not talk about that, please." Does she not want the mood of this moment spoiled? Does she not want the gap between her faraway lover and her present circumstance bridged? Does she imagine herself falling back into her arrangement with Ben as if nothing has happened, nothing has been learned? Prosper's fingers cease circling and come to rest at the top of her pubis, as if waiting for direction.

He says, "Is it all right if I say that I love you?"

Her eyes tear, and she turns to kiss him.

Maddy is astonished when she wakes up, peers at the clock radio, and sees that it's already nine thirty. She doesn't even sleep this late on weekends. She's on her left side, facing away from Prosper and the window; Prosper, who's still out like a light, is curled up facing the window, oblivious to the bright sunshine. If she expects to be in East Harlem by noon they'll have to leave before eleven; if she goes back to sleep now, that'll never happen. She extricates herself from the little bed (it's *still* cold in this room) and hurries upstairs.

Her clothes are dry and not terribly wrinkled. She removes Prosper's t-shirt and puts on her purple top and denim skirt; the tights can be done without for the moment. In the living room she admires the view yet again. The bird feeder has attracted nothing exotic this late morning; the water is calm. To the right, to the south, there is a gardening crew pruning a tree and working on what appear to be rosebushes in the vast yard between Catherine's and the seawall. She walks out the front door onto the patio. It's spring, for sure. There are several little planting areas out here among the bricks, and lots of stuff is in bloom. She's not really sure what much of it is. She has managed to grow up in suburban New Jersey with an avid gardening mother and two avid gardening sisters and somehow miss the magic, the tending, and the nomenclature of plants. Not that she has anything against all these gorgeous bushes and treelets; she just doesn't know what they are, or how to take care of them.

But what a beautiful day it is--not quite summery, probably about sixty degrees, and still. She concentrates on the quiet: she can hear the tree pruners maybe a hundred feet away, and nothing else except that mockingbird--or some rival of his-- singing his lovely, disjointed song somewhere to the north. She stretches, feeling a moment of pleasant, exciting anxiety. What the hell is she doing here, and why does she feel so good about it?

She strolls to the end of the brick path and onto the gravel driveway, beyond which is an empty, forested lot; she turns right, her bare feet crunching cautiously on the gravel, and then right again, onto the parallel brick path that leads to the kitchen door. She picks up the *Times* that sits just in front of the door.

Should she wake Prosper? He can sleep for another half hour. In truth, she wouldn't mind spending a few days or a few weeks in this house, but there's no way that's happening now. What she would like to do is get something to eat; excepting snack food at Chip's, she's had nothing since late yesterday afternoon. She leaves the newspaper on the kitchen table and cruises through the dining room, the living room--pausing again

309

to look out at the Sound--and down the stairs. Prosper's head is buried in his pillow. He's had a tough week.

Back in the kitchen, she inspects the refrigerator. It's devoid of edibles: a few cans of Schlitz, plenty of condiments, two re-corked bottles of French white wine. She checks the cabinets and the best she can come up with is a box of Cheerios. No milk to eat them with, so she pours a bowlful and begins munching on them dry.

Unfolding the *Times* on the kitchen table, she reveals a banner headline:

## NORTH VN AND U.S. AGREE TO CONTACT; JOHNSON CONSULTS SAIGON, TO GO TO HAWAII

This would appear to be extremely good news. The fact that Lyndon Johnson is willing to have any communication at all with North Vietnam seems a giant step in the right direction. There is a subhead:

### President Sees Kennedy, Then Talks to Humphrey

She reads the story, which turns out not to contain much more information than was in the headline, yet outlasts her bowl of Cheerios. She imagines herself sitting across the table from Ben on 91st Street, hears him explaining that this is nothing more than a cynical attempt on Johnson's part to take the wind out of Kennedy's sails. He's dragged us into this war, this stupid, pointless war, and now he's unable to pull us out, so he's pulling himself out, and handing the reins over to Hubert Humphrey. He hates Kennedy's guts, so he'll do anything to create the illusion of an imminent peace, anything to help Humphrey get the nomination in August. But what does Ben

310

*The Mountaintop*

know, really? Certainly more than she knows, but that's not saying much.

Near the bottom of the front page, another headline catches Maddy's eye:

### Reagan Is Not Quitting Politics, Aides Say of Report He Might

She has never been to California, and offhand can think of no one she knows who lives there, but she wonders what sort of a state it is that could have elected Ronald Reagan governor. Whenever she sees him on television she is struck by that strange hairdo and that oddly vapid smile. He seems to speak in platitudes, as if someone had implanted a tiny tape recorder in his head while he slept, and now presses the proper buttons by remote control. Not quitting politics? What future could he have now that he's served his two terms in California? If Richard Nixon somehow wins in November, would he actually appoint a gregarious idiot like this to his cabinet? Well, possibly. But as what? Secretary of B-Movies. Secretary of Cretins.

Here is a story of more immediate relevance:

### Court Bars March in Memphis; Dr. King Calls Order 'Illegal'

She hadn't wanted to think at all about Ben, but now she recalls their attenuated telephone conversation Tuesday night, when he woke her at two in the morning and then hung up on her. He'd said there was a possibility he and Randall might meet with King. The story quotes King as saying there is a "real possibility" he might not obey the federal court order, and just

311

go ahead with the march. She feels adrenaline course through her midsection. Is it out of concern for Ben, who might be in the front lines when the police or the National Guard or both descend upon the illegal marchers? Or is it concern for herself, because Ben is such an unfaithful bastard?

On the other hand, does Ben's unfaithfulness justify her own? Her own *single* infidelity. Prosper in fact is only the fourth boy she's ever slept with; she imagines Ben's conquests to be ten times that number, or twenty. But Ben has never had sex with her best friend. Probably.

She has an urge to call him, right now, and tell him everything that's happened in the last fifteen hours or so, and see what he says. But of course he's never even told her where he's staying. She could call Kennedy headquarters downtown; she's got a number that goes straight to Ed McCaffrey, who's Randall's superior and would certainly know where they are.

She begins flipping the pages of the newspaper, not paying much attention to them as they pass, until she gets deep into the second section, where there are reviews of two new movies. One is science fiction, by Stanley Kubrick, called *2001: A Space Odyssey.* What a pretentious title. The other is *La Chinoise*, by Jean-Luc Godard, who is Prosper's favorite director. The three of them went in January to a Godard double feature at the Thalia, a stuffy little theater on 95th Street just west of Broadway: one movie with Brigitte Bardot and Jack Palance, which was quite strange and intriguing when it wasn't boring, and one black-and-white movie about a prostitute, played by Godard's wife, or perhaps ex-wife, which Maddy thought was wonderful. Ben walked out of the first one, the Brigitte Bardot one, and didn't come back. Perhaps she and Prosper will go see *La Chinoise*.

312

## THIRTY-SIX

Leroy Telford, as Randall and Lee Floyd have predicted, is great. The band comes out first--wearing iridescent blue jackets and black pants tonight--and does eight or ten minutes worth of instrumentals, tunes familiar but nameless to Ben. At the conclusion of their second number the bass player steps to the microphone and says, "Thank you, ladies and gentlemen. Thank you, Memphis, Tennessee. And now we gonna bring out the star of our show--the one, the only, the *toast* of soul music up and down the Atlantic Coast, the lean and luscious lover man...*Leroy Telford*!" Whereupon there is enthusiastic but hardly deafening applause from the crowd that has grown by now to fifty or sixty people, and Leroy Telford struts slowly onstage. To Ben he suggests a young Chuck Berry: tall and thin, chocolate-skinned, with a strong chin and pronounced cheekbones. The bass player steps back from the microphone and plays a familiar progression; Telford seizes the mike from its stand and begins singing "My Girl." To Ben's ears the band's rendition is letter-perfect, and Telford if anything sounds a little richer, a little more mercurial than the record Ben has heard a thousand times.

"What you think?" Floyd yells in his ear.

"Sounds fantastic to me," Ben yells back.

Telford finishes "My Girl" with his back to the audience, holding the final note for a good thirty seconds against the bass player's vamp. Then he turns to the crowd's applause, does a quick little bow, and says, "Since we're in

313

Memphis, why don't we do a little Memphis tune," and the band launches into another song Ben knows, "Knock on Wood."

Randall yells to Delphine, "Could I interest you in a dance?" And Delphine nods her head in response. Just before rising, she brushes her hand across Ben's knee. He's not quite sure what that means, but assumes it's some sort of reassurance that even though she's dancing with the man who's just been treating him like shit, her heart is still his. He finishes his second glass of beer and pours himself a third.

Randall isn't that great a dancer, despite his athleticism. Among the five couples currently on the floor, Ben judges Randall--who tends to flail and overstate his moves--the worst dancer, and Delphine by far the best. Delphine is fluid and lovely. Ben considers himself a pretty good dancer, a very good dancer, for a white guy. Would he even be permitted to dance with Delphine here? Perhaps not if it were a white club; perhaps she wouldn't even be welcome in a white club. Probably she wouldn't want to go in the first place.

Again the Leroy Telford version gives life to a song Ben has heard hundreds of times, mainly on car radios. It's another tune with a catchy bass line, and he watches the bass player for a while, then watches the two horn players swaying in rhythm to the music, watches the drummer keeping the beat, finally can't keep his eyes off Delphine: it's a mid-tempo song, way too fast for a slow dance, but not fast enough for abandonment; it leaves Randall looking like some kind of marsh bird with its feet stuck in the mud, while Delphine's arms and legs work in marvelous harmony, and the rise and fall of her breasts at once reminds him of their intimacy and causes him to crave it.

Midway through the next song, the up-tempo "Funky Broadway," Lee Floyd excuses himself, leaving Ben alone at the table--alone with the dregs of a pitcher of beer. The dance floor is much better populated by now; there are twelve, maybe fifteen couples out there, and Randall doesn't look nearly as ridiculous doing what Ben assumes to be the Funky Broadway itself. He watches Floyd make his way to the bar, then to the side of the stage, where he spends some time shouting in the ear of the young man who untangles wires and adjusts amplifiers. A minute later "Funky Broadway" winds down, and during the ensuing applause Ben sees the wire/amp guy quick-walk onto the stage and speak to Leroy Telford. What's this about?

"Thank you very much," Telford says from the front of the stage. "Thank you, people." He wipes sweat from his forehead, makes a show of catching his breath, and says, "Hey, what you know but the boss man here tells me we got some celebrities in the house." At this moment the waitress arrives with a new pitcher of beer; Ben reaches for his wallet and grabs a couple of bills, but she shakes her head, seizes the nearly empty pitcher, and departs, as Telford continues, "We got two gentlemen down here from New York City, two gentlemen workin' to make Robert Kennedy the next president of the U-nited States!" And Ben, in the process of pouring himself his fourth beer, realizes that he, sitting alone at a table in Memphis, listening to a smattering of applause plus a whistle or two, is one of the celebrities in question.

"*Hey*," Telford speaks into the microphone, "y'all can do better that *that*. You want that old cracker Johnson to keep sendin' brothers to Vietnam to get themselves killed?" There is laughter all around Ben, and a few cheers.

"Damn right, you don't," Telford continues. "So we got a couple of *ded*icated brothers here tonight, doin' *good* work, goin' round the country tryin' to get somebody elected get us the hell *out* of Vietnam. So give the brothers a hand!" Now there is enthusiastic applause, and Telford stands at the edge of the stage. "Randall...Ben...where you at? Stand up! Take a bow!"

Ben sees Randall, standing some five feet in front of the stage, wave his hand, whereupon a spotlight hits him and the crowd applauds. Randall then points at Ben and raises his hands, palms up, urging him to stand. In an instance of doing something that's against his better judgment, Ben gets to his feet, and feels the bright light hit him a second later. It seems to Ben that there is a hush--an ever-so-brief moment of absolute silence while all these black people take in the recognition that one of the "brothers" is a white boy--before everything returns to normal. There is applause; there is some cheering and hollering, and then Leroy Telford turns to his band, counts out a rapid beat, and they break into the Otis Redding version of "Respect." Ben sits down.

Delphine and Randall rejoin him after "Respect." Now the band is in the midst of another old Otis Redding song, "Mr. Pitiful." Sweaty and grinning, Randall says, "I was hopin' for a slow one. Gettin' too old for this."

Ben pours Delphine a fresh glass of beer as she plops down next to him. In her ear, he says, "You looked great out there."

"Did I?" she says. She has a large swallow of beer and says, "Did you enjoy your moment of fame?"

He nods energetically. "Took me by surprise, a little."

"Hey," Randall shouts, "Leroy Telford not only leads the world's greatest cover band, the dude's got the right politics! I gotta talk to him after the show, man. I'm serious. Get him to do some Kennedy gigs. Could be good for both sides--get him some exposure, get us some great music."

    Just below table level, Ben touches Delphine's left arm,
feels its warmth, its cover of dewy moisture, which like nearly
everything about her he finds erotic, and runs his finger from
her wrist to her elbow. He shouts to Randall, "Sounds good to
me!" And Randall makes a wide-eyed, palms-raised gesture of
*why not?*

    Everybody's in a better mood now, it's clear. Ben says
to Delphine, "Can we dance?"

    "How do you mean?"

    "Can you and I dance here, now?"

    "You want to dance?" She says. "Sure. Why not?"

    "Let's do it, then."

    "Don't I get to rest?"

    "All right," Ben says, "you've got a minute."

    Delphine drains her beer and slams the glass down on
the table. "Okay," she says, "show me your stuff."

    If Ben has felt a sense of communion with Delphine
previously--the ease with which they've gotten to know each
other, the way they meshed in bed--it's nothing but underscored
on the dance floor. At first he simply does what she does. It's
not an easy thing to do, absorbing someone's style and motion
so quickly that it's almost as if you're anticipating every move.
It's not something most people can do. She knows that,
obviously. She makes eye contact, which isn't something his
dance partners have done in the past. Self-conscious white girls
look at the floor, or close their eyes. Maddy hardly dances at
all. Delphine grins at him as they get into this incredible
groove, moving to "I Second That Emotion" as if they've been
choreographed. If this were a movie, everyone else would clear
a space for them and stand off to the side in appreciation, in
awe.

"You can *dance*," she says to him, breathless, and he shrugs modestly. Leroy Telford, a little breathless himself, says, "Hey, y'all, we gonna slow it down a little now. Gonna do a tune written by the great Curtis Mayfield..."

It's a song Ben doesn't know, a ballad, just too slow for dancing apart. He puts his arm around her waist and she draws close to him, as if contact this intimate is permissible even between a colored girl and a white boy as long as they're on the dance floor. A few seconds in he realizes that Delphine is reacting to the song's slightly Latin beat, syncopating her steps; he joins her, and their dance evolves into a slow rumba. "Who does this song?" he says in her ear.

"The Five Stairsteps," she tells him, and she sings along, "We can overcome, and make two strangers become as one." As Ben considers whether she's simply chosen to join in at this point in the song or whether there's greater significance, he's jolted from behind, causing him to stumble and Delphine, in reaction, to lurch backward. They both manage to stay upright, and when Ben turns to look for the truck that hit him he sees nothing but apparently oblivious dancers. "You okay?" he says, as he and Delphine resume the dance. "What the hell was that?"

"I'm fine," she says. "That boy in the black satin jacket." She turns them around. "You see him?"

The young man about Ben's size and age is now ten feet from them; he and his partner have matching Afros, and they're the only couple on the floor currently, inappropriately, dancing apart. "Drunk," Delphine says. "Don't worry about it."

The next song is even slower. Ben and Delphine are now virtually stationary on the floor, swaying more than dancing to the music, when he's again clobbered from behind, if anything a bit harder this time, but higher up, so it's not a question of keeping his balance as much as feeling a sharp pain in the middle of his spine. He releases Delphine and turns quickly, to see the young man in the black satin jacket and the elevated Afro facing him. Ben says, "I think you want to watch where you dance."

The young man smiles fiercely, "I was gonna say the same thing to you."

"Okay," Ben says, doing his best to ignore the adrenaline that's starting to surge. "Why don't we both do our best to stay out of each other's way?"

"That ain't what I'm talkin' about," the young man says.

Delphine seizes Ben's left arm. "Don't pay him any mind, Ben. Let's go sit down, please."

"Yeah," the young man says. "Listen to that half-white bitch, Ben. Sit your honky ass down, motherfucker."

"Ben, come *on*," Delphine urges.

Ben is conscious that people around them have stopped dancing. The music continues, but at least on this portion of the floor more attention is being paid to the shouting match that involves the only white guy in the club. And as far as he's concerned, everything was tolerable until the "half-white bitch" part. "Who the hell do you think you are," he says, "saying something like that?"

"Who the fuck you think *you* are," the young man replies, "comin' in a place like this?"

Delphine tugs on his arm. "Ben, for God's sake." Her voice has risen in pitch. Ben figures he could hit this kid on the jaw once, and that would be it. Not that the kid isn't muscular, not that they wouldn't be fairly equally matched in some sort of formal fight. But the kid is drunk, and Ben could deck him with one quick punch. He has a feeling, unfortunately, that it wouldn't be a great thing to do. As well, just at this moment he perceives one body in motion, someone making his way

319

through all the other immobile figures on the floor, and recognizes Randall. "Okay," he says to Delphine, "let's go then." He makes a half turn and waves to Randall, and presently feels what he assumes to be the young man's shoe striking his right buttock with great force. Whereupon Ben wheels around and delivers an uppercut to the young man's jaw and--just as he'd anticipated--his antagonist falls to the floor in a heap.

"Who the *hell* do you think you are--John fucking *Wayne*?" Randall has asked Delphine if she might wait in the car while he had a talk with Ben. "Do you have any fucking self-control at all? Are you just *stuck* in your fucking adolescence?"

"No," Ben says, standing here in the rapidly cooling night air.

"No, what?"

"No, I'm not stuck in my fucking adolescence, and no I'm not gonna take this from you. I don't deserve this."

"Jesus *Christ*, Ben." Randall has lowered his voice, at least. "Jesus Christ. Do you have any idea what you're doing half the time?"

"Yes. Yes, I do have an idea what I'm doing, when some son of a bitch keeps bumping me intentionally, calls the girl I'm with a bitch, and then kicks me in the ass, I'm gonna retaliate, and I don't see what's wrong with that. I didn't see anybody flocking to that asshole's defense. Did you?"

"Look, we're not here on spring break." Randall's tone is almost down to normal. "That wasn't a frat house...I'm sorry, an *eating* club. It amazes me that I have to tell you shit like this, but, one, we are down here representing a man who wants to become president of the United States, and two, you are the only white guy in a room full of black people."

"This is so fucking hypocritical!" Now it's Ben raising his voice. "What's the story, Randall? Are black people worse judges of character than white people? Are black people gonna jump all over some white guy because he puts a drunk, out-of-line black guy in his place? Look at what happened, for Christ's sake. That guy had it coming, and everybody there felt that way."

"I wouldn't be so sure," Randall says.

Ben feels himself starting to shiver; it's certainly not because of the weather, which tornadoes or no tornadoes is still remarkably warm this late night. "What are you talking about?"

"Did you happen to notice the jacket that kid was wearing?"

"Sure. Black satin jacket. So what?"

"The kid was an *Invader*, Ben. Or at least he was wearing an Invaders jacket."

"So?"

"So maybe there weren't any other Invaders at Corinna's tonight, but you can bet your ass the story's gonna get around town, that the white guy from the Kennedy campaign cold-cocked one of our boys last night. And you can bet your ass the story's gonna get better with each retelling--how the honky was messin' with some black chick, and the honky hit what's-his-name when he wasn't lookin'." Randall pauses, catches his breath. "*And*, how the hell we gonna meet with the bee oh pee guys tomorrow night when they know you've been punchin' out their brothers?"

"Okay," Ben says. "Okay. I get the point. I had no idea the guy was an Invader, obviously. If I *had* known, I have to say I don't know if I would've acted differently. If we're talking about stuff getting around town, what are people gonna say about the white guy from the Kennedy campaign who gets kicked in the ass and just walks away as if nothing happened?"

"I've got a simple question for you, Ben," Randall says. "Did we see someone speak tonight?"

"Yes. Of course we did."

"Do you profess that this man is one of your idols?"

"I profess that. I *believe* that. Of course."

"What do you think *he* would have done if that drunk Black Power asshole kicked him in the ass?"

Delphine drives them back toward Mason Temple, and Ben, having no sense of perspective from this direction, can't remember where he parked the car. As Randall grumbles in the passenger seat (it's past one a.m., and they've got to be up at seven), Delphine must drive directly to the Temple for Ben to get his bearings. He suspects that at this point Randall *wants* him not to be able to find the car, but once he's oriented Ben leads Delphine directly to the Mustang.

He lingers in the back seat after Randall has left the Comet. He rests his left hand on her right shoulder and says, "Can we see each other tomorrow?"

"I'm not sure. I've got a real busy day."

Is she brushing him off? "I'm sorry about all this."

"About what in particular?" Her voice is pleasantly gentle.

"At the club. I shouldn't have hit that guy."

"Far as I'm concerned, you did the right thing," she says. "I'll try to call you tomorrow. Maybe in the early afternoon. I might be free around four or five."

## The Mountaintop

They drive back to the Holiday Inn in silence. At stoplights Ben glances at Randall, wishing to speak, but finds him with eyes closed. He guesses that Randall is not sleeping. They walk from the garage to the elevator, still not a word; they ascend to the second floor, and only as Randall inserts the key in his door does he speak. "Up at seven, right?"

"Right," Ben replies.

"Don't forget--good chance we meet with King tomorrow."

"Got it," Ben says. The important word in that last sentence was *we*.

In his room, exhausted and a little drunk, he flops fully clothed on the big bed, and thinks of Maddy. Odds are he'll miss her again in the morning, because she leaves the apartment so damned early. But can he bring himself to wake her for the second night in a row?

He dials for an outside line, then dials their number and listens to the telephone ring: four times, eight times, twelve times, rehearsing his apology and his explanation, getting more anxious because with each successive ring he imagines Maddy in a deeper sleep. Finally, when she hasn't answered after twenty rings, maybe twenty-five, he hangs up. Obviously she's covered the phone with pillows, or done something to muffle the ringer so he *couldn't* wake her up, which means she's probably pretty pissed off at him.

Which means he'd better make an effort. What time does she leave the apartment in the morning? Seven thirty or so, which would be six thirty here. He dials the front desk and asks for a six o'clock wake-up call.

## THIRTY-SEVEN

Two blocks up Columbus when he heard the sirens, Alex told himself to be cool, to maintain his fast-walk pace but not to run, not to give the cops reason to suspect he was anything more than a white guy in a blue summer suit hustling through a predominantly Puerto Rican neighborhood at one thirty in the morning. By the time he got across Cathedral Parkway onto Morningside Drive he felt a great deal more secure, but couldn't help noticing he was breathing heavily and covered with sweat, which made the night air and the cool wind all the more biting.

What am I going to do with the gun? He asked himself, realizing how foolish it had been not to wipe it down and toss it into a trash can or under a parked car, that if the cops *had* happened to stop him back there his ass would've been grass. Now he thinks that when he gets home he should change clothes and go down to the car, drive over to Riverside Park and throw the damn thing in the river. In fact, the foolish thing would've been to ditch it back there, because if the cops found it they could trace it to Elliot through the serial number.

But what if Flaco's not dead, or what if one of those other guys—the huge fat one Julio or the one with the leather jacket Rafael—comes after him? Wouldn't it be good to have the gun?

He's freezing when he gets back to the apartment, trembling as if he'd been stranded on an ice floe off the coast of Greenland. He takes a long shower, during which he thinks a lot about what Flaco had said just before he shot him: *He's ballin' your old lady*. The concept is so complex that he has to study its various aspects in isolation. One, that Lydia would be with that Puerto Rican asshole in the first place, when she was so pissed off about the whole thing; two, that she would be *spending the night with him*, sleeping with him; three, that if Rafael heard what Flaco was telling him over the intercom, all that shit about the *maricón gringo*, then Rafael and Lydia both would have figured out that it was Alex who shot him; but, four, that Lydia would never believe in a thousand years that Alex could shoot anybody; five, if he wants her back, and he does most certainly want her back, he's got to downplay the jealousy and be really cool about the gun and not even let her know about the car; except, six, if Rafael or Julio decides to take revenge, then he's got to have the gun at the ready.

It's all too confounding, too self-contradictory to make sense of.

Back in his jeans and work shirt, he takes the Walther and the baggy of marijuana from his jacket and leaves the gun on the bed while he hangs his suit in the closet. He stuffs the pistol under the mattress, at the foot of the bed. Bullets? They're in the knife drawer in the kitchen. He retrieves them and squeezes them in next to the gun. His pulse is still racing—it's got to be about a hundred and ten. He rolls a good-sized joint and puts Miles Davis's *Porgy and Bess* on the stereo. It's the most soothing thing he can think of.

*****

Lydia can't get back to sleep. Thank God she and Rafael had gone to bed early—like about ten o'clock—so she'd slept a while before all hell broke loose. Then she drifted off maybe an hour afterwards after talking with Rafael about Flaco, but she woke up when he got out of bed and now she lies here

325

in a semi-stupor, not quite willing to lift herself out of bed to go into the other room and comfort him. Granted, she only met him for about half an hour, but as far as she was concerned Flaco was the scum of the earth, the epitome of everything that was wrong with Latin men—you want something, you take it, whether it's a girl or Alex's movie camera. Rafael of course remembers the kid he grew up with, how Flaco was always like a foot taller than him, and his protector when things got rough. Flaco got suspended from junior high when he was caught screwing a girl in a stall in the boys' bathroom. He would have been kicked out altogether, but Rafael—who was an A student and a starting guard on the basketball team—convinced the principal that Flaco had good qualities and that his life shouldn't be ruined because he made one mistake, and besides the girl in question had done it with every other boy in school. This part of the argument didn't sit particularly well with Lydia, even if it was true. She can still feel the bastard's fingers sliding down her torso and she has no regrets that he's dead. Except that Rafael does, and he wonders whether if he'd buzzed him in Flaco would still be alive. More likely, whoever killed Flaco would have killed them all. Unless it *was* Alex. The idea remains insane to her: Even if he really got himself fucked up, he'd just get crazy and mystical. Maybe he'd decide some lady's car belonged to him and he wouldn't move, but he wouldn't lay a finger on anyone.

Listening to Rafael pace in the living room, finally she musters the energy to get out of bed. Seeing her, he stops in mid-passage. "Did I wake you up?"

"Sweetie," she says, "just come to bed with me. Maybe you can fall asleep."

He shakes his head. "You think he could've done it?"

"Who? Alex? You know I don't think so."

"Yeah, but that *maricón gringo* thing. It just keeps going through my head."

"You're telling me Flaco never called anybody else that?"

"It's a hell of a coincidence, don't you think? Flaco rips off this guy's shit, humiliates him…"

"How do you know he humiliated him?"

"Julio says. He pushed him around, said all kinds of shit to him. Then a couple of days later some white guy shoots him. It kinda adds up, don't you think?"

"Yeah, except if you know Alex. His dad is, like, a big shot business guy in Florida, and he's into hunting and everything. Alex hates guns and all that shit." She stands in the doorway, wearing just her shirt. The heat's off and it's cool, if not cold. She thinks what a good idea it would be to call in sick this morning, but she did Tuesday morning, and union or no union she doesn't need Mrs. Sálazar on her case. If she called in sick she could go over to the apartment at eight or so and confront Alex, if he were confrontable, if he weren't stoned out of his mind. She says, "What would you do if it was him?"

"I don't know," Rafael says. "Like, would I go to the cops? I don't think so. Flaco pulled so much shit—probably I don't even know half of it—that somebody would've killed him next month or next year, or five years from now. But maybe it just wouldn't have happened outside my door."

She has convinced him to lie down, and now at six thirty he sleeps soundly, next to her. She, on the other hand, is wide awake.

She dresses in warm clothes, moving about quietly, checking on him every few seconds to make sure he isn't

327

stirring. She writes him a quick note and leaves it on the bathroom sink.

She could probably find a taxi on Broadway, but it's only a twelve-block walk to the apartment, so she should be there in plenty of time to talk to Alex and still make it to school by eight. If he's even there.

She lets herself in; the apartment, as usual, is stifling— both windows shut tight. She finds him stretched out supine on the bed, fully clothed, down to his shoes. Surprisingly, the place is fairly neat, and except for a slightly stale marijuana odor, there's no evidence of drugs. She sits on the bed and touches his forehead. "Alex? Hey, wake up."

\*\*\*

He's aware that someone's speaking to him, rubbing his head, but he's been in a deep sleep and he's not sure whether he's dreaming. He's exhausted and wants very much to remain asleep, but the other person in this dream or non-dream is persistent. Can this be Lydia? In fuzzy semi-consciousness he remembers the other night when either she came in the middle of the night or he dreamed that she came in the middle of the night, and he concludes with the logic of the half-asleep that it's happening again, that dream of visitation, and there's no real need to awaken. But she keeps at it. "Babe," he says, "don't wake me up."

"Wake *up*, Alex, for Christ sake!" She says.

He opens his eyes, and there she is, in her coat, sitting on the side of the bed. "It's you," he says.

"You're fucking right, it's me," she replies.

"Hey," he says. "How've you been? I missed you."

"Listen, I've just got a few minutes and I have to talk to you. Are you all right? Can you make sense?"

What does she mean? What does any of this mean? "Of course I can make sense. Where've you been?"

"Where have *you* been?" She says.

"I've been right here, babe. Did you talk to Maddy? I've been going to class. Those fucking Puerto Rican guys came back and stole my stuff."

"Alex," she says, "what did you do last night?"

What a terrible time to have to make important decisions, when you've just woken up from a sound sleep and there's so much at stake. "What time is it, babe?"

"It's seven o'clock, a little after. Where were you last night, please, Alex?"

"I went to a party," he says. "You've met Chip Boyle, from Princeton, has a place on the East Side. I *missed* you, babe. I didn't have any way to get in touch with you."

"Alex, for Christ sake, you could've called me at school..."

"Yeah, I did. Or I tried to. But I saw Maddy last night, with Prosper. I smoked some dope...I got this really incredible grass from upstate New York. I smoked some with these guys I knew from college. We had a good time."

"Is that all you did?"

He can't tell her about Nicola, about the car, about the drive down to Delaware, about Elliot's license, about the Mafioso car salesman, any of the adventures of the last two days. "Yeah, well, I came home. I walked home. It was good to be out." She sits on the bed, staring at the wall above his head. He puts his arm around her. "Why don't you come to bed with me?"

"I have to go to school, Alex, for Christ sake. Why are you sleeping with your clothes on?"

He sits up and puts his arm around her shoulder. "I'll take 'em off for you."

She moves away, sliding a couple of feet down the bed. "You know that guy who ripped you off, Alex? The tall one, Flaco?"

"Sure, I know him."

"Well, he's dead. Somebody shot him last night."

Alex sits in silence for a few seconds, absorbing two momentous discoveries: that he's actually killed someone, and that the man he killed was telling the truth just before he killed him. "It couldn't happen to a nicer guy," he says. His brain begins to lurch as he considers what he isn't telling Lydia versus what she isn't telling him. He says, "How do you know that?"

"How do I know what?"

"That somebody shot Flaco last night. Was it on the news?"

She moves still farther down the bed. He wonders whether he's put an end to the conversation, or whether she'll confess. After a very long time she says, "I was there, Alex. Flaco was trying to get into Rafael's building, and I was upstairs with Rafael."

Playing dumb to the hilt, he says, "Who's Rafael?"

"Jesus, Alex," she says, "are you fucking brain dead? Rafael was one of the three guys Monday morning. You spent the whole fucking night with him."

"Okay, okay. I remember. What the hell were you doing with Rafael? I don't recall that you and he were the best of friends."

"Things change," she says.

"How did they change, in this case?"

330

"You were stoned. He was nice." He'll grant her the first part. He still doesn't really get the second. She says, "On the intercom, Flaco said he was outside with the *maricón gringo*. That's what he called you Monday morning."

"I'm sure I'm not the only white guy he calls that."

"Yeah," she says, nodding.

There is another silence. Alex feels a great longing for her, wishes he could undress her and pull her into bed with him. There's a little bit of anger, a little bit of jealousy, a small sense of betrayal, but not nearly as much as he might have expected, perhaps because he realizes his role in driving her away. He says, "Will you come back?"

She shakes her head. "I don't know. We'll talk about it, okay?"

"Let's talk about it now. Let's talk about it in bed."

She stands up. "No. I have just enough time to get to school."

## THIRTY-EIGHT

Maddy speaks to him. "We should go soon."

He's barely conscious, but awfully glad to see her. She's back in the clothes she wore to the party, sitting on the edge of the bed. He woke up briefly a couple of hours ago, found himself alone under the covers, and wondered if last night and

331

this morning were just a dream. He touches his chin and feels a
day and a half's worth of stubble. His tongue feels as if it's been
replaced by a dust cloth. He says, "What time is it?"

"Ten thirty."

"Jesus Christ," he says. "How did it get so late? What
have you been doing all this time?"

"Walking around. Reading the paper. Enjoying myself.
It's wonderful here."

He feels a curious mixture of anxiety for the lost time,
time that he could have spent with her, and pleasure that she's
been having a good time even without him, where he lives, and
something close to elation that she's here, sitting on his bed.
He sits up, and puts his hand on her knee. "I'm extremely glad
you're here," he says.

She leans in to kiss his cheek, his stubble. "That's very
nice of you to say, but we should be going."

The hand that was on her knee now strokes her leg.
"Hey," he says, "I'll call Martin at the radio station, you call
Mrs. what's-her-name at school, and we'll tell them we were
abducted by aliens."

"I'm sure they're on to that one."

"Seriously. Not the aliens part, but we could just spend
the rest of the day here. Whatever excuse you made before, it
turns out it's just taking you a little longer."

"That's not our deal," Maddy says. "You're supposed to
get me to school by noon. And you don't want to lose your
job."

"I won't lose my job. This isn't even part of my job.
Martin wants me to help him prepare for Cousin Brucie."

"From what you've told me about Martin, I'd say you'd
better go to your meeting."

Slowly, he slides his hand from her hip to her shoulder, feeling the sleekness of her ribs, the softness where her breast begins. "Even if I lose my job, what difference does it make? In a few weeks I've got to get out of here, one way or the other."

"You don't know that."

"I can be pretty sure."

"We can talk about this later," she says. "Now we should get going."

He runs his hand now past her collarbone and across her breast. "We've got plenty of time to spare," he says. "Why don't you let me take your clothes off?"

She moves away and stands up; his hand drops to the bedspread. "Let's go," she says.

They're on the Hutchinson River Parkway when Maddy says, "Prosper, what *are* you going to do?"

If he tells her how much his life has changed in the last fifteen hours or so, will she burst his bubble immediately? "What would you like me to do?"

"I'd like you to figure out something that doesn't involve getting drafted or going to jail. I don't understand why you've gotten fatalistic all of a sudden."

"I haven't gotten fatalistic at all."

"Last night in the living room you said you could file for conscientious objector status..."

"But by their definition there's no way I'd get it."

"You said you could delay the whole process for a few months, until Kennedy's elected."

He shakes his head. "Maybe I'd delay it for three months, five months. *If* Kennedy's elected in November, he doesn't take office till January. By that time my goose is cooked."

333

"It sounded like a pretty good plan to me."

"Ever since I graduated I've had this thing hanging over my head. Go to graduate school or you'll get drafted. Go to *divinity* school so you'll be sure you won't be drafted. Get married and have a kid fast, and then they'll never draft you. I'm sick of all that. That's why I took the job with Martin..."

"I know. And you were convinced you could fail the physical. But you didn't."

Minutes pass. Prosper steers the Valiant onto Bruckner Boulevard. He says, "What's going on between you and me?"

It takes Maddy half a minute to reply. "I'm not sure."

And Prosper easily as long again. "The reason I ask is that I'd go to Canada tomorrow if you'd come with me."

"I couldn't do that," she says.

"I don't mean literally tomorrow."

"I know you don't. But I've got a job. I've got a place to live. I'm settled in. I've got relationships with teachers and kids..."

"And Ben," Prosper says.

"The hell with Ben."

"Do you mean that? Are you fed up with him? Because if you're not, I could give you about twelve reasons why you should be."

"Don't do that," Maddy says. "He's your friend."

The light turns green. "I wasn't *going* to do it," he says. "It was a rhetorical device. I *could* give you twelve reasons, but I don't need to, because you know them already."

"So it's not that you've been counting the girls he's slept with since we've been together?"

"No, but I'm sure *he* has."

"You're sure he's slept with girls or you're sure he's been counting them?"

334

"Both."

"So then you *are...*"

"I am what?"

"You are giving me reasons not to stay with Ben."

"No," Prosper says. "No, for Christ's sake, I'm not. He doesn't confide in me, Maddy. He certainly doesn't brag about sleeping around to me, because he knows I care about you."

They're both silent now for several minutes, driving through increasingly heavy traffic in the Bronx, heading for the Triborough Bridge. Once they hit the bridge, they'll be about ten minutes from P.S. 72. He says, "Do you know when he's coming back?"

"Prosper, for God's sake, I've told you, I don't even know where he's staying." There's no anger in her voice--at least none directed at him.

After another brief silence he says, "Are you going to tell him what we did?"

"What do you think I should do?"

"I think you should come away with me."

"What do you think I should do about telling Ben?"

"Tell him," Prosper says without hesitation.

"It'll probably put the slightest little crimp in your friendship."

"That's not very high on my list of priorities right now."

"Why not? What's he done to you?"

"Nothing," Prosper says. "That's not the way I mean it. I mean that I don't care about me and Ben nearly as much as I care about me and you."

On the bridge, he hands a quarter to the man in the tollbooth. He says, "Maddy—what about tonight? After the TV stuff with Martin we've got to do some real work, and I

335

should be done about six thirty or seven. This guy I made friends with in New Haven, Leotis, may be coming into town. It would be great if we could all go out to dinner."

"Oh, God, not tonight, Prosper..."

"We could make it an early night..."

"No, I mean, I'm not free. I'm doing parent conferences tonight. I meet with all these moms and dads—*mamas y papas* who get to be puzzled by my accent. It probably goes till about eight or eight thirty..."

"Late dinner, then. Dessert."

"I'll be really wiped out by then."

"I'd accept you in any condition."

"We'll see. Okay?"

"It works even better if you're really wiped out. I park the car in your neighborhood. If Leotis comes into town, we meet at the school. There's got to be a good place to eat nearby, right?"

"Depends on your definition of 'good.'"

"Okay, *decent*. If Leotis can't come, I drive out and pick you up. Either way, you get a ride home

"I can't guarantee anything," she says.

He takes the ramp onto the East River Drive--a long, sharp downhill curve. "Okay... there's one more thing I need to tell you now." Her lips form a minor frown, and he says, "It's not about you and me. It's a little-known fact about Carl Orff. You know about Carl Orff?"

"Of course I do. He wrote *Carmina Burana*. And some other thing—you told me once—that Sonny of Sonny and Cher plagiarized for 'I Got You Babe.'"

"Exactly," Prosper says. "I just found out that right around the turn of the century, when Orff was a child prodigy in Munich, Annie Oakley visited Germany..."

"You're kidding."

"This is in the historical record. You can go down to the main library tomorrow and look it up on microfilm. Annie Oakley did a show in Munich, and she heard about this amazing piano-playing kid, and she convinced his parents that they should go on the road together. So first he'd play some Beethoven, then she'd do her trick shooting, and all in all it was quite a show. And they were billed as Little Orff and Annie."

Maddy laughs--one quick, explosive burst. "But wouldn't it have been *Kleine Orff und Annie*? Wouldn't that have ruined the joke?"

"It was close enough, for the Germans," Prosper says. Stopped at a red light at Second Avenue and 106th Street, he reaches across the transmission hump to her bucket seat and strokes her leg. "Maddy, I wish I could tell you.... This has just been..." As he pauses, searching for words, she sprawls across the gap and kisses his neck. "It was a great night," she says. "A great, wonderful morning. I wouldn't have missed it."

*Peter Delacorte*

## THIRTY-NINE

Ben is semi-conscious when the phone rings,
anticipating the wake-up call. "Six a.m., sir--time to get up,"
says a pleasant, lilting female voice. "Thanks," Ben replies. He
sits up in bed and tries to clear his head. He never needs much
sleep and hasn't had much, but he must have consumed a full
pitcher of beer at Corinna's, and he's more than a little fuzzy.
What's he going to tell Maddy? That things have been really
busy, and exciting. That he had to hang up night before last
because of an impromptu strategy session. That he's not sure
when they'll be getting back, but there's a good chance they'll be
meeting with Martin Luther King tonight or tomorrow. And of
course that he saw King speak! With this huge fucking storm
raging outside: thunder and lightning you wouldn't believe, and
King likening himself to Moses.

He clears his throat and shakes his head, feeling a little
buzz, as if something isn't connected quite right. He gets an
outside line and calls the apartment. Three rings, four, and no
answer. Is she in the bathroom with the water running? Five
rings and six. She should already have taken her shower by
now. Is she *really* angry at him, making him suffer, or thinking
she's making him suffer? Twelve rings, fifteen. Could she have
spent the night somewhere else? In Short Hills? Could there
have been a family emergency? After twenty rings he hangs up.
He gets out of bed and trudges to the bathroom, where it takes
him about five minutes to empty his bladder, then returns to bed
and falls back to sleep right away.

338

## The Mountaintop

Up again at seven, no less fuzzy. Randall is his usual
ball of fire at breakfast, laying out the day's schedule: They'll
return to Memphis State at nine, to meet with a convocation of
Political Science classes until eleven. Then some kind of
gathering with faculty, and depending on how long that lasts
somewhere between ninety minutes and two hours free for
lunch, unless they're having lunch with the faculty. Randall's
not sure about that. Then maybe if MLK can squeeze them in
they'll see him in the early afternoon at the Lorraine Motel. If
not, maybe they'll see Ralph Abernathy, who droned on
interminably last night. Randall has spoken to Abernathy at
some point, and Abernathy has indicated that King would truly
like to get together with representatives of the Kennedy
campaign because there is clearly so much common ground. So
if not this afternoon, almost certainly tomorrow morning, before
King is off to Atlanta, or somewhere. This evening at eight
thirty there is a tentative meeting with the leaders of the radical
group, the Black Organizing Project and Randall's friend
William Marchand, and possibly some of the ministers Randall
has befriended.

Ben stares at his half-empty plate of scrambled eggs and
hash browns; he has little desire for the rest of his breakfast, an
uncommon absence of appetite. He spears a bit of potato with
his fork, wondering what he'll say to Martin Luther King when
the time comes, or whether as usual he should just let Randall
do all the talking. He imagines that one-on-one he could have a
lengthy, spirited conversation with King. Possibly he'd tell him
about the confrontation with the guy in the black satin jacket
last night, and ask him what *he* would have done. As a young
man. A young man dancing with a white girl in a room of
whites? No, that wouldn't be analogous at all.

339

"So, tell me, Ben," Randall interrupts his reverie, "how do you see the next few months of your life?"

What kind of question is this? Randall's tone of voice seems neutral, unaccusing. Ben finds himself lifting the fork to his mouth and ingesting the bit of potato; it's cold, salty, and greasy, and for a moment he's on the verge of nausea. "The campaign," he says. "It's gonna be exciting."

"You think so?"

"Sure, I think so. Don't you think so?"

"Yeah, I think so." Randall pauses. "Tell me about your role in it."

What's Randall after? Should Ben be candid, be modest? "A lot of that depends on you, doesn't it?"

"Just tell me what you'd like to happen. If things worked out best."

"Well, I'd be on staff, first of all, so I wouldn't be living off savings, and so I'd have some authority. And after that, hell, it's hard to say. But if we win in Indiana I figure that's gonna give the campaign a big boost. I'm just guessing here, but I'll bet there'll be a lot more kids volunteering, and campaign offices opening up where there haven't been any, and somebody's gonna have to be in charge of them. That's something I think I'd be good at. Maybe out west..."

"California?"

"Yeah, California would be great."

"You been there?"

"Just a quick visit when I was fifteen, or sixteen. With my parents. My mom and my stepfather. San Francisco. It was really cool. Really something."

"You figure Maddy would go with you?"

Is this a trick question? "She's got school till what, the middle of June. California primary's the first week in June, so no, she'd stay in New York."

"Figure Delphine might fly out and join you?"

Is that what all this has been leading up to? "Come on, Randall. I thought we were gonna go easy on that."

"I'm interested to know what you're about, Ben."

"You *know* me, for Christ's sake. Something's happening here. I don't know exactly what it is yet. Whatever it is, I don't think it has anything to do with the campaign, so why don't we just drop it?"

Randall's gaze has remained riveted on Ben. "You haven't told Delphine about Maddy, would be my guess, and I *know* you haven't told Maddy about Delphine."

"No. I will, in good time."

Randall smiles, and Ben makes an effort to discern what *that*'s about. "Let's say we go back to New York early next week," Randall resumes. "Let's say they send us somewhere new. Boston. Cincinnati. Detroit. Who the hell knows where. Are we just gonna have a repeat of this? Are you gonna zero in on some chick and spend half your time gettin' her into bed or thinkin' about it?"

Has it just been another of Randall's tests? Is there a right answer? Ben tries to balance reason and a growing sense of irritation. "Look--you're not listening to me, are you? This is not a casual thing for me, okay? But even if it were, what the hell difference would it make? It doesn't affect my work. I've got free time, right? Why should it bother you how I spend my free time?"

"It bothers me," Randall says, coolly. "It raises all kinds of questions with me. Maybe I get too wrapped up in the job, but I don't think so. I think this is the kind of gig you have to

341

work about twenty-three hours a day. I've got serious doubts whether I want to travel around the country with somebody who might not have a lot in the way of principles."

Principles! What in God's name does this have to do with principles? Ben feels a tightening in his abdomen, adrenaline running rampant. Does Randall speak as his friend or as his boss? His former friend, his soon-to-be former boss? Ben takes a deep breath and concentrates. "What does that mean?" He says.

"Food for thought," Randall says, smiling again, glancing down at the congealing remains of Ben's breakfast.

On the car radio Ben hears Martin Luther King say, "We are not going to be stopped by Mace or injunctions." A Memphis judge has granted the city a temporary restraining order against King's planned second march. "He's right," Randall roars. "He's got a goddamn constitutional right to march, no matter what some redneck judge says."

It's a nice spring day, a normal spring day by Ben's New England standards, probably about sixty degrees. There are remnants everywhere of last night's storm--huge tree branches on sidewalks, great random accumulations of leaves and debris here and there on streets, and small ponds collected where storm drains have clogged. What must it be like to live in a climate where a blizzard is followed by a few days of summer, then by a storm that sucks barns and tractors into the sky?

As usual it's Randall who addresses a group of perhaps a hundred Memphis State students. Ben counts the black faces in the audience: nineteen, a far higher number than he would have expected. Randall lets him take a major part in the question-and-answer portion of the program, and by his own evaluation

Ben does a pretty good job. He notes that none of the Negro
kids are wearing black satin jackets.

They sit with twelve teachers (seven white males, two
white females, three black males) in a comfortable faculty
lounge. Here Ben gets to play a bigger part; there are actually
several of these people who seem more interested in talking
with him than with Randall, including one blond assistant
professor of history who could be no older than twenty-six or
twenty-eight and whose corduroy skirt stops just short of her
knees. They have a spirited discussion of the future of civil
rights legislation in a Kennedy administration, versus a Nixon
administration, and Ben imagines that in different
circumstances they might enjoy each other quite a bit.

At noon, en route to the Mustang, Randall says, "You
hungry?"

"Not particularly."

"Me neither. You want to just go back to the hotel and
see if Abernathy's called?"

"Sounds good."

"And if he hasn't, I wouldn't object to taking the rest of
the afternoon off. I'm kinda wiped out."

"Fine with me," Ben says.

There have been no telephone messages for Randall, but
the chipper young man at the desk hands him an envelope that
he says was dropped off moments earlier. Ben can see the
Southern Christian Leadership Conference letterhead on the
single page Randall holds. "Tomorrow," Randall says,
grinning. "We've got ourselves an audience tomorrow
afternoon at two, at the Lorraine Motel. What do you think
about that, my man?"

"Incredible," Ben says, his smile just as big as Randall's.

343

"*Credible*," Randall says, and slaps Ben on the back. "We're gonna do it! We're gonna sit down with the great man and we're gonna lay the foundation for one hell of an alliance."

In his room, Ben calls the desk and speaks to the same young man. "I forgot to ask if there were any messages for two one six."

"Yes, sir. From a Miss Delphine Ennis. Please call her before two o'clock."

It's now twelve thirty, and he doesn't waste any time.

"Hi," she says. "How are you doin' today?" It strikes him that her voice is warm, welcoming, as it was day before yesterday.

"I'm okay," he says. "Guess I was a little hung over this morning. How about you?"

"I'm fine." She pauses for a couple of seconds. "I keep thinking about you just turning around and putting that guy on the floor. That was a very cool thing to do."

"Not to Randall's way of thinking."

"I know," she says, and stops again, long enough for Ben to wonder if it's his turn to speak. But she resumes. "I think Randall might have a little bit of a conflict."

"How do you mean?"

"Last night, when you were parking the car, when he met me in front of the Temple, he was kind of feeling around, I think trying to find out what's goin' on between you and me..."

It flashes into Ben's mind that Randall has *told* Delphine about Maddy. That's what her coolness was about last night, that's why Randall was playing games at breakfast this morning. But if he *has* told her about Maddy and Ben's now correctly interpreting the sound of her voice, evidently Randall has done

344

a great job of breaking the ice for him. "What did he say?" Ben asks, innocently enough.

"It wasn't so much what he said. It was the way he was acting, like it was the first time he and I were alone with each other, and he was kind of sweet talkin'. I had the impression he was romancing me a little, which was why I had some doubts about goin' to the club with you all, with both of you."

Ben has just been getting accustomed to the likelihood that Delphine knows he lives with a girl in New York, has been formulating the beginning of a strategy, and now, faced with the necessity of switching gears fast, he's paralyzed.

Delphine says, "You didn't know that? You weren't aware that he'd kind of...had his eyes on me?"

"No," Ben says. "No, I didn't have any idea."

After a few seconds she says, "Well, I don't think I'm wrong about that." Ben is silent, still trying to get his bearings, and Delphine says, "I don't want to mess things up between the two of you, if you have to work together."

"No," he says, "don't worry about that, please." She has of course screwed things up between him and Randall, and it's not as if he's just figured that out; it's that he didn't know entirely *why*. He says, "Have you had lunch yet?"

He possessed the keys to the Mustang, so he could have driven over to her house and picked her up, but that would have required knocking on Randall's door--waking him up, probably--and telling him he was taking the car. Surely Randall would have asked where. It did cross his mind that he could just go without telling Randall, and it was sixty-forty or maybe even seventy-thirty that Randall would never have missed Ben or the car. But there would've been hell to pay if Randall had

suddenly needed either one. Accusations of deceit, more fuel
for the fire.

So instead Delphine has picked him up and they've
returned to Charlie's, the joint near Southwestern where they
had dinner two nights ago. Nearly deserted then, Charlie's is
packed now--fifty or sixty white college kids all yelling to be
heard. There's no place to sit and even if they could find a table
they wouldn't be able to have a conversation. Ben says, "Can
we get it to go?"

"To go where?" Delphine asks.

"Back to your house?"

"I'd just as soon not."

"My room, then?"

She shrugs; she smiles. "Why not?"

He wants to tell her about Maddy. He wants to say,
"Look, there's something you should know. I've been living
with this girl, and it's been pretty serious, but I've never felt
what I feel with you." He runs variations of this through his
mind, searching for a conclusion, and for just the right way to
say it. But then he considers that he's known Delphine for not
quite a hundred hours, and he wonders how much of what he
feels has to do with the circumstances, the romance of the
exotic. Perhaps after a week or two that accent would wear on
him, that lack of sophistication would make him yearn for
Maddy. And then he looks at her, at the green eyes and slender
legs, at her cheekbones and the way her body moves when she
reaches for her Coke, and he resumes trying to phrase the
revelation.

Delphine sits against the bed's headstand, Ben across
from her at the bed's foot, down to the last few bites of his steak
sandwich, which is not nearly as tasty cold as it had been fresh

and hot at Charlie's. He says, "There's something I want to tell you," and she looks at him expectantly. It's going to be a shock, no question, and she might just get up and walk out the door. It would be better, all things considered, to tell her later, in more intimate circumstances. She's waiting, meanwhile, for him to tell her what he wants to tell her, so he says, "We're meeting with Doctor King tomorrow."

Her eyebrows rise simultaneously with the corners of her lips, and she says, "You *are*?"

"We are," Ben says. "Two o'clock at the Lorraine Motel."

She leans across the bed and slaps his foot. "*Damn*, Ben, you sittin' there all smug and content! I don't suppose you could bring along a guest?"

"If it were up to me," he says.

"Well, you know I'm not serious. But would you, if it were up to you? Would you let me come?"

"Sure I would. I don't think *he'd* object. Why would he object?"

"I don't know. I sure don't know much about the Kennedy campaign. I'd just sit there with my mouth open."

"That would be fine."

"Well, it's too bad," Delphine says.

"What's too bad?"

"It's too bad about Randall."

"You want me to ask him if you can come with us?" Ben says, surprised as he utters the words.

Delphine's eyes widen. "Are you *serious*? Come on, Ben, let's not make things completely crazy."

"Am I serious?" He flips the empty take-out carton to the floor, where it lands upright. He crouches in Delphine's direction and removes her right shoe, then her left. "You bet

347

I'm serious," he says, and he runs the fingers of his right hand up her calf, pauses briefly at the knee, then traipses up her inner thigh. She does not protest.

## FORTY

"Where were you?" Lydia says. "You look like you just got back from a party."

In reality, Maddy's just gotten back from a relatively painless five-minute session with Mrs. Sálazar, and now she sits across the usual little table from Lydia--who looks like someone who hasn't slept in a week, and has as well been saddled with twice the usual number of five-year-olds for the past three hours. "I'm sorry," she says. "Really, it couldn't be avoided."

"Something nasty?" Lydia says, tilting her head as if to avoid incipient bad news.

"No, not at all. I had to drive Prosper home, to Connecticut…"

"What—so you spent the night at his house?"

She doesn't feel like opening up to Lydia, not just yet, anyway. "At his aunt's house. It's a big place. How about you? You look kind of…weary."

"Yeah, strange shit in my life, Mad. I almost called in sick too. That would've been something. The bitch Sálazar would've tried to get us both fired..."

"I can't tell you how grateful I am," Maddy says. "It was so selfish of me, but he was pretty wasted. I didn't trust him to drive." Is Lydia buying any of this?

"Listen, Mad—did you see Alex last night?"

Now things are going to get complicated. Maddy's already regretting her pledge of silence to Alex. "I did. He was at the same party I went to with Prosper. Ben was supposed to come too, but he's still in Memphis."

It's apparent that Lydia has other things on her mind than whatever might be happening among Maddy, Ben, and Prosper. "What time did he leave?" She says.

"I didn't really notice him leave. He said to make sure to tell you he was going to class. He said he missed you."

"But you didn't tell him where I was?"

"No. Of course not."

After a few seconds Lydia says, "What time did you leave?"

"After eleven. Maybe quarter after, eleven thirty..."

"Was Alex still there?"

"No, he'd left." She pictures Alex talking with Nicola in the kitchen, Nicola stalking away, but that was before her own brief chat with Alex. "I don't remember seeing him after, maybe ten-thirty." Grateful that the conversation has veered away from her and Prosper, Maddy finds herself curious about Lydia's interest in Alex's whereabouts, but constrained in that she can't honorably mention anything about the bedroom scene with Nicola. So she says nothing further.

And it's a good half-minute before Lydia speaks again. "Mad—you remember when I first met Rafael..."

349

"Alex was stoned and he was trying to give those guys his stuff…"

"Right. And the one guy, the tall, shitty guy, felt me up?"

"I remember."

"Somebody shot that guy last night."

"My God."

"Right outside Rafael's building. He was buzzing Rafael's apartment, trying to get in. And Rafael thinks it was Alex."

"He thinks Alex *shot* the guy? That's the craziest thing I ever heard."

"Yeah," Lydia says. "That's what I thought. But I wish I knew for sure."

"He's a *pacifist*, Lydia. He hates guns. He used to get after Ben for going hunting with his stepfather."

"I talked to him this morning…"

"You called him?"

"No, I went over there. He was sleeping in his clothes…"

"That's not so unusual, is it?"

"Not when he's been tripping. But he hadn't been doing any of that shit. There was something about him, about the way he kept changing the subject from him to me…"

"I think he really misses you…"

"Yeah, I know," Lydia says. "But there might be something else going on."

***

What she really wants to do is go back to Rafael's and sleep until he comes home after his shift at the store. But she finds herself turning north instead of south when she gets off the bus, and walking up Morningside Drive toward 118th Street.

She doesn't particularly want to have a confrontation with Alex now; in fact it's not entirely out of the question that she'd move back in with him at some point. Right now she can't imagine walking out on Rafael, but how long is the romance going to last? How long will she be able to tolerate the grungy walk-up and the piss-stinking entryway, the scummy friend across the hall?

If nothing else, she can pick up a few more days' worth of clothes so she doesn't have to spend Saturday morning hauling stuff back and forth from the laundromat four blocks away.

Alex isn't home, which is a relief. The windows in the kitchen and the bedroom are open several inches; the bed is made. There is a note on the coffee table in Alex's upper-case scrawl:

DEAREST LYDIA
IF YOU HAPPEN TO COME BY AFTER SCHOOL & I AM
NOT HOME IT IS BECAUSE I'M AT CLASS. I'LL BE
BACK BY 4/4:15 & WOULD LOVE TO SPEND SOME
TIME WITH YOU. HOW ABOUT DINNER AT THE WEST
END OR ONE OF THE CHINESE PLACES? ON ME.
TU HOMBRE,
A.

Does she want to wait for him, or does she want to make a quick exit? She's made no specific plan with Rafael, but it would be heartless to stand him up tonight in particular, so any contact with Alex would have to be quick and polite. Better, then, to gather her clothing, reply politely to his note, and get out of here. It's twenty minutes to four.

351

*Peter Delacorte*

There's a stack of grocery bags in the kitchen cabinet next to the sink. She finds one with handles and—back in the bedroom—transfers two bras and three pairs of panties from her underwear drawer, then a couple of blouses formal enough to wear to school from the drawer below. From the closet she selects a knee-length wool skirt and a cotton one in case the weather warms up, and…what else? She takes a step back so she can eyeball everything hanging, almost all of it hers, and she notices that Alex's blue summer suit, his only suit, is no longer in the dry cleaner's plastic bag. Why? Would he have worn it to that party on the East Side last night, in the cool April air? It's a mess, in any case, the pants slung unevenly over the hanger's crosspiece, so they'll be even more rumpled. She pulls the hanger from the bar and, by habit as much as out of curiosity, goes through the pockets. In the outer left pocket there are a folded piece of paper and a pair of keys on a makeshift wire ring. The swatch of thick yellow paper on the key ring reads 64 STUD LARK, which at first makes no sense to her. The piece of paper, unfolded, is a receipt from Sonny's Sport Shop in Wilmington, Delaware, dated 4/2/68. In a meticulous hand, it reads:

1 WALTHER PPK    $100

1 PKG .38 AMMO    $15.50

It's such a small amount of information, but so much to interpret, to decipher. First: does this receipt even belong to Alex? Why would he have been in fucking Delaware? *How* would he have been in Delaware, two days ago? What is a Walther PPK? The giveaway, of course, is the word AMMO, which unmistakably stands for "ammunition." Lydia is a New York City girl who has never in her twenty-four years sat behind the wheel of an automobile and might never deduce that STUD stands for Studebaker, but she knows what car keys look like, and she's able to put together the unlikely story: Alex somehow acquires the keys to a car, drives down to Delaware, and buys a gun and bullets. The rest isn't too difficult to figure out, and it leaves her slumped on the bed in tears.

\*\*\*

Just inside the front the door, Alex senses more than hears someone in the bedroom. Hopefully, he calls, "Babe, you here?" When there's no immediate reply he takes the fifteen steps that lead him to the bedroom doorway, and sees Lydia on the bed. Is she crying? "You okay, babe? Something wrong?"

She looks up at him, her expression suggesting something between sadness and anger. She pushes a slip of paper across the bedspread in his direction. He picks it up; it takes a few seconds for him to figure out what it is, whereupon he decides that the best tactic is to resume this morning's mien of ignorance. "What's the matter?"

Her voice breaking, she says, "You know what the fucking matter is. You *did* it."

"Did what?"

"You killed that son of a bitch, Alex."

It's remarkable how things can change, how one's world can turn upside-down, in a matter of seconds. He's thinking, at once, *how did she find that receipt; where did I leave it?* And *there's no reversing this, there's no convincing her that she's wrong.* He says, "Okay. It's true. But two things…I didn't mean to do it. He jumped off the fucking stoop on me and it was just kind of a reflex. And he *was* a son of a bitch."

"Why didn't you just tell me this morning?"

"I don't know. Because I still don't really believe it happened." He sits down on the bed, next to her, and she moves away. He says, "What are you gonna do?"

"About what?"

353

"About this. About us."

"Do you mean am I gonna tell the cops? No, I don't think so. Am I gonna tell Rafael? Yes, I have to. And *us*? You're more fucked up than I ever dreamed. You drove to Delaware and you bought a gun! Did you steal somebody's fucking car, Alex?"

"No, babe, absolutely not. I paid for it." Even as he's speaking, he realizes he has to get rid of the car as soon as possible. Take it back to New Jersey, to the lot, and leave it there. Forget about the money. Get rid of the gun, too. Or maybe not, if this guy Rafael is feeling vengeful…

Lydia lifts herself off the bed and picks up a shopping bag he hasn't previously noticed. He says, "What's that? Where you going?"

"That's my clothes, and I'm leaving."

"Don't go, babe. Please." He stands up. She walks past him, into the living room. He says, "You don't have to tell Rafael. What's the point?"

Opening the front door, she says, "Don't press your luck, Alex."

## FORTY-ONE

In order to make the journey from the elevator bank to the offices of WABC-FM, one must pass the splendor that is WABC-AM, whose principal broadcasting studio is a carpeted room perhaps thirty feet by thirty feet, its walls covered with thick soundproofing. The disk jockey--the "personality"—sits at a sleek hardwood desk in the middle of the room looking at his engineer, who is fifteen feet away behind a thick glass panel in the control room, which is stuffed with state-of-the-art electronics. The deejay wears headphones that would be the envy of NASA, and has little more to do than talk and make hand signals to the engineer. WABC's deejays are rumored to be the highest paid in the country, befitting the station that has the greatest listenership in the world's biggest market.

While the FM side is hardly Tobacco Road, its main studio is about eight by ten, uncarpeted, in need of a paint job. Technically, for the moment at least it is not truly a broadcasting studio, but a taping room, where an ex-Lutheran minister named Brother Ned sits for five hours a day, five days a week, saying in a pleasantly deep voice things like, "Hey, that was the Buffalo Springfield saying sit down, I think I love you, and before that a little solo thing from Neil Young. Did you know Neil was from Canada? That's right. I wonder if they ever thought about calling themselves the Toronto Springfield. Heh heh. Well, probably not. But I'll tell you what: we're gonna come back in just sixty seconds with something from Richie Havens, so stick around, my good people."

Brother Ned works primarily with Paul Grossbaum, an engineer who is younger than Prosper, and a genius. Prosper and Martin work primarily with Harvey Weiss, a competent engineer and a very nice man who enjoys his work, likes the music, and often expresses to Prosper his enthusiasm for working in this new medium. When there is a difficult job to be done, when Martin has interviewed someone drunk or stoned, or simply very inarticulate, then Martin insists that Paul be called in, which means Prosper must spend anywhere from a couple of hours to parts of several days with this surly perfectionist, who makes it clear to Prosper that he thinks Martin is scum, a talentless opportunist, and the entire FM operation is an aesthetic disaster--a commercialization of something that must remain free-form to thrive, but will doubtless end up making the American Broadcasting Company bundles of money.

This afternoon at a few minutes past one o'clock, Prosper passes by the studio, where Brother Ned looks up, and they exchange waves. On the AM side, it's exhilarating to stand by the studio window and watch the deejay as his words boom out of overhead speakers, knowing those same words are being heard by, say, half a million listeners. On the FM side there are overhead speakers as well. At this moment, for instance, Brother Ned's voice intones, "Hey, how about that Peter Green's guitar? Can that guy play? Did you know the group was originally called Peter Green's Fleetwood Mac over in England? And no, kids, Mick Fleetwood was not a member of the Fleetwoods, the group that did 'Mr. Blue' back a few years ago. They were actually named after the type of Cadillac." But the real-time, flesh-and-blood Brother Ned inside the studio is saying something altogether different, something that won't be broadcast until next Monday or Tuesday.

356

## The Mountaintop

By Prosper's calculation, Brother Ned is "on the air" about eighteen hours a day in seven cities, but fortunately for his vocal cords and his sanity the vast majority of that time is filled by music. Still, if you figure he's got to speak the name and artist of maybe twelve to fifteen songs per hour, read a few national commercials, and make all sorts of semi-hip small talk, that's an awful lot of time spent before the mike. And the marvelous thing is that it all does manage to sound spontaneous, as if Brother Ned really is sitting in a studio in your town, grooving on the music.

If some wretched artist--someone a rung or two lower on the culture ladder even than Peter Max--were to paint a picture of the quintessence of hip at this moment, it would bear a great resemblance to Martin Snyder. He is a tall man, perhaps six feet three, and angular, with a sharp, pronounced chin and an aquiline nose, a Zapata mustache, and a great mound of sharply curled black hair in the style that--were Martin a black man-- would be called an Afro.  And he was born to wear this clothing: this impeccable buckskin jacket with its fringes, beneath it a blue silk shirt studded with white five-pointed stars; black wool bell-bottoms with broad white stripes descending to...saddle shoes. *Wide* bell-bottoms descending to saddle shoes with extra-thick soles, so they add at least an inch to Martin's height.

Along with Paul Grossbaum, they're in Martin's office-- nothing more than a cubicle, actually, and a bone of contention between Martin and Allen Simmons, the young program director. To underscore his displeasure, Martin has chosen not to augment the decor, which consists of two rolling office chairs and a coffee table with a stained Formica surface. Martin has offered Prosper brief condolences, then begun giving an account

357

of his hardships in Prosper's absence, as if the New Haven debacle had been nothing worse than, perhaps, a bad job interview. Martin is in the midst of an analysis of Harvey Weiss's editing shortcomings when Grossbaum says, "Hey, Harvey's my friend, for God's sake."

"So what?" Martin replies. "Take it as a compliment to you. You know what you're doing. The other guy, not so much."

Grossbaum—who is twenty-two but could pass for thirty, with five-o'clock shadow and thick black hair--blows a kiss across the table. "That's the sweetest thing you've ever said to me, Martin. Probably the sleaziest compliment anyone's ever given me, too. Do you want to tell me what I'm doing here?"

"We're gonna go through the tapes from the Morrison interview."

"You mean two hours of you talking to a drunk rock and roll guy? Why are we gonna do that?"

"Because I need material."

Grossbaum looks in Prosper's direction. "Didn't you and Harvey do about twenty spots from that interview?"

"Twenty exactly," Prosper says.

Grossbaum looks back at Martin with a shrug. "Why do you need more?"

Martin doesn't reply immediately. "I'm gonna be on Cousin Brucie's TV show."

"Congratulations. What does this have to do with me?"

"Harvey's working with Brother fucking Ned and your union won't let me play the tapes on my own. Or Prosper."

"Yeah," Grossbaum says, "well, I work for the radio station, not for you, and I'm not gonna waste my time on this bullshit."

358

"Martin," Prosper says, "I can practically recite that interview by heart. You don't need Paul."

"Okay," Martin says. "I'll tell you guys why you're really here..."

Prosper suspects that they're really here because Martin was hoping to con Grossbaum into playing the tapes—which, thank God, is not going to happen. But he's inevitably intrigued when Martin gets this look of incipient conspiratorial revelation: His eyes widen and the corners of his mouth curl in what is too Mephistophelean to be called a smile. "You're not gonna believe this," Martin begins, leaning forward, "but there's this guy I know from way back, from like nineteen fifty-*eight*, who's kind of a hanger-on artist type, a guy without much talent but he talks a good game, and what the hell, in art you never really know anyways. So I run into this guy the other night at the Café Reggio. He calls *me* over, and we're rappin' about this and that, and he's telling me some boring shit about how I should put some conceptual artist in my column because she's gonna be the next big thing, and how Yoko really digs her stuff. And I say, *Yoko*? And he says, yeah, of course, Yoko. So I'm cool about it, and after a while I say yeah, sure I could put this chick in my column, but could I get a quote from Yoko? And he says, sure, you want her number?" Martin's eyes now become huge. "So I've got fucking Yoko Ono's phone number!"

"Wow," Prosper says. "You sure it's real?"

"*Real*? I *spoke* to her!"

"When did you speak to her?"

"Just now. I called a few times, there was nobody home. I was starting to think maybe the guy was just fucking with me. But just, like, twenty minutes ago I called and there's this chick with an Oriental accent. I can't believe it. Yoko? This is

359

Martin Snyder--and she says, yeah, I read your column in the *Voice*. She reads my fucking column! I mentioned I was a friend of this guy and I was gonna do an item about the artist, and could I get a quote from her, and she said sure." Martin pauses, his eyebrows at an impossible height. "Now, tell me, am I gonna leave it at that?"

Is this a rhetorical question? Prosper decides it isn't. "I'll bet you're not."

"You're fucking right I'm not. I said, oh, by the way, I do this little radio gig, too. We're tryin' to get rock and roll on the FM dial. We're on seven stations, blah blah blah, and it would really be a shot in the arm if we could maybe get an on-air interview with you and John."

"Wow," Prosper says, with genuine zeal. "So?"

"So, she said she'd have to talk it over with John, but she thought it was a good idea."

"Fantastic," Prosper says.

"No shit, it's fantastic. Think about it. We can go in depth on FM. I can get Allen to give us an hour...*two* hours on a Friday night. And can you *imagine* how many spots we could get out of this? The guy's a fuckin' walking quote to begin with. On all seven stations. On the AM side they'd go nuts for this, but we're gonna get it!"

Grossbaum says, "I wouldn't count my chickens."

This is not something Prosper would say to Martin, in part because he tends to avoid confrontation, but more because Martin seems incongruously vulnerable in these moments of great enthusiasm. Martin, his eyebrows back to normal level, says, "Why not?"

"Because at this stage in his career I don't think John Lennon's a publicity hound. So why should he want to spend any time with you?"

## The Mountaintop

"Not a *publicity* hound?" Martin's voice falls just short of shriek level. "Whaddayou call inviting the press to see you and your old lady laying in bed? Whaddayou call what this guy spends about half his life doing?"

Grossbaum has just now bothered to look at Martin. "Yeah, but that's all for peace, not to sell records anymore. He doesn't need to publicize his records. They sell themselves."

"Paul, for Christ's fucking sake, who says I'm even gonna talk about his records? He wants to talk about peace, we'll talk about fucking peace."

"That's gonna be a pretty short conversation at your end," Grossbaum says.

"What the hell are you *talking* about? Where does a twenty-year-old-kid get off talking to me like that? I've interviewed Doctor Spock! Abbie Hoffman! Jerry Rubin!"

"Where, at parties?"

"Jesus!" Martin looks at Prosper, wishing for a partner in disbelief. "Who does this fucking kid think he is? At *parties*." He returns to Grossbaum. "Right on the shelf above your head is the tape with my interview of Hoffman and Rubin. You wanna listen to it, see if I asked them about peace?"

"I'm trying to make a point, Martin," Grossbaum says. "You're in a position of power. You're in a position where you can actually influence people, but all you want to do is talk to rock stars about how much money they make and how many girls they screw. So why should John Lennon talk to you?"

"*Jesus!*" Martin looks at Prosper again. "Do you have any idea where this guy is coming from?" Prosper is at least mildly shocked by the intensity of Grossbaum's assault, but it's hardly out of character, and certainly most of what he's said is true. Prosper says, "I think Paul enjoys getting under your skin, Martin."

361

"What Paul needs," Martin says, turning his head toward Grossbaum, "is a lesson in economics. In how to run a radio station. In what people want to listen to. In when it's sensible to take a stand. And if he wasn't such a fucking good engineer, on how to look for a new job."

Ignoring Martin, Grossbaum speaks to Prosper. "It's not just about getting under his skin. I'm *serious* about this. All three of us in this room are against the war, right? Probably everybody who works at this station is against the war, including Allen, and he's the program director. What kind of audience are we trying to reach? People in their teens and twenties, and *they're* against the war..."

"I know where you're going with this," Martin interrupts. "And it's bullshit. Sure, we're all against the war, and Allen's against the war, but Allen's not the boss. The American fucking Broadcasting Company is the boss. They own the station, all the stations, and if we try to turn this into our little anti-war gig, they'd fire our asses in five minutes."

Grossbaum smiles ruefully and shakes his head. Martin says, "It's easy to be an idealist when you're twenty and you know you can get a job anywhere."

"What about you?" Grossbaum says. "You think if ABC fired you because you did something controversial, some other station wouldn't pick you right up?"

"What station? No *AM* station, that's for sure. Who would fucking pick me up?"

"I don't *believe* you," Grossbaum says. "You're the guy that's supposed to be on top of everything--all the trends, what's happening--and you don't have the slightest idea what's going on. In two years there's gonna be rock and roll all over FM, Martin. And there's a movement, if you haven't noticed, that's *against* the war and *for* rock and roll, that's hungry for stations that play eight-minute album cuts and guys like you who supposedly know what's hip. You think people are gonna blackball you because you're the guy ABC fired when he called Lyndon Johnson a baby-killer on the air?"

"That's exactly what I think," Martin says. "I know how this business works. I know how this *country* works. How old were you during the McCarthy hearings? Five?"

"You're hopeless," Grossbaum says.

"Hopeless! I'm gonna get John Lennon a national forum, and I'm hopeless. Prosper, is this kid full of shit?"

Prosper has been hoping against this turn of events. But what, really, does he have to lose? "I wouldn't say that."

Martin raises his eyes ceilingward. "Oh, Jesus. A *pair* of idealistic maniacs." He glares at Prosper. "Would you have said that a week ago, when you were gonna fail your physical and be free and clear of all this bullshit?"

"I might not have said it, but I would've felt it."

"Felt *what*, for Christ's sake?"

"That somebody's got to take a stand. Lots of people have to take a stand."

"Bobby Kennedy's taking a stand," Martin says. "That opportunistic, cold-blooded little son of a bitch is taking a stand, so why should I put my job on the line? Bobby's gonna get elected, and he's gonna end the war."

Grossbaum says, "What makes you sure of that?"

Prosper manages to get away shortly after three o'clock, and calls Leotis's number in Stamford. He gets a woman he assumes to be Mrs. Telford, introduces himself, and asks if he can leave a message for Leotis. "Why don't you just talk to him?" His mother says. "He's standing right here."

"Didn't expect to find you home," Prosper says.

363

"Yeah, I got finished early."

"How's everything going?"

"About like usual, except now I got this thing hangin' over my head."

"I know what you mean," Prosper says. "You still feel like coming into the city tonight?"

"Yeah, I'd like that."

"I told Maddy I'd meet her when she's done with these parent conferences she's got, probably about eight o'clock…"

"Maddy, huh? That sounds good."

"It is good, really good."

"Wow. That mean what I think it does?"

"It pretty much does," Prosper says.

"Damn! So one good thing happened the last couple of days. Where's her school at?"

"A Hundred and Fourth Street, Between Lexington and Park. Why don't I call you back when I'm sure about the time?"

"You got it," Leotis says.

## FORTY-TWO

When she would normally have been enjoying an early, leisurely dinner—between three thirty and five this afternoon— Maddy chose to stretch out on the couch in the break room and have a nap. Good thing she did. The conferences last half an hour and come one after another; usually one parent or set of parents is ready to begin just after the previous set has finished. They would be difficult enough if she were dealing with a homogeneous group, but that's hardly the case. Half the time, more or less, it's just a mother; she's had a couple of lone fathers, one tonight, and the rest both parents. She never knows exactly what to expect in the way of literacy or accent. She may have assumed that one of her students was from the Dominican, say, and then discovered that the family was from Cuba, which meant various key words would be different, there would be misunderstandings, embarrassing moments of silence or confusion.

So when her seven o'clock parents—Rodrigo and Elvia Morales—haven't shown up by ten after, she feels a sense of relief. There's only one more conference scheduled, at seven thirty, and she's been eager to talk to her sister Jill all day. There's a pay phone in the hallway outside the break room, about twenty feet from her classroom, so if the Moraleses do show up she'll see them. She dials O, gives the operator Jill's number and tells her she wants to charge it to her home phone. The call will cost a king's ransom, but Ben pays the phone bill and she's not feeling very charitable toward him just now.

"Jill? Hey, I've just got a few minutes between conferences, but I thought I'd say hi."

365

"It's preposterous," Jill says, "to think of you as someone who has conferences."

"Yeah, I know. Imagine how *I* feel about it…"

"So…what's going on? Any more word from Ben?"

"Nope."

"You don't sound too upset about that. How was the party?"

"The party was fine."

"Mad—why did you call me? There's something going on with you, isn't there?"

"I went home with Prosper. I spent the night."

"Are you *kidding* me, Maddy? You went to *bed* with him?"

"I did," Maddy says. "I went to bed with him."

"God," Jill says. "You're a *slut*, Maddy."

"I didn't go to bed with him right away, though. First we did this amazing thing. You'd have to see the house. I can describe it to you, but I can't do it justice. You're standing there in front of this huge window, and the moon's out, and the water just stretches out forever, and you're pleasantly drunk, and there's this guy standing behind you that you've always really liked, but not *that* way, and all of a sudden he's doing these amazing things to you, I mean it's as if somebody gave him my instruction manual…"

"Do you mean Ben?"

"No, for God's sake. Ben wouldn't talk to Prosper about stuff like that. At least I don't think he would. And Ben didn't ever do anything like that to me, anyway."

"Like *what*, Maddy?"

"Just…touching. Just touching all the right places."

"You're not gonna tell me anything more than that?"

"I can't. I can't put it in words. It was just really wonderful. You had to be there."

"Would have been kind of strange if I had been."

Maddy laughs. "In my place," she says.

"So you *didn't* go to bed with him. You just did stuff in the living room, looking out at the water."

"Then we went to sleep," Maddy says. "Separate beds. Then I got up and called in sick and did the laundry. And then we went to bed."

"You actually did it?"

"We did it."

"Was that as good?"

"That was pretty good. Pretty damn good."

There is a brief silence, except for fuzz on the line between Cambridge and Manhattan. Jill says, "So, what now? You're not gonna tell Ben about this, are you?"

"*Tell* Ben? I'm not sure I even want to see Ben again."

"Why? Because of Prosper?"

"No," Maddy replies immediately. "Well, partly, I guess. But mainly I'm just fed up with him. That phone call was the last straw."

"So…you went to bed with Prosper because Ben's an asshole?"

"No…It wasn't as if I planned it. I mean, maybe if I'd been feeling more of an…
allegiance to Ben I wouldn't have been there in the first place, but it wasn't tit-for-tat by any means."

Several seconds go by. "So what happens now, Mad?"

"I'm not sure," Maddy says quickly. "I just can't..." She stops. "When you make a commitment to someone, when you move *in* with someone, it seems so melodramatic to just kind of end it. I mean, what do I do? Do I have the right to kick him

367

out and stay here? Should I leave? Should I go out this minute and start looking for a place of my own? Could I afford a place of my own? And then, you know, I wonder if somehow I just misinterpreted the whole thing, like maybe that was his long-lost Tennessee cousin, or some friend of Randall's."

"I don't think so," Jill says. "I mean, you can pretty much be empirical here, can't you?"

"Yes. Of course. I know."

There is another silence before Jill says, "What about Prosper?"

"How do you mean?"

"Well, if you're not interested in him, I wouldn't object if he invited me out to that house and did amazing things to me."

Maddy laughs, and briefly pictures Jill, in her inevitable dirty jeans and boots, standing in front of the picture window. Then she has a flash of herself there, and the sensation of Prosper's hands making their way down her torso. She says, "It's so hard--when you've thought of someone in a certain way for so long--it's so hard to just turn that on its head."

"Hasn't he kind of done that for you?"

"Sort of. I guess. I wish I could figure things out."

"What about him? Does he have a girlfriend? Was he cheating on someone too?"

"No," Maddy says. "No, I think he's pretty serious about me."

"So he's just kind of been in the background all this time, waiting for his moment? I think that's pretty cool."

"Yeah, but Jilly, it's so weird. It's so strange. He's only, what, the fourth guy I've slept with, and I'm so *used* to Ben, to his body, and to expecting what he does. I don't mean it's boring, or repetitive, just that I know him so well, so maybe it's just the novelty with Prosper..."

368

"That turned you on?"

"But it wasn't just that it turned me on, whatever it was, it was that it turned me into a jar of Stuckey's strawberry jelly. It was ecstatic."

"Maddy--I have to tell you, I don't see what the problem is."

Maddy searches for the words, trying to convey her sense of wonderment that a relationship could make the transition from fraternal to...whatever it is now. She's still searching when she becomes aware of a sort of commotion at the other end of the line, of at least one new voice in Jill's room, a shrill voice that suggests alarm, and then she hears Jill's voice saying, not to her, "*What*? Are you *kidding*."

"Jill?" Maddy says. "Jilly? What's going on?"

When she speaks to Maddy, Jill's sentence is punctuated with sharp, quick sobs. "Kirsten says...Kirsten says somebody...just shot...just shot Martin Luther King."

Maddy sits in the break room, listening to the clock radio, for several minutes. It's a rather pointless exercise because the people on the radio--on each of the five stations she's tuned into--keep repeating the same information. What it boils down to is that they know King has been shot, they know the shooting occurred on the balcony of a motel in Memphis, and they don't know anything else. So possibly it's not a serious wound, a bullet in the hand, the fleshy part of the arm. Even if it *is* serious, this is 1968, this is Martin Luther King, so an ambulance pulls up in record time and in a few minutes he's in the emergency room and the best doctors in Memphis have been summoned--surgery, transfusions, lives are saved miraculously every day.

She can't help thinking of Ben--not so much that he could have been right there, in the motel, on the balcony, but that he's *somewhere* nearby and Memphis is going to be in chaos.

It's seven thirty-three and Vera Echevarria has not appeared for her conference, so Maddy returns to the pay phone with the little address book she carries in her school bag. She dials the Kennedy headquarters number that bypasses the receptionist. After the first ring a male voice answers, "Yah?"

"Is this Ed McCaffrey?."

"Who wants to know?"

"This is Maddy O'Connor. I have to get in touch with Ben Shelton and Randall Briscoe."

"Look," the voice says, "Ed's very busy now. Extremely busy now. You want to call back in the morning?"

"No," Maddy says. "This can't wait till morning. If Ed's busy maybe you could find out for me how I can reach Ben or Randall. They're in Memphis."

"Who are you again? Are you a relative?"

Who is she? A little hyperbole is in order. "I'm Ben's fiancée."

"Okay," the voice says. "Wait."

It is not a minute before a new voice says, "McCaffrey."

Surprised, having assumed that the anonymous man was searching in one way or another for a telephone number in Memphis, Maddy is speechless for a couple of seconds, then talks a mile a minute. "Ed, this is Maddy O'Connor, Ben Shelton's friend, and I desperately need to reach Ben, because I just heard what's going on in Memphis..."

"Hold it," he cuts her off. "It's all right. Slow down."

"I know you're really busy," she says, realizing as she says it that it's a complete non sequitur, feeling as if she's on the verge of losing her breath entirely.

"We're trying to track down the senator," McCaffrey says. "He's in Cleveland and he's got to make a statement about King. We just missed him."

"I'm sorry," Maddy says.

"Don't be sorry." McCaffrey's voice is comforting, less abrupt. He is a large man with a Boston accent. Maddy has seen him three times and on each occasion he wore a bow tie that seemed inappropriate to her.

"Do you know yet," she begins, and stops, and starts again, "Does anybody know yet what King's condition is?"

"No. We know it's serious. I think he was shot in the neck. I don't have a confirmation on that. Evidently he was standing out on the balcony of this motel and some son of a bitch shot him in the neck."

"Someone else on the balcony?"

"No. Across the street. I don't have any verification of this, but what I hear is he was standing on the balcony and someone with a rifle must have been in a building across the street."

Maddy wonders where McCaffrey hears these things, whether there's some sort of magical network, telepathic network, that broadcasts bulletins to important people. As well, she has a picture in her mind of Martin Luther King standing on a generic motel balcony, a bullet zooming toward him from across the street, its lethality diminished by the distance it must travel. But there isn't any vacant space in the neck, isn't any area terribly far from important arteries, or tissue, or spinal cord. Again she is speechless, and after several seconds McCaffrey says, "Did you try calling the Holiday Inn?"

"The Holiday Inn," she repeats.

"I'm sure if they're not in you can leave a message."

"In Memphis?"

"Yeah. As far as I know they were still there this morning. Do you know something I don't know?"

"No, no," Maddy says, overwhelmed by the moment, unable to admit that Ben hasn't told her where he's staying, although if he chose to focus on this trivial detour McCaffrey could certainly make that deduction. "Thank you, Ed. I'm sorry to bother you."

"Don't worry about it, kid," McCaffrey says, and he hangs up.

She feels tears running down both cheeks, and she catches her breath to avoid sobbing. She dials the operator and asks for information in Memphis, Tennessee. Speaking to a second, more distant female voice she requests the number for the Holiday Inn. There are several, so Maddy chooses the one identified as being downtown. Her first impulse is to press the disconnect cradle and call immediately, but after dialing O she begins to cry. At first she sobs rather gently, but within moments she finds herself weeping convulsively, like a child caught in a vortex of irrational despair. She pounds the receiver into its cradle, gets to her feet, and walks compulsively around the hallway. As she does so, she sees a small, thin, chocolate-skinned woman standing outside her classroom.

"¿Señora Echevarria?" She says between sobs.

"Sí...¿Señorita O'Connor? ¿Usted está bien?"

Maddy holds her breath for a few seconds. In her elegant Castilian she says, "I've just heard someone shot Martin Luther King."

"No! Oh, my God! Is he dead?"

372

"I'm not sure. I don't know. But can you excuse me? My boyfriend is in Memphis and I have to call him."

Señora Echaverria excuses herself and disappears down the hallway. Maddy's voice breaks only slightly when she asks the Holiday Inn man for a guest named Ben Shelton. The next thing she knows, a phone is ringing: once, twice, three times.

"Hello?" It's a girl who answers, and Maddy is struck dumb. She has anticipated not being able to find Ben, or calling the wrong Holiday Inn, or listening to a telephone ring endlessly in an empty room. "Hello?" The southern voice says again, and Maddy forces herself to speak. "I'm trying..." She stops, sensing that she's again on the verge of crying.

"Yes?" The girl in Memphis says. "Are you still there?"

"Is this Ben Shelton's room?" She speaks rapidly, but can't keep her voice from breaking.

"Yes it is. Do you need to speak to him?"

"I do, please." She inhales deeply to keep from sobbing. If she were more together she might ask this girl who she is. What her name is, at least.

"Hold on," the girl says. "It'll be a minute." The stress is on the word *be*, perhaps to indicate that it will be well more than a minute. Maddy hears the receiver being clunked down, then listens to fuzzy long-distance silence for what seems ever. It's been more than a minute already. Again tears fall. Maddy has an impulse to hang up the phone and call Prosper at the radio station. Who is this girl? Obviously she's the one whose voice Maddy heard in the background when Ben called her in the middle of the night. Obviously, but maybe not. Maybe she's a friend of Randall's, or possibly there's some kind of impromptu gathering in reaction to the shooting. *He's there*, anyway; he's not dead, or caught up in some sort of street

373

violence. He's safe and he's probably just down the hall somewhere, doing something vital.

Have two minutes passed now? Three? The notion of calling Prosper once more crosses her mind: a much easier, more pleasant thing to do. Perhaps she'll never have anything to do with Ben again. Perhaps she'll just move all her stuff to Prosper's aunt's place, temporarily. Ben would return to an empty apartment. The thought gives her a thrill, followed by a plunge into guilt, that she should be sitting here immersed in vindictiveness when she really doesn't know what's happening, except that Martin Luther King has been shot in the neck.

Suddenly there is sound in her ear: first a scraping noise as, presumably, the receiver is picked up, and then Ben's voice, saying, "Hi."

## FORTY-THREE

Ben *is* serious. Maybe not about working Delphine into the meeting with King; that would be pushing things too far with Randall. But he's serious about her. It's only the second time they've been in bed together, but just as they coalesced on the dance floor, they seem to sense each others' needs here. Ben isn't lacking in experience, but he's never experienced anything like this. It's not like an adolescent's fantasy of fabulous sex, with lots of rolling around and changing positions, nor is it a taking of turns, of separate pleasures, as his lovemaking with Maddy. And again, he's had no real complaints about his lovemaking with Maddy. If he were to list, say, his twenty greatest moments in bed, maybe seven or eight would be with Maddy, which is actually pretty amazing. But this is an entirely new territory. If he and Maddy had been singing sweetly together, it's as if he and Delphine have invented a whole new kind of harmony. And it's a given that when he sings a note she's going to respond with the perfect complement, and vice-versa.

For a long while Ben does not notice the time. Neither of them is constrained by time. It's been established that Delphine isn't expected anywhere this afternoon or this evening; Randall might knock on the door when dinnertime approaches, but that won't be for several hours. Ben is astonished, then, when after they've made love, and talked, and slept, and made love again, he glances at the clock radio and sees that it's a quarter after six. Delphine sleeps on her side, facing him. He slides out of bed, not to disturb her, and walks to the window, opens the drapes a foot and looks out at the darkened city. A police car, its siren wailing, zooms along Third Street. In fact, Ben has been remotely aware of many sirens for the past few minutes. It's something New Yorkers become inured to.

What if Randall comes knocking? Shall he ignore it? Shall he simply open the door and the consequences be damned? Another police car speeds down the wide street. In the building across the way there are numerous lighted windows, people looking down at the street. Ben is suddenly conscious of his nakedness, and pulls the drapery closed.

Delphine is motionless, silent, dead to the world. Ben pads into the bathroom and turns on the shower.

375

He's got a head full of lather and he's trying to remember the words to the slow Five Stairsteps' song when, first, the glass shower door rumbles, causing him imprudently to open his eyes, and second, Delphine speaks his name in a voice suggesting something other than serenity. He swings the door open and sees her for an instant before the shampoo sting becomes intolerable; she's wearing his shirt and her panties. He says, "Hold on a second--I've got to get the soap out of my eyes."

Delphine says, "There's some girl on the phone for you."

Oh, Jesus. But he hasn't even told Maddy where they're staying. His back to Delphine, the shower spray hitting him full in the face, he says, "Did she give you her name?"

"I don't know," Delphine says. "She's all, I don't know, she's crying. She's all upset. She said she had to talk to you."

"Okay," Ben says. So it's got to be Maddy. She's called Kennedy headquarters and gotten the number, so something's going on. Did Randall call *her*? "I'll be out in a second." The stinging has stopped, but his head is covered with shampoo.

"You want me to tell her?"

"No." He shuts off the shower, turns around, and gets a good look at Delphine. He'd interpret her expression as curious, surprised. Not angry. Not angry yet. He slips past her and seizes an oversized bath towel from the rack, swathes himself in it, grabs a smaller towel and slaps it across his head. Is there anything he can say to Delphine at this moment? Ask her to go get them some dinner? He says, "Thanks for getting the phone," and immediately it seems an inane thing to have said.

"You were in the shower," Delphine says, almost apologetically.

He slips past her again and walks moistly onto the carpet, to the bed. The receiver sits sideways on the night table, and he picks it up, sucking in his breath. "Hi," he says, not speaking her name on the off chance that it's someone else: his mother, his sister.

"Ben," Maddy's voice says, "is everything all right there?"

There's definitely distress in her tone. His instinct is to soothe, but how telephonically intimate can he afford to be with Delphine standing in the bathroom doorway, in his shirt and her panties. "Fine," he says. "Everything's okay."

There is the slightest of pauses. "Do you know if he's still alive? Is he going to be all right?"

What's this? It's as if she just started having some other conversation, speaking some other language. He says, "I don't know what you mean."

"I just heard it on the radio," Maddy says. "I was talking to Jill when her roommate walked in and said he'd been shot. So I turned on the radio, and it's all over the radio, but they didn't know how serious it was. And then I kept thinking about *you*, wondering where you were..." She stops. He has no idea what she's talking about, and he's too concerned about the logistics, about the peril of his immediate situation, to make the obvious deduction, so he says nothing, but catches a glance at Delphine, who remains stationary by the bathroom door. "I called Ed McCaffrey," Maddy says. "Thank God he was still there. I guess it was a miracle I got through to him, because he was trying to track down Kennedy in Cleveland or someplace..."

"Indiana," Ben says, thinking he's correcting her, thinking at least he knows where the primary is.

377

"No," Maddy says. "Kennedy's at some event in Cleveland, and they didn't know how to reach him." She stops again. "What am I talking about? Anyway, that's how I got the number. And I was afraid for a minute I got the wrong number, or the wrong room. It's all so awful...'

"It's okay," Ben says, staggering in the dark. On the street below a siren shrieks, and Ben is reminded of all the sirens just before he got in the shower. Things are starting to add up.

"Is it okay?" Maddy asks. "Have you heard? Is he going to live?"

He begins to tremble; his feet feel amorphous. "I haven't heard," he says.

"Are you right near there?" Maddy asks. "The Lorraine Motel?"

"Maybe a mile, or half a mile," Ben says. "Not far away." He glances again at Delphine, who has begun to look quizzical, or so it seems. He motions for her to switch on the television; she appears to understand, and moves in that direction.

"Is Randall okay?" Maddy asks. "Is he there with you?"

"Right next door," Ben says. The television has flickered to life; a somber-looking man sits at a desk, the image of Martin Luther King behind him, to his right. The sound comes up just as the man at the desk says, "...at this moment whether the wound is life-threatening, but we will keep you informed of the terrible event here in Memphis tonight..."

Delphine raises her hands to her head and turns to Ben with horror in her eyes. "Oh, my God, no!" She says, in a loud voice.

Maddy says, "Is that the girl who answered the phone, Ben? Who is she?"

## The Mountaintop

\*\*\*

Maddy's first thought is that this girl, this woman, whoever she is, has just learned something terrible about Martin Luther King. Immediately thereafter--almost simultaneously-- she realizes why Ben has been so laconic and evasive, and feels foolish for not having recognized it earlier. The tears well again as she says, "Is that the girl who answered the phone, Ben?" There is no response. "Who is she?" Still Ben is silent, but Maddy hears the female voice in the background--dull and unintelligible, but unmistakably there. "Ben, for Christ's sake, will you *talk* to me?" Maddy shouts into the phone.

"Listen, sweetheart," Ben says, "listen, I'm so sorry to do this, but I've got to get off the phone now. I'll call you back later, okay? There's some stuff going on here right now. I'll call you back later tonight, all right? I promise you."

"*No!*" Maddy says at the top of her lungs. "*No*, Ben, it's *not* all right! Talk to me now, for God's sake! Tell me what's going on, please!"

There is a loud click, and silence on the line, and then the dial tone. He's gone. Maddy drops the receiver in its cradle and slides into a squatting position, weeping without restraint. Martin Luther King is surely dead and Ben, in the company of some southern floozy, has just called her "sweetheart" and hung up on her again.

\*\*\*

Prosper re-enters the ABC building with a brown paper bag containing two orders of falafel—Martin's favorite entrée after a long day at the station. Indeed it has been a long day. It's past seven thirty now, and they've spent the last two hours "brainstorming" after Paul Grossbaum's departure. Martin managed a magnificent end run following the John and Yoko discussion, electing to redo all twenty Jim Morrison spots, which allowed him to listen to the entire ninety-four-minute interview again. Thus were Grossbaum's union objections superseded, and thus was Martin able to take notes for his incipient appearance with Cousin Brucie. Now they're all but done. Prosper hustles by the AM studio noting that while Bruce Morrow sits in the deejay chair, the speakers are blasting news instead of music. It's a bulletin, evidently, someone reporting live from somewhere, talking about the police being ready for anything, the National Guard having just been here. Normally Prosper would stop and listen, but his intention now is to deliver the falafel, take care of whatever last-minute business Martin might have in mind, and wait for Maddy's call, which should come in twenty or thirty minutes. On the FM side it's business as usual: in this case, the Buffalo Springfield's "For What It's Worth."

"Some chick called you," Martin says, grabbing the falafel.

"When?"

"Just now. Like, five minutes ago."

"Who, Martin? Did you get a name?"

He hands Prosper a scrap of paper with a seven-digit number he doesn't recognize. "I think it started with an M," Martin says. "She didn't sound too happy."

She answers on the fifth ring. "Prosper? Oh, thank God…"

"Maddy? What's the matter? Where are you?"

"On a pay phone here at school. I just talked to Ben, and I don't think he even knew…"

"Knew what?"

"Oh, Jesus…I figured you'd be on top of things, at a radio station…"

380

*The Mountaintop*

Things come abruptly into focus: Cousin Bruce sitting silent in the AM studio while ABC's national news blasted through the speakers. He says, "My God, no...King?"

Across the room, Martin sits bolt upright. "King what?"

On the phone, Maddy is sobbing. "I thought you'd know if he's alive..."

"What happened, for God's sake?"

"Somebody shot him, at his motel in Memphis. Jill's roommate heard it on the news. I called this big wheel at the Kennedy campaign to find out where Ben was staying, and all they knew was that he'd been shot in the neck..."

Martin says, "What the fuck is happening, Prosper?"

"And Ben didn't even know if he was alive?"

"No— some girl answered the phone. She had to go get him somewhere." Maddy pauses, sobs coming in spasms. "He didn't seem to know anything. Then he hung up again."

"Wait a minute--King has been *shot*, Ben's right there, he didn't know about it, and he hung *up* on you?"

Martin gets to his feet. "I'm going to AM," he says, and he's out the door.

Prosper says, "Martin just went to find out what's happening. You don't have a radio there or anything?"

"I turned it off." Her sobs have abated somewhat. "I'm here with the janitors and the security guard. I scared away my last parent a few minutes ago."

"Maddy," he says, "I'm gonna go down to AM to see if they know anything, and I have to call Leotis. Let me call you back in about five minutes."

"I think maybe I'll just go home," she says.

"I don't think that's a good idea. We don't know what's happening on the streets."

381

"I was thinking I'd take the subway down to Grand Central and cross over to the West Side…"

"Just wait there, okay? You're safe and sound in the school."

"Prosper, it's about a block and a half to the subway."

"Just give me five minutes, please…"

In the luxurious AM broadcast studio, Martin sits across from his employer-to-be, Bruce Morrow, both of them listening to the national news feed. Martin waves for Prosper to come in and join them, but he shakes his head no. On the air, a Memphis police official is being interviewed: King has been rushed to a hospital; he was shot once in the neck, his condition is critical. "Is he expected to live?" asks the interviewer. "I couldn't comment on that" is the reply.

Prosper hastens back to the FM side, finds Leotis's card in his wallet, and calls. It's Leotis who answers. "You've heard?" Prosper says.

"Yeah, man. We're all around the TV. My mom and my sister can't stop cryin'. It's a bad, bad thing. Where you at—down at the radio station? You up on all this? You know how bad he's shot?""

"No…we're just listening to the news, like everybody else."

"Funny," Leotis says, "you at the radio station, listening to the radio."

"I don't suppose," Prosper says, "you still want to come into the city?"

"Yeah, man, why not? Sittin' here ain't gonna do nobody any good."

"How soon can you leave?"

"Five minutes, more or less."

"Okay—it's P.S. Seventy-Two, on a Hundred and Fourth Street. You figure you can get there by eight thirty or so."

"Yeah, if there's no traffic. It ain't but about thirty miles, right? Just tell me how to get there."

## FORTY-FOUR

Is Randall even in his room? Ben has begun knocking gently, gradually increasing the volume. He's about to turn around when he hears Randall's voice: "Yeah...a minute!"

Randall opens the door, in stocking feet, suit pants, and rumpled white shirt. "Jesus," he says, "I guess I didn't know how tired I was. What time is it?"

"Seven, give or take."

Randall scratches his head and peers at Ben. "So...what's up? What's the matter with you? You look like your grandma just got run over by a bus."

"Just about," Ben says. "Somebody shot Martin Luther King."

Randall's mouth hangs open. "You're kidding me."

"No. Afraid not."

"Jesus Christ, Ben....When? Is he all right?"

383

"I don't have a lot of the details, but it's all over the TV. He was standing outside his room at the Lorraine. Somebody, apparently with a high-powered rifle, apparently from across the street, shot him in the neck."

Randall stomps his stockinged right foot on the floor and slaps the side of his head with his right hand. "Jesus!" He says. "*Shit*...that ain't good at all. In the *neck*?" His voice chokes and his eyes well. He turns and walks rapidly across the room, stopping at the television. He fumbles with buttons and after a moment the set pops to life; it is several seconds before the tubes warm up and the picture appears. A different man from the one Ben and Delphine have been watching is on this screen. Ben walks cautiously into the room. He has left Delphine sitting on the edge of his bed, waiting for shoes to drop.

Looking grim, the man on the television says, "We do not have confirmation of this, but we believe that Doctor Martin Luther King Junior, who was shot by an unknown assailant here in Memphis shortly after six o'clock tonight, is near death."

"Jesus *Christ*," Randall says. "Jesus fucking Christ!" He slumps down on the edge of the bed. "Oh, *damn*...this is just unbelievable. Am I dreaming, man? Tell me I'm dreaming, would you, Ben?"

Silent, Ben still stands by the door, arms crossed in front of his chest.

The man on the television repeats the information Ben has heard on a different channel minutes earlier, information that channel is doubtless now repeating itself, as are whatever other channels and radio stations there are in Memphis. Gently shaking his head, Randall listens to the particulars Ben has already given him: high-powered rifle, probably from a rooming house across the street, King standing on the balcony outside

384

his room at the Lorraine Motel, where many civil rights leaders and other prominent black Americans have stayed when in Memphis. Still staring at the screen, Randall speaks in a low voice that gradually rises: "He knew it. He goddamn well knew it. I don't how he knew it, but he knew it." Randall turns his head in Ben's direction. "You were there. You heard him, right?"

"Heard what, Randall?"

"I may not make it to the promised land with you, the man said. He said he'd been to the mountaintop, he'd like to live a long life, but he didn't figure he'd be around much longer, is what he said. You were there. You heard him as clear as I did. I don't know how the man knew it, but he knew it."

Standing by the door, unable to focus on King's words of the night before, faced with a side of Randall he's never before encountered, the depth of whose emotionality stuns him and somehow confronts him, Ben wishes to retreat. But to go next door is to go to Delphine, and another set of problems. Suddenly, out of nowhere, Ben has a vivid image of himself at age eight or nine, waking in the middle of the night in a strange bed during a sleepover at a friend's house: feeling terrified, apart, and alone, without any of the comforts of familiarity. What did he do then? He got out of bed, wandered around the alien house until dawn, and fell back to sleep on the living room couch.

What does he do now? He recalls all at once King's words, can in fact picture King's very expression as he spoke them, and now that Randall has provided the interpretation he must acknowledge a degree of prescience, of eerie foreknowledge. Ben wishes at this moment, wishes fervently, that he could feel what Randall is feeling, what Delphine just on the other side of that wall is feeling. He was fabricating nothing when he told Randall that Martin Luther King was one of his heroes, and yes, of course he has been shocked as much as anyone else by the gruesome news. But grief doesn't come easily to him; it's something he believes he can understand, just not something he experiences.

The telephone rings, startling him, and Randall as well. Randall jerks his head toward the nightstand where the phone sits, as Ben instinctively makes a move in its direction. He stops abruptly when he sees Randall make a gymnast's vault across the bed and seize the receiver before a third ring.

He answers with "Yeah," and a moment later says, "William. Jesus, this is unbelievable, isn't it?" It's Marchand, Ben deduces. Randall says, "What've you heard? Is it as bad as it sounds? Any chance he's gonna pull through?"

Ben watches as Randall slowly moves his head from side to side, listening, and as tears begin to fall quite profusely down his cheeks. "No, man, don't tell me. Jesus, William, this is such a fucking tragedy, man. You were there last night, right? You heard what he said about not getting to the promised land?"

Randall listens again, takes a glance up at Ben and shakes his head; Ben shakes his own head in return, and holds his hands apart, palms up, in a gesture of sad frustration. Randall then says, "Yeah, well I reckon we're not gonna be doin' that, right?" And listens. And says, "Yeah, okay. I can see the wisdom there, I guess. You think it's a good thing?"

Randall listens for well over a minute now, looking up at Ben occasionally, before finally saying, "Okay, buddy, you got it, man. See you there."

To Ben he says, "King's dead."

At that precise moment the man on the television says, "We've just received this tragic bulletin from St. Joseph's

Hospital. Doctor Martin Luther King Junior has died of his wounds..." and Randall vaults back across the bed, gets to his feet, and slams his fist against the television's on/off switch. He turns to Ben and says, "King's dead, and that meeting with the Bee Oh Pee guys is on."

Is it the finality, or is the one-two punch from Randall via Marchand and then the white man on the TV, or is it something else? Ben doesn't know, but something has pierced his defenses and he feels himself choking up, eyes watering. "I'm sorry," he says, in a little boy's voice.

"What the hell are you sorry about?" Randall's voice is far gentler than his words.

Ben shakes his head, unable to hold back the tears, unable to speak, and even if he could speak, unable to put his finger on what it is he's sorry about, or for. Randall gets to his feet and pads toward him. "Hey, man, it's okay. It's all right, Ben." He clasps his arms around Ben's waist and holds him tight. "We all react different ways, my brother. We're gonna get by this. You, and me, and the movement, and the country. I don't know what the fuck it means. I don't know why God chose to pull this particular move, but we're gonna get through this."

"I believe it," Ben manages to whisper, not at all sure what he means.

Randall releases him, and steps back. "You okay? You gonna be all right?"

"Yeah, I'm fine."

"You heard what I said? William tells me we're still gonna meet tonight. Those three Bee Oh Pee boys and a few of the ministers. I guess everybody's afraid the roof's gonna blow off this city tonight."

"What time?"

387

"Eight thirty. Out on their turf, where I went Tuesday night. You don't have to come. Matter of fact, maybe it would be better if you didn't."

Ben is in the last stages of regaining his composure, and this seems a challenge. "Why?"

"Hey, if we were meeting someplace else...if we were meeting here, I wouldn't think twice. I'm just afraid that tonight there might be even more, shall we say...*polarization* out in the neighborhood."

"If you go," Ben says, "I'll go with you."

Looking sad and weary, Randall says, "I don't know, Ben."

Ben raises his voice only slightly. "I'll *go*, for Christ's sake."

He lets himself in to 216, opening the door cautiously, as if there were some delicate life form nestled against its inside. Delphine is on the floor in front of the television, her back against the foot of the bed. She looks in his direction as he enters, and it's clear that she's been crying. Weeping, perhaps. In a soft voice, almost a gasp, she says, "He's dead."

"I know." Ben walks toward her. "I'm sorry I was gone so long. Randall was asleep."

"He all right?" Delphine asks.

"Yeah. Well, he took it pretty hard." Above her now, Ben sinks first to his knees, then sits so he's parallel to her, and slips his arm between her neck and the bedspread.

"He's *dead*," Delphine sobs, and Ben pulls her against him. "Two hours ago he was...gonna lead a *march*. He was gonna go back to Washington. We *saw* him last night. Now some son of a bitch shot him, Ben, and now he's dead!"

388

She resumes weeping, and he embraces her ever more tightly, stroking her back with his right hand. "I know," he says. "It's the worst thing that could have happened."

"What now?" Delphine whispers. "What are we gonna do now?"

He doesn't have an answer, but he needs to answer. "Carry on."

"How?"

"Keep doing what he would have done," Ben says, fearing that his words are misplaced, obvious, fatuous.

"Without him? Who's gonna speak to the people?"

Who, indeed? Ben has a sudden perception that a chain has been broken, that the master link has been brutally disjoined, that there might just be no way to repair it. Who is there with King's mixture of presence, and understanding, and compassion? "Someone will fill the void," he says in her ear, not believing it for a second. "Someone will step in."

"God, I hope so," Delphine says.

And then he has a second revelation, a recognition, a recollection: that the man he works for has that mixture of presence and understanding and compassion. He's not a black man, and hasn't played any active role in the civil rights movement, but if anyone has King's gift for bringing people together it's Bobby Kennedy. So it is that in this moment of dread and apprehension Ben has his epiphany. While he has until now genuinely admired the man referred to within the campaign as either "the Senator" or "the Candidate," he has never previously thought of him in this light. He has considered Kennedy the best man for the job, to be sure. He has considered Robert Kennedy potentially a better president than John Kennedy, better perhaps than anyone since FDR, but not until this moment has Ben seen him as the Savior.

"Bobby Kennedy can do it," he says.

"You really think so?"

"No doubt in my mind."

"I wish I could believe that."

Still stroking her back, he kisses the tip of her earlobe and whispers, "We're gonna get there, sweetheart."

He feels a change in her bearing, a stiffening; after several seconds she says, "Why did you call me that?"

"What?" Ben replies, in the dark.

"Sweetheart." She's pulling away from him. "That's what you called the girl on the phone. Your girlfriend in New York."

So this is the way it happens, with a mindless slip, a misplaced term of endearment. "I'm sorry," he says, preparing for his punishment.

She has somehow switched her body around so she's turned ninety degrees to him--he with his back still against the bed, she with legs crossed, cheeks moist, nose running ever so slightly. Behind her, the television murmurs on, more people talking morosely about the shooting, the death. Delphine says, "Sorry for what?"

He suspects that his answer to this question may have a tremendous effect on his life. What's he sorry for? His instinct tells him to get right to the point. "For not telling you about her."

She takes a deep breath. "It's kind of a big thing not to tell me about, isn't it?"

"Right," he says. "It is."

She wipes her index finger across the base of her nose, without apparent self-consciousness. "But I guess I didn't ask you, either. I guess I just took for granted you weren't serious about anybody."

"It's my fault," Ben says, maintaining eye contact. "There were a couple of times I was going to tell you, but one thing or another got in the way."

"Like what?"

"I figured Randall might have told you, for one."

She considers this for a moment, then says, "He didn't say a word."

"Yeah...I guess I'd pretty much figured that, too."

"You're all good friends, then--you and Randall and her?"

"Not good friends, really. They like each other."

Delphine looks briefly at her lap, then fixes her eyes on Ben's. "What's her name? You never said her name."

"Her name is Maddy."

"You and Maddy aren't married, are you?"

Ben shakes his head. "No."

"Engaged?"

"No." He could avoid imparting this other information now, but ultimately she'd know, so he might as well get it over with. "We've been living together," he says.

Her eyes widen. "*Living* together? That's pretty much the next thing to being married, isn't it?"

"I wouldn't say that."

"So...you've just been tyin' Maddy up till something better came along?"

"I don't think that's the way I planned it," he says. "But that's the way it's turned out."

She laughs. Although it is not a laugh of great cheer, Ben imagines that if nothing else he has taken her mind away from the grim matter at hand. She says, "And I'm the something better."

"You are."

*Peter Delacorte*

## FORTY-FIVE

Lydia doesn't think it's necessarily going to do Rafael any good to tell him about Alex—to confirm his suspicion—it's just that she can't imagine the dishonesty of keeping the secret. So she's waiting for him at the market when his shift ends; he smiles when he sees her, but he appears pale and sleepless. As he embraces her he says, "Cop came here today."

"You told them you worked here?"

"Yeah. Today it was a guy in street clothes. A detective. He asked me all the same shit. I told him I didn't know anything more."

They move slowly down Columbus Avenue. "I talked to Alex," she says.

"Yeah, I got your note."

"I talked to him this morning, then I went back after school, to get some clothes. I found a receipt for a gun..."

Rafael stops in his tracks. "No shit?"

"Then I talked to him again. He did it."

His eyes become huge. "He *told* you he did it?"

"He told me."

"Did he say why?"

She knows that her choice of words is going to be extremely important. She can't lie; the whole point of telling him was to avoid deception. Maintaining eye contact, she says, "Why do you think? If some nasty son of a bitch a foot taller than you is about to beat the shit out of you, and you happen to have a gun, wouldn't you use it?"

His hands on her shoulders, he says, "Is he still there?"

"Who? Alex?"

"Yeah. Is he still at his place?"

"How would I know? I left two hours ago."

"I'm gonna talk to him," Rafael says.

"No, you're not. What's the point?"

"I want him to tell me what happened."

"Don't be crazy, Rafael. He's..." She searches for a word that will at once describe Alex and deter Rafael. The best she can do is "...unpredictable."

"You think he's gonna shoot me too? Last night you said he was a fucking pacifist."

"He won't let you in," she says.

"Then give me your keys."

She struggles with the conflicting images of Alex in her mind: the old one, a self-destructive, occasionally brilliant but generally irrational drug fancier who would avoid violence at all costs, and the new one, which is quite a lot like the old one except that he's just killed somebody. The notion of *driving down to Delaware to buy a gun* strikes her as the bridge between the old and the new. It wouldn't have surprised her if he'd somehow acquired a car and driven to Delaware to buy a revolutionary hash pipe, or a new strain of morning glory seed. But here's the question: Is there even a remote chance he'd use the gun on Rafael? She says, "I'll go with you."

"No," he replies. "Not a chance."

"He won't do anything if I'm there," she pleads.

"Yeah, but if you're there he won't talk to me. This is for me to do."

***

Alex's mind has been racing out of control. As much as he tries to calm himself, sitting in the lotus position and taking deep breaths, trying to clear his brain of all this negative clutter,

393

he keeps falling into these grim, downward spiraling trains of thought. Lydia's left him and she's not coming back; she's going to tell the Puerto Rican guy with the leather jacket that he shot Flaco; he'll go to the cops and Alex will be busted; he'll go to jail for what, for some kind of manslaughter, or he'll have to go to his father to get the money for a good lawyer and he'll beat the jail term but surely Columbia will kick him out, nobody else will let him in, and then he's draft bait. So either he's getting gang-raped at Sing Sing or he's getting shot at by Viet Cong. Or Lydia's wrong about Rafael, and one night Alex is on his way back to the apartment and somebody steps out of the shadows and cuts his throat. She doesn't even have to be wrong about Rafael. Maybe he's the nicest guy in the world, but he fills in his big friend Julio, who comes by and beats the living shit out of Alex.

He needs to talk to someone. It keeps flashing through his mind that Lydia will be home soon, but then he remembers that she won't be back. He pictures himself calling his mother from military school in Indiana when he needed comfort, before she killed herself.

He's got to do something, but as fast as his brain is working it's as if his body is paralyzed. He's got maybe an eighth of an ounce of Elliot's marijuana left, and the way things are going he may not be getting anything more from Elliot, but what the hell—when will he ever be more in need of a little relaxation?

He's smoked half the joint, settled down just a little bit, when the buzzer sounds—somebody downstairs wanting to come in. Not Lydia. Jehovah's Witnesses? The cops? His first instinct is to ignore it, but when there's a second and a third buzz he goes to the intercom and shouts, "Who is it?"

"It's Rafael."

He can't have heard that right. "Who?"

"Rafael, man. You know who I am."

Alex's heartbeat has re-accelerated. "What do you want?"

"I want to talk to you."

"I don't want to talk to you. Get the hell out of here."

There's a pause. "I've got Lydia's keys. Buzz me in or I'll let myself in."

"I don't believe you," Alex says.

"Okay." Rafael says, "I'm coming in."

Alex licks his thumb and forefinger and squeezes the joint to extinguish it; he zips into the bedroom and fumbles for the pistol under the mattress, finds it just as there's a series of rapid knocks at the front door. "I've got a gun," he shouts.

"I know you've got a fucking gun," replies Rafael.

This isn't good—two people yelling at each other about guns within earshot of several sets of neighbors. "Come in," Alex calls. "Let yourself in." As he hears the key fumbling in the lock, he wonders whether to leave the Walther's safety on or off. Did he remember to switch it on after he fired it? He can't recall, and here's Rafael opening the door—just a little guy, in the good-looking leather jacket with the fleece collar.

"You gonna shoot me too?" Rafael peers down at the gun, then up at Alex.

"Probably not," Alex says. "What did you want to talk about?"

"You want to invite me in? Put the gun down?"

Alex lowers the Walther and moves sideways, making a sweeping gesture with his left hand. Rafael walks by him and sits at the far end of the couch. He says, "Do I smell weed?"

"Yes, you do." Alex removes the half-joint from his shirt pocket. "You want some?"

395

"I wouldn't mind it."

Alex hands him the joint. His Zippo is in his right-hand pocket; without much thought he rests the gun on the coffee table, perhaps four feet from Rafael, in order to remove the lighter. He sits on the couch and proffers the Zippo. He says, "It's pretty amazing stuff."

Rafael inhales deeply, holds the smoke in for what seems like half an hour, and exhales. He says, "Okay, tell me what happened."

"Lydia already told you, right?"

"I want you to tell me." He passes the joint back to Alex.

"Okay, you know those guys stole my stuff, right?"

"I know all about that."

"You have anything to do with that?"

"No. I told Julio not to do it. Obviously he wasn't the one who made the decision."

After a quick toke, Alex hands the joint back. "Okay, I'm trying to get my life together. I'm at film school. I need a camera and I need a tape recorder, a particular kind of expensive tape recorder..."

"It didn't seem that way Sunday night, Monday morning. If it wasn't for Lydia, you would've handed over that stuff to us then."

"I was high. You know how it is."

"No, I don't. If I had shit like that I wouldn't be giving it away to guys I just met on the street." Rafael returns the joint to Alex. He says, "But get on with it."

"It's pretty simple," Alex says. "I found him at the bar. He said he was gonna take me to where the stuff was. We're walking down Columbus and he hits me up for money. That's when I showed him the gun..."

396

"Where were you?"

"About half a block from your place."

"He was taking you there, to my place?"

"Right. He wanted to distract me. I didn't know about you and Lydia. So we're gonna walk in on the two of you, I'm gonna be all surprised and fucked up, and he'll—I don't know—grab the gun, or hit me with a lamp, or just take off..."

Rafael reaches for the joint, which is approaching roach status, and has a quick hit. He says, "Loyal fuckin' friend, huh?"

"Yeah," Alex says. "I don't know how close you guys were, but I don't think at that moment he had your welfare in mind."

"You weren't planning on shooting him?"

"Not until he jumped on me..."

"So...he jumps, you shoot, he lands on you?"

"Right. I've got this huge fucking bump on the back of my head."

Rafael smiles grimly. "That's more than you can say for him." He gets to his feet. "You better get rid of that gun."

"How about the other guy--Julio?" Alex says.

"Don't worry about him." Rafael offers his hand to Alex. "Thanks, man. That's some fine weed. No hard feelings, all right?"

No hard feelings? Alex may feel a grand sense of relief that there's no revenge in the making, but what about the other matter? "You and Lydia," he says. "Is that a serious thing?"

"Far as I'm concerned," Rafael says.

What time is it? Just past eight o'clock. Surely Leonia Ford-Mercury will be closed by the time he gets across the bridge. He'll park the car on the lot or as close to it as possible,

397

and dump the gun in a corner garbage can. Perhaps it would be safer to toss it into the Hudson, but that would involve a trip to Riverside Park in the dead of night. This way it will almost certainly end up buried in landfill, but even if it gets into the hands of the Leonia police, what are the chances they'd link it to a shooting in upper Manhattan?

The radio is turned down to a murmur as he heads west on 121$^{st}$ Street. The deejay, Frankie Crocker, is rambling on about something, not playing music. Alex hits the other buttons he's set on rock and roll stations—WMCA, WABC, WINS— but everybody's talking. It angers him that he'd have such bad luck. Somebody somewhere should be playing music, which would make it easier for him to regain the marijuana mellowness he'd begun to achieve before Rafael's visit. He makes the light at Broadway, but at Claremont Avenue just misses the next one, and then he sits there as the seconds pass. He runs through the radio buttons again: It's all news, news, news, and Frankie Crocker on WWRL not his usual ebullient self. There's no traffic heading in either direction on Claremont and he's been stuck here for so long he wonders if the signal is broken, so what the hell, he turns right against the light, which is a legal move in most civilized areas anyway.

There are two cops standing on the east side of the street, as if they were waiting for him. Indeed, one cop steps out onto the street and motions for Alex to pull the car over. Not a chance. He keeps right on going, but realizes that he's not going to get too far because the light at LaSalle Street, two blocks up, has just turned red. The obvious thing, then, is to take a right on 122$^{nd}$ Street. A quick look in the rearview mirror reveals one cop still standing in the street, hands on hips, the other holding a walkie-talkie to his face. Jesus Christ. Stay

398

cool, Alex tells himself. He'll be on the West Side Highway in
two minutes, on the bridge in five, and in New Jersey in ten.
The cops have better things to do than send a platoon after
somebody who ran a red light.

Halfway down the relatively short block he checks the
rearview again: no cops in sight, but the street isn't very well lit.
The light at Broadway is green; he's got the Lark up to forty-
five or so and he's maybe thirty feet from the intersection when
the light turns yellow. He's got to keep moving. Either stop
here and then hang another quick, illegal right, which would
take him in the wrong direction, or don't stop at all. He chooses
the latter option, and makes it safely across the two southbound
lanes of Broadway, then hits the brakes as he recognizes
northbound vehicles have already started moving. But he's
going way too fast to stop in the median area, so he turns the
wheel hard left and swerves onto Broadway, where the Lark
smashes into a late-model Buick Electra 225. It's not quite a t-
bone collision, as his right front fender hits the Buick's rear
door at about a fifty-degree angle, but it's very loud and it's
powerful enough to send the Buick several feet sideways.

Adrenaline coursing, Alex has a quick look at the
Buick's driver, a black man who's glaring at him while banging
his shoulder against the inside of his car door, which evidently
has jammed. That's good news for Alex, who needs to get out
of here as fast as possible. He floors the accelerator, but
nothing happens because the engine has stalled. He shifts into
neutral and turns the key; the engine turns over but doesn't
catch. Meanwhile, the Buick's driver has slid across the front
seat and opened the passenger-side door. Alex turns the key
again, and again the engine fails to start. The other driver is
about Alex's height, but stocky and considerably older,
probably around forty. Why won't the car start? Damage to the

carburetor on impact? Or did he flood it when he slammed the gas pedal to the floor? The Buick driver has made it around the front of his car and pounded the Studebaker's hood with his left hand. He's yelling at Alex: "Motherfucker! Crazy stupid white motherfucker! You gonna pay for this, you bet your white ass!" Alex gives the key one more turn, carefully laying off the accelerator, and the engine turns with healthy vigor but doesn't catch.

Alex locks his door an instant before the Buick driver grabs the handle. It's dawning on him that he can't afford to sit here and try to start the car. Soon the cops will arrive, or worse. A small crowd has gathered under a streetlight on the sidewalk adjacent to the accident, and the Buick driver now whacks on the Lark's window with the side of his large right hand, yelling, "Open your window, you fuckin' coward! Get out your damn car!"

Alex takes the pistol from his jacket pocket and doesn't so much point it at the Buick driver as show it to him, and the man immediately backs up several steps. Alex checks his wallet, which contains three twenties and a ten, and opens the car door. The Buick driver has retreated to the iron railing on the periphery of the median strip. Alex says, "Hey, man, I'm sorry about the car." He tosses two twenties in his direction. "I know that's not enough, but it's all I can give you right now."

"You a cop?" The Buick driver asks, unaccountably. It seems the sensible thing to do to nod yes. Alex turns and walks rapidly around the Buick—which actually doesn't look too badly damaged, unless the frame is bent. Traffic has backed up on Broadway, headlights and taillights glowing a block back at least, horns blaring as two lanes try to squeeze into a space barely wide enough for one car, and the crowd on the sidewalk now numbers thirty or forty. He looks over his shoulder to check if the Claremont Avenue cops have appeared; they haven't. He switches the gun to his left hand and holds up his right to signal the slow-moving single file of traffic to halt, and makes his way toward the sidewalk but not quite onto it. People, all black, seem to regard him with curiosity and respect, but it's not as if he can just blend into the crowd, so he moves parallel to the sidewalk. A teenage boy says, "Hey, you got a badge?"

"Sure," Alex says.

"Don't look like no po-lice gun to me," the boy says.

Another boy says, "You pick a bad night to be fuckin' around in Harlem."

Alex picks up his pace, gets beyond the crowd and hops up onto the sidewalk. Most stay behind, but a few people, kids, follow him, staying fifteen or twenty feet behind. Where is he going? Everything, the whole plan, was based on getting the car to New Jersey, and now that's not going to happen. He's only about half a mile from his apartment, but heading south would mean getting through that crowd and risking a rendezvous with the cops who'd flagged him down. A glance over his left shoulder reveals the Buick driver, still up against the median, moving parallel to him. Alex speeds up a little more, so he's almost trotting, passing 123$^{rd}$ Street, revving it up a little more, figuring that he'll turn right on 125$^{th}$ where he can hail a cab or duck into anyplace that's open. But what's this— LaSalle Street? He takes a right and breaks into a jog. Fifty feet down the street he looks back and under dim street lights thinks he sees the small group of teenagers not too far behind, and is that the Buick driver just now turning the corner? Alex stops and holds the gun over his head; his pursuers stop as well. Nearly breathless, he shouts, "Hey, you guys think this gun isn't real?" He pauses for breath. "I'm gonna ask you to stay back,

401

all right? Do *not* fucking follow me!" He considers pulling the trigger for emphasis, but decides that might provoke unwanted attention, so he turns and begins running full-bore down the street. By the time he gets to Amsterdam Avenue he seems to have lost his pursuers.

There is a bar at the corner of Amsterdam and 125$^{th}$: Moe & Eddie's. If he ducks in here and waits for a while, fifteen or twenty minutes, he will certainly be lost to the world. Then he can walk another long block down to Morningside Avenue, take a right, and cut through the park back to his apartment.

There are perhaps fifteen patrons sitting or standing at the bar, a large man with a white apron standing behind it. All eyes are trained on a color television that sits on a platform high on the wall. When Alex closes the door behind him—a disheveled young white man, sweaty and breathing hard, in blue jeans and an unseasonal cotton jacket with a bulge in the right-hand pocket—several men turn to look at him, and there is some muttering.

## FORTY-SIX

Prosper ascends from the subway to the piercing wail of nearby sirens. As he reaches the sidewalk on Lexington Avenue, three fire engines rumble by on 103rd Street. In the northwest night sky are what appear to be two separate plumes of smoke, perhaps a mile from where he's standing. That, he thinks, is not a good sign. In the immediate neighborhood, the streets—Lexington and then 104th Street—are virtually deserted, but there seem to be sirens everywhere.

He knocks on the broad front door of P.S. 72 and after a minute or so it's cracked open from within and a voice says, "You Miss O'Connor's friend?" Prosper answers in the affirmative and a broad-shouldered man in his forties, in janitorial garb, lets him in and directs him to the break room.

Still in her party outfit—which gives him a kind of thrill—she sits on a vinyl sofa with a stack of papers on her lap. "Hi," she says. "Come sit." Her eyes are bloodshot, but she smiles as he plops down next to her. He's not sure what degree of intimacy the moment calls for, but he puts his arm around her and kisses her cheek. She says, "Did you hear?"

"I haven't heard anything but sirens."

"He's dead," Maddy says.

"Oh, my God. Do they know who did it? Did they catch the guy?"

"No." She shakes her head.

He can't think of anything to say other than "Leotis should be here any minute."

"I hope he doesn't have any trouble getting here. The sirens have been nonstop for the last half hour or so. Mostly fire engines, I think."

They sit in silence for fifteen seconds and then she says, "What's the plan, Prosper? What do we do from here, when your friend gets here?"

"I guess we'll go and get something to eat. Is there anyplace near here?"

"At this hour? There's a sort of greasy Puerto Rican restaurant a block down. That's about it for the neighborhood."

***

Leotis looks very young, very strong. He shakes Maddy's hand with a gentle grip and says, "I've heard a lot about you."

"Same here," she says. She imagines he's heard a lot more about her than she has of him, but how are you supposed to reply when someone says that?

"I parked my van right downstairs, right in front of the school. Is that okay? They gonna tow it away?"

Leotis's van says JIFFY CARPET on both doors, with an address in Bridgeport. "Yeah, they get free advertising from me, but it don't do 'em a lot of good because they went out of business." He laughs in his pleasant, throaty way. "That's how I got the van. Bankruptcy sale. Two hundred and fifteen dollars. Didn't have but sixty-three thousand miles. Good clutch, pretty good tires. Got the big V-eight in it. I could haul two standup pianos up the steepest hill in America in this rig. Problem is that's all I could fit. Like the one time I had a job to move a whole house, I had to make seven, eight trips from Stamford up to Fairfield. Took me the whole weekend. I could've done it in four hours with a truck."

Maddy says, "How much did they pay you?"

"Three hundred."

"It wouldn't have cost you more than about thirty to rent a truck, right?"

Leotis squints at her. "Who's gonna rent a truck to a twenty-year-old Negro?" He uses the word *Negro* ironically, or at least Maddy thinks so. Such things can be hard to tell.

Prosper says, "Everybody's hungry, right? Leotis--is a greasy Puerto Rican place just down the street all right with you?"

"First time for everything," Leotis says.

Maddy looks at the sky. "I don't want to seem alarmist, but shouldn't we get out of here?"

"I think that's all farther uptown," Prosper says. "Like, above a Hundred and Twenty-Fifth Street. What did it look like driving in, Leotis?"

"I don't know one street from another," Leotis says, "but it looked to me like all the fires and all the sirens was about a mile or two up from here."

Prosper looks at Maddy. "Okay," she says. "Let's eat."

\*\*\*

The Sol y Luna has some twenty tables and booths and stays open till midnight. Tonight at quarter after nine, the three of them are its only customers. A small black-and-white television on a table in the back of the room shows a Spanish version of events in Memphis. "Do we want to watch that?" Prosper asks.

"I don't," Maddy says, and Leotis shakes his head.

Maddy has a brief conversation with the waitress, a rotund, copper-skinned woman, who tells her that the *arroz con pollo* is good tonight and that the radio says to avoid West Harlem.

405

"This is all like a dream," Maddy says. "A strange, bad dream. I remember when Kennedy was killed it was the same sequence. We were in school, and we heard he'd been shot. I don't think offhand any of us even knew he was in Dallas. He was the president and we were seventeen- or eighteen-year-old kids. You just took for granted that wherever he was, whatever he was doing, he was protected..."

"Right," Prosper says. "There was that same element of...incredulity..."

"I wouldn't have believed it, except there was this *nun* telling me it was true. And then when it sinks in, you think maybe it's not too serious. Then you find out it *is* serious, and you still try to convince yourself that somehow it'll be all right, that the doctors will save him."

The waitress brings a giant bottle of Schaefer beer and three absurdly small glasses, which she fills. Leotis says, "This one is different to me."

"Why is that?" Prosper says.

"Lotta things. Maybe cause I'm older now. I wasn't but sixteen then. Maybe cause I was home. I was at school too with President Kennedy--vice-principal came into math class and broke the news, and everybody let out a gasp, and some girls started to cry. But today my mom and pops were watchin' the news and all of a sudden my mom lets out this *scream*, and my sister Ella comes runnin' down the stairs cause she thinks somebody broke into the house, and I'm in the kitchen tryin' to concentrate on my book, waitin' for Prosper to call me, and I hear my pops say, loud enough so you could hear it down the street, 'Some son of a bitch just shot Doctor Martin Luther King.' It's the first time I ever heard him use language like that in front of my mom. So now we're all in front of the TV: Mom is cryin', but Ella's hysterical, she's shakin' and sobbin', and

Pops is huggin' her. So I sat down next to Mom, put my arm around her, and we watched, and when we heard they shot him in the neck, I knew he was dead..."

Prosper says, "So...this is different because you're older? Because you were home?"

Leotis grimaces and shakes his head. "No, man, not just that. I mean, Kennedy meant a lot to me. I think he meant a lot to black people in general. Eisenhower was this old bald white dude that I knew was president, you see his picture up on the wall every day at school. But it was like he was president of some other country that had nothin' to do with me. Kennedy, we had his picture up in our *house*. Still, much as I admired him, much as I got excited hearin' him talk, there was like...a separation. This man may do good for me, but he *ain't* me. Now, Doctor King, with that way he had, all cool and reserved, but then fiery all of a sudden, he'd say, 'Okay, you can knock me down, but I'm gonna get up. You can knock me down again, but I'm gonna get up again. You can knock me down many times as you like, but I'm gonna get up every time and keep tellin' you it's wrong to knock me down, and finally you're gonna get the message. Trouble is, they finally figured out the way to keep him down was to kill him."

Prosper says, "But people did get the message. He got the job done."

"Did he?" Leotis says. "I'm not sayin' he didn't. I just don't know if he finished it. And if he didn't finish it, who's gonna take over?"

As the question hangs in the air, Maddy is on the verge of pointing out that Lyndon Johnson, of all people, pushed through most of the important civil rights legislation after the Kennedy assassination, finishing that job. But she thinks better of it, inasmuch as she's sitting here with two young men

407

who've suddenly become eligible to participate in another project Johnson inherited, and transformed into something much grander.

It's Leotis who speaks after the lull. "When Kennedy was killed, did y'all feel that something was over? That it wasn't ever gonna be the same again?"

Maddy says, "Right then, right afterward maybe, yes."

Prosper says, "I think I was just in a state of shock through the whole thing."

"I don't know how much of it has to do with the draft," Leotis says. "That's been sinkin' in to me all day. But now I just feel like somethin's been chopped out of me. Everybody in my house was so damn sad, I had to get out of there. But I can't run away from that feeling."

The *arroz con pollo* arrives, and they order another quart bottle of Schaefer. Sirens have sounded intermittently, occasionally quite close by. "I hope it ain't like Detroit," Leotis says, "when people burned down their own neighborhood."

"It's probably just abandoned buildings," Prosper says.

Maddy says, "Leotis, you don't know the city very well?"

"Been here maybe five times in my life. My pops took me to a Mets game when they played at the Polo Grounds, and to a Yankee game when they had Mantle and Maris. Last couple years, I've come in with my sister to see my cousin at the Apollo."

"Who's your cousin?" Prosper asks. To white fanciers of rhythm and blues the Apollo is a legendary but dangerous shrine. It's where virtually every great black music act appears in New York, and it's said that certain audience members often disapprove of white people in their midst. Prosper has been to

# The Mountaintop

the Apollo perhaps fifteen times and never encountered anything worse than surprise. He says, "Who's your cousin?"

"You probably never heard of him. Leroy Telford?"

Prosper grins. "Never heard of Leroy Telford? Are you kidding me? I *know* Leroy Telford."

Leotis grins back. "You puttin' me on, right?"

"Leotis...my God, your cousin has the world's greatest cover band. He can sound like just about anybody. I saw him at the Uptown in Philadelphia three years ago. He opened for Sam and Dave. I tracked him down and hired him to play Saturday night of some big weekend for the club I belonged to at college. He called me about six o'clock that night and said his car broke down, would it be all right if he played Sunday afternoon instead. I said, where are you, I'll come pick you up. He said no, there's five of us, and all our instruments. I said I'll get two friends and we'll pick you up in three cars. He said okay, I'll tell you the truth: My manager double-booked me and I'm doing a gig tonight in Camden. But I'll come up tomorrow afternoon and play your club for half price."

Leotis continues to grin. "So did you let Leroy take advantage of you?"

"I did. We had kind of a dull Saturday night, but Leroy showed up about two o'clock Sunday afternoon. It was a beautiful day, so we ran a couple of big extension cords out to the porch and hooked everything up, and they did the best show we ever had. Better than Wilson Pickett. Better than Bo Diddley. Better than Howard Tate."

"Damn!" Leotis says. "You had all those people play at your club? I didn't know white people went in for that kind of music."

"I kind of imposed it on them," Prosper says. "Until they got the hang of it."

409

"That radio station you work at--they don't play soul music, right?"

"No. Not at all."

"So, how come you work there?"

"I ask myself the same question," Prosper says.

Maddy has run back into the school to retrieve paperwork; Leotis sits inside the van, and Prosper is about to join him when a green and white police cruiser pulls up behind them. The first thought to enter Prosper's mind is that Leotis won't have to pay the ticket because the van is registered in Connecticut.

Initially, only the cop in the passenger seat gets out of the car. He's a tall, thick white guy, and when he's still several feet away he says, "This your van?"

"It belongs to my friend." The cop is now close enough so that Prosper can read his name—MAGLIE—and see the TPF pin on his uniform. The Tactical Patrol Force are the storm troopers of the NYPD.

"Where's your friend?" Asks Officer Maglie. "In the van," Prosper replies. Maglie looks back toward the car and nods his head, whereupon the second cop emerges, hand ominously on his holster. Prosper says, "We were just about to leave."

"You can't park here," Maglie says. "There's signs all over the place. It's a school zone. I can have this van towed away."

The second cop—shorter, solidly built, also white--has paused between them and the van; his nameplate says PAZ. Prosper cannot help thinking first that it's "zap" spelled backwards, then that it's the Spanish word for "peace." And for that matter, that the only other Maglie he's known of was Sal the Barber, who pitched for both the Giants and the Dodgers, and was on the losing end of Don Larsen's perfect game in the 1956 World Series. What food for small talk, at a different time and place. He says, "My girlfriend is a teacher at the school. We just stopped for a minute so she could pick up some papers."

"Is that right?" Maglie says, in a voice heavy with skepticism.

Having eavesdropped for a moment, Officer Paz now makes his way toward the front of the van, and Prosper takes a step in that direction. "You stay right here," Maglie says. Then, "I want you to put your hands up against the back of the van, and spread your feet apart."

Prosper obeys, and as Maglie pats him down he strains to hear any conversation that might be occurring up front. What he hears is Paz's voice, loud and clear, "This one's a colored kid."

Maglie says, "I'm gonna reach in your pocket, okay? Don't you move a fuckin' inch." The pocket in question is on the right side of Prosper's sportscoat, his work jacket, and Maglie removes his keychain. He says, "One of these open the back?"

It takes him a moment to realize the cop is talking about the van. Still leaning against it, with his feet a yard apart from each other, he says, "No, they're my keys, and it's not my van. You mind if I stand up straight now."

"I'll tell you when you can stand up. Where'd you get this van?"

"It's my friend's van."

"What's your friend's name?"

"Leotis."

411

"Where did Leotis get the van? He work for Jiffy Carpet?"

"He bought it at a bankruptcy sale." Where is Maddy? Actually, it's difficult to say whether her arrival at this point would be good or bad. Maybe she could flash an i.d. card and put this nonsense to a quick end, or maybe she'd be considered a co-conspirator and all three would spend the night on Rikers Island.

"Hey, Ricardo," Maglie calls, "bring that one back here."

Leotis appears seconds later, with Paz's nightstick resting against the small of his back. Prosper shakes his head and says, "Sorry about this."

Paz says, "You shut the fuck up," and Maglie, almost simultaneously, says, "What're you sorry about?"

"Inviting him down here," Prosper says.

Maglie says to Leotis, "You steal this van?"

"I *own* it. Your partner's got my registration in his hand."

"That right?" Maglie says to Paz, and Paz gives a quick nod and hands over the little greenish paper. Maglie peruses the registration. "Tell me what you're doin' in Harlem tonight? Why'd you come down here from Bridgeport?"

"Stamford," Leotis says. "I just finished tellin' your partner that I came in to have dinner with Prosper here and his friend Maddy."

Maglie shakes his head almost imperceptibly, as if it is unfathomable that this black boy and this long-haired white boy could be up to anything but no good. "I want you to open up the back of this van for me," he says, pointing his thumb as if hitchhiking, signaling for Leotis to pass in front of him.

Prosper stands back until Maglie nods at him, indicating that he's to be part of this investigation as well.

The four of them stand behind the van, Leotis searching through his pockets, Maglie's fingers on the butt of his pistol. Leotis says, "Keys in the ignition." He stares into the cop's sullen visage, waiting for further instruction, and Maglie doesn't fail him. "Get the fuckin' keys, then."

Leotis and Paz return whence they'd just come, Prosper standing next to Maglie, the two of them like party guests during an awkward moment when no one can think of anything to say, Prosper all the while fearing that the longer this goes on the greater the possibility that something will go wrong, that someone will make a false step.

But Leotis reappears, still in one piece. With a steady hand he turns the key on the van's right rear door, swings the doors open and reveals exactly what one might expect to find in a mover's vehicle: lots of rope, lots of pads, plus a spare tire and a jack. "There you go," he says.

Maglie pulls out his nightstick, leans into the van, and pokes at the furniture pads, looking no doubt for *plastique* and Molotov cocktails. But he's not quite satisfied. "What's all that rope for?"

"I'm a *mover*," Leotis says. "I'm in the *movin'* business. How'm I gonna tie shit up if I don't have rope?"

Maglie takes a step toward Leotis, slapping the nightstick into his own left palm. Prosper says, "He's just answering your goddamn question."

"Was I talkin' to you?" Maglie says to Prosper, with a glare of scary intensity.

It is at this point that Maddy appears, in her black tights and short denim skirt and purple top, carrying a stack of manila folders, exuding respectability. Prosper says, "Here she is."

413

"You know these guys, Miss?" Maglie calls to her when she's still twenty feet away.

"Of course I know them. What's the matter?"

"Could I see some identification, please, Miss?"

With a terrible sinking feeling, Prosper recalls that any identification Maddy might normally have is back at her apartment, because she spent the night with him. He envisions the three of them sinking deeper and deeper into Tactical Patrol Force quicksand. "Why do I need to show you identification?" Maddy says in her best Irish-Spanish patrician manner. "My name is Magdalena O'Connor. I'm a kindergarten teacher at P.S. Seventy-Two, which is right behind us. I've had a very long day. Doctor Martin Luther King has just been killed, and my two friends have been kind enough to wait for me here while I went inside to get these folders. I'm sure you gentlemen have something better to do than make me prove who I am."

Prosper's eyes have remained fixed on Maglie, whose expression is ambiguous: It might connote a combination of surprise and bewilderment, or it might be the foreshadowing of a great explosion of rage. As for Maddy, clearly she's deduced the basic nature of the situation, but Prosper wonders if she'd have played her hand so strongly had she realized the degree of the cops' antipathy. There is a profoundly heavy moment of silence, of immobility--as if they were all involved in a sinister game of red light, green light—broken finally when Maglie says in a low growl, "I don't need you to tell me how to do my job."

Beyond the tone, it strikes Prosper as a weak rejoinder, as a sign that it's just occurred to Maglie that he and Leotis are not in fact terrorists. Before anything else can happen there is a loud crackling from the police car's radio. "Better get that," Maglie says, and Paz walks the several steps to the cruiser.

"Somebody in the school now that can vouch for you?" Maglie says to Maddy.

Prosper watches Paz as he sits in the car and speaks inaudibly into the transponder. Maddy says, "Of course."

Paz ducks out of the cruiser, "Somethin' goin' down on a Hundred and Twenty-Fifth and Eighth. They want us."

"It's your lucky day," Maglie says to Prosper. "You and your colored friend."

## FORTY-SEVEN

Delphine says, "I think you're both crazy. I think your friend William is crazy, and I think those ministers and anybody else that wants to get together tonight is crazy. And if y'all do have to meet, then for God's sake don't go and do it out on McLemore."

The three of them are in Randall's room, finishing off a room service dinner of cheeseburgers and cold French fries. Randall sits by the window in one the room's two chairs, his plate on the circular table between the two chairs; Delphine sits across from him, while Ben is cross-legged on the bed, his plate in his lap. She has had a brief, tearful telephone conversation with her mother, who has urged her to come home as soon as possible. It's not far from the Holiday Inn to her part of town--a couple of miles--and as Randall has pointed out, "The cops aren't likely to stop someone as light as you."

"What about that?" Ben says to Randall. "What if we were to call William and get in touch with everybody? Hell, we could meet here, right? Holiday Inn's got to be considered neutral territory." Ben knows Randall's reaction ahead of time, but it's no matter. He's spoken for Delphine's benefit. He understands that, objectively, it's not a sensible thing they're planning to do, but he's feeling determined and dedicated and invincible, as if this is his moment to take care of something, to be a part of something.

"Don't think the bee oh pee boys would come within five miles of downtown tonight," Randall says. "You can't blame 'em. Probably half the cracker police force sittin' out there waitin' for some militants to stir up trouble." He pronounces the word *militants* as if it's within quotation marks, as if the Black Organizing Project really aren't militants, or as if the word might have a different connotation within the ranks of the Memphis Police Department.

"Randall," Delphine says, "I hope you understand I'm not just bein' cautious here. I'm not just bein' the voice of reason. Ben's new to all this, but you should know better."

"I've been around the block a couple of times."

"That's what I'm saying."

"Yeah, and we've got a job to do. We came down here to take care of business. This ain't exactly the kind of business I expected, but when duty calls, you answer."

Delphine says, "Well, I get the feeling you've been away from this kind of business a little too long."

"How do you mean? I've been in this business all my life, by definition."

416

"Right," she says, "from what I understand you spent the last ten years in Boston and New York."

"But you don't forget, sister. Believe me--you don't forget."

"Maybe you get a little spoiled, though?"

"Tell me about *spoiled*, Delphine...growin' up in the biggest damn house in Memphis."

Does Ben have any right--does he have the ability--to step in here? If he had time to analyze the rancor that's just sprung up it might make some sense, but he doesn't. It's been difficult dealing with Randall's anger toward him the past couple of days, but this is worse; his urge is to protect Delphine, but he wonders first how much he might endanger his already shaky standing with Randall, and second whether she needs any protection at all.

"Don't give me that shit," she says to Randall. "I'll bet you can live in the nastiest apartment in New York and nobody's gonna give you a hard time when you want to use the bathroom in the restaurant down the street."

Randall guffaws, and slaps the table, sending his plate dangerously close to the edge. He glances at Ben. "You think she might have a thing or two to learn about the big city?"

"Stop it," Ben says. Randall glares at him for the briefest of moments, then smiles. This much Ben knows: Randall had expected some sort of concurrence, some sort of teammate affirmation of Delphine's ignorance regarding the accessibility of public facilities in New York. Ben wonders if Randall knew how angry he sounded in his exchange with Delphine, and if there was something cryptic in that anger, one of those things that transpire between black people, thus that it was a kind of fake anger, or play anger; and Ben wonders finally if he's chosen a bad time to speak those two harsh words to Randall.

"It's cool, Ben," Randall says. "Don't sweat it, okay?

Judging by the look on Delphine's face, it isn't cool at all, but then maybe Ben is entirely out of his depth. He tries to catch her eye, but her gaze is fixed sternly on Randall. Ben says, "If there's something I don't understand, you can tell me what's going on."

Randall chuckles. "There's a lot you don't understand, my little brother."

"I'm sure," Ben says.

"Don't call him your damn little brother," Delphine says. "Don't patronize him."

"It's okay, Delphine," Ben says, and sensing that she's a few seconds away from tears he puts aside his plate and pushes himself off Randall's bed. "It's all right. It's under control." He stands behind her chair, hands on her shoulders. "Will you excuse us for a minute?" He says to Randall.

"You have every right not to go out there with him," she says, standing just inside the door to Ben's room. "If he wants to go out to that part of town tonight, let him go. But you don't have to. Come to my house with me."

"I told him I'd go," Ben says. "We can take care of ourselves. Each other."

She shakes her head; tears emerge from those extraordinary green eyes and roll down her cheeks. She speaks in a low voice, just above a whisper. "Don't be crazy."

"It's not as if I'm gonna be the only white person there."

"The others would be as crazy as you."

He embraces her and says, "Look, it's my job, okay?"

It would be inaccurate to say that the drive is uneventful, but fair to say that--just as Ben had anticipated, had *sensed*--it is not fraught with peril. He's at the wheel, as usual.  Now it makes more sense, or at least it seems to make more sense, for the white member of the pair to be driving the shiny new Mustang through the dark streets of Memphis. They head south, in the direction of Mason Temple, where less than twenty-four hours earlier they had seen Martin Luther King in all his serene majesty. The danger, if there is any, would come in the form of police, because in this all-black part of the city there is virtually no civilian on the street. What would the cops do to them? They've discussed this, Randall and Ben, before setting out. The worst they could expect would be getting pulled over, detained, searched, and ordered to return to the Holiday Inn, or to New York City.

They head south, and then east, and the neighborhood dilapidates: unpainted frame houses, some abandoned, plenty of broken windows, derelict cars on the streets. The Mustang's radio is tuned to Delphine's station, WDIA, which between gospel songs urges its listeners to stay inside and respect the teachings of the assassinated leader. But evidently not everyone is doing so; through the closed windows of the car and above its radio the wail of sirens is constant. There are four...six...*eight* fires of apparently major proportion in Ben's field of vision, most of them so far away he's aware only of the great trails of smoke, but two are nearby enough so their glow is perceptible.

As they cruise along East McLemore at a steady thirty miles per hour, Ben says, "The stoplights seem almost irrelevant."

"Yeah, I know," Randall responds. "But stop anyway."

"I wasn't planning not to stop. I'm just pointing out how weird it is out here. How surreal."

419

"You got that right," Randall says.

And indeed, the light at the next intersection goes red just as they near it; a police car turns right onto westbound McLemore a block away, and glides past them, through the red light, its driver and his partner having a good look at the Mustang and its occupants. Ben watches in the rear-view mirror as the car proceeds west; he wants to be prepared if the cops make a U-turn and pull him over.

"Let's go," Randall says. "Green light. Wakey-wakey."

"I didn't realize we were in a hurry," Ben says.

"You're the one talking about ignoring the red lights."

"Jesus Christ, Randall...you know that's not what I meant."

Randall says nothing in response.

In its stark decoration and in the nature of various objects that strike Ben's eye as he enters the house--the ratty furniture, the basketball in the corner of the living room--this could be an off-campus home to any college students anywhere in the United States. Except for the portrait of Marcus Garvey over the fireplace, and the huge map of Africa on the opposite wall. Randall introduces Ben to Edwin, and Edward, and finally to Charles. There is some hesitation as to which protocol to follow; having raised their fists in Randall's direction, Edwin and Edward both nod sullenly in Ben's direction, not seeing fit to include him in the Black Power salute. Charles manages a weak smile and offers his hand, whereupon he and Ben engage in a standard American shake. Charles is a sturdy man about Ben's age, perhaps a year or two older; Edwin and Edward, Ben guesses, are younger, but it's hard to tell. Edwin wears dark glasses, a black t-shirt and black jeans; if he weren't black and didn't have a sprouting Afro he

420

could pass for a vestigial beatnik. Edward has hair nearly identical to Edwin's, a scruffy, mustacheless beard, and a shirt with broad stripes in orange, purple, tan, and black that Ben presumes to have some African significance. Charles wears slightly frayed blue jeans, a blue work shirt, and a tan jeans jacket.

William Marchand is here, as are the black Baptist minister, the black Church of Christ minister, and the white Methodist minister from Tuesday's lunch meeting. The prevailing mood in the room, it's Ben's perception, is not anger but a mixture of shock and sadness. That, and the disparity of background and direction, gives rise to a period of uneasiness, as if several vaguely similar species of mammal had just been placed together in a cage by some half-witted zookeeper.

Ben's urge is to talk to the Methodist minister, to ask him whether his liberal views on race relations are shared by his parishioners, but how unseemly would it be for the only two Caucasians in the room to gravitate to each other? So Ben instead approaches Edwin, the black man in black, searching for an entrée as he does so. Edwin stands in a corner of the living room, smoking. "Terrible day," Ben says.

"Yeah. Guess so," Edwin replies.

"I'm Ben Shelton." Ben resists the reflexive action of offering his hand. Edwin nods and says nothing, his eyes invisible behind the shades. Ben says, "Charles an old friend of yours?"

"We go back a ways," Edwin says.

"Must be tough," Ben says, "to go to a school that's just integrated. It must feel like everyone's eyes are on you all the time."

"I wouldn't know," Edwin says.

Ben takes a deep breath and plows ahead. "You're not with the Bee Oh Pee?"

Edwin shakes his head almost imperceptibly, and after several seconds says, "Invaders."

Ben nods studiously. "I thought they were affiliated. I thought the Invaders were an offshoot of the Bee Oh Pee."

"Yeah...kinda," Edwin says.

It's an impasse. Where can he go from here? His impulse is to ask Edwin whether he has a job, what are his interests, his hobbies, as if he were chatting with an exchange student at one of his mother's parties. But he can be pretty sure that Edwin would be no more forthcoming to such a line of trivial questioning. So--what's next? Just say, nice talking to you, and back away?

Edwin provides the answer, after an uncomfortable gap. "Hey...you the dude that punched Dwayne over at Corrina's last night?"

Taken completely by surprise, Ben says, "I'm not sure."

Edwin's lips form a wisp of a smile, the first time his face has registered anything other than indifference or contempt, and he says, "You ain't *sure* you punched him?"

"I punched somebody who kicked me when my back was turned," Ben says. "I'm saying I don't know what his name was."

Edwin chuckles. "Ain't the way I heard it."

"How did you hear it?"

Edwin shakes his head ever so slightly, as if to say that it wouldn't be worth his trouble to tell a different version of the story. Instead he says, "I heard you was dancin' with a black chick."

"What if I was?"

Edwin leans in, so his lips are no more than ten inches from Ben's left ear. "You ain't from around here, are you?"

"No, I'm not."

"Well, that explains it."

Ben is as curious as he is angry. "Explains what?"

"I'll tell you one thing. Dwayne's my little brother."

It's so confounding. Does he mean that the guy who kicked Ben in the ass last night is literally his brother? Ben says, "How do you mean that?"

"Shit," Edwin says, extending the word so that it's at least two syllables, cocking his head backward in exaggerated astonishment. "Leave it at that," he adds, with another shake of the head. "Quit while you ahead." And he walks away, toward the kitchen.

It's not long before William Marchand claps his hands for silence and--as the only person here who's connected to everyone else--calls the meeting to order. Marchand stands by the front door; Randall and the two black ministers share the ratty sofa; Ben and the white minister flank the sofa, standing against the wall on either side of it; Edward sits in the armchair to the left of the sofa, Charles on a small wooden chair next to it; Edwin has not emerged from the kitchen.

"I don't think I need to express how we all feel about what happened this evening," Marchand begins. "I don't think we're going to know for many years what effect this murder will have on our lives. I think right now we're all dealing with the sadness of it, with the tragedy of it. But I hope to God that in some way it will draw us together, that in some way we will benefit from it. Maybe that's stupid, maybe it's wishful thinking, but I hope not." He pauses, choked up a little, catches his breath, and resumes. "Ralph Abernathy was going to drop by tonight after dinner, and I'm sure you all understand why he's not here. I managed to talk to Reverend Abernathy for a couple of minutes tonight and he told me the march is still going to happen, that Mayor Loeb and the powers that be are still making noises about stopping it, but that now it's a memorial to Doctor King and they know that the world would look very unkindly upon them if they made more than a token objection. So the march *will* happen."

Marchand now introduces the Baptist minister, who thanks everyone for gathering at this difficult time and then recalls the career of Doctor King. Ben at first wonders if this portion of the evening is necessary: surely all present are familiar with the details of the struggle. But as he listens he is impressed anew by the bravery and the fortitude of the man who's just been killed, and of the extraordinary progress that's been made in the last decade. The Baptist minister leads the group in prayer, and when at the end he recites King's closing words of the night before verbatim, and in a cadence eerily similar to King's-- "*I may not get there with you, but I want you to know tonight that we as a people will GET to the promised land. So I'm happy tonight. I'm not worried about any thing, I'm not fearing any man. Mine eyes have seen the glory of the coming of the Lord.*"--Ben feels tears emerge spontaneously and profusely, and spill from his lowered head onto the threadbare carpet below; it is the second time he has cried this evening, as well as the second time since, perhaps, 1954.

The Baptist minister waits what seems like two or three minutes before speaking again. "And now I want to turn things over to our host, a young man who was gracious enough to have us all out here tonight. We may have some differences of opinion with this man and his organization, but I think we want to listen carefully to what he has to say."

## The Mountaintop

Unlike Marchand and the Baptist minister, Charles doesn't assume a place in the front of the room, but remains in his slat-backed chair, and simply begins speaking in a low, resonant voice. "I want to tell you that I grew up idolizing Martin Luther King. If you were black and you lived in this part of the country and you had a brain in your head, that's what you did. The reverend here talked about progress, and it's true. When I was growin' up, black people didn't have no piece of the pie at all, and now we do. But I want you to think of a time when you were 'bout as hungry as you ever been, you been workin' hard all day and ready for a big meal, and somebody brings you this little, tiny piece of pie and says, 'Here, boy, this for you.' Now...are you gonna be grateful for that piece of pie? Are you gonna say, thank you God, now I'm satisfied I finally got me somethin' to eat, or are you gonna stand back and say, wait a minute--that's all I get? Over there I see people eatin' a big damn slice of pie. I see people gettin' *full*."

In the big armchair next to Charles, Edward in his shirt of many colors nods emphatically, as if keeping the beat. Charles resumes after a short pause. "That's the way I started to feel two, three years ago at Memphis State University. Much as I admired Martin Luther King, I didn't have patience for his methods no more. We had integration, yes. And a few of us were allowed to go to this fine school, to have this little slice of pie, which we would not have had except for Doctor King and men like him. But I felt we had to step up the pace. I felt like Doctor King all these years had been tryin' to prove to white people that we were entitled to everything just as much as they were, and that was the wrong way to go about it. I felt that it's a *given*, in that we're citizens of the United States of America, that we're entitled. It ain't somethin' we got to prove. What we have to do is go out and claim what's ours."

425

"Say it, Charles," Edward intones. Ben notes that the black Church of Christ minister has begun nodding his head, perhaps more in appreciation of the style of Charles's oratory than its content.

"I didn't meet Martin Luther King until a couple of weeks ago," Charles says, "and I have to guess that in some way he thought of me as the enemy, cause he knew that I stood for this thing called 'Black Power' that was threatening to break up his movement. If he felt that way, he never let on. And *I* felt that a line had been drawn, connectin' me to my childhood, because in that moment I felt exactly about Doctor King as I did when I was fourteen, or sixteen, except in his *presence* I was exposed to a kind of serenity and composure that you don't experience on television or in the newsreels. And I realized that day that we're still fightin' for the same thing. And that when my brothers in the Black Organizing Project mock Doctor King, talk about him like somebody whose time has passed, they could not be more wrong."

Now when Charles pauses the room is all astir; there are *amen*s from both black ministers, simultaneous to a *tell it!* from Edward, and spontaneous applause from the white minister, who is immediately joined by Randall, then Ben, and soon everyone is clapping. Charles nods in acknowledgement, waits for silence, and speaks again. "I've been thinkin' a lot today, in the last few hours, about what Doctor King said last night, like he knew somehow his time was up. And I had a thought a few minutes after I learned that some vicious, racist son of a bitch had shot this man. I thought, maybe Doctor King did know, and maybe he knew it would somehow be for the better--that his death would bring us together. I wish I *knew* that's the way it's gonna go down. All I can tell you right now is that when that march happens sometime in the next few days, all of black

426

Memphis will be united. There won't be nobody out on the streets breakin' windows, givin' the cops a chance to run wild. I can guarantee you that."

It takes a moment for Ben--and everyone else in the room--to recognize that Charles is done, that his guarantee is his final word. Now the reaction is less spirited; it's almost as if everyone has been left stunned. Surely no one was expecting the direction of Charles's words, and Ben at least, especially after his encounter with sullen Edwin, was hardly prepared for eloquence. He wonders, though, whether Charles's guarantee that there will be no window-breaking at a second march amounts to a tacit admission that the B.O.P.--or the Invaders-- were responsible for the actions that set the police off during the first march. And he wonders what's going to happen next: unless one of the other ministers plans to say a few words, it would seem to be Randall's turn, and Charles is going to be a tough act to follow.

Still standing against the wall, Ben is suddenly conscious that Randall, below him and just to his right on the sofa, seeks his attention. "You want to say a few words?" Randall's voice is just loud enough for the room to hear.

"Me?" Is this just another test, or is it Randall's payback for his supposed malfeasances, offering the callow white boy the floor, or the opportunity to back down?

"You," Randall replies.

So this is how it is. It's more than a little bit like the anxiety dream in which he finds himself taking the final exam in a course he thought he'd dropped, and he has no idea what the questions are about. What is there to do but begin? "My name is Ben Shelton," he says, astonished at the sound of his voice, "and I'm with the Kennedy campaign." He pauses, searching for a heading. He looks down at Randall. "Randall and I are

427

with the Kennedy campaign, and we were scheduled to meet
with Doctor King tomorrow. It was going to be one of the
thrills of my life. I hope I don't sound like some silly white kid
when I say that, but Doctor King was a hero of mine...maybe he
was my greatest hero, and I can't think of anyone I'd rather be
able to spend a few minutes with. Now that's not going to
happen. So I guess the question that Randall and I have to ask
ourselves is--what would we have talked about with Doctor
King, what kind of bond could we have begun to establish
between the Kennedy campaign and everything that Doctor
King represented? The SCLC, the sanitation workers here in
Memphis and, I guess, the civil rights movement as a whole..."

Is he doing all right? Is he getting carried away? He
glances down at Randall, who nods almost imperceptibly. "I
think you all know," he resumes, "that Senator Kennedy
considered Doctor King a friend. A close friend. And that civil
rights is high on Senator Kennedy's agenda. Next to ending the
war, I'd say that it's his highest priority. And of course we
know that ending the war in itself is an important issue to black
America, because a disproportionate number of our soldiers in
Vietnam are black..."

Ben hears a *Yeah, right on* from Edward, and knows that
he's winning over at least part of the audience. "I think it's
Senator Kennedy's idea that if we can take all the money and
energy we're expending in Southeast Asia and put it into our
inner cities, this country's going to be a lot better off." As he
scans the room he sees Charles nodding in apparent
appreciation, and Ben realizes that he's probably just
paraphrasing what Randall had told Charles two nights earlier,
and of course he was present when Randall far more eloquently
made his presentation to the assembled ministers at lunch. So
this is all for show, like letting the rookie quarterback play the

last few minutes when the game has already been decided. But what the hell--he's not just going to run out the clock.

"I want to talk a little bit about words now. There's a saying that's popular in some circles: Jesus Christ was a communist. Of course Jesus Christ wasn't a Communist with a capital *C*, but he was a man who believed in equality, and sharing the wealth. If you were to stand up in certain churches and shout that Jesus Christ was a communist, you might get your brains bashed in. By the same token, Robert Kennedy can't go out on the campaign trail and say he believes in black power, because that term has taken on a certain connotation, and if he spoke those words millions of white people wouldn't vote for him. But just the same you'd better believe that Robert Kennedy *does* believe in black power, with a lower case *b* and a lower case *p*. In Robert Kennedy's America black people would have just as much power as white people. I think that's the goal that Martin Luther King was working toward, and that everybody in this room shares."

He would sit down now, but short of slumping to the floor there's no way he can do that, so he simply stops talking. There is brief but enthusiastic applause, and Randall gets to his feet. He leans over and whispers into Ben's right ear, "You pushed that about as far as it would go, my brother." Ben has no idea whether he's been chastised or complimented.

## FORTY-EIGHT

It doesn't take Alex long to figure out why all eyes are glued to the television high above the bar. Despite the fact that no one at the bar talks above a murmur, the TV volume is turned way up—this because it seems that every fifteen seconds or so a siren, or a clutch of sirens, blares by. Martin Luther King has been shot. Is he dead?

Alex stands some ten feet away from the bar, trying to puzzle out as much as possible. Memphis. Someone else is in Memphis. Ben, for the Kennedy campaign. King shot in the neck, so he must be dead, or as good as dead. Fire engines wail not on the TV but here in Harlem, maybe two blocks away. Someone at the bar says, "Niggers tryin' to burn they own houses down. Don't do nobody no good."

"Hey!" the bartender calls, and Alex realizes he's talking to him. "What you want here?"

Several patrons have swiveled on their stools to check him out. "How about a beer?" Alex says.

"I don't think you want to be in here right now," the bartender says.

"Let me stay for a few minutes, would you? I just had some trouble outside. Need to catch my breath."

"What kinda trouble?" The bartender says.

"Car trouble."

The bartender looks askance. A middle-aged man in a porkpie hat says, "How come you all sweaty? You look more like you been pushin' a car than drivin' one."

"Yeah," Alex says. "I had to push the car off the road, get it out of traffic."

"Where you live at?" Porkpie hat says.

"A Hundred and Eighteenth Street."

"Well, why don't you take your ass and get back to Hundred and Eighteen Street, leave us to mourn in peace."

More sirens, accompanied by thunderous fire engine horn blasts, drowning out the TV audio. This time there is no Dopplering, but rather a winding down of one set of sirens while others approach. A man with processed hair and a brightly checked jacket says, "Shit—that's got to be right nearby."

The bartender says, "You want to check, Ellis—see if we gonna get burned down?"

Ellis slides off his stool and zips out the door, soon followed by five or six other patrons. Porkpie hat says, "Why don't you go see where the fire's at, white boy? Maybe you can push one of them fire engines at it."

"I'll just stay here, if that's okay," Alex says.

"Well, it ain't okay," the bartender says. "I don't want you in my place of business. Somethin' wrong with you, comin' in a bar on the main street of Harlem the night Doctor King gets shot."

"I didn't know," Alex says. "I swear, I had no idea till I came in here."

"Somethin' wrong with him he didn't know," Porkpie says to the bartender.

Ellis re-enters, breathing hard. "Right down on Amsterdam," he announces. "Block and a half down, just past LaSalle Street. Big motherfucker! They got about six engines, hook and ladder, people out on the street, police..."

"Look like it gonna spread?" The bartender says.

"No, man, looks like they already got it under control."

431

There is a break in the siren clamor, at least. On the television, a familiar-looking black man in a suit, probably someone from the Civil Rights movement, says that he has lost a friend and a mentor, that the country has lost a leader and lost its way. A couple of the other patrons who'd left with Ellis now return, followed by someone else who looks familiar. This beefy, fortyish man catches sight of Alex and stops in his tracks, at which point Alex realizes who he is: the man whose Buick Electra 225 he collided with twenty minutes ago.

"That motherfucker has a gun on him," the Buick driver intones, and instantly Alex feels every eye in the place on him.

"That white boy?" The bartender says. "Shit no."

"I ain't lyin'," the Buick driver says. "He held it on me not half a hour ago. Wrecked my Deuce and a Quarter and then he pointed his gun at me. Call the police, Franklin."

"I don't reckon we gonna get no police out here just now," the bartender says.

Alex begins taking baby steps toward the door. The last thing he wants to do is employ the pistol again, but it might be the only way to get around the Buick driver.

"That true, what the man's sayin'?" The bartender says. "Why don't you just put that gun down on the floor and get outta here?"

"Bull-shit," the Buick driver says. "What about my car?"

Alex reaches into his back pocket for his wallet, and the Buick driver takes an apprehensive step toward the bar. "It's cool," Alex says. "Write down your information for me and I'm gonna give you my driver's license."

"Man, why the hell should I trust you? You left your car sittin' there all banged up on Broadway."

432

## The Mountaintop

"I'll pay you for your damages," Alex says. "If I had the money on me, I'd give it to you now."

"That's gonna be two, three hundred dollars."

"I'm good for it." As he speaks the words, Alex thoroughly believes them. The accident was his fault, the guy deserves to have his car repaired, and three hundred dollars is a small price to pay for getting out of this. The Buick driver is in the midst of scribbling on a Rheingold beer coaster supplied by the bartender; Alex sidles closer to him, and to the door. He stays just beyond arm's length, so the guy can't grab him, until he's between the burly man and the door. Right hand above his jacket pocket, he accepts the coaster with his left, then hands the Buick driver Elliot's Delaware license. "No hard feelings," he says.

"We'll see about that," the Buick driver replies.

He gets a whiff of smoke leaving the bar; it's a nasty smell, as if something toxic has been burned and extinguished. Too bad Amsterdam Avenue is closed off, because he could have taken it straight down to 118th Street and been practically home. Now he's got to walk the long block down 125th to Morningside Avenue and cut across steep Morningside Park, which separates Harlem from the environs of Columbia. He's the only white face on 125th Street, to be sure, but there aren't that many black faces around, either. It seems as if there are sirens coming from every direction, and there are several clouds of smoke on his left, to the north, and straight ahead, to the east. It's a good night to be inside, unless someone's burning down your building. A police car speeds by him, heading east, and again he encounters the quandary of the gun. No one's following him. The Buick driver's back at Moe & Eddie's, and the little gang of kids is God knows where. Should he hold on to it until he can toss it in the Hudson, or dump it in a random trash can here in Harlem? What if the bartender went ahead and called the cops the minute he walked out the door? What if the cops stop him for any number of other reasons—just for being a long-haired white guy in the most famous black neighborhood in America on the night Martin Luther King got killed?

He turns right on Morningside Avenue, having engendered nothing more than some dirty looks so far. Between 124th and 123rd he ducks into a doorway and takes the Walther from his pocket, removes the clip and spends a couple of minutes rubbing every square millimeter of the pistol's surface, then the clip. No fingerprints on this gun. Standing there, he has an inspiration: Will the gun fit between the grates of a storm drain? At the corner he looks in all directions; there's no one around. He kneels and fits the gun between the grates, and lets it go.

It's past eleven o'clock when he cuts into the park at 120th Street. The terrain is flat for the first fifty feet or so, then begins to rise gradually, and finally becomes quite steep at the park's western edge, culminating in a flight of stairs leading up to Morningside Drive. Alex has never given much thought to the politics involved in Morningside Park. He's figured: If the university wants to build a gym or whatever it is they want to build, and plans to let neighborhood kids use it, then what's the problem? Despite the fact that he's lived a few yards from the park for the better part of a year, he's never actually set foot in it, although he and Lydia furtively made love under a statue overlooking the park on a warm night last September. Now, ascending the incline and looking up, it strikes him that if Columbia has the high ground, then the park logically belongs to the people at the bottom, and the gym would represent a kind of invasion.

He's a bit winded when he gets to the base of the stairs and sees three boys perched five steps up. They're black, maybe fifteen or sixteen years old. He stands, catching his breath, and one of the boys says, "You intend to come up?"

"That's my plan," Alex replies.

"Well, we got a tollbooth here. Cost you a dollar to get through."

It wouldn't be such a bad thing to hand these kids a dollar, except Alex recalls that after flipping two twenties to the Buick driver right after the accident, all he's got left is a twenty and a ten, and he's not about to part with ten dollars to climb a flight of stairs. He fishes in his pants pocket and comes out with change: a quarter, two dimes, and two pennies. "I've got forty-seven cents," he says. "How's that?"

"Ain't enough," the boy says. "I told you a dollar."

"I don't have a dollar. I've got forty-seven cents. You want it or not?"

A second boy gets to his feet. He's tall, taller than Alex, and built fairly wide. "You got a wallet, Mister?" The third boy has begun sliding down the steps on his buttocks.

Alex takes a couple of steps back. It's been a long and frustrating evening, and this little coda is too absurd. If he'd offered them the ten right off the bat, they probably would've taken his wallet anyway. If he acknowledges possession of a wallet now, it's gone for sure. If he runs, where does he run to? Back down the hill? Surely one of the boys—if not all three—is faster than he is.

The third boy, short and wiry, gets to his feet and says, "Why'nt you just hand it over? We take the dollar and be on our way."

435

"Stay back," Alex says. The two boys still on the stairs laugh and jeer as the short boy stalks him.

The short boy, grinning, repeats something like "gimme, gimme, gimme," while the first boy—evidently the brains of the bunch, shouts, "Hey, honky, you afraid of a little midget like Curtis?"

In fact, Alex isn't afraid of Curtis at all. He's already planning on how to arrange things so he can fight these kids one-on-one. To be sure, he got his brown belt in karate when he was eighteen—almost six years ago—and when he tried to face off against Flaco on Monday morning he ended up on the floor. But he was out of it then, woozy on Seconal, while now he's sharp and as alert as can be. Alex calculates that if he can make quick work of Curtis, the big kid will be next; if he can take care of *him*, then maybe the smart boy will have the sense to take off.

Curtis, who has a high, frizzy Afro and wears boots with elevated heels, begins hopping around like a shadow-boxing kangaroo, rhythmically repeating, "Gimme that wallet, hon-kee, gimme that wallet, hon-kee." Alex raises his hands and slightly bends his knees, eliciting laughter from the boys on the stairs, one of whom shouts, "Hey, Kato, don't hurt him!" Curtis, still bobbing and weaving, gets close enough for Alex to reach him, and he aims a quick chop at the boy's nose. It connects, and Curtis tumbles to the ground, screaming in pain.

The two boys on the steps rise as one. The leader shouts, "Curtis, you all right?" While the large one begins descending the stairs. Curtis cries, "Motherfucker broke my nose!"

"Why you want to hit him?" Says the large boy, advancing on Alex, who holds his ground.

"Keep away," Alex says.

436

"Hit a little boy like that, didn't do shit to you? Pick on someone your own size, how about?"

Alex's glance shifts rapidly from Curtis, still on the ground, bleeding, to the leader, now making his way down the stairs, to the large boy, who's just about too close for comfort. "I'm warning you," he says, but the large boy keeps coming. He's too tall for a chop to the face, and the last thing he'll expect is a foot in the groin, so Alex puts all the force he can muster into a right-footed kick. But it's a little premature, a split second early, so his heel catches the boy in the abdomen. Indeed it's a surprise, but it's also only a glancing blow, and it serves to further infuriate the large boy, who lets loose a howl of pain and anger as he lunges toward Alex, who has barely recovered his equilibrium when the large boy tackles him around the waist. He has the frightening sensation of breathlessness as the wind goes out of him, and before he can resume breathing the large boy has begun battering his face with both hands.

Helpless, Alex keeps struggling to take that first breath, but the large boy's bulk is centered on his midsection and the huge hands keep pounding away at his face. After a while, the tollbooth boy stands above them, shouting, "This is what you get! This is what you deserve!" Then, almost simultaneously, Alex manages to take a quick, gasping breath, and plunge into unconsciousness.

*Peter Delacorte*

## FORTY-NINE

Maddy has found a bottle of cheap New York State burgundy lying on its side among the canned goods in the cabinet above the sink. They've sat for half an hour watching the little television in the living room and drinking wine. The television alternates pictures of fires in Harlem with reports of greater violence in Memphis and degrees of mayhem in other cities around the country. After a while it becomes repetitive.

It's near midnight and a stern white man on Channel Four describes Mayor Lindsay's attempts to quiet the natives by appearing at Eighth Avenue and 125th Street, which drew a large and restive crowd. "Hey," Prosper says, "that must be where the cops who were hassling us went."

"*Hasslin'* us?" Leotis says. "That's what you call it? If Maddy didn't show up, we'd be locked up right now."

"On the other hand, if I hadn't gone back into the school, we wouldn't have been there in the first place." She refills Leotis's glass; they're down to the dregs of the bottle. Ben has about half a fifth of Wild Turkey under the sink, and in his sock drawer is a bag with the bare remnants of what had been six months earlier an ounce of marijuana. Shall she offer either, or both? If she's in bed by one she can still get six hours of sleep, if the dogs don't go crazy tonight. "Anybody want some good bourbon?" she says.

"Not for me," Leotis says. "I should be headin' back to Connecticut. Got to be at a lady's house in Norwalk at nine."

Maddy says, "Leotis, do you have a plan?"

"A plan?"

"Are you just gonna let them draft you?"

438

"Broke up with my girlfriend a few months ago. She broke up with me, truth be told, because I didn't want to get married. Now it don't seem like such a bad idea."

"Is that even a deferment anymore, for sure?"

"Maybe if she got pregnant right away..."

"Even then," Maddy says, "are you sure it's automatic?"

"I told him he should talk to the War Resisters League," Prosper says. "He's got a history of high blood pressure in his family. I'll bet he could get a doctor's note."

"Now? After he's already passed the physical?"

"I think you can appeal, if they overlooked something really outrageous."

"Then why don't *you* appeal?" Maddy says.

"On what grounds? That the Dexedrine wore off?"

Leotis laughs his throaty laugh, and then for several seconds everyone is silent, as if the gravity of the day has again descended upon the room. Maddy finally says, "Leotis, why don't you go to Canada with Prosper?"

He smiles. "They got black people in Canada?"

"That's what I hear," Maddy says.

"I didn't know Prosper was for sure goin' to Canada."

"It's not such a bad idea," Prosper says. "I mean, whether I'm going or not. You could take your van up to Toronto--set up an instant business."

"You think they'd accept my college credits up there? I've got a year in."

Maddy shrugs and Prosper says, "Maybe."

"I wouldn't have to learn French?"

"English in Toronto," Prosper says.

"You know people there?"

"Not really. Couple of people I went to school with."

Maddy says, "Are you interested, Leotis?"

439

*Peter Delacorte*

He takes a deep breath. "Well, it's not like it's
something I've spent a lot of time thinkin' about. I don't know if
I could just pick up and say goodbye to everybody and start
over again. But I guess if I get drafted, that's what I'm gonna be
doin' anyway, right?"

"Right," Prosper says. "And if Kennedy's elected
president, you could probably come back to Stamford before
this time next year."

"Something to think about," Leotis says. "Damn!
*Canada.*"

Leotis has left and Prosper has just put on his jacket. He
says, "I don't suppose you'd want to come back to Catherine's
house with me?"

Maddy smiles, and shakes her head. "It's too late. I
can't miss another half day."

"My car's only about four blocks away. I could be back
here in ten minutes."

"God, Prosper," she says, "why don't you just stay?"

"Stay here?"

"Yes. I've changed the sheets."

As she rinses out the wine glasses, Prosper grabs the
dish towel slung over the refrigerator handle and dries them,
something Ben would not deign to do if the Queen of England
had dropped by.

Prosper says, "I'm working with Martin tomorrow,
starting around noon. I'm pretty sure we'll be done by
dinnertime. Let's do something."

"I don't know," she says. "I'd love to. I don't know
what's going on with Ben..."

440

*The Mountaintop*

"I don't see how Ben comes into this." There is more than a scintilla of irritation in his voice.

"Don't misunderstand me," she says. "If he comes back here tomorrow, and God knows he may not come back here ever again, but if he comes back here tomorrow night he and I have to clear the air and figure out what's going on--like who's gonna be living where, and who's gonna be paying for what."

"Sorry," Prosper mumbles. "I..."

Maddy interrupts, "You know how I felt yesterday. What do you call it when there's a last straw, and when the camel's lying there with a broken back somebody drops a whole bale of hay on him? I have to track Ben down, just to find out where he is...'Please, Mister McCaffrey, can you tell me where the hell my deceitful boyfriend is staying in Memphis?' And then when I get him on the phone I'm crying my eyes out and it doesn't even dawn on me for I don't know how many minutes that he doesn't have the slightest idea what I'm talking about! Martin Luther King, his *hero*, has just been shot, and he's shacked up with some tootsie at the Holiday Inn, having such a great time that he's completely unaware of what just happened right down the street!"

She feels tears welling in her eyes for about the eightieth time in the last six hours, and the next thing she knows Prosper has embraced her, enveloped her. It's not exactly what she wants right now, but it's not all that bad, either. He says, "I'm sorry...I didn't mean to set that off."

"*You* didn't set it off," she says.

She's about to slide into her side of the bed, against the wall, when Prosper says, "You have to get up at seven, right? Why don't I sleep on the inside?"

"You don't have to twist my arm," she replies.

441

It's twenty past two, her brain is going a mile a minute, and her bladder is sending her a signal she can't ignore. Naked, she pads into the bathroom. She returns just as the dogs make their nightly foray into the backyard; first she hears them scrambling and snuffling through the plants--the acoustics involved in this always astonish her, that a couple of small creatures two stories down can be heard so clearly--and then there comes the inevitable, unknown stimulus that sets the dogs off. They're little terriers of some sort, but they could give Leontyne Price a run for her money in a decibel contest. What could it be that makes them go nuts? A mouse? A rat? A rustling breeze? Or a sadistic cat who lies in wait for them every night, then strolls before them, just out of reach, at two or three o'clock in the morning, or whatever hour the thoughtless Stillmans choose to let them out.

She makes her away along the narrow space between the bed and the wall to the window; the barking might continue intermittently for fifteen or twenty minutes, and she'd rather fall asleep sooner than that. She tries to pull the sash down gently, but it falls with a thud. Prosper stirs, and turns, and looks up at her. He rolls over and embraces her ankles.

She kneels and strokes his hair. "Go back to sleep."

"What's happening?" His hand now cups her right buttock.

"The Stillmans let their goddamn little dogs out. I was just closing the window."

After a couple of seconds he says, "What if this is the last night we ever spend together?"

"Why do you say that? Why would it be?"

He sits up, his hand sliding between her thighs until it has removed itself from erogenous areas and rests on her knee.

442

"I don't want to keep you up," he says. "I know you have to go to work in the morning. I just want you to know how I feel. With everything that's happened in the last couple of days, I just want you to know that this is much more important to me than everything else."

She says, "It shouldn't be."

"Why, Maddy?"

"Because you have to figure out what to do with your life. Because you have huge decisions to make. Because the world seems to be turning upside down."

"I don't see why all that and the way I feel about you should be mutually exclusive."

After a moment, she says, "You may have to make some major changes in your life pretty soon, and I don't want you to do anything stupid on my account."

"Like what?"

"Like staying here when you should go to Canada."

"Look...I may not get my induction notice for six months. I may *never* get my induction notice. The point is that I don't have to *do* anything until I get my induction notice..."

"You may not have to do anything, but it's probably a pretty good idea to have everything planned out so that when the time comes you know what you're doing."

Prosper doesn't reply immediately, and Maddy sits back on her haunches, taking the pressure off her knees, Prosper's hand as a result sliding down to her ankle. He says, "How about this--your spring vacation is next week, right?"

"Right."

"Come with me. Let's drive up to Toronto. We can do it in a day if we leave early in the morning. Get a sense of the place. It's a great city. It's a lot like New York, except it's

443

cleaner, and the taxi drivers aren't as homicidal, but everything else is exactly the same."

"I'm sure. Lots of Spanish-speaking kids there?"

"Lots. And they've got a lake just like ours."

"Where's our lake, Prosper?"

"Central Park. Theirs is a little bigger, but essentially it's the same thing. We can spend four or five days there, and maybe ask some questions about schools, and jobs, and apartments..."

"I don't think so," Maddy says. "I've got stuff to do. My sister Bridget's's birthday is a week from Saturday."

"I'm sure she'd understand."

Maddy shakes her head, all the while wondering whether a drive up to Canada might not be fun, and eye-opening. She's starting to feel a little chilled now, sitting naked on the floor. The dogs have stopped barking. She says, "I'll think about it," and gets to her feet. She slides adroitly under the covers, appreciating the warmth of Prosper's presence here in her bed.

**FIFTY**


"I wouldn't try something like that again," Randall says.
They're standing on the front steps of Charles's house. Sirens--
fire engines' probably--sound as if they're no more than a mile
distant; there is a slight aroma of wood smoke in the air, and to
the northwest a small portion of the sky is charcoal, blotting out
the stars. The meeting has ended. Randall was last to speak,
assuring the small assembly that Robert Kennedy would be
paying special attention to Tennessee and to Memphis in
particular, that yes, all things being equal, he would participate
in the march next week, but that he had a primary to win in
Indiana.

No one has left yet; people are chatting; the black-and-
white television in the living room has been switched on and
tuned to images of fires and violence in cities around the
country. There's nothing else on in Memphis.

"Like what?" Ben asks.

"You had 'em. You didn't need to go to the Jesus-was-a-
communist bit. You got up, you said your piece, and then you
took a chance, and you almost fucked it up."

"Who's to say I almost fucked it up, if it worked?"

Randall recoils in mock astonishment. "Ben, hey, I
know it's been a long and bad day, but half your audience in
there is men of the cloth, and this ain't exactly a seat of
sophistication, okay? You're pushin' it with the Jesus stuff, and
then after Charles, Mister Black Power, has told us how
moderate he really is, you tell everybody that our candidate is in
favor of black power."

445

"Randall...my *God*," Ben feels his adrenaline rising, and feels he's about had it with Randall, having just performed a thankless task and now getting far worse than no thanks.

"Your God *what*?"

"You bend stuff...you twist stuff. We're not dealing with idiots here. Those people understood what I was saying, from start to finish. Give me some credit, for Christ's sake."

Randall places a hand on Ben's shoulder. "Maybe they did, my brother. Maybe they did. But why do you want to take risks?"

A car cruises down McLemore, coming from the west. It's a long, low coupe with a growling motor and a noisy exhaust--a Dodge Charger, Ben thinks. The Charger stops directly in front of Charles's house, double parking, and two men emerge. Ben recognizes the outfit of the driver--it's Edwin, the sullen Invader--and the passenger looks familiar as well, in his black satin jacket.

"You gonna answer me?" Randall asks.

"Will you tell me something?" Ben says, as the tall, wiry young men approach the lawn. "Is that the guy who kicked me at the club last night?"

"Oh, shit," Randall says. "I believe it is. Why don't we make ourselves a subtle retreat?" Randall edges toward the door to Charles's house.

"Where are we gonna go?" Ben asks.

"We'll think about that when we get inside." Randall takes a step forward and seizes Ben's arm. "Come on."

Edwin and what's-his-name...Dwayne...are no more than twenty feet from them, walking on the slight uphill slope of the flagstoned path through the dead-grass lawn. "What's the point?" Ben says.

446

"If we're in the damn house," Randall says, "they're not gonna try anything."

"Do you *believe* that?" Ben says.

"I wouldn't have said it if I didn't believe it." Randall tugs on Ben's arm, but Ben will not budge. He pictures them backing into the house, and then what? Would they head for the back door, and flee? Would they mingle with the ministers, seeking safety in numbers, or the protection of the clerical collar? Neither is an alternative Ben would begin to consider. If there's an issue to be decided, let it be done here and now, honorably.

"Ben," Randall says in a voice brittle with urgency, "Will you remember what I told you last night, for Christ's sake?"

"I need to take care of this," Ben replies. Randall releases his arm and Ben, whose eyes have met those of his antagonist, is only vaguely aware of the door slamming behind him when Randall goes inside.

Edwin and Dwayne stand at the base of the steps, Edwin grinning and Dwayne glaring. From this close, Ben can see the wide bruise in the area of Dwayne's chin, blue on brown, and the swelling of his lower lip. Looking up at Ben, who's on the top step, Dwayne says, "Where your high yella bitch? She inside?"

Ben shifts his attention to Edwin, the matchmaker, who stands slightly behind Dwayne and just to his right. "If you'd stuck around you would've heard people say some pretty good things about making peace. Keeping peace. You could ask your friend Charles about that."

Edwin says nothing, but Dwayne growls, "Peace? What you talkin' about peace, you sucker-punchin' motherfucker?"

It's a little too much for Ben, coming from the guy who kicked him when his back was turned, and he starts to feel that competitive rage so valuable to star athletes. He fixes his attention on Dwayne. "You want me to turn my back to you? Is that your idea of a fair fight?"

"Fair!" Dwayne ascends the first of four steps to the porch, and Ben clenches his fists. "Fair would be honkie assholes stayin' where the fuck they belong."

There is a commotion behind Ben and he's aware of people--how many he's not sure--joining him on the porch. He hears Charles's voice. "*Dwayne*...cut it out! Get the hell outta here, or you gonna mess everything up."

Dwayne shakes his head. "I ain't goin' no place till I get some satisfaction." Ben is close enough to Dwayne that he can see the veins in his forehead pulsing. This is a man, Ben estimates, who would be deterred only by a dart from a tranquilizer gun.

"Edwin," Charles says, "did you go and bring this crazy nigger here?"

Edwin nods, smiling. "I recognized that white boy as the one that hit my little brother, Charles. Hit him and knocked him out."

"Then you drag his ass away from here," Charles says.

Ben is now aware of Randall's voice, speaking quietly, directly to him. "Why don't you just back up, old buddy? We're gettin' this thing under control. You just back up and you and I will go in the house."

"Not yet," Ben says. "I don't trust this guy at all."

Dwayne continues to glare at Ben, even as Edwin seizes Dwayne's left arm and says, "You heard the man, brother. Maybe we take care of this shit later." Dwayne flails his arm, dislodging Edwin's hand, and at this point Charles rapidly crosses the porch and descends the steps.

Randall says to Ben, "They called the police."

"Who did?" Ben watches as Charles places himself in front of Dwayne.

"One of the preachers. Baptist dude. As a precaution."

In a very loud voice Dwayne says, "I just want a fair fight with the motherfucker." And Charles replies, "You ain't gonna get no kind of fight here, so forget about it." Charles gives Dwayne a shove, and Dwayne stumbles several steps backward.

That's it, Ben guesses. Dwayne's forward progress has been stopped. "Okay," he says to Randall.

"You know what?" Randall says. "You remind me of a dog my uncle owned. Would never back off. He wasn't that big a dog, but you put him face to face with a damn Rottweiler and he wouldn't give any ground."

"He was protecting your uncle," Ben says.

"The hell he was. He had some fucked-up notion he was the baddest dog in the neighborhood, and he wasn't."

Ben watches as Charles, Edwin, and Dwayne make their way from the edge of the lawn to the street, to the low-slung Dodge. Standing in front of the car, Dwayne's captors release him, as Ben considers Randall's analogy. He doesn't particularly appreciate being likened to a feisty little dog; he doesn't think of himself as an underdog, by any means. The Baptist minister appears on the porch, trailed shortly by his two colleagues.

"All over," Randall says. "Can we call the police and cancel that invitation?"

"Don't think it works that way," the Baptist minister says, with a chuckle. "You watch--they gonna show up about three, four in the morning." He speaks to Ben, "What's that boy got against you, anyway?"

Ben, who has been keeping on eye on the three men by the Charger, turns to respond, but Randall beats him to it. "Jack Dempsey here decked him last night on the dance floor. And evidently he's the little brother of Edwin, one of our hosts."

Better Jack Dempsey than Randall's uncle's dog, but still Ben is compelled to give some context. "He was drunk. He insulted the girl I was with, and he kicked me." Ben sees the Baptist minister's eyebrows elevate, sees Randall turn clockwise, toward the lawn, and exclaim, "Oh, shit!"

By the time Ben himself has turned, Dwayne is three-quarters of the way across the lawn, Charles in pursuit, Edwin still back by the car. Dwayne is sprinting, right hand in black satin jacket pocket, emerging now with...what is it? Ben steels himself at the top of the stairs. It's not a gun, thank God. It's small and black...a jackknife? Ben is conscious of Randall moving diagonally, toward the stairs and Dwayne, shouting, "Hold it right there," and further conscious of a car moving down McLemore, pulling up beside the Charger.

*If that is a jackknife*, Ben thinks, *Dwayne will have to stop and open it. If he does that, Charles will tackle him from behind. If he doesn't do that, he'll have to climb the stairs to get to me, which gives me the advantage.*

The only problem is that Randall continues his diagonal and at the bottom of the stairs intercepts Dwayne, who with a wild swing strikes Randall in the abdomen, knocking him to the ground. Now Dwayne, stationary, fumbles with the knife. Ben moves cautiously toward the stairs as Charles stops just behind Dwayne and shouts, "Put that thing *down*, nigger!"

Edwin too now comes running from the Charger. *Is he a peacemaker or his brother's ally?* The blade now exposed,

450

Dwayne lurches around to see who's giving him orders. This is clearly Ben's moment to act, but only after he's made the decision to leap and it's unretractable does he recognize the new car on McLemore as a police cruiser.

From the top of the stairs he vaults with perfect accuracy, his head striking Dwayne in the small of the back, and a split second later his right arm makes violent contact with Dwayne's, causing the open jackknife to go flying. The only complication--for the moment--is that Dwayne has been propelled into Charles, shoulder versus shin. Charles collapses with a howl of pain onto Ben, who has become in effect the center of a sandwich.

He can see nothing, his face pressing downward into Dwayne's back, all the weight of Charles on top of him. He can hear: car doors slamming; Dwayne moaning, sounding at best semi-conscious; Charles continuing to bellow in pain; and Randall's voice. "Drop that! Come on, put it down!"

"Charles!" Ben says. "Can you move?"

"My *leg* is broke, man!"

"Okay. Can you slide off me? I don't want to hurt you."

Someone, perhaps the Baptist minister, is calling, "Be cool! Be cool!" A white voice, deductively a cop's, shouts, "Y'all stop and stay where you are!" Ben feels Charles trying to shift his weight, and helps him, until Charles has slid far enough so Ben can lift his head and see Randall and Edwin struggling for control of the jackknife, and two burly white policemen-- one with his nightstick raised, one with his gun drawn--bearing down on them.

"I'm tryin' to take the knife from this son of a bitch!" Randall shouts, as Ben struggles to his knees.

"Y'all *quit*, you hear me?" The cop with the nightstick yells, as the struggle continues.

Ben concentrates on the cop with the gun, figuring he's the one to worry about, catching his eye. "It's under control," he shouts. "Don't shoot anybody!"

But perhaps Ben's priorities have been misplaced. The cop with the nightstick begins beating the two intertwined black men indiscriminately--Edwin in his black satin Invaders jacket and Randall in his charcoal Brooks Brothers sport coat--despite progressively louder calls of protest from the ministers, still on the porch, and from Ben, until ultimately they both crumble to the lawn.

For an infinitesimal moment everything is frozen, as if in a painting made from a photograph: Ben now kneeling alongside the prostrate Dwayne, Charles supine behind him, Edwin and Randall unconscious, or close to it, on the grass, the two cops above them like victorious gladiators awaiting a signal from the emperor.

But instead they hear the wrath of the Baptist minister, who sets a new scene in motion when he descends the stairs and shouts, "What did y'all have to do *that* for?"

"Mind yourself, preacher," says the cop with the gun.

The minister proceeds. "Can't you boys *tell* when somebody's tryin' to uphold the peace? Tryin' to take a knife away from somebody else? You just bring your damn clubs and your damn Mace and what all weapons you got and beat up any colored man you run across?"

"I'd hold my tongue, preacher," says the cop, nevertheless holstering his gun.

The Baptist minister is by now within a couple of feet of the policeman whom he harangues. "*You* hold your damn tongue! You're in trouble now--the both of you! You know who the man is you just beat up? Hell, maybe you *killed* him. You know who he works for? Senator *Kennedy* is who, and

452

you come in here and bash his head in like you caught him robbin' a liquor store."

Is Randall stirring? Ben gets to his feet, cautiously, his eyes for an instant meeting those of the cop with the club, who then returns his attention to the Baptist minister, as if having acknowledged that Ben, by virtue of being well-groomed and caucasian, poses no threat.

"Just another nigger!" The minister continues his rant. "Bet if Martin himself was here, back from the dead, y'all would beat *his* head in, just for the sake of it."

Having made his way across several feet of crisp lawn, Ben kneels by Randall, whose eyes are open but not necessarily seeing. He says, "Can you hear me?"

Very slowly, Randall nods. Ben slips his right hand under Randall's head and feels it immediately immersed in blood. There is a huge welt on Randall's forehead. "Can you talk?" Ben says.

In a tiny, hoarse voice Randall says, "Yep."

"Think you can get up?"

"Don't think so," Randall whispers. "Can't feel my legs."

"Okay," Ben says. "We're gonna get you to the hospital." He looks up at the cop nearer to him, the one who'd drawn his gun. "All right with you guys if we get out of here?"

The other cop, the one who clubbed both Randall and Edwin unconscious, says, "Hell, no. Not your colored friend, anyway."

"Let 'em go, Ernest," the first cop says. "What are we gonna take 'em in for--disturbing the peace?"

"Assault!" The second cop shouts.

The first cop turns to Ben. "You want me to call an ambulance?"

"Just tell me where the hospital is, if that's okay."

The Baptist minister says, "I'll tell you. Hell, I'll ride with you."

"That'll be good," Ben says. He slides his right arm under Randall's lower back, his left under his upper thighs, lifts him in one smooth motion, and carries him toward the car.

*The Mountaintop*

# APRIL 16

It's just before noon when Prosper finds Alex's room at St. Luke's. He's not fond of hospitals, and his ten or twelve minutes' wandering around this one has done nothing to change his mind. He's relieved, though, that this section doesn't match what he'd expected--Alex to be spread out on a narrow bed in a room full of moaning injury cases, people in thick casts and traction. The door to room 817 is closed. What's he supposed to do now? He knocks gently and waits, then slowly pushes the heavy door open.

It is in fact a single room, and Alex (or someone) is supine and not apparently conscious. Prosper says, "Alex?" and approaches cautiously. Had he not expected to see Alex here, he would not have recognized this person with the grotesquely swollen face. "Alex?" He speaks the name a bit more loudly, and Alex's purple eyelids gradually open. His face breaks into a semi-smile and he says, "Hey, man." His lips move but his mouth remains closed. "How the fuck are you doing?"

"Better than you, I'd say."

"Yeah, listen, they got my jaw all wired up. Hard to talk."

"I would've been here earlier but I just found out. They called my aunt's house and she called me at the radio station. What the hell happened to you?"

"Long story," Alex says. "Black kids beat the shit out of me in Morningside Park. Broke my jaw in two places."

"Jesus."

"You're supposed to say, okay, Morningside Park was one place, what was the other?"

Prosper doesn't get the joke right away, but he chuckles

455

about five seconds late, still assessing the state of Alex's face: stitches here and there, a hodgepodge of purples, browns, and yellows. He says, "You were in a coma?"

"Yeah, for a week. Little bastards took my money but they left my wallet. Cops figured out to call my father. He came up here and got me transferred into this room. I woke up...what day is it today?"

"Tuesday."

"Okay. I woke up Thursday."

"Jesus, Alex. Did they know you were gonna wake up? Was there some question?"

"I guess they knew, or they expected. Doctors explained the whole thing to me about five times, but these drugs, man....I can't remember anything. I *hope* it's the drugs."

"You serious?"

The half-smile again. "The drugs are cool, man. I have these, like, Samuel Taylor Coleridge dreams. I want to write everything down, but I can't focus. But my brain is okay. They did all these tests while I was out. You know my dad--nothing but the best. They said, okay, kid has a sublime skull fracture and broken jaw, but his brain is groovy."

"Sublime skull fracture?"

"Something like that."

"And where's your dad now?"

"At the Plaza, I think. Or maybe down on Wall Street."

"You're getting along all right?

"Sure. Long as I'm like this, I don't pose any problems. And he's happy it's over with Lydia. Did you know we split up?"

"I heard from Maddy." So much has happened in the last two weeks, it crosses Prosper's mind, and Alex has been lying here like a cabbage. "Did you know Martin Luther King

456

was killed?"

Alex's laughter is abrupt and explosive, and evidently quite painful, as he stiffens against his pillow. He seems to catch his breath before saying, "Yeah, I knew."

"What's funny?"

"Not that he's dead. Just...how I found out."

"Your dad?" Prosper imagines what it would be like to emerge from a coma and have your father relate to you with something resembling glee that one of your heroes has been murdered. But then Martin Luther King--neither a creator of comic books nor a director of obscure art films--wasn't one of Alex's heroes.

"My dad's fucking *happy* about it, but no, I was up in Harlem."

Harlem, Prosper muses, is a few hundred yards and a few million miles from Alex's apartment. "What the hell were you doing in Harlem?"

"It's a long story, man. I don't know if I can even remember everything now. I'll tell you sometime. Do they know who did it? Did they catch the guy?"

"They have a pretty good idea who did it. He left his gun in a rooming house across from the hotel, fingerprints all over it. They don't know where he is, though."

Alex laughs softly, wincing just the same. "Another *lone gunman*, what do you bet? Just like JFK....If they ever figure out what really happened, it'll be long after we're dead."

There is half a minute's silence; Alex shifts in bed, and grimaces. Prosper says, "What are you gonna do now? When you get out."

"My dad wants me to go back to Florida and go to law school, or business school..."

"That's what he always wants."

"Right. I think the cool thing about all this..." Alex points to his face. "...is that I'm sure Columbia's gonna let me do the semester over. I was really fucking up--that's why Lydia split. So I figure I'll be out of here in a few weeks, maybe I'll sublet the place, go to California, go to Hawaii, go to Paris, come back in January with a clean slate."

"What about the draft?"

Alex's laugh is briefer and gentler. "Look at me, man. Coma! Brain damage! Would you want me over there mixing it up with the Viet Cong?"

"No, I guess not," Prosper says. "Actually, not you or anybody else."

"Right." Alex draws in a quick breath. "I forgot you passed your physical. What's going on with that?"

"Nothing, so far. I talked to the War Resisters League again. They're a little unclear about Connecticut, but they said in New York guys are getting induction notices three to six weeks after they're reclassified. It's been just about two weeks for me."

"You thought anymore about what you're gonna do?"

"Canada, I'm pretty sure. Toronto. I was up there all of last week, and I liked it a lot. Of course, it didn't hurt that Maddy was with me."

Alex's eyes widen. "*Maddy*?"

"Yeah, she was on vacation, so we drove up there together."

"What the fuck, man? What about Ben?"

"Ben's kind of...out of the picture."

"Wow!" Alex looks as if he'd be grinning if it didn't hurt too much. "So...Ben's down in Memphis saving the world, and you move in on Maddy?"

"It's not like that," Prosper says, although he knows that

458

to a good degree it is.

"But she's gonna go to Toronto with you?"

"I don't know. I hope so. I'm working on it."

"And what's going on with Ben?"

"He's still down in Memphis. You know Randall, the guy he was working with?"

"The black guy. Sure."

"A cop beat him up the night King was killed. He's still in the hospital, so Ben's in charge of whatever the Kennedy people are doing down there. Sort of a weird way to get a promotion."

"Jesus." Alex leans back on his pillow. "How the hell did all this happen? Does Ben know about you and Maddy?"

"It's a long story," Prosper says. "I'll tell you sometime."

He's a few steps down the hallway, toward the elevators, when he hears a voice call his name. He turns to see a stocky, good-looking man of about fifty who brings to mind an older, wider, fairer version of Alex. Prosper stops in his tracks. "Mister Hayes. How are you, sir?" He would never in a million years call his own father "sir," but somehow it seems the proper appellation for Alex's.

"Very well, thank you." Mr. Hayes gives an extra-firm handshake, for which Prosper, mercifully, is prepared. "You're looking well, too--except for that haircut." He chuckles and adds, "Just kidding." Prosper, of course, knows that Mr. Hayes isn't just kidding, that he considers long-haired men to be communists, anarchists, or homosexuals. "And Alex, thank God, seems to have survived this crazy business."

"I just found out about it," Prosper says, "or I would've been here earlier."

459

"I wouldn't worry about that. He's only been awake for a few days. Listen, could I buy you a cup of coffee?"

"Can you talk some sense into him?" They sit in molded plastic chairs in St. Lukes' cafeteria, at a formica-topped table. The room is vast and surprisingly quiet, despite the presence of fifty or sixty other people--some in swabs, some in custodial uniforms, others clearly visitors like themselves.

"I don't think I've ever been able to do that," Prosper says.

"Do you think he's got a future in this film thing? Do you think he's just wasting his time?"

What Prosper thinks is that while Alex probably has zero chance of making it in Hollywood--which would doubtless be his father's definition of a "future"--he would be miserably unhappy at law school or business school, and with a film degree he'd get to hang out with an arty set in New York, maybe pick up a job here and there, maybe even slap together some avant-garde nonsense that would be well reviewed in the *Voice*. Prosper says, "Yes, I think he could definitely have a future."

Mr. Hayes nods, has a sip of coffee, and grimaces. "Well, at least he's not with the Spanish girl anymore. I imagine you approved of her?"

"Not really, sir. I don't think they were right for each other."

"Well, that's a relief. I don't know--there's something so *perverse* about all this. Boy grows up in a community like Palm Beach, goes to Culver, goes to Princeton. Lives with a girl who grew up in a slum, lives right on the edge of the damn jungle, where these animals can beat him to within an inch of his life! They'll never catch those kids, of course."

460

Prosper has nothing to say to any of that. If Mr. Hayes is right about anything, it's not just that Alex's muggers will never be caught. There is a perversity to Alex, but by Prosper's accounting it's that his rebellion against Palm Beach and military school has so far stopped short of being complete, or at least of being constructive--that it's manifested in a sort of druggy nihilism.

"What about you?" Says Mr. Hayes. "Alex has always looked up to you. What are you doing with your life?"

"Kind of in limbo at the moment."

"Alex says you're one-A."

Thanks a lot, Alex, Prosper thinks, imagining that this turn in the conversation can lead to no good. "Yup...just recently."

"Military was the best thing that happened to me. Taught me how to be a leader. I wasn't in combat, but that was just the luck of the draw. My men and I were all set to ship out when things ended in Europe. We missed out on the Pacific because Harry Truman dropped the A-bomb on the Japs. Only decent thing he ever did. I had mixed feelings because I would've liked to kill a few of the bastards myself. But I suppose it's all for the better. My dad left me a million dollars, and I turned it into ten. If it hadn't been for the military, for the discipline, for the sense it gives you that you have to take these aimless kids and turn them into a *force*, I think I might've been more like Alex--content to sit around and spend my money."

Once more lacking a congenial reply, Prosper is wondering if this is the time to excuse himself and flee the cafeteria when Mr. Hayes resumes. "I'm going to make an educated guess and venture that you don't think much of this war."

Prosper nods. "How do you think this war compares to

461

your war?"

"Apples and oranges," says Mr. Hayes. "Do I think communism's as much of a threat as fascism? In some ways, worse. Joe Stalin was just as much of a murderer as Hitler. Do I think we have to worry about this new Oriental in Hanoi? Anybody's guess. But we're over there and we damn well better finish the job, or the consequences are severe."

"How so?"

"Because in the world's eye we've got to be *winners*. That's what America's about. What does the rest of the world think of us when we let a little two-bit country make a fool of us?"

It's a rhetorical question for sure, but it deserves an answer. "Most of the world would admire us, I'd say, if we made a graceful exit."

Mr. Hayes shakes his head ruefully. "Generation of spoiled brats and cowards," he says.

## APRIL 21

Maddy has spent the past seventeen nights with Prosper: three here in the apartment, then the week in Toronto, then back here. Most of his things are still at Aunt Catherine's house in Connecticut, but he's brought several days' worth of clothes, plus his toiletries and his typewriter, to the apartment. At first Maddy pushed Ben's clothing as far to the side of the closet as she could, making room for Prosper's five shirts and two pairs of corduroys, figuring it was up to Ben to dispose of his stuff whenever he saw fit to return. Finally, over the weekend just finished, she took all his clothes from the closet and piled them neatly on a corner of the couch, along with most of his other possessions. He could go through the process of segregating his records and books--if he wanted to--when he got back.

He'd called three times since the night of the assassination; only one conversation lasted more than ten minutes, and that was the first one, when he gave her a blow-by-blow of the events that led to Randall's beating and paralysis. The second and third calls were mostly taken up by the doctors' latest views of Randall's condition, and by descriptions of how incredibly busy he was, having suddenly become the Kennedy campaign's main man in Tennessee, and dealing with the ongoing question of whether to file a suit against the Memphis police department. The first call had begun with profuse apologies--for not having let her know where he was, for not being the one who answered the phone when she called that terrible night, for being generally self-absorbed and inconsiderate. But there was never a mention of the girl who had answered the phone, or what their relationship was. And of course for her part, she hadn't pursued the question, nor had she mentioned that Prosper had pretty much moved in.

The trip to Toronto had gone well. They'd left early Sunday morning, spent the night on the Canadian side of Niagara Falls, which she'd never seen before, gotten to Toronto Monday afternoon. It wasn't at all like New York, but then she hadn't really expected it to be. It was... *nice*--lots of green space and not too much traffic, a huge lake, a ferry that took you to a quaint island with an amusement park, taxis unadorned with jingoistic American flag decals, cabdrivers who yielded to

463

pedestrians. It was as if a whimsical supreme being had seized
Philadelphia or Cleveland and made a few arbitrary changes,
like making it virtually impossible to buy a six-pack of beer or
a bottle of wine, putting Queen Elizabeth on the money,
spelling "labour" with a *u*. She wasn't as taken with the city as
Prosper, who must have spent a full day, all told, examining
every frequency on the radio dial, loved parking somewhere off
the beaten track and wandering the neighborhoods. The movies
were pretty much the same as in New York. They found
Godard's *La Chinoise* at a dumpy little theater (theatre) in
Yorkville and even Prosper had to admit it was boring.
Yorkville, where they spent much of their time, was like a very
tame version of Greenwich Village. The restaurants were good,
and cost about half what they would on Broadway or in the
Village. There were Spanish-speaking communities--Cubans,
and Spaniards, of all things. Prosper urged her to make some
phone calls, even found the number for the Board of Education,
but she put it off, never did it, for reasons not entirely clear to
her. If she discovered that she *could* transfer that part of her life
here, would it mean she was edging that much closer to a
commitment?

Footsteps coming up the stairs. This would be Prosper
returning from the Pez Dorado with moo goo gai pan and ropa
vieja, plus whatever else occurred to him when he ordered. But
wait...the climber is taking the steps noisily, two at a time.
That's not Prosper, and although she's been through this
moment many times in her head, she's not prepared for it.

She opens the door as he takes the final four steps. He's
carrying his brown leather suitcase, as if he's intending to stay
awhile. "Wow," he says, smiling, "I'd forgotten we don't have
an elevator." He's hardly breathing heavily.

464

*The Mountaintop*

"I wasn't expecting you," Maddy says, smiling despite herself.

He drops the suitcase on the landing and stands there for a second, as if expecting her to come to him. "I had a chance to get away. They sent a couple of people down to help out. It was all kind of sudden."

"You could've called me from the airport."

"Randall's doing better," he says. "'Stabilized' is the word they use."

"Can he walk?"

"Nope. They say he might, might not. They can see the vertebra's fractured but they're still not sure about the spinal cord damage." He takes a step forward. "You gonna invite me in?" He extends his arms a bit, but she steps aside and he walks through thin air into the apartment. Should she pick up the suitcase and bring it in? She elects to leave it on the landing.

Of course he spots the pile of clothing on the couch straightaway. "I was about to say you're not too happy to see me, but I guess that's an understatement."

"I'm glad you're all right," she says, still standing by the door. She can feel herself trembling a little. In his absence, in her confusion and rage, she had ceased thinking of him as so tall and good-looking. And despite the absence of it in the last two phone conversations, she'd expected some semblance of penitence when she saw him again.

He sits on the couch, next to his clothes. "Is this some kind of symbolism? I'm capable of taking my own things out of the closet."

"You understand that you don't live here anymore?"

"Listen, sweetheart, I'm sorry about everything. I'm just here for a couple of days. I have business to take care of, and I thought you wouldn't object if I stayed here. On any terms you like."

465

If he'd called from the airport, she could have left him a note and gone out with Prosper to the Pez Dorado, or someplace farther away. But this encounter would still have been necessary at some point. She says, "Do you have your car?"

"Jesus, that's another thing," he says. "Do you know what it costs to leave a car in short-term parking for three weeks? It was supposed to be a week, and Randall would've used his credit card. I felt like an idiot asking them if they'd take a check. So there went all my cash."

"I can lend you ten dollars, or twenty. I'll help you carry your stuff down to the car. You've got friends all over the city. If you like, there's no one staying at Alex's place on Morningside Heights, and Lydia still has the key."

"Maddy, for Christ's sake, what's the big deal? I'll sleep on the couch, if that's what you want. I'm tired. I just flew from Memphis to Atlanta to New York, got hassled by the parking guys, drove from the airport to the West Side of Manhattan in rush hour traffic, and I'm asking you if I can spend the night in a place I pay half the rent for. I don't think that's unreasonable."

Now she hears a second set of footsteps on the stairs and knows for sure it's Prosper this time. Should she meet him on the next-to-last landing and tell him to retreat? No--better to get the whole thing over with at once. But at least fair warning is called for. She takes two steps onto the landing and shouts, "Ben's here!" The footsteps stop for a moment, then resume.

"Who's that?" Says Ben, getting to his feet.

"It's Prosper, with dinner."

The man in question appears in the doorway, holding a large brown paper bag, and says in a voice lacking affect, "Hey, Ben."

Has Ben recognized the situation? He says, "Hey, man,

466

how've you been?"

"I've been okay, all things considered. And you?"

"About the same," I'd say.

Prosper's a step inside the door, Maddy stands just to his right, Ben across the miniature living room next to his stack of clothes. "Well, hey," Ben says, crossing the room in five steps and giving his oldest friend Prosper a quick hug, which is even more awkward than it might seem because Prosper still clutches a big bag of Cuban-Chinese food. There's still been no physical contact between Ben and Maddy. Ben moves back a step and Prosper says, "How's Randall?"

"Might be permanently paralyzed, waist down, might not be. He thinks he has some feeling in his toes, but he can't move anything."

"Damn," Prosper says. "You guys suing the cops?"

"It depends. I don't know. What's in the bag?"

"Pork lo mein, ropa vieja, pepper beef, and a thing of steamed rice. There's enough for all of us." Maddy tries to catch his eye and makes the slightest negative movement of her head. She's not sure whether it got through.

"What about you, man? Maddy told me the other day you passed the physical. Any news?"

"Not really. I got letters from the army, the navy, and the air force telling me that because I did so well on the test I was officer material, so if I wanted to enlist they'd send me to OCS right after basic training..."

"Just what you wanted to hear, right?"

"Yeah, well, the funny part is I really fucked up the test. Not on purpose, but because I couldn't tell one tool from another, and I couldn't figure out what all those shapes would be if they were three-dimensional. I don't think I'm exactly what they're looking for in an officer."

"Right. You know they just want to train you for a few months and then put you in charge of some angry Puerto Ricans in Da Nang. So either the Viet Cong or the Puerto Ricans will shoot you after a week or so."

Prosper smiles. "Alex's father tells me that if I join the army he's got connections. He can get me a nice desk job in Germany, or Korea."

"Why the hell are you talking to Alex's father?"

"It's a long story," Prosper says.

So...everything is in suspension. When Ben goes to pee, Maddy says in a low voice, "I didn't want him to stay," and Prosper replies in an equally low voice, "Does he know about us?"

"No," she whispers.

"Well, it's not a big deal. What do we have to worry about?"

Of course Prosper has known Ben much, much longer than she has.

The dinner table isn't really big enough for three, but they squeeze in. Prosper gets each of them a can of Schlitz from the refrigerator, and Ben says, "You storing your beer here?"

"Pretty much," Prosper replies, and launches into the story--as much as he knows of it--of Alex and the black kids in Morningside Park, Alex in the hospital, Mr. Hayes in the cafeteria. Maddy tells what she's learned through Lydia of the breakup, and Lydia's new romance with Rafael.

Ben says, "I've got some news," and Maddy thinks for a moment he's going to tell them about the girl in Memphis, which would make everything much easier. But he says, "I'm on payroll now, retroactive to April first, and I've got benefits

468

and everything, which means in all probability I've got a job in the administration, which is really cool."

"If there's an administration," Prosper says.

"Yeah, I know you're still holding out for McCarthy, but let's be serious. How about this--Kennedy at the top of the ticket, McCarthy as vee pee? A double anti-war ticket."

"Have you heard something?" Prosper says. "Because I don't think that would ever happen. I think McCarthy hates Kennedy too much."

"Maybe so, maybe not," Ben says. "But the *extremely* cool thing is...as soon as everything gets straightened out, all the tees are dotted and the eyes are crossed, I'm going to California."

"Wow," Prosper says.

"It was supposed to be Randall's job--managing the L.A. headquarters. Not running the California campaign, but in charge of two or three hundred people until the primary in June..."

"Going with your new girlfriend?" Maddy says.

There is a moment of dead silence. Prosper then clears his throat and says, "Ben..."

"Hold on a second." Ben gets to his feet and strides into the bedroom. The closet door can be heard sliding open as by great force, and shortly thereafter Ben stands between bedroom and living room holding Prosper's blue denim shirt. "Storing your beer *and* your clothes here?"

"I don't think that's any of your concern at this point," Prosper says.

Ben's voice rises. "Somebody might have mentioned something to me."

Maddy says, "Right! The way you called me from Memphis and told me where you were staying. The way you told me about the girl who answered the phone? And God knows how many other times you cheated?"

Ben continues to glare in Prosper's direction. "Is this what best friends do? Explain that to me, if you don't mind. You're just lurking around, waiting for the moment when she's vulnerable?"

"You've got no fucking right, Ben," Prosper shouts back. "You can't be a spoiled brat your whole life. You can't have everything your own way!"

Ben stalks back to the table--Prosper facing him, Maddy squeezed between the little table and the refrigerator. He snatches his can of Schlitz, flecks of beer flying into the air. "Who's to say it's over between us?" Still facing Prosper, he points at Maddy with his free hand. "Not *you*, for Christ's sake..."

"*I* am," Maddy yells.

Ben continues staring at Prosper, as if there was much more to say but it has escaped him. He makes a demi-turn to the south, facing the living room window. And with the power and accuracy of the prep school quarterback he was, he hurls the nearly full beer can at the closed sash window, which is no match for it. Glass spews everywhere as the Schlitz can flies into the cool evening air where, Maddy imagines, if there weren't obstacles in between, it would reach the Statue of Liberty. Outside, the Stillmans' loathsome little dogs begin to bark.

Ben wheels and stomps out the front door, slamming it behind him. Prosper puts his right arm around Maddy's shoulders and says, "That wasn't so bad, was it?"

## JUNE 1

It had been determined that the assassin of Martin Luther King was a drifter and prison escapee named James Earl Ray. The object of a worldwide manhunt, Ray was still at large, thought to be somewhere in Europe.

The induction notice arrived on May 8, five weeks to the day from Prosper's final encounter with Corporal Dybzinski. By then he'd virtually made up his mind that Canada was his best option. Catherine called him at Maddy's to give him the news, and even though he'd known it was all but inevitable, it came as a shock. He asked Catherine's permission to charge a call to Dakar to her number. In the middle of the night, when it was early morning in Senegal, he had a twenty-minute conversation with his parents, who assured him that the decision was his to make, that it would have little or no effect on his father's status in the diplomatic corps, and that they would feel much more at ease having a son in Toronto than having one in Vietnam.

Earlier in the evening he'd called Leotis, whose notice had arrived the day before. Leotis had first broached the subject of Canada with his father, who had served (as a cook) in the Pacific in World War II but did not have high regard for the miltary or for the current war. He told Leotis that the essential approval would have to come from his mother, and that turned out to be a piece of cake. "I can come *visit* you in Canada," she said. Leotis had a couple of jobs to be completed, but would be ready by the weekend, Monday at the latest.

Thursday night, Maddy and Prosper met Catherine for dinner at Manero's in Greenwich, where Catherine gave Maddy an Air Canada ticket from New York to Toronto, so she would have no excuse not to spend Memorial Day weekend there.

Prosper left Friday morning, May 10, and drove straight through to Toronto. He returned to the once elegant, now somewhat seedy Ford Hotel, where he and Maddy had stayed, and spent a restless night listening to muffled voices, slamming doors, distant merriment. Saturday morning he busied himself with the classified section of the *Star*, circling twelve apartments for rent in the Yorkville area. The third place he visited, shortly after noon, was a two bedroom, one bath furnished apartment (really half the lower floor of a two-story house) on Charles Street between Yonge and Church, for $180 a month, which Prosper calculated to be about $168 in U.S. dollars. It was easily three times the size of Maddy's walkup on 91st Street; the living room was big, the furniture ancient but not ratty, the bedrooms not too small, the bathroom fixtures serviceable, kitchen appliances seemingly from the mid-1950s, plenty of street parking. Why look any further? The landlady was a pleasant middle-aged woman named MacMurray who lived upstairs. He gave her $360 in Canadian bills newly acquired from the foreign exchange place on Yonge Street, then asked if, by the way, she'd object to his fellow tenant being a Negro. If he pays the rent on time, she said, I don't care what color he is.

Canadian coins were exactly the same size as American coins, or close enough to fit in the pay phone at the post office. With a pocket full of Washington quarters and Roosevelt dimes, money he wouldn't be needing for months or years, or possibly ever, he called the Telford house in Stamford and spoke to Leotis's mother, gave her the address, described the place to her, and she seemed pleased. He called Maddy and talked with her until his American change ran out.

## The Mountaintop

Memorial Day falls gracefully on Thursday, May 30. There's no Friday school in New York, so it's a four-day weekend, and Maddy catches a six p.m. flight from Kennedy to Toronto International. By now Prosper has a telephone and a rudimentary stereo system that sounds pretty good; Catherine has shipped a box of his records. He has registered with Canadian Immigration and obtained Ontario license (licence) plates for the Valiant; he and Leotis have both been regular visitors to the Toronto Anti-Draft Programme four subway stops up Yonge Street. There the tidings have been mixed. Canada's immigration policy, it seems, runs on a point system that favors those who score well in certain categories, such as college education, occupational demand, and the rather vague "personal assessment." The consensus is that Prosper will have no trouble gaining legal immigrant status, but Leotis is advised that his best prospect is to remain "underground." He'll hardly be alone in that respect, according to the TADP, which estimates that there are several thousand American draft evaders living illegally in Canada, more coming every day. Leotis has already hustled a job delivering furniture for a store on Queen Street, where he's paid by the delivery, in cash; it's not legal and the money isn't very good, but at least the cost of living here is close to negligible. Prosper has concentrated on finding a job for Maddy, which he figures, or he hopes, will be the last step in convincing her to come live with him.

He meets her just outside the Customs area; she's carrying her little plaid suitcase and she's just as beautiful as the person he's been seeing in his mind for the last three weeks. It's a half-hour drive to the house on East Charles Street, then

473

about two minutes to get into bed. Leotis is out to dinner with a girl from Addis Ababa who works at a coffee shop on Queen.

At ten o'clock they sit in his double bed, each of them with a bottle of Labatt's. Prosper says, "How important is it to you to teach?"

"I'm not sure I like the sound of that," she replies.

"It's not out of the question. There's a private girls' school that's looking for a Spanish teacher for next September. I think if you really impressed them, it wouldn't bother them too much that you don't have immigrant status yet. They'd just assume that you'd get it, and of course you'd have to get it."

"Pretty iffy," she says. "What about public schools?"

"Then you'd have to be a legal immigrant before you could even apply, and you'd have to take some courses, but after that I'd say it would be a sure thing."

"For September nineteen sixty-nine. What would I do till then?"

"Well, that's the great thing. There are all these jobs going begging for translators and interpreters--federal jobs, provincial jobs, city jobs, private jobs. Because French speakers are a dime a dozen, but *Spanish* speakers..."

"I'd have to do the legal immigrant business first, right?"

"Right. But you could probably walk into Berlitz tomorrow, for instance, and get hired right on the spot, with your Castilian accent."

"I'll bet they don't pay much at all."

"It would just be temporary, and it's so cheap to live here. And we could do it together."

"I don't want to just bide my time, though." She's silent for a moment. "If I stayed in New York, I could come here for

vacations, some weekends, all summer. And maybe you could
come back next year..."

"Talk about iffy," Prosper says. He thinks: That would
be better than nothing, being with her about a third of the year,
but the other two-thirds would be tough.

"What about Leotis?" Maddy asks. "What's he going
to do if he can't be a legal immigrant?"

"Work, and lie low. He can live a pretty normal life.
Evidently lots of guys are doing it."

"But he can't do anything that would make him
conspicuous, right? He can't go back to college, he can't get a
real job, with benefits?"

"I think there are ways around those things."

"He's gonna be driving that van every day. What if he
gets stopped for making an illegal turn, or something petty like
that?"

"He's got a legal Connecticut driver's license. He pays
the ticket, that's the end of it."

"And the van's got Connecticut plates--what about
that?"

"All figured out. I'll register the van in my name, buy
the insurance."

She shakes her head. "It's not fair. It doesn't seem
right."

"It's not," Prosper says, "but consider the alternative."

***

Perhaps because she's more at ease, perhaps because the
weather's warmer, perhaps because she's staying in this cute
little quarter of a house, she's growing fond of Toronto.
They've explored some more, taken long walks through the
green, gothic university, spent an afternoon at the Royal Ontario
Museum. On Friday they dropped in at Berlitz, where Maddy

475

had an impromptu interview with the assistant to the director, who gave her every indication that she could have a job at a moment's notice. Thursday night they saw *Belle de Jour*, which was very strange, and Friday night they saw *Hour of the Wolf,* which was more than grim, but she wouldn't have missed either. They spend Saturday night with Leotis and his friend Amina, who is an Ethiopian Christian and a legal immigrant. She's quite pretty, with a complexion lighter than Leotis's, and a big fan of American rhythm and blues. She's never heard of Leotis's cousin, Leroy Telford, but recommends various clubs in Yorkville that feature soul music. Prosper, of course, already knows them all.

"What if they get married?" She asks him. "Would that help him with the immigration business?"

"They've only known each other for ten days," Prosper says.

When the telephone wakes her from a light slumber, she checks the glowing face of the clock radio: five minutes after one. She has one association when it comes to middle-of-the-night phone calls, although in this instance it doesn't make much sense. Prosper sits up in bed a few seconds later. "Who's calling you at one in the morning?" She says.

"Don't know. Might be for Leotis, might be a wrong number."

***

He pulls on his pants and barefoots his way to the living room. In its two weeks of existence, the phone hasn't rung often, and never after eight o'clock. The first thing he senses, when he picks up the receiver, is that it's long distance.

"Hey, man! Did I wake you? I figured you'd either be up or out on the town, on Saturday night."

His first thought is that it's Alex, out of the hospital. But even though the voice is indistinct amidst blurry static, he realizes it's not. "Ben? How did you know where I was?"

"I called the apartment...Maddy's place. No answer. So I called your aunt in Connecticut. She was awake. She gave me this number."

He sounds a little drunk. It's just after ten in California. "So...what's on your mind?"

"I wanted to apologize for last month. I was pretty messed up. It was a tough time. I acted like an asshole, and I'm sorry."

"Apology accepted," Prosper says.

"You took the big step, then. How's Canada?"

"Pretty good so far. We haven't gotten to the cold weather yet."

"Can't be any worse than New Hampshire, right? We made it through four years there."

"How's Randall?" Prosper says.

"Doing well. Back in New York, back at work, doing physical therapy. He can't walk yet, but he's got some feeling in his legs. And Delphine--the girl I met in Memphis--she'll be out here tomorrow. She'll be here in time for the primary, and there's gonna be a hell of a party afterwards."

"Everything's good, then?"

"Oh, Jesus--you wouldn't believe it. Everything's rolling along so beautifully. Did you read about the debate with McCarthy?"

"A little."

"Bobby kicked his ass, or that's the way we all felt. He's gonna win big here, Prosper, and that means momentum. McCarthy's gonna drop out and I don't think Humphrey has a chance of catching up."

"What about Nixon?"

"Nixon can't fight the old Kennedy mystique. He might carry the south, but that's it."

"I hope you're right, about Humphrey and Nixon, anyway."

There is a short silence before Ben says, "How's Maddy?"

"She's great."

Another short silence. "She there now?"

"She is," Prosper says, hoping Ben won't ask to speak to her.

"Well...don't wake her up. Tell her I said hello, okay? And Prosper, I'm gonna have a permanent phone number later this week. I'll call and give it to you. We should stay in touch. And tell Maddy I'll take you both out to dinner in New York a year from now."

"It was Ben, wasn't it?" Maddy asks.

"It was," Prosper replies, getting back into bed. "He said to say hello."

"Anything else?"

"He said Kennedy's going to win big in the primary on Tuesday, so he'll have momentum and he'll be unbeatable."

"I hope he's right," Maddy says, snuggling up. "Then we could all go home."